# A
# Different Kind
## of Honor

The Honor Series
by Robert N. Macomber

*At the Edge of Honor*
*Point of Honor*
*Honorable Mention*
*A Dishonorable Few*
*An Affair of Honor*
*A Different Kind of Honor*

# A Different Kind of Honor

Lt. Cmdr. Peter Wake, U.S.N.
in the War of the Pacific, 1879

Robert N. Macomber

Pineapple Press, Inc.
Sarasota, Florida

Inquiries should be addressed to:

Pineapple Press, Inc.
P.O. Box 3889
Sarasota, Florida 34230
www.pineapplepress.com


Library of Congress Cataloging-in-Publication Data

Macomber, Robert N., 1953-
  A different kind of honor / Robert N. Macomber. — 1st ed.
      p. cm.
  "The sixth novel in the Honor series following the exploits of Lt. Peter Wake, United States Navy."
  ISBN 978-1-56164-398-1 (alk. paper)
  1. Wake, Peter (Fictitious character)—Fiction. 2. United States—History, Naval—19th century—Fiction. 3. United States. Navy—Officers—Fiction. 4. War of the Pacific, 1879-1884—Fiction. I. Title.
  PS3613.A28D54 2007
  813'.6—dc22

                                                          2007015832

First Edition
10 9 8 7 6 5 4 3 2 1

Design by Shé Heaton
Printed in the United States of America

This novel is respectfully dedicated to

Commodore Ronald Warwick

and to

the outstanding officers, staff, and crew
of the legendary R.M.S. *Queen Mary 2*

—wonderful shipmates,
with whom I have voyaged in splendor
across the oceans of the world.

Pacific Coast of South America in 1879
Panama south to Guasco, Chile
(Including the coasts of
Ecuador, Peru, and Bolivia)

# Foreword

In this sixth novel in the Honor Series of naval fiction, the year is 1879. The European empires are carving up the world among themselves with the ostensible motive of spreading civilization. America is still recovering from its self-slaughter, mired in the very worst kind of politics after the disputed presidential election of 1876. The nations of Latin America are stunned by an economic dispute over bird-droppings that has escalated into a deadly international conflict for domination of the Pacific coast of South America—known to history as the War of the Pacific.

The U.S. Navy is still dilapidated following the collapse in congressional funding after the Civil War. Changes are in the wind, however, in this time of tremendous technological advancement—Wake will use his first typewriter, telephone, and elevator. The United States Naval Institute has been formed, naval observer assignments overseas are being made, and forward-thinking officers are starting to plan for the future. Peter Wake is one of them.

A lieutenant commander now, Wake is on staff assignment at the Bureau of Ordnance at the Washington Navy Yard. His routine work has been interrupted by a special assignment to the bottom of the world as an official neutral naval observer in the War of the Pacific.

Wake leaves his family behind in Washington and heads south, intrigued by the mission and excited by the prospect of going to sea again, even if only as a passenger on other officers' ships. It is a difficult assignment—part naval, part diplomatic, part intelligence gathering—but he is determined to carry it out to the best of his ability.

However, Wake is about to find out that seemingly simple orders when given in a opulent office in Washington have a way of embroiling the recipient in situations he never imagined, with consequences fearful to contemplate. And, in addition to his own professional peril, Wake's family fights a mortal danger 10,000 miles away in Washington. 1879 is not a good year for Wake.

His life will never be the same.

Onward and upward,
*Bob Macomber*
Serenity Bungalow
Matlacha Island, Florida

# 1

# Make Them Understand . . .

**8 October 1879
in the South Pacific Ocean
off the coast of Bolivia**

**71 degrees West Longitude
23 degrees South Latitude**

"Difficulty sleeping, Commander Wake?"

In the cold fog of a Southern Hemisphere spring night, Rear Admiral Miguel Grau, commander of the Peruvian warship *Huascar,* absentmindedly stroked his famous bushy side whiskers, waiting for a reply. Swaying easily with the roll of the ship, the two men stood on the afterdeck, Wake's lanky frame leaning against the port boat davit. In the diffused moonlight, both men peered at the northeastern horizon on the starboard bow. A thousand men aboard other warships were out there, searching for *Huascar.*

"Well sir, considering that we're surrounded by overwhelming forces bent on destroying us, yes, I'll admit that I *am* having trouble sleeping," answered Lieutenant Commander Peter Wake, United States Navy. He shook his head. "Admiral, you know that as a neutral naval officer I'm forbidden from being involved in hostilities. Now I've managed to end up right in the middle of them. You've got the entire Chilean navy looking for you."

The ship's bell rang out five times, signaling that it was two-thirty in the morning as the quartermaster of the watch called out the traditional "*Todo está bien.* Wake thought that ironic, for the situation was far from being "all well."

He wasn't supposed to be aboard any Peruvian warship, but especially not *this* Peruvian warship, the scourge of the Pacific coast of South America. Sinking the *Huascar* was the primary goal of every Chilean military and naval man. And Grau was their most hated enemy, having humiliated them for five months with his daring raids.

Grau shrugged and allowed a grin. "Quite true, Commander. The enemy will find us sooner or later. And you are also quite correct, of course, that Washington would not be amused if you were involved in a battle—even though your presence here is not by your choice."

Wake nodded agreement to *that.* A day before he'd been a neutral passenger aboard a Chilean merchant ship captured by *Huascar,* and since had been the privileged guest of the Peruvians' wardroom. The officers enjoyed telling him how *Huascar* had defeated the Chileans at Iquique in May, and how Peru's navy had brought the cost of the conflict home to the aggressors who had started the war. Young fresh-faced Lieutenant Diego Ferré, the admiral's aide, regaled the American with tales of the admiral's decisiveness and bravery, and grim Lieutenant Palacios, the gunnery officer, gave a blow-by-blow account of the battles thus far.

It was clear to Wake that Grau's men were devoted to him and equally obvious why. He had defied the odds and won—so far. Incredibly, this man and his ship had been Peru's sole protection against the pending Chilean invasion for five long months. But Wake knew that the odds were building against these men as the war dragged on. And by the yellow cast of the swinging wardroom lamps he could see in the stoic faces of the older officers that they knew it too. As they ate from china and silver and drank from crystal chalices in the richly paneled wardroom, it was as if they were savoring the richness of their last meals.

Wake saw no end to the bloodshed. Peru's enemy was stronger than ever. It was now October eighth and the War of the Pacific had thundered incessantly since Chile occupied the Bolivian coast at Antofagasta in February. In April the Bolivian leaders invoked their secret mutual defense treaty with Peru and soon thousands of miles of the South America's Pacific coast had become anything but its namesake. The Chileans were continually victorious ashore against the ragtag allied armies of Bolivia and Peru, but the Peruvians were victorious afloat along the sealanes. And so the stalemate continued.

While on a mission from the Navy Department to assess the naval developments of the war, Wake had been scrupulous in maintaining his neutral stance between the warring countries. For four long months he never betrayed his opinion nor what his report to Washington would contain. That document was locked in his valise with the only key in his pocket. It had been difficult to remain nonpartisan, but his position—and at times his safety—demanded it.

Wake wasn't fluent, but his Spanish was good enough for basic conversation, earning him information a non-Spanish speaker would have missed. He was considered an enigma by both sides—an enigma who was seen as important, possibly crucial, to the formation of the United States' policy regarding the conflict.

Wake had been bound north from Valparaiso to Panama in transit to the United States to present his report when the cargo steamer was captured. His homeward journey, already started a month late, was now in jeopardy of substantial delay and Wake knew that the naval leadership in Washington, waiting for a professional assessment, did not suffer fools or laggards easily. There were too many officers for too few billets in the dwindled navy, and incurring the displeasure of senior officers frequently meant going on half-pay for the rest of your life. That depressing image spurred Wake to take a chance.

"Admiral, is there any way to put me ashore? I know you're roaming the coast but I really need to get on my way. They're waiting for my report in Washington, sir."

The admiral's eyebrow raised. "Ah yes, Commander, you must never keep admirals waiting! Regretfully, *Huascar* is no longer going close to this particular coast." Grau paused and looked to windward. A tiny light on their sole accompanying ship, the corvette *Union,* could barely be seen through the swirling fog as both ships steamed northward eight hundred miles to their home naval station at Callao. "Perhaps there is a way. Yes, I think there is. We will transfer you to *Union* and you will not be tethered to this ship and her old admiral."

Wake realized he might have been too abrupt. "Thank you, sir. But I meant no disrespect."

"No, no. No offense meant and none taken, Commander." Grau put his hand on Wake's shoulder. "I know you need to report to your superiors. I will ask of you a favor though, if I may be so bold?"

"Certainly, sir. If it's within my power."

"It is. I want you to tell them about us. Not just the facts, but about these men. My men. They have done the impossible and held off the Chileans for five months. The world predicted they would fail. They didn't."

Grau leaned closer. "You will be the one to tell the truth about all of this, Commander Wake. Of why this war was started, and how it progressed to this point. You must get your naval secretary to understand and convince President Hayes to help us end this madness. More will die unless this is stopped. Many more."

Wake felt the man's fingers grip his shoulder again, this time with strength. The barrel-chested Grau was forty-five years old—five years older than Wake—but had the strength of a man twenty years younger. The faded moonlight showed the admiral's face tighten, his eyes locked on Wake's. It was an image that burned into Wake's memory.

"Make them *understand*, Commander."

"Aye, aye, sir," Wake replied, unable to look away from those eyes. "I'll . . . make sure . . . they understand."

Grau eased his grasp. "Very good. And now I will quickly tell you how this sad war came about. You will forgive me if I repeat the obvious. I want to make sure you comprehend."

Wake nodded while the admiral continued with a sigh.

"It is all because of bird excrement on the coasts and some nitrate-rich sand in the desert behind the coast. Men are dying for guano and some gray powder. Incredible, isn't it, Commander?"

"Yes, sir. I hear that guano and sand are worth a lot of money, though."

"Yes, they are. The guano is used for fertilizers around the world, especially in your country. The nitrate is used in making explosives, mainly in Europe. We here on the Pacific coast of South America have a unique treasure—the largest concentration of guano in the world. That is due to our huge sea bird populations that feed on the nutrient-rich waters provided by the Humboldt Current, which comes up from Antarctica. The nitrate deposits in the Atacama and Tacapacá coastal deserts, brought down from the high Andes eons ago on long-gone rivers, are the richest on the globe.

"The guano became valuable only thirty years ago, and the nitrate was discovered only twenty years ago. But in that time they have eclipsed all other industries of Peru and Bolivia. Fortunes are made overnight each year, as with your gold rushes, in a desolate place where people have never lived or wanted to live."

A rueful laugh escaped from Grau. "God blessed us with something most people didn't want, until scientists found a way to make war with it. Guano is now worth millions of dollars a year. Nitrate is worth even more. Thousands make their living directly or indirectly from it, all over the world. Who would have thought that not so many years ago?"

"But why war, Admiral? There's enough for all the countries here." Wake had heard several explanations for the start of the war—from Bolivians, Chileans, and Peruvians. He wanted to hear this man's opinion.

"Yes, it was once thought that there was enough guano for all of us. But it is being depleted, quickly. And it takes money to *make* money from guano and nitrate. Machinery, skilled man-power, transportation, masses of unskilled labor. The Chileans and the British are the ones with the money. Peru has a little and the Bolivians have none, so we, and they, charge the Chilean-British companies a tax for the right to come in and harvest the resources God gave us. Bolivia signed a treaty with Chile to that effect, including a clause that the already existing Chilean mining concerns were exempt from the tax since they were building the economy. Chilean money and efforts were creating jobs and infrastructure, like railroads and water-making facilities, along the desolate Bolivian and Peruvian coasts. So it is fair to give them an exemption, I say.

"But then, late last year the Bolivians got greedy. They raised the tax to ten cents per hundred pounds and included the exempt companies. The companies, especially the Antofagasta Nitrate and Railway Company, owned by British and Chileans, were angry. And that too is fair, I think. The company said no to the tax, that they were exempt. The Bolivian government became enraged, making the tax retroactive and demanding that it must be paid by February fourteenth of this year—on the feast of Saint Valentine of all things—or the company's assets would be seized by the government."

Grau sighed. "Fools that they are, the pompous leaders in La Paz, led by their incompetent army dictator Hilaron Daza, thought they could intimidate the Chileans. They were wrong. Dead wrong. That company has high-placed friends in Chile's government who responded by having her navy and army occupy the Bolivian city of Antofagasta on the twenty-fourth of January this year.

"Bolivia was frightened. Her army is a joke and she doesn't even have her own tug, much less a navy, on her coast. Suddenly Bolivia's big threats were empty. Not only was she not getting the tax, she lost the biggest town on her Pacific coast. By the way, only ten percent of the population on the Bolivian coast is Bolivian! Eighty percent are Chilean workers, so they welcomed the Chilean occupation. The Chilean *rotos*—peasants who came to the coastal deserts to mine guano and nitrate—were the only people the companies could get to do the work. Bolivians wouldn't work in those terrible conditions. They wouldn't even descend from the highlands into the coastal deserts.

"Daza, as everyone knows, is a bully whose main aim is to fill his own pockets. Uh oh, the Latin American world thought, Daza finally went too far and picked the wrong country to bully with that tax. The Chileans are known for their military prowess—they were trained by the British. There was nothing the Bolivians could do, everyone thought. You may have noticed, Commander Wake, that Peru is not a part of this ridiculous story at this point."

"Yes, sir."

"Ah, but the Bolivians had, as you Yankees say, a playing card hidden up the sleeve of their shirt. That card was a secret treaty with Peru. A treaty of defense against invasion, concluded back in 1873 as a sign of mutual respect and amity. Few people were supposed to know of the treaty, but there were many rumors. I had heard them, but they were always vague, nothing I could trust. I thought it was just another silly treaty no one would really care about." Grau harrumphed in disgust. "I hope it's the last of those we sign."

"So Bolivia invoked the treaty and Peru's leaders were honor-bound to come to their assistance?" offered Wake.

"Precisely, Commander. If we didn't, and Bolivia made peace

by allying with the Chileans, that combination of forces would have been fatal to Peru's independence. So, against the wishes of many in Lima, including all the army and navy officers I know, we went to war. It was as if we were watching a landslide coming our way, knowing what was about to descend upon us, but not able to turn away. We just stood there and waited. And now we are here, surrounded, waiting for the inevitable."

"Admiral, you've had victories for five months over the Chilean navy."

"In May we beat them toe-to-toe at Iquique, but during the battle, Moore, captain of one of our two ironclads, *Independencia*, ran her on an underwater rock and lost her—destroyed. In minutes, we lost half our strength in ironclads. Now the only ironclad Peru has is *Huascar*. We have been following a guerilla war at sea since then, hit-and-run. It was effective at the beginning, but has become a case of roulette odds. Now the Chileans outnumber us on land and sea, the Bolivian army is a joke, and our Peruvian army is tiny. We are getting no support from our shore forces in this area. Sooner or later we will lose as the Chileans grow even stronger and overwhelm us."

"Only if they catch you, sir." Wake wanted to say something more encouraging, a supportive word, but knew that would cross the line of neutrality.

Grau flashed his disarming smile. "They *will*, Commander. The Chileans are good warriors and sailors, trained and equipped very well. They know where we've been striking, so they know our approximate location. They know that by now our hull is foul with growth and slowing down our speed, our boilers need overhaul and can't operate at the highest pressure for very long, and our men are tired. So because of all that, they know we will be heading home.

"We will do our best, but we will lose. And that is why you need to tell Washington what is happening. That is why I am diverting *Union* right now and putting you aboard. Time is not on my side."

Captain Elias Aguirre, *Huascar*'s taciturn executive officer, was summoned. Aguirre glanced over at Wake as the plan was explained by Grau, then asked his admiral in rapid Spanish, "What if this man gets ashore and gives away information to the enemy regarding us, Admiral?"

Wake understood most of it, particularly its tone. Grau was dismissive in his answer. "He won't. He follows the rules of war, honor, and neutrality. Make ready his transfer. I want it done immediately."

Half an hour later the *Union* was close alongside and several officers had come up on deck to say goodbye to their American colleague. MacMahon, the Anglo-Hispanic chief engineer who spoke English with his father's Scottish accent, passed him a letter to cousins in Edinburgh. Young Ferré laughed and wished him luck on his journey. Lieutenant Garezon, a serious-looking man with constantly furrowed brows, shook his hand silently and strode away.

Wake took one last look around the main deck of *Huascar,* the giant white turret showing her massive double Armstrong 250-pounder muzzle-loading cannons forward, the narrow bridge deck spanning the main deck above them with the officer of the watch pacing back and forth, the helmsmen aft in the steering alcove under the antiquated sterncastle. A feeling of dread swept over Wake as he dropped down the ship's low freeboard into the *Huascar*'s gig.

The boat crew rowed over to the corvette in the choppy waves, the bosun calling the cadence but no one else talking. Suddenly a speaking trumpet rose above the creaking of the oars and rush of the seas—the words coming out deliberately, sounding like doom itself in the hazy murk.

"*Remember,* Commander Wake."

A shiver went down his spine as Wake called out "Aye, aye, sir," and watched the ironclad warship's outline soften in the night, until it faded away. Then he was balancing his sea bag on one shoulder as he climbed up the heaving hull of the wooden corvette. On the main deck he met the ship's commanding officer, Captain Garcia, a tired man who appeared less than enthused about his new passenger.

Garcia explained in broken English that the corvette was being used as a lookout and dispatch vessel for *Huascar*. No match for the enemy warships prowling for them, *Union* was unarmored but fast, and had orders to run if the Chileans appeared. The captain opened the envelope from his admiral and read the note, then told Wake with an icy glare that Grau had made him personally responsible for making sure the American naval officer made it to shore in Peruvian-held territory and was able to deliver an important message to Washington.

*Union* then sheered away from *Huascar*, engine revolutions increasing, bound to the northwest away from her big sister. Within minutes even the few faint lights aboard *Huascar* were lost to view in the haze and Wake thought of his last sight of Grau—the admiral had merely nodded goodbye from the afterdeck, but with a sad mien that unnerved Wake. There was no doubt about it. It was a final farewell.

*Union* began rolling in the seas as she plunged ahead doing an easy ten knots. *Huascar's* foul hull and patched boilers made her top speed only eight or nine knots for any sustained length of time. As the scout, *Union* was deployed forward and to the west, both ships stayed off the coast and away from Chilean army spotters.

After thirty minutes of steaming, *Union's* watch struck the ship's bell seven times just as the lookout yelled something from the foremast. Wake checked his pocket watch. Three-thirty in the morning. Men peered off to the starboard, pointing. The officers focused their telescopes, concern evident in their hushed comments.

Staring in that direction, Wake saw the mist clearing, lifting with an increase in the northwest breeze. Stars became visible and soon he could see, far to the east, *Huascar's* black silhouette against the loom of the starlight. Signal lights on the *Huascar's* quarterdeck flashed. An officer next to Wake said they meant "enemy in sight." Officers grimly pointed to the northeast. Even without a glass, Wake saw what they were looking at. A line of smoke smudges was spread across the horizon, blotting out the stars.

Then the lookout called out that there were more ships—to the northwest. Wake borrowed a telescope and swung it in that direction. Four more ships were charging through the night.

And all of them were steaming directly for *Huascar*.

Garcia ordered *Union* to battle quarters. In seconds men were jostling and calling out in the darkness, swearing grimly as they rigged splinter nets and manned guns, opened ammunition boxes and broke out small arms. When all was ready seven minutes later the commotion stopped, all eyes on the main deck looking aft at the officers. The engine's rumble and the swish of the bow wave were the only sounds as quiet descended over the corvette.

Garcia held his course and increased speed, hoping to draw off some of the enemy. An enemy signal lamp winked in the distance. Two of the smaller Chilean ships went for the bait, diverting toward the corvette. The others held their course for *Huascar*.

On *Union*'s starboard quarterdeck an older officer scrutinized the clearing sky, shaking his head. He muttered something to the cadet beside him, then looked aloft again, his arm tracing an arc through the night. Wake followed his gesture, not seeing anything at first. Then it jumped out at him.

From the west, near the horizon, upward to the overhead zenith, he saw several planets in a line. Jupiter was about to set, then above that he saw Saturn. Little Mars was next in the line, directly overhead and next to the Seven Sisters of the Pleiades. Even the moon was in the alignment. Wake searched his memory, but couldn't remember ever seeing anything like it before. He followed the imaginary line across the sky to the eastern horizon and felt his heart miss a beat. The line ended at the Chilean warships.

Next to him, Wake listened as the officer patiently explained the Greco-Roman mythology of the planets in line to his junior: Jupiter, ruling god of them all; Saturn, god of time and former ruling god of them all, whom Jupiter overthrew; Mars, the god of war; Luna, the moon, also known as Hecate, the three-headed goddess and fearsome traveler with the dead at night. The officer added that it appeared Mars, the god of war, was leading the Seven Sisters of the Pleiades, ending with the opinion that this conjunction of planets was clearly an omen. A bad omen.

The cadet glanced up at the Pleiades, then stared at the enemy vessels, counting them out loud. There were seven. The officer nodded dourly and walked away. Wake didn't believe in mythology. He believed in science. But that didn't stop his blood from going cold at the sight of the cadet shuddering while gripping the rail.

Watching the Chilean ships grow closer—now able to smell their acrid funnel smoke racing downwind ahead of them—Wake thought about the prospects of dying here, at the bottom of the world, in a frigid ocean during a sad, ridiculous war that wasn't even his own. A few months ago, at this time of night he would have been blissfully asleep in Linda's arms. His wife and kindred soul had been beside him through good times and bad for fifteen long years, quietly showing a strength of spirit that Wake had seen in few men. He knew how lucky he was to have her.

Auburn-haired, with lively green eyes that still captivated him, Linda Wake was all that a naval officer could ask for—beautiful, intelligent, and incredibly soft and gentle at night when they were alone. She was opinionated but not arrogant, loyal but not subservient. But still, for all of that he'd almost lost her because of his profession.

Five years earlier their marriage had nearly ended from Linda's frustration with the navy's arcane ways and her husband's long absences. She was exhausted trying to raise their two children alone at Pensacola naval yard on the pay of a junior naval officer. Linda was sick of sleeping alone and worrying about whether he was dead or alive in some far-off corner of the world. Pleading letters for him to return home from sea were met with equally heart-felt notes in which he tried to explain his need to go to sea, to be a naval officer. It was a need he didn't understand fully himself. The fear and frustration in Linda had culminated in an angry ultimatum for Wake when he was stationed as a flag lieutenant to the squadron admiral in the Mediterranean—leave the navy or lose your family.

Wake had always considered the luckiest day of his life the one when he married Linda at Key West during the war. The second-luckiest was the day she unexpectedly showed up in Italy, just as he returned from northern Africa a seriously wounded hero, and they renewed their love affair. His subsequent awards and promotion had gotten him a shore job back in the States and since then neither had brought up that dark period of sad letters and heartbreak.

For the last five years they'd been home together, stationed at the Washington Navy Yard. Wake had been nominally attached to the Bureau of Ordnance, but increasingly he had been sent on various special assignments for senior officers and the secretary of the navy. Most were short and he was gone only a few weeks, a mere nuisance for their marriage. Professionally, it wasn't sea duty, but those assignments kept him busy with intriguing challenges—a rarity in a moribund navy that had declined to a shadow of its former strength in the fourteen years since the war.

In their tiny home in eastern Washington, D.C., they raised their family. Fourteen-year-old-daughter Useppa was bright and fun-loving, with a serious thirst for knowledge that reminded him of her mother. She was named after the lovely island in Florida where she was born near the end of the war. He could see Linda's beauty emerging in Useppa, which made her worsening limp seem all the more cruel.

The pain in her left leg had never been fully understood by the doctors. A birth-defect, they callously told Linda. Wake would hold his wife for hours as she cried at night, wondering what she had done wrong while pregnant. The medical opinions were divided—some said she might get better, some that she might decline in her ability to walk. No one knew, so Useppa and her parents waited to see how her ailment would evolve.

Sean, their twelve-year-old son was another matter altogether. Named after Wake's best friend, Irish-American bosun's mate Sean Rork, little Sean was a rambunctious fellow, always getting into mischief while exploring new things and places. His laugh reminded Wake of Sean's namesake, and the boy frequently talked about joining the navy, which Linda quietly ignored. Still, Wake thought his son might make the kind of officer that was needed, and he allowed himself the fantasy of imagining his own son gaining the rank of admiral. That was a professional plateau that Wake knew he—one of the few serving officers not graduated from the academy at Annapolis—would never know.

In the evenings after dinner, the little family would sit in the parlor and Useppa would ask her father about the different cultures and peoples he had seen, practicing her Spanish and French and Arabic. Sean would ask him about his ships and the storms and enemies he had faced. Then, at bedtime, in her gentle way of returning the conversation to a less bellicose nature, Linda would ask her husband to describe the sunset over one of the various seas he had sailed, or the beach of a tropical island. Wake would spin a yarn, the end of which would have them all sighing as the sun set in a far-off sea at the end of a wonderful day on a coconut palm–clad beach.

He loved those evenings and his mind traveled back home now. They were on that old sofa in the parlor. The children were in their beds, only red embers left in the fireplace. Linda was in his arms, smelling of jasmine, her softness making all the tension in his body go away. Wake reveled in the sensuousness of her. . . .

*Zaaak!*

Wake was jerked back to reality as a shrieking sound ripped through air, the fall of the Chilean shot lost in the dusk of early morning. Captain Garcia muttered a vile oath. The other officers stood silent.

It had begun.

The shot had come from the *O'Higgins,* one of the Chilean ships that had diverted from *Huascar* to chase *Union. Loa,* the other ship, also opened fire, the shot disappearing in the gloom. *Union* was not losing ground, however, and the pursuers' long shots were without effect.

Garcia frowned. "Montt, he is the captain of the frigate *O'Higgins* over there. Good sailor, good ship. British-built. Molinas of the *Loa* is good too, but she is small. No, I am watching Montt. He might get lucky with one of those shots. They have hundred-and-fifteen-pounders."

A lieutenant reported *Union's* speed as now thirteen knots by the log, that the chief engineer advised they were doing their very best. Then he reported the relative bearing on both Chilean ships was opening. The distance was increasing.

A slight smile crossed Garcia's face. "Thank God for our speed. They cannot do more than maybe nine or ten." He cocked his head as another wild shot rent the air. "Still, we must take time to swerve occasionally. I don't want Montt to get promoted at *our* expense."

The eastern horizon was brightening quickly now, the mist lifting completely. An ominous blood-red sliver appeared, then grew into a giant eye as it rose over the mountains near Punta Angamos, burning the haze away. More gunfire flashes erupted to the starboard. Then a continuous thunder of explosions began, echoing across the water. The men aboard *Union* knew their brethren on *Huascar* were fighting for their lives.

The sun changed from red to golden. The air warmed quickly and the remaining clouds parted, sunlight illuminating the ships around them like players on a field in a deadly game of sport.

"Just perfect," Wake grumbled with a growling epithet as he held the rail though a roll. "Now I'll get to see exactly who's going to kill me. Oh Lord, I wish I was home," he said to no one around him.

They paid no attention anyway. Everyone was looking east toward their admiral's ship. A collective gasp came from the officers and someone moaned, "*Dios mio . . .*"

# 2

# Washington

## District of Columbia

Two older men relaxed in an ornate second-story office on the east side of the new State, War, and Navy Building. It was an unusual meeting on a Sunday morning, a quick get-together before they both walked next door to a White House prayer breakfast, with attendance expected at church afterward.

"I'm still getting lost in this place," muttered Richard Wigginton Thompson, secretary of the navy for President Hayes. "Not used to it yet, Admiral. Looks like some oriental potentate's palace. Nothing like it back in Indiana, I can tell you *that*." Thompson folded his hands together and gazed up at the elaborate molding on the ceiling above the tri-level chandelier. "Say, Admiral, speaking of getting lost, don't we have an officer down there in South America checking on that war? Where is he? The president asked me the other day about the naval aspects of the war and I told him we were expecting a report soon."

Admiral David Dixon Porter, one of the naval heroes of the War between the States, President of the Board of Inspection, and

17

senior admiral of the U.S. Navy, lounged back in a winged chair facing the desk. He'd asked his chief of staff the same thing two mornings earlier. Porter shook his long beard, now thinning and gray. "I don't know *exactly* where he is, Mr. Secretary. Last telegram had him in Valparaiso, embarking on a merchant ship northbound for Panama and home. Said he had some very interesting observations, both naval and political. Should here in three or four weeks."

"Hah. I'll believe it when I see it. When was it that we sent him down there?"

"Left in May, sir. He arrived in June."

"And still no word, no report of what he's seen, through telegrams?"

"No, sir. His telegrams said the lines weren't private enough for his report."

Thompson pursed his lips. "Evarts over at State is making noises about wanting more ships stationed down there and getting the president to be more involved in that part of the world. Evarts is getting what he calls *intelligence* from his sources. Wish I could get 'em from mine, Admiral."

Porter considered that comment, then said, "Secretary of State Evarts is getting *opinions* from his ministers who have vested interests in the countries they're accredited to, Mr. Secretary. I'm not certain that is good intelligence, however. Our man is not tied to anyone or anything down there. He knows the culture and language, but is only loyal to our navy and our country. Thus, I believe his report will be more valuable."

Thompson returned his gaze to the admiral who had spent the last fifty years in the U.S. Navy. Porter was an icon politically, but Thompson was hearing grumbling third-hand from inside the navy: Porter was old school. Porter was tired. Porter was against innovations.

"Do you personally know this man, Admiral? What's his name again?"

"Lieutenant Commander Wake. Peter Wake. I do know him

professionally but not personally. Augustus Case spoke well of him and that was good enough for me. Admiral Case is a steady man, so I picked the man he recommended to do the job."

"Well, I hope this Wake fellow's not lollygagging about on holiday in the tropics with department funds, Admiral. And he'd better have a darn good reason for his tardiness when he gets here. Evarts is making me look the fool in front of President Hayes. We'll being seeing him this morning over there, by the way."

Porter's eyes showed no emotion as he regarded the man before him. Thompson was just another politician sitting in the secretary's chair, overseeing a navy he couldn't ever fathom. Porter'd seen them come and go over the years. He mentally added up all the secretaries of the navy he'd seen since he'd started his career—was it really twenty-one? Thompson, like most, understood his home state and Washington, but was hopelessly ignorant of the world. "It's a long way to Chile, sir. Bottom of the world. He'll have a squared-away report when he does arrive."

Secretary Thompson stood and stretched, then opened the book lying on his desk—*The Papacy and Civil Power.* He glanced at the title page. It was his personal exposé against what he considered the world-wide Catholic empire's threat to secular governments, which he had convinced Harper and Brothers to publish. But sales were dismal and now he gave copies away. "I wonder if anyone can really understand those papists down there, Admiral? It's a strange culture. Their leaders are illogical. Completely alien to us. Is this Wake one of these Catholic papists?"

Porter, whose half-brother was the late Admiral David Farragut—of Spanish descent—submerged his disgust. "Well, I never asked him, sir. I consider that sort of thing to be personal, Mr. Secretary. And I don't care if he is a papist. To me that is politics and politics isn't my bailiwick. That's what *you* understand and do."

Porter let a few seconds go by. "Wake is a warrior. And I'm a warrior—in charge of maintaining and then *using* America's warships."

Thompson headed across the room to the double doors to his private balcony overlooking the White House. He stepped out and looked east to the mansion next door. There was a whiff of burning leaves in the crisp air, a welcome change from the fetid stink of Washington summers. Thompson turned and faced inside the office, mildly irritated at Porter's reply and the fact that he hadn't joined his superior on the balcony. Porter still relaxed in his chair.

"Yes, well if others around here get their way, Admiral, you just might get the chance to do exactly that."

A little over two miles away on the eastern side of Washington, fifteen-year-old Useppa Wake turned the front page of the *Washington Post*. A three-cent daily begun two years earlier, the *Post* was in desperate competition with four other dailies in the capital and already doing well, with press runs of ten thousand. Useppa looked over at her mother putting the fried eggs onto their plates next to the buttered grits. Little brother Sean eyed the breakfast closely, licking his lips and sniffing the air as bacon sizzled on the griddle.

Sounds of the city drifted into the window. A baker's cart clattered by three floors below on Tenth Street. The Baltimore & Potomac eight o'clock rumbled by along Virginia Avenue. A Marine sergeant thundered out an order at the barracks a block over to the west. Rhythmic hammering on heavy iron came echoing up from the Washington Navy Yard.

Sean's attention wandered briefly to the window when a steam whistled shrieked at the yard's foundry shed. He knew that was unusual on a Sunday and wondered what was going on over there—his imagination conjuring up a man-o-war being fitted out hastily for some dangerous foreign service on orders from the president. Useppa turned another page, folding it so she could read something. The crinkling noise turned his scrutiny onto Useppa. She'd been changing lately, he noticed. Reading newspapers a lot, especially stories from some lady named Calista Halsey, and talking with their mother about adult things like politics.

"Mama, I wonder what they say behind Mrs. Hayes' back at those White House functions? From some of the things in this article, I imagine it's not kind," said Useppa, trying to sound grown up after reading the social column of the *Washington Post* for the first time. It described the state dinner given by the president for the British foreign secretary two nights earlier, with most of the space devoted to the first lady's attire and anecdotes from a few of the guests regarding the hors d'oeuvres. Some of them were disapproving, though veiled in polite words, suggesting that really it wasn't the first lady's fault the affair was so provincial. She was, after all, from Ohio. There was also a comment from the Italian ambassador's wife on the lack of wine or champagne.

Carrying two plates to the table, Linda Wake smiled. "Well, that is all to be expected, dear. A person in charge is frequently ridiculed, even when their policy is for the best, or at least won't hurt."

Sean giggled. "Hey Useppa, you talking about mean ol' Lemonade Lucy's temperment rule? No Devil's rum in my house!"

His mother rounded to him with narrowed eyes. "*Sean Rork Wake!* I will *not* have a twelve-year-old son of mine speaking so crassly of the first lady of our land. You just forfeited your eggs to Useppa for that remark, young man. And it's temperance, not 'temperment.' "

Useppa cast a sideways glance at her brother while she slid the eggs off his plate onto her own. "Why, thank you, Sean. I've a big day today and ever so much appreciate the extra breakfast," she said with assumed gravity. She added in a whisper when her mother returned to the stove, "Nice going, Seannie. Open your mouth again so I can have the *rest* of your breakfast." That elicited a fraternal kick to her shin.

Their mother continued on, ignoring the commotion under the table. "The *Post* ridicules President and Mrs. Hayes because they are Republicans, Useppa. That's because the newspaper is owned by Stilson Hutchins, who started it to voice the Democratic Party's opinions. So, you see, dear, they will search for uncomplimentary comments about the social affairs at the White House and print them."

"That's not fair."

"No, Useppa, it's not. But it's human nature. They see things their own way at the *Post*. Like that horrid cartoon they had recently against the president."

"The one about President Hayes vetoing that law that the Democrats passed to stop federal protection for black people voting down South?"

Linda paused, her brow furrowed. "Yes, that one. Your father fought for that freedom. I'm glad President Hayes stood firm on that. Too many good men died."

"Why do the papers make fun of Mrs. Hayes, though? Is she dull?"

"No, not at all," said Linda. "She's just a temperance lady. Her no-alcohol rule doesn't mean there isn't gaiety at the official functions, it just means no one is going to be rude or boorish on account of liquor."

Sean gave her the puppy dog look he knew she loved. "Daddy drinks rum, Mama. Does he get rude?"

"Certainly not. Your daddy is an officer and a gentleman. He never drinks too much, just a taste now and then."

"Do you drink rum, Mama? I've never seen you drink anything like that."

Linda couldn't help smiling, remembering when she and Peter were younger and occasionally shared a rum punch or wine. "Yes, sometimes I do when I'm with your father. But not often, and not in a long time, Sean."

Useppa chided her brother. "Sean, you're not supposed to ask a lady such things. Especially your own mother." She turned to Linda at the end of the kitchen table. "I'm sorry he's so very rude, Mama. Lord knows we've tried to teach him better than that."

"Useppa, he's at that age. You were at that age not so long ago."

"Mama, sometimes he embarrasses me so at church. I was never that . . . that . . . *ill-mannered!*"

Sean glared at his sister. "I'm not *sick,* Useppa. And you're not grown up yet, so stop acting all uppity and bossing me around."

Linda was about to tell them both to stop when the pain that had bothered her for the past few months hit again. It clenched her abdomen, seeming to twist her organs. She tried to stifle a gasp, but Useppa saw it and rushed to her mother.

"Mama, is it the pain again? What can I do to help?"

"It's gone now. Just a sharp ache. Nothing really, dear. I'm all right."

Useppa didn't believe her. "Mama, I'll get the doctor at the navy hospital."

"No. Right now you both should get ready for church. We've gotten behind time this morning."

Linda touched her daughter's hand. "I'm fine, dear. Really. Thank you."

The girl nodded slowly, unconvinced. "If you say so, Mama. Sean and I'll be ready right away. Come on, Sean."

The pain gripped Linda once more, but this time she turned away so Useppa couldn't see her face.

## 3

# Una Leyenda Heróica

Now that the mist was gone, Wake could see the battle unfolding. Standing next to the Peruvian officers, he could hear their gasps and sighs, helpless spectators desperate for another miracle. They had seen it happen before.

*Huascar* was firing quickly, but Wake could see that most of the shells were not hitting their target, which a lieutenant next to him identified as *Cochrane,* one of the Chileans' best ships. Wake thought about what he had heard in *Huascar's* wardroom at dinner just ten hours earlier—the gun crews of *Huascar,* while full of élan, had little experience with gunnery practice at sea.

The war had caught Peru unprepared and the navy took in men from the fishing and merchant fleets who were still learning how to shoot accurately. Ammunition was in short supply so training was limited while they were far from resupply. Luck and bravery had played larger roles than skill in their hit-and-run victories to date. The officers knew that and said they had planned more gunnery practice once they returned home to Peru, but there was the unspoken worry of what a major confrontation beforehand might bring. Even the enthusiastic Ferré had admit-

*24*

ted their green crew was *Huascar's* biggest liability.

*Cochrane,* a newly built armored frigate with four times the firepower and twice the protective armor of *Huascar,* was firing slowly, deliberately. An explosion rumbled across the water from the bow of the Peruvian ship but she kept on, smoke billowing as the two ironclads still raced toward each other like gladiators in an insane death match. Wake couldn't see how it could end in anything but annihilation for the Peruvians—the other Chilean ships were firing at *Huascar* now too. Grau's ship was surrounded by geysers, the close misses shredding the decks with clouds of shrapnel.

The range between *Cochrane* and *Huascar* was dropping rapidly—Wake calculated the closing speed as close to twenty knots—and the Chileans' renowned proficiency with naval gunnery was becoming apparent to the hushed crowd on *Union's* deck. *Cochrane's* identical sister, *Blanco Encalada,* came into range and began pummeling away from another side. *Huascar* was now being beaten down continuously by eight times her weight in guns, as the smaller Chilean ships moved toward the flanks and added their fire.

Suddenly, a huge blast of smoke erupted on the main deck of Grau's ship. When the wind cleared it away, Garcia cried out, "Dios!"

*Huascar's* turret, with her main guns, was mangled. Seconds later two explosions amidship destroyed the bridge deck where Wake knew Grau would have been standing, red flames lashing out across the deck and transforming into roiling black smoke. This time it didn't blow away, but spread along the main deck.

But *Huascar* was not done. She was firing her small secondary guns, the panicked shots going wildly into the sea around her. Steam shrieked from her stack as it toppled. Wake thought it all horrific, like a beast in the bullring being killed slowly, but he couldn't turn away.

"She is not dead yet," uttered Garcia through his tears. "Look at that! She is ramming."

Wake stood there stunned at the bravery he was witnessing. *Huascar* had altered course toward *Blanco Encalada* with the obvious intent of impaling her with the ram bow, but the Chileans understood the move and were able to swerve away.

"Now comes the end," mumbled the lieutenant next to Wake as *Cochrane* and *Blanco Encalada* turned in unison to ram *Huascar*, their courses describing circles in the sea as they settled on collision courses with their determined enemy. The Peruvian ironclad's secondary guns were mostly silent now but her speed was still considerable and Wake's eye told him that the Chileans might miss.

Grau must be dead though, thought Wake. No one could have survived that barrage of explosions on the bridge deck. He wondered if young Ferré was alive, and whether Aguirre or Garezon was commanding now. Whoever it was, the warship was still moving fast, still maneuverable, and her ram still very dangerous to an enemy. Incredibly, *Huascar's* speed and a quick swerve to port let her escape the mortal ramming blow meant for her by her two biggest assailants and she steamed on, smoke pouring from her decks and her shattered funnel, still heading north for Peru and home.

But then, as Wake was beginning to think nothing could sink Grau's ship, the Chilean ships fired broadsides from a mere two hundred yards away. Blasts rippled along the main deck and stern of *Huascar*, massive sections of deck and hull and spars flying as if from a child's model. She heeled over on her port side, almost to the point of capsizing, in a violent turn to starboard. The turn never ended and she kept on in a circle, clearly out of control. *Huascar's* decks were hidden now beneath the black cloud of smoke, and a chilling moan came from her steam whistle, diminishing to a hiss as her boilers lost their pressure and she slowed down.

"The rudder . . ." choked out Garcia.

"She's slowing," said the lieutenant. "Low in the water."

The Chileans were close alongside, turning with her, firing incessantly, smashing her down as she veered to the east. The Peruvian ensign had been shot down several times, but he saw it go up again on the stump of the main mast, fluttering above the smoke.

Good God, Wake thought, they've got to strike their flag and surrender. It was insane not to surrender. "Strike the damn flag. Please strike the flag!" he yelled, tears filling his eyes. They were dying for nothing now. They had to surrender.

Garcia shook his head. "They will not give up, Commander Wake."

*Cochrane* turned toward *Huascar*, Wake thinking it the prelude to another ramming attack, but it wasn't. The Chileans were boarding. In a scene out of the Napoleonic Wars, they were going to *capture* their greatest nemesis. Wake gripped the stern rail as he watched the Chilean ensign rise above Peru's. Towing hawsers were sent over and the smoke gradually diminished. Grau's premonition had been fulfilled, but with even worse symbolism. The Chileans under Admiral Riveros had not only won the battle, but had captured Peru's last ironclad. Wake predicted that they would probably repair her and use her against her former owners.

The bright sun was making the sea glitter as *Union* raced away from the scene of the battle. She was still receiving fire from *O'Higgins* but it was slowing as the range increased. Eventually *O'Higgins* gave up the chase and slowed down.

Wake knew that what he had just witnessed had been cataclysmic. The war, and history, was completely changed forever. Peru's final defense was gone, her resupply routes from North America and Europe eliminated. Bolivia's last hope to retain her three-hundred-mile coastline, and only outlet to the sea, had literally gone up in smoke. Along the *seven thousand miles* of South America's Pacific coast, Chile was now invincible.

Wake turned to a dazed Garcia, whose eyes remained on the southern horizon where his hero's ship wallowed. "What now, Captain?"

Garcia came out of his trance. "What now? We go home, Commander. And then we wait for them to come for *us*."

On the tenth of October *Union's* foremast lookout sighted Peru, inciting the only spark of positive emotion felt in two days. The corvette's crew was exhausted, Garcia keeping them eating and sleeping at battle stations the entire time in case more enemy ships should appear. Her engine gang below labored incessantly in the heat and grime to keep up her speed at ten knots, the chief engineer realizing it was her last defense and that if her boilers and condensers should fail after reaching port, at least her crew would be alive. The deck and gun sailors realized it too, and for the first time the coal heavers and oilers and boiler firemen were treated as first among equals.

The Peruvians went about quietly, mourning for their lost friends and countrymen, but Wake saw something that he recognized during those several days after the battle. Officers and men—old regulars and recently conscripted, Hispanics and *mestizos*—they all periodically glanced back at the southern horizon. Wake noticed that when they did, their faces would harden, eyes would grimly narrow, and after a moment they would return to their task. The Peruvians may have started out as inexperienced, but Wake knew that look from his own time in war. No matter what their age, the men of *Union* were no longer young. They were veterans now and would carry the memory of what they had seen until the day they died. And their eyes would always show it.

When *Union,* in a lifting fog, finally came within sight of the blocky headlands off Callao, the port of Peru's capital of Lima, Garcia visibly relaxed. His shoulders sagging after a long exhale, he allowed himself a lopsided smile, appearing almost lunatic in his haggard face.

"It appears that you will be able to carry that important message to your superiors after all, Commander Wake." He waved a tired hand toward the port. There was no energy left in Garcia's voice.

"This is our home, Commander. We will stay and repair and reprovision as best we can, to be ready for the enemy attack. You will probably have to go overland to Ecuador, unless a neutral warship comes into port that you can seek passage aboard."

Wake noticed the anchorage was practically deserted. Where in the past dozens of ships used to lay on their hooks with cargoes from around the world, only a few small coasting schooners could be seen. Just then the report of a cannon echoed off the town. The duty lieutenant reported that a previously unseen British frigate over by the navy docks had run up her ensign and was rendering the required naval salute. Wake could barely see her in the mist, the British naval ensign a clump of limp color on its halyard.

"An English warship? Hmm. The friends—and the eyes, no doubt—of the Chileans." Garcia sighed. "Yes, return the salute, Lieutenant, though I hate to waste the powder."

In a corner of the Peruvian naval yard, by a shed near the boiler works, Wake saw some men crawling over a large iron cylindrical object with oddly shaped appendages. He guessed it as a boiler tube, but had never seen one that long. It sat on a cradle, had pointed ends and some sort of box perched atop it amidship, with a large pipe standing up near each end. He asked an officer standing nearby about the contraption. The man offhandedly said it was an engine under repair, then changed the subject to the artillery emplacements being constructed around the harbor. But to Wake's eye it wasn't a boiler or an engine, but something else. What exactly, he couldn't fathom. That bothered him.

After *Union* had edged alongside the pier, Wake faced Garcia. "I'll be leaving now, sir. Thank you for your assistance."

Garcia nodded. "Good luck on your journey, Commander. I suppose your superiors need to have a professional assessment of the naval developments in this war."

"Yes, sir, they do. But rest assured that along with my professional assessment, I will tell them what I have personally seen of the considerable bravery of the men of the Peruvian Navy. I have never seen anything like it, Captain. It's the stuff of legend, sir. A heroic legend."

The captain nodded gently. "*Una leyenda heróica.* Yes, Commander, I think you are right about that. Perhaps that will be the lasting legacy of Admiral Grau's final battle, and a unifying rallying cry for our people in the difficult times to come."

Wake held out a hand. "As a neutral naval officer, I must professionally wish you only *safety*, sir, and not victory. I'm not allowed to tell you my personal wishes or show bias, but I suspect you can imagine them."

"I hope your country's leadership will share them, Commander. For if they do not, soon my country may disappear."

# 4

# *El Toro*

## November 1879

The U.S. legation was squeezed between tenements on a grimy side street off the Plaza de Armas in dreary central Lima, almost three hours by rickety cramped coach from the naval docks at Callao. Not a breath of afternoon air, or anything else, was stirring in the city—it was siesta—and a morose Wake thought the limp American flag outside the building a perfect symbol for his country's lack of power and influence in the region. He didn't anticipate much help from the legation, but knew he was expected to at least ask them.

Gibbs, the head of the legation with the rank of minister, was off trying to find President Prado at a Peruvian army camp outside the city, so Wake talked with the chargé d'affaires, a twenty-year careerist named Kronburg with a flaccid face and condescending attitude.

"There aren't any ships to get you out of Peru, Commander. I suppose you could go overland to Ecuador through the mountains, but that would take a month. At least a month. I hear an

American warship might stop by sometime early next year, though." He smiled. "You could always wait for that boat."

Wake swallowed the rebuke forming in his mouth. "Look, you know from my previous visits to the legation that I'm on official duties here. Time is of the essence—Washington's waiting for this report and I need to get to Panama. You've got no influence with anybody?"

"The only influence around here right now is money, Commander, and this office doesn't have much of that at all. Of course, if we had any kind of real American naval presence on this coast perhaps we could do more, but then you wouldn't be here asking *me* for a ride, would you?"

Wake sighed. He wanted to smack the smirk off the man's face. "All right. I'll try the Brits. I saw one of their ships in the harbor at Callao when we came in."

"Don't think you'll have any luck there either, Commander. They aren't exactly alongside us on this one. They're on the Chileans' team."

The sun was setting into the smoky sky of the city as Wake marched out of the building carrying the bulky sea bag on his shoulder. He was tired, hot, and angry, mostly at himself. He should've left Chile earlier, thereby avoiding the delay of being captured by *Huascar*. Then he could've gotten to Panama before chaos gripped Peru and transport disappeared.

Cursing, he walked toward the Plaza de Armas to seek a cab for the long ride back to Callao. Siesta was over and the streets echoed with shouts and hoofs in the shadows of late day. As he rounded the corner by the giant Cathedral de Lima, his eye was drawn to a landau clattering by. It had a Union Jack painted on the side, which reminded him of something. An idea flashed in Wake's mind.

"You there! In the British carriage! Please stop for a moment."

The landau slowed, then stopped as the driver turned around in his seat cautiously. "You speaking to me, sir?"

An imperious gray head emerged out of the curtains and

yelled, "Keep going, we don't have all day!" The head turned and registered the American naval officer. "Good God, now what!"

Wake recognized the man and thought it too good to be true. It would save time. He nodded politely to the driver, leaped up to the carriage step and opened the door. The lone man inside recoiled, obviously expecting lunacy or worse. "What the bloody hell are you about, man? Do you know who I am?"

Wake knew, or at least hoped he knew, exactly who and what the man was. If he was wrong, this could get bad. Very bad. Dungulph Egglestone was the British commercial attaché—officially. But Wake had deduced two months earlier that Egglestone was actually a political operative and the local spy for the Foreign Office. And for the Chileans.

His mind flashed through the points of his deduction beginning with the man's behavior around the Peruvian naval officers at a banquet in July, where he had frowned while they described their navy's victory at Iquique. Egglestone insistently asked detailed questions of them about the disposition of the Peruvian fleet, and about any innovations they were working on. On the other side of the conflict, in Valparaiso, Wake had heard Captain Patricio Lynch of the Chilean Navy mention Egglestone's name in a conversation, saying that he wished the American diplomats understood Chile's needs and grievances as well as Egglestone— an unusual compliment about an officially neutral diplomat who was stationed in your enemy's capital.

And the final and most compelling point—Wake had learned that Egglestone had arranged a shipment of three hundred Winchester Model 1876 repeating rifles to a militia regiment of ex-patriot Chileans that had been raised in the occupied Bolivian coastal town of Antofagasta. Clearly flaunting neutrality and his diplomatic immunity, the Englishman had facilitated the shipment from a surplus supply at the Canadian Northwest Mounted Police via a Mexican merchant. Over rum in a Valparaiso harbor tavern back in August, Wake had learned about it from the Colombian schooner captain who transported the rifles to Antofagasta.

Wake leaned forward into the carriage. "You aren't the commercial attaché and you aren't neutral. I know that and so will the Peruvians if I don't get a passage request to Panama from your office to HMS *Shannon* within the next hour. Tell your driver we're going to your office. Now."

"This is preposterous. I am the attaché for commerce and am bloody well offended by your behavior. The American minister will most certainly hear of this! Now who the hell *are* you?"

The man wasn't weakening and Wake's doubt was growing. Was he wrong? It didn't matter anymore, he had to continue the bluff and get passage on that ship. "Lieutenant Commander Peter Wake, but you knew that already. You've kept track of me all along the coast. The passage request for my silence. A simple *quid pro quo*."

Egglestone looked down. "A request from me means nothing. They probably wouldn't take you—"

"An official request from the political officer to take a fellow naval officer aboard? They'll take me and you know it."

"I don't know where they're headed—"

"Panama, and they get under way at dawn. The whole harbor knows that. Stop delaying, Egglestone. If I get out of this landau my first stop will be Peruvian naval headquarters. It'll take them about thirty minutes to track you down. You won't get away."

The driver called back. "Sir, continue onward or a new destination?"

Egglestone brought his gaze up from the floor, his eyes boring into Wake. He wasn't playing the confused bureaucrat anymore. The voice was graveled, the contempt spewing from him. "You will regret this, Wake. You are way beyond your depth with this."

"Time will tell on that, Egglestone. I'm a *real* neutral and have kept my mouth shut so far. This isn't my fight. You've nothing to fear if you help me."

Egglestone leaned out of the curtain and called forward. "Take us to my office. Quickly."

It was a silent, brooding ride to Egglestone's legation as Wake tried to exhale slowly, without showing his relief.

"Lieutenant Commander Peter Wake, United States Navy, with a passage request from Dungulph Egglestone of the British Legation. Permission to come aboard, sir?"

The lieutenant on HMS *Shannon*'s deck watch took the proffered document, read it, and one more time surveyed the tall American standing before him on the quarterdeck. A Yankee naval officer here on a British warship? Wanting passage? With official support?

"Please wait here, Commander. I'll need to inform Captain Nagle immediately."

Wake smiled to himself—I'll bet you do, he thought. Moments later the gold-braided arm of a full commander in the Royal Navy grasped the coaming of the after hatchway and the captain appeared, causing a commotion among the watch standers. The captain made for the American.

"Lieutenant Commander Wake, is it? I'm Commander Nagle, captain of *Shannon*. How exactly can the Royal Navy help you?"

Commander John Nagle stood ramrod straight for all of his five and a half feet. His eyes and speech were direct and Wake decided quickly that candor was the best policy.

"Sir, I am on an official fact-finding mission regarding this war and need passage to Panama. I'm required in Washington as soon as possible. Mr. Egglestone of your legation was kind enough to officially request that passage aboard *Shannon*. Word is that you're getting under way at dawn for Panama City."

Nagle pulled out Egglestone's letter from a pocket and read it again. Finally he spoke. "Fact-finding mission, hmm . . . This is quite unusual, Commander Wake. I'm not sure I understand, but

I suppose there is a good enough reason for Egglestone to make this request." He turned to the watch lieutenant. "Lieutenant Carter will be sharing his cabin with Commander Wake. See to it that Commander Wake is welcomed in the wardroom and given every consideration."

Nagle resumed his examination of Wake. "I'm not happy our departure and destination are so well known, but am looking forward to your company, Commander. Yes, our destination is Panama—but not directly. Circumstances have changed and we'll get there by way of various ports. We should be in Panama City in three weeks, if all goes well, which it seldom does on this coast. Good evening to you."

Wake's attention was diverted by a shout that came up from the ship's launch bumping alongside. The midshipman boat officer leaped up the entry port steps, braced up straight and first saluted the ensign floating off the stern staff, then the lieutenant of the watch. "All crew members accounted for and back aboard now, sir. Oh, also, there was a bit of a blowup ashore, sir. Seems somebody did in one of our senior diplo's. Did him in frightfully efficient—shot him dead as a doornail right outside the building where he lives."

Nagle stopped in his course and spun around. "Mr. Quail, who was killed from the legation?"

The youngster suddenly paled at being addressed by the captain. "Sir, a man named Egglestone. Murdered on the street beside his home just now. Shot four times in the face, sir."

"And the murderer?"

"Nobody knows, sir. But the legation clerk who handled our reprovision orders thinks it's got something to do with Peruvian fanatics and the war."

Nagle shifted to Wake, his tone even. "Looks like you got that official request just in time, Commander Wake. How very fortunate. Say, when was it that Mr. Egglestone signed that for you?"

Wake felt his cheeks flush. This was an incredible turn of events. "Not more than an hour ago, sir. Mr. Egglestone signed it in his office at the British legation. Once I had it, I came out to the ship straight away. Mr. Egglestone must've gone directly home."

Nagle nodded pensively, holding Wake in his gaze. Then he walked aft.

HMS *Shannon* was a good ship. Built only a couple of years earlier, she was unlike anything Wake had seen in the U.S. Navy. Her iron hull had an armor belt nine inches thick protecting her central vitals, backed with another thirteen inches of wood, and her steam engine—as her Welsh engineering officer proudly pointed out—drove a lifting propeller for a speed of up to twelve knots. Her main guns, shown to Wake by the gunnery officer, consisted of two eighteen-ton, ten-inch rifles that were deeply embrasured in the iron hull near the foremast so that they could fire forward as well as abeam. The sail plan was a full square-rig, but Wake learned she was a poor sailer and only carried five hundred fifty tons of coal, not nearly enough for that station. That meant that her long-distance transits would be slow, which was significant from a naval strategy point of view.

He admired the easy way her crew worked the vessel, without confusion or threats, and the competence of her officers in handling her. They had been on the coast for about six months and were beginning to know it well, having repeatedly traversed from Chile to Peru to Panama on a routine patrol route.

Dinner that evening was a stilted affair, with conversation limited to events of that day, and polite inquiries and references to Wake's career. He got the impression they were far more curious but were counseled or ordered to refrain from any in-depth discussion with him. No one would talk about Panama or *Shannon*'s route there, nor their opinion of the war raging along the coast.

And no one asked him about Egglestone.

*Shannon* got under way the next morning as the sun flared over the peak of Cerro El Cristóbal, east of the city of Lima. Callao's harbor front was quiet except for heavy clanging coming from the naval yard. A steam hammer echoed deeply off metal, the staccato beat interrupted by the occasional shout of a workman. Wake thought it odd to hear such industrious effort so early on a Sunday morning. As they steamed slowly past he peered through the gloom to find the source of the noise.

"Their new submersible craft," said Nagle as he offered his telescope and pointed. "Over there, by the shed. The fools think it's a secret but everyone knows about it."

Wake swung the glass and focused. It was the boiler-tube thing. It hardly appeared threatening, or even able to float.

"Thank you, sir. I saw it when I arrived yesterday, but couldn't deduce it's meaning. I was told it was an engine under repair. So it's a real submersible, eh? With torpedoes?"

"Yes, they've had a crew of men working on it for some time, since June. The theory is that they'll use timers in torpedoes placed under the hull of an enemy—not automotive torpedoes like a Whitehead. If it works, it could prove a nuisance for the Chileans. If it works."

Wake remembered Egglestone asking Peruvian naval officers about any innovative ideas they had. He wondered if the British spy had gotten too close to the secret project. "Well, sir, if the Royal Navy knows about it, I imagine the Chileans do."

"Yes, I would think they do. A German engineer named Othon's been working on the design for years. He started during Peru's war with Spain in the mid-sixties, but that ended before he could get it built. Othon continued off and on since then, especially since the Peruvian rebel pirates' run-in with HMS *Amethyst* back in seventy-seven. You may remember hearing of that—we used a Whitehead torpedo for the first time in combat. Somewhat successfully, I might add. It made the enemy turn and run."

As Nagle paused, Wake recalled an article about some sort of maritime dispute during a military coup in Peru where the *Amethyst* had battled one of the revolutionaries' vessels that had been harassing British ships. There was some concern at the time that use of a Whitehead automotive torpedo might be considered against the rules of war, and the captain receiving the order had asked for it in writing. The torpedo missed the target but forced the other ship to flee the scene. Then he recalled which ship the British had used it on—it had been *Huascar.*

"Well, since then, this Othon chap's accelerated his project. Since last June he's gone into high speed to complete it. Worked on it in a guarded location at the railroad's property in Paita. We heard he tested it in the water there three weeks ago and actually managed to get the bloody thing down to around seventy feet below the surface. Then they even got it back up, with all eleven crew alive. Germans—amazing engineers, aren't they? Remarkable, really . . ."

"And now it's here, sir," said Wake, his mind reeling with the possibilities for the use of such a weapon. It could turn the war around.

"Yes, quite so. They brought it here a week ago, hidden in a transport, the *Limeña*. Been keeping it in the shed and putting the finishing touches on it since then. Yesterday was the first time they've had it out of the shed. I should think it'll be in the water soon."

"Ready for action?"

Nagle ruminated for a moment, then shook his head. "I think not. But they'll have to get it ready soon, now that *Huascar's* gone. They don't have much left. The Chileans went behind the Peruvian army lines and landed 10,000 troops in the area of Pisagua a few days ago."

"They did?"

"Yes, the Chilean navy has been working well on moving their army troops forward along the coast—leapfrogging them, as it were, around the enemy. The Peruvian army in Iquique under General Buendia is now cut off from reinforcements."

"So after Iquique maybe Arica is next, then here?"

"That's the measure of it, Commander. Won't be long now. And when the Chileans do come here I think that little bull will certainly see some action. Probably its last . . ."

"Little bull, sir?"

"That's the submersible's name, Commander Wake. *Toro.* The bull. Hard for me to think of a bloody tube of iron as a bull, or even as a 'she.' More of an 'it.' The art of naval war is becoming an infernal science. Shame, really. Where's the art in it all anymore?"

Wake had seen war close up and thought it the farthest thing from art, but ignored the comment. He decided to press the question in his mind. "You seem to know quite a bit about a Peruvian secret project, Captain Nagle. I find that impressive, sir. Very impressive indeed."

Nagle gave the slightest of shrugs, his eyes neutral. "We had our ways. It's not hard around here."

Wake marked the use of the past tense and nodded, smiling in reply. Another addendum would be needed for his report.

An hour later he realized why no one would comment about their altered course the previous night. It was because they weren't headed north. *Shannon* turned south when she got out about ten miles offshore. The watch lieutenant merely shrugged when Wake asked him why, saying it was the captain's orders and one direction was as good as another.

Nagle didn't come on deck until the second dogwatch in the

late afternoon, when Wake picked a quiet moment to approach him on the windward rail. The captain wasn't in a good mood.

"Sir, it was my understanding we were heading north to Panama with various ports along the way. Why are we steering south?"

"Necessities of the service, Commander."

"Ah, then when will we be heading northward, sir?"

"When our activities are *completed,* Commander." Nagle glowered up at Wake. "You are not in charge and are aboard under my sufferance because of a British diplomat's request—a British diplomat who was murdered within minutes of meeting you. Kindly do not forget that and keep your impertinent questions to yourself. You are along for the ride. Nothing more."

Wake saluted and said, "Aye, aye, sir," as Nagle strode off and the officers gathered to leeward exchanged glances. This will be a frosty voyage, he muttered to himself with a sigh. A very frosty voyage.

# 5

## *La Ciudad de Panama*

### December 1879

"Lieutenant Commander Peter Wake, United States Navy, sir," announced the senior yeoman to the crowded great cabin aboard HMS *Triumph* as she lay drifting off the port of Arica on the Peruvian coast. Around her loitered the other ships of the Royal Navy's Pacific Squadron—*Shannon, Amethyst,* and *Shah*—as their captains assembled to meet with their commanding admiral. Each held a glass of port and a cigar. When Wake entered, the conversation dwindled.

"Good afternoon, Commander Wake," greeted Rear Admiral Frederick Henry Stirling as he shook Wake's hand. He was a large man with small, dark eyes and a vicelike grip. "I hope your voyage aboard *Shannon* was professionally illuminating and personally interesting."

"Yes, sir. Very impressive, Admiral."

"Good. I heard your time in Peru was short but not dull."

"Very short, sir. I presume you're speaking of Mr. Egglestone's death?"

The cabin got quiet. Wake noticed Stirling's eyes narrow even more. "You mean his *murder?* Yes. Quite a bit of speculation going on about that. I suppose you were *lucky* not to be there when he was attacked. You might have been killed too."

They were all watching Wake. He didn't like Stirling's inference. "From what I've heard, Admiral, it was a targeted assassination, probably by Peruvian nationalists. I wouldn't have been a target, since the United States is neutral in this war."

"So is Her Majesty's government, Commander."

"Most of the Peruvians believe otherwise, sir. They believe your government, and this navy, is siding with the considerable British economic interests in Chile."

Stirling tilted his head to one side. It was an odd mannerism, out of character with his domineering image. Wake could tell the man was seething inside. Stirling answered flatly, "Well, that's just so much rubbish."

He glanced around at his officers with a condescending smile. "I suppose the drubbing we gave the Peruvians a few years ago still stings." Stirling turned back to Wake, smile gone. "In fact, it was *Shah* that administered the lesson, assisted by *Amethyst.*"

The subordinates murmured agreement. Like so many trained dogs, Wake thought. He'd seen the same fawning in the American navy.

Nagle held up a hand. "Sorry to change the subject, sir, but if I may? Commander Wake is impatient to reach Panama. I regret that *Shannon's* duties have interfered with his itinerary. He wanted to go directly there, but our duties took us the other way. He's lost about three or four weeks, sir."

"Indeed? Three or four weeks . . ." Stirling replied. "Why, we mustn't have that. I've heard you were trying to get home to Washington posthaste, Commander Wake. Reports of the war and such for your national leadership. Very sorry for any inconvenience we may have caused."

Wake had a quick reply for the sarcasm, but swallowed it. "Sir, I was stranded in Peru and greatly appreciated the passage out of the country on board *Shannon*. But yes, I really do need to get to Panama and then home as soon as possible."

"Yes, of course. Well, we can get you to Panama now. Right after this little fight they're having at San Francisco, over by Iquique, ends."

A staff lieutenant who had just entered the cabin raised his hand. "Sir, we just got word on the battle ashore. Our consul at Iquique reports that General Escala's Chilean army forces have completely routed the Bolivian militia. The Peruvian regulars are retreating northbound, toward Tarapacá. All resistance in the Atacama region is expected to collapse within days."

The news was met with sage bobbing of heads by the naval officers. Several commented it was no surprise. One laughed. Stirling noticed Wake's reaction.

"The Bolivian peasants didn't have a chance, Commander Wake. And the Peruvians have no experience, modern weapons, or equipment. Most of all, they've got no leadership. They are doomed too."

"I wouldn't count them out just yet, Admiral. The Chileans've beaten them on the Bolivian coast and Peru's southern frontier, but once they fight in the Peruvian heartland it may be different."

Nagle interrupted. "Commander Wake's passage northbound, sir?"

Stirling sighed. The head tilted again. He didn't even look at Wake but turned to another officer. "*Shah* is heading north this afternoon. That departure will be expedited. Captain Thorncroft, have Commander Wake's things taken aboard your ship *immediately*. Commander Wake, you should be in Panama in ten days or so. Just in time for Christmas."

With a thick Scottish accent Thorncroft said, "Aye, sir. Said and done." He glanced at Wake, then jerked his head toward the cabin door and put down his glass.

"Thank you, sir," Wake said to Stirling, who was already speaking to Nagle about something else. The admiral waved a dismissive hand in reply as Wake followed Thorncroft out of the cabin and along the passageway.

Panama was reached in twelve days, the first distant landfall after Ecuador's volcanic Cabo Blanco being the island of Taboga in the Islas Perlas. At dawn the next day they were at anchor off the old city of Panama, the southern terminus of the trans-Isthmusian railway and the soon-to-be French canal linking the Caribbean Sea and the Pacific Ocean.

La Ciudad de Panama was a beautiful sight from a distance. This was the fabled place where for three hundred years the incredible treasures of the East Indies arrived in the Americas, halfway en route around the world to Sevilla in Spain. Balboa had discovered it and was later beheaded by the governor there. Pizarro had used it to launch his expeditions to Peru. Drake and Morgan had descended upon it. And now the world of commerce came to this city, not as a destination, but as a waypoint to somewhere else.

The graceful forms of the city's ancient pink and yellow colonial edifices—churches and treasury buildings and mansions—rose from a flat peninsula in front of the imposing heights of Cerro del Ancón, with an ancient fortress dominating the waterfront in the foreground. Lesser structures emanated away from the city center, gradually giving way to modest homes that sprawled for miles along the outer curve of the bay. Red and brown spires and green coconut palms rose above the glittering blue of the sea, combining Spanish imperial elegance with the languid ease of the tropics.

The sun was high overhead and glaring mercilessly when Wake departed the ship without ceremony and rode ashore on a harbor bumboat. The old wherryman landed him near the market at a wharf jammed with fishing boats. By the time he had climbed over the boats and made the wharf's stone deck, Wake was soaked with sweat from the humid air. He walked east through the throng of sellers and buyers in the market square, remembering it all—the people in motion, the sewer stench, the conflicting noise of laughter and screams.

Wake knew Panama City well from his duty with the 1870 United States naval expedition commanded by the famous Selfridge that surveyed Panama for a canal route. He didn't like it. It was the crossroads of ne'er-do-wells and human parasites from North and South America, from Europe and Asia. A dozen languages could be heard shouted along the waterfront, many slurred by rum. Every hue of skin, every class of man, was all around him as he trudged through the three-hundred-year-old city. The air of the city was always the same, filled with a sense of excitement offset by a sense of hopelessness.

In the *mercado* of Panama City one could see ashen-faced Chinese coolies, sharp-eyed Japanese merchants, sunburned French and German construction engineers, swaggering musta-chioed Colombian administrators, wild-looking half-drunk American filibusterers, and mixed-breed seamen, all of them watching muscled black laborers carrying impossible loads—the streets were full of men without illusions.

And there were women, too. Some of them very dangerous women, their haughty eyes evaluating a man in seconds as he approached, then turning sultry if they thought it worth the effort. These were women with red lips and dirty hair who could outwit, out-cuss, and out-fight most of their prey.

Wake shifted his sea bag to the other shoulder and kept going in the rolling gait of a sailor, eyes focused on the uneven street twenty feet in front, ignoring the mass of humanity around him. He'd seen it all before anyway, in Colón, in Cartagena, Havana, Cádiz, Genoa, and Kingston. Same look in the eyes and sarcasm in their words.

Once through the gateway of the Carrera de Cordoba the crowd thinned out. Wake was now in the winding streets of oldest section of the city, where the important people lived. Gentlemen strode along in white linen suits topped with the broad-brimmed woven hats that were becoming the rage up in the States. Elegant ladies were glimpsed within carriages, clattering by to a luncheon or church social. Watching the elite go by, Wake had the odd feeling that something was different about the city.

Now it registered. It was the buildings. They were cleaner, as were the streets. There was whitewash on the walls, with increasingly more cosmetics applied to the buildings the further he walked into the upper class district. It must have been a tremendous effort, he realized, especially after the horrendous fire of the year before when a third of the city was burned. But he hadn't noticed any of the new paint and cleanliness when he had been through in June. He wondered why they had suddenly renovated the city.

Ahead he saw the mansion of the provincial president-elect, Demaso Cervera—servant of the Colombian national government in Bogotá and the man who oversaw the swirling mess that was Panama. Colombian soldiers in white dress uniforms with blue caps stood at parade rest at the grand entrance overlooking the bay. Bunting in the yellow, blue, and red of the national flag was everywhere. A nervous-looking officer stood nearby watching the American naval officer approach.

A block before the mansion Wake made a right oblique into a tiny alleyway. It angled off and took him on an incline to the Carrera de Sucre, where he made another right and soon saw his destination, with the great cathedral of Panama looming up behind. A red, white, and blue cloth draped over the second-story balcony announced its ownership even before one saw the eagle on the large brass plaque next to the massive paneled door.

Wake lifted the latch and swung the door open. Inside it was at least ten degrees cooler. He stood there for a moment, savoring the slight breeze flowing through the room from a shaded courtyard beyond the far wall. Voices echoed. A fountain gurgled in the courtyard. From a doorway in the shadows an older man interrupted Wake's reverie.

"Lieutenant Commander Wake, I presume? Welcome to Panama. We've been expecting you—*for two months.*"

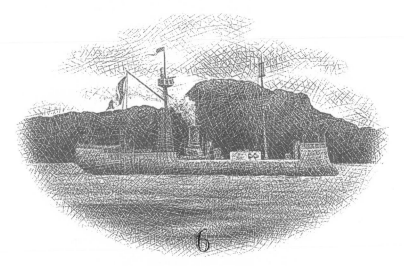

# 6

# The Bridge at Barbacoas

"Bridge over the Chagres is partially out at Barbacoas. It'll take a few days to get the railway fixed," said Deputy Consul General Bernard Ford, after ushering Wake into a private office. Wake had met him on the way south to Chile in June. The man was your average diplomat, no more, no less. He had listened patiently while Wake explained his convoluted route and eight-week delay, and his urgent need to get to the other side of the Isthmus and get a ship home.

Wake asked, "The Rio Chagres is in *full* flood? I can't even get through on foot?" The Chagres was the main river traversing central Panama. It was also a barrier when in a torrent.

"Yep, full enough flood that it overwhelmed that iron bridge that was forty feet above the river. Nobody ever thought it would get that high, but it did. The road and railway are closed. The water's going down slowly, so you'll be delayed only a few days. Maybe a week. Guess you'll be here for Christmas."

Wake had forgotten about Christmas—one day was like another at sea and he'd lost track of the date. A fleeting image of his family in Washington flashed in his mind, which reminded him of his naval superiors. He forced himself to think.

"What about the telegraph line?"

"Last I heard the telegraph is still working, though for how long is always God's guess. You want to use it?"

"Yes, sir. I need to communicate with my leadership."

"Yep, I bet you do, Commander. I bet you do."

Wake drained the coffee, wondering what that meant but was too tired to pursue it. "Anyplace I can hole up till the bridge is open?"

"Not too many decent places with vacancies. Suppose we can put you in one of the legation's reserved rooms at the Grand. Town's pretty much full up in anticipation of the big event. You'll have to be out by then, but that'll give you a week."

"What big event?"

Ford grinned. "Oh, you really have been out of touch, haven't you?"

The clerk took the smudged form from Wake's hand and studied the block letters. Overhead a fan slowly turned by way of a jute string that crossed the ceiling and ran down the wall to the moving toe of a yawning boy in the corner. The effort didn't move much air and the squeak of the pulley was aggravating Wake's headache.

The clerk clucked as he counted the letters in the message to add up the cost, glanced at Wake, and walked off. The clatter of telegraph keys started up in a back room behind a louvered door. A few minutes later the clerk reappeared, signed the form with a flourish, then returned it to the American, who scanned it again.

23 DECEMBER 1879
URGENT ROUTING FR PANAMA CTY, COLOMBIA
TO USNAVY DEPT, WASH DC, USA
TO: COMMODORE W.N. JEFFERS, USN
CHIEF OF BUREAU OF ORDANANCE
FR: LTCMDR P.WAKE, INDPNDT ASSGNMT

XXX AM IN PANAMA CTY NOW XXX MY DELAY
DUE TO CAPTURE OF MRCHNT SHIP BY PERU NVY
XXX THEN PAX IN TRANSIT WITH ROYAL NVY BUT
DIVERTED OUT OF WAY XXX NOW WAITING FOR
ROAD TO COLÓN TO OPEN XXX MAYBE 1 WEEK XXX
ETA 15 JAN 1880 XXX IMPORT INFO IN RPT XXX

Wake wanted to ask Jeffers to let his wife know where he was
and when he'd be home, but that wasn't done in official
telegrams. Still, he hoped Jeffers, who was his nominal boss at the
Navy Department, would understand and take care of that anyway.

Since he was frequently on assignment for other senior officers in the department, Wake hadn't seen much of Jeffers and
sometimes worried that his official commanding officer was
offended by his odd duties and unavailability to the Bureau of
Ordnance. But Jeffers had never hinted at any animosity, so Wake
assumed he was used to having his officers siphoned off for special jobs.

Without enough left over for a separate personal telegram to
Linda—he needed what he had left for travel money—Wake paid
the telegraph bill out of his own pocket, knowing that at some
point, probably six months later, he would get reimbursed.
Afterward, he emerged into the harsh white light of the afternoon, heading to the central plaza and his room at the Grand. He
had the legation's last vacant one, before the anticipated influx of
guests the following week.

By then, Wake hoped to be long gone on his way home.

Christmas was depressing. The combination of loneliness and worry for his family, concern about his career, and memories of the look in Grau's eyes as he spoke those last words produced a melancholy that kept Wake in his room, reading and rewriting his report. The day after his telegram went off he received the terse reply—"RPT ASAP"—which did nothing to lessen his anxiety. Even the Christmas Eve service in the little Methodist church added to his depression and sense of failure. Claustrophobic in the hotel room, he felt overwhelmed outside in the crowds.

As was common in Latin America, the initial repair completion estimate for the railroad was hopelessly inaccurate. It wasn't a few days, or six or seven. It was eight days of waiting. And even then the railroad wasn't open for the whole route—the main vehicle span of the bridge was still out, but people were crossing on foot along planks laid across the remaining framework. Trains waited at either side of the river to shuttle people and light cargo between the bridge and each coast. But the Isthmusian transit, and the way home, was open. He was leaving that morning.

December 31, 1879, was a day that Wake later would remember as one of the most important in his life. It was day of the big event for which everything in the town had been in turmoil—Panama City would meet the great French canal builder, seventy-four-year-old Ferdinand Marie Vicomte de Lesseps, constructor of the Suez Canal and heralded architect of the much greater Panama Canal. De Lesseps and his entourage had arrived in Colón on the Caribbean side the day before. They were scheduled to cross half the isthmus on the train to the bridge over the Chagres that very morning, cross the bridge on foot, then board another train to the Pacific coast, arriving that afternoon.

Wake's plan was to vacate his hotel room—it was already allocated to incoming visitors that day anyway—then take the train from Panama City to the Barbacoas Bridge at Rio Chagres. When the triumphant de Lesseps parade took the Pacific-bound train from Chagres, Wake would take the Colón-bound train. He'd been warned by the hotel's manager that the train to Barbacoas Bridge would be jammed with people with influence, that all passage on the train had been reserved, and that he'd never get on board.

He left the room before dawn in his best uniform, which he had cleaned and pressed the day before. By seven that morning he was ensconced in the Panamanian presidential car of the train at the yard north of the city, having informed the watchman that he was a special American advisor to President-elect Cervera. The best car in the train, the mahogany-paneled salon stank of stale cigar smoke and greasy food leftovers.

By nine o'clock, when the train crew sauntered aboard to ready the cars, Wake was reclining on the sofa and making do with what he found lying around that would give the impression he wanted. In spite of the shabby condition of the car, he discovered some pleasurable items and ended up smoking an apparently expensive cigar, sipping some very decent rum, and nibbling some pineapple and oranges. Wake didn't like smoking, but it was part of the façade he needed to create. The rum he did like, however—Pampero from Venezuela. He played the part, banking on the fact that in Latin America if you looked the part of a *jefe,* others would be subservient. It worked. The conductor shrugged and went about his business, smiling at the *yanquí* sailor and getting ready for a long day with obnoxious people.

Those people started boarding before lunch, by which time Wake was in a pleasant mood. Things were changing. His earlier travails were over. He was going home. By that evening he might very well be on a ship at Colón. In two weeks he would be in bed with his wife in America. Wake stood in the corner away from the revelers, keeping out of the way, but his mind was visualizing Linda.

His train-mates, mostly Panamanian politicians and businessmen in their finest white suits, along with a few influential local

Americans in dark attire, were also in a good mood. After ten years of economic downturn the future looked bright for Panama. The smell of money was in the train car—money from construction of the new canal, planned to take at least six years; money to support the infrastructure of the construction; and money from the ongoing operation of the new canal. It was going to be more money than anyone there had ever seen—money that would go on forever. In fact, they said with knowing grins, they would get richer than anyone could even estimate. And the people in that private car were the ones who would be getting richest.

Wake stayed in the background once the car filled, not wanting to chance a confrontation and subsequent eviction. It was a long ride, almost three hours to go the twenty-five miles to Barbacoas. They chugged alongside the Rio Grande through cheering crowds in the villages of Miraflores, Pedro Miguel, and Paraíso, then the locomotive struggled slowly farther up into the mountains, smoke and cinders belching up then settling down in their path. Swaying along at little more than a walk, the train made the big curve of the track around the western slope of Gold Hill, where the French had hopes there was enough gold to finance the whole project.

From there it went through the central highlands, chugging past Bas Obispo to the banks of the notorious Chagres River. From there it turned west and followed along the edge of the river to Matachín, the village where Chinese laborers working to build the railroad twenty years earlier had committed suicide en masse. It was the only place they passed where the inhabitants did not cheer, the few left in the village glancing up sullenly as they watched the train struggle by.

Wake studied the river he knew so well from his work on the 1870 Selfridge Darien Expedition. During the mission, he had transited the Isthmus several times on that very same railroad and knew each village, each hill, every swamp. Nothing had changed. Matachín was said to be haunted, but it was the Chagres that truly scared Wake. That chasm through tentacled jungle was a deceptive monster that could change from placid dream to treacherous nightmare in minutes during the rainy season, flooding entire valleys, wiping out villages, destroying roads and bridges. He shuddered at the memories: slithering snakes, droning clouds of mosquitoes, river waters rising more than a foot a minute. And the physical dangers he'd endured paled in comparison to the malaria that had eaten out his guts and set his brain afire—nearly killed him—not so far from that exact spot.

Seven miles farther west they saw the bridge at Barbacoas. The shanty village itself was on the other side, bamboo and palm thatch huts perched on a reddish-brown bank of mud. Wake saw why the rail line was cut—both entry ramps to the bridge were partially washed away, making the roadbed unstable. Gangs of laborers, black and Asian, were hauling mud and timbers along the slope to fill in the gaps even as the water raged by them.

The train slowed and Wake saw a group of well-dressed people standing near the bridge on his side. Others were walking gingerly in a single file, arms outstretched for balance, across planks laid on the iron bridge deck, the line snaking back to another group of people waiting on the far bank. Gray smoke wisped up from another train—Wake's ride to Colón—on the Barbacoas side.

The Panama City train's whistle shrieked as the cars jerked to a stop, eliciting an ovation from the elite in the salon car and half-hearted applause from the waiting crowd. The important foreign guests of honor standing in a clearing by the track were trying to keep up the appearance of gaiety, but Wake thought their smiles a bit worn, gestures sadly lethargic. Several ladies in fancy dresses with bustles and flowered hats were surveying their surroundings with undisguised horror. A howler monkey in the tree above them screamed out, bringing forth a similar reply from the ladies and making the men laugh nervously. Standing in ankle-deep brown ooze off to the side, a Colombian army band in spattered dress whites tooted out some unfamiliar tune as the leaves of the triple canopy forest dripped all over the entire affair. It wasn't raining—it was the permeating humidity reminding the attendees that they lived at the sufferance of the jungle. The sight, the sounds, and smell—Wake thought it all a rather pathetic show. And pure Panama.

Wake disembarked last, his eyes on the bridge, trying to figure out if he could stem that line of crossers and walk past them to the Colón train. Steam hissed from the other train and a cloud of smoke erupted from its stack. It was getting ready to leave. Wake decided he'd just have to be rude and force his way through the oncoming pedestrians and over the bridge—there was no time for delay. He heard shouts from the other side in Spanish, catching the words, "*Vamos ahora!*"

On the near side of the bridge, the president-elect of Panama stepped forward from the assembled Panama City people and embraced a grandfatherly man in a crumpled white linen suit who strode out from the entourage grouped around him. Wake thought Ferdinand de Lesseps looked just like the drawing he'd seen in the *Star & Herald*—the English language newspaper in Panama City. The Frenchman appeared confident, no easy feat while standing drenched in sweat in a jungle next to the torrent that cut the only lifeline for the new project, and whose noise filled the background so that the two men had to shout to be heard.

Wake caught all this only peripherally as he made his way, sea bag on his shoulder, around the throng to the railroad ramp. His back now to the ceremony, he was stepping onto the bridge when he heard a voice calling him.

"Wake? Peter Wake! I say, is that you?"

It was an American voice, one that sounded vaguely familiar. Wake turned around and saw the source. George Muirson Totten—one of the men who had led the effort to build the railroad in the early 1850s and who had designed and built the Barbacoas Bridge—stood there, hand out, beaming. His large eyes set in a plain face, atop a tall frame, Totten was the image and spirit of American enterprise.

"It *is* Wake, what a coincidence! To meet you here at Barbacoas, of all places."

"Mr. Totten, good to see you again. Yes, it is a coincidence, isn't it? Same place we last spoke, what, nine years ago—"

"And the river flooding then too. But not this bad. Never this bad. And look at this bridge. I never dreamed it would flood this high when I built the damned thing."

"It never had." Wake heard the far train's whistle sounding, a plaintive shrill like some giant wounded rainforest bird. He was running out of time. Totten was gesturing for someone to come over. Wake tried to get Totten's attention while moving backward across the bridge. "Sorry, Mr. Totten, but I really must go—"

"One of Selfridge's officers!" Totten shouted to the man in the crowd, then nodded. "Yes, from the survey, right here!"

Several men in the crowd pointed at Wake. They started heading his way.

Wake was almost at the point on the bridge where the single file crossed when a Colombian soldier held up a hand. His words weren't discernible above the din of the water rushing by below. Then he pointed behind Wake. The three men in suits were walking fast toward him, gesturing to him, close enough now that he recognized them. He stopped, energy leaving his body, debating whether to keep walking away, maybe even running, over the remaining part of the bridge. The hesitation lasted a few seconds while the soldier looked at him quizzically, but he knew he didn't dare be rude at this point—not to these particular men.

Wake turned and faced them, trying to smile pleasantly as Totten; Thomas Brown, the American consul general; and none other than Ferdinand de Lesseps himself came up and shook his hand.

Wake knew his plan was falling apart.

# 7

## *Le Grand Français*

"Yes, Commander Wake here was on the survey party. He knows the rail route, the canal route, and the local situation," Totten explained to the Frenchman. De Lesseps scrutinized Wake for a moment, then nodded pleasantly.

Wake still edged slowly across the bridge. "It was awhile ago, Mr. Totten. I'm sure things have changed since I was here back in seventy. And I really need to get on that other train for Colón before it leaves."

Brown was adamant. "Nonsense. You'll come to Panama City with us. Catch the train tomorrow. The United States is here to assist in the French effort and Ferdinand will want to ask you some questions. Won't you, Ferdinand?"

"Yes. I would like that opportunity," the Frenchman said slowly, his eyes darting down at the river, then at Wake. "It will assist me in my planning. Thank you very much, Commander."

Totten patted Wake's shoulder. "It's settled then, you're coming back with us. Besides, you don't want to miss the grand soirée we've got planned for the guest of honor tonight, do you?" He glanced at a pocket watch. "Oh, times a-wastin' men, let's get going."

"No, gentlemen, I can't," Wake said levelly, trying to control his anger. "I have specific orders and need to be on that train—" Above the crash of a floating log against the bridge piers below, he heard the hiss of steam blowing, then iron squealing on iron, and finally another shrill whistle as the Colón train started moving. It was too far for him to run and make it now.

Totten chuckled. "Looks like your train over there's gone without you anyway, Wake. Might as well grin and bear it, son. You're just going to have to go to a New Year's Eve party tonight and have *fun.*"

De Lesseps did not talk with Wake on the train. Totten, explaining that de Lesseps had duties to perform, said the Frenchman wanted to speak with Wake at his leisure later that evening. Then Totten headed off to de Lesseps' personal car, where the president-elect, consul general, and others were discussing politics over drinks. Wake was left with the bureaucrats in a general car, swaying with the incessant motion, trying to get comfortable and not slide off the worn wooden benches.

The train pulled into the station at Panama City amid fanfare and blaring music from the presidential honor guard band. Several politicians spoke, then de Lesseps' entourage departed in a line of carriages and proceeded through the city streets to the central plaza, where thousands of people were waiting for the main speeches. Along the way, the inhabitants gathered to catch a glimpse of the Frenchman. Balconies and windows were full, streets had to be cleared for the procession, and even the rooftops had spectators. The whole city wanted to see the great man who was going to bring such wealth and fame to them all.

The central plaza was dominated on the western side by the great brown-stoned Cathedral of Panama, the spires of its twin bell towers piercing the sky. Also on the plaza were the bishop's residence, provincial government headquarters at the Cabildo, and the Grand Hotel where de Lesseps, et al., would stay. It was a huge park, overflowing with people and ringed for this occasion with French flags adorning every lamppost, doorway and window. Wake had never seen anything like it. The feeling in the air was almost religious, as if the savior were coming. *Perhaps he is, at least economically,* decided Wake.

Fed up with his plight, he decided not to attend the speeches in the plaza and instead ended up back at the Grand. A back room was found for him, this time shared with a newly arrived pasty young French engineer with spectacles who appeared permanently bewildered. Wake stretched out on his cot, listened to the crowd outside, and fumed quietly. He looked at the youngster, sitting there reading a manual, and calculated that Panama's diseases would take him in six months, once the rains started again.

"Thank you for taking time to talk with me, Commander Wake," offered de Lesseps as he entered through the red damask curtain into the alcove set aside for their conversation. The curtain screened them from view but didn't really diminish the loud dance music just beyond.

The Frenchman looked tired and spoke softly, his English much better than Wake had anticipated. "I apologize for this most unusual locale and time, but it has been . . . very busy. Everyone wants to talk to me, to tell me things they think are important."

Wake was tired too. It was after eleven o'clock in the evening and the guests were getting noisier as the night went on, fueled by rum and champagne and ecstatic predictions for their future. He was hot and sweaty in his full dress uniform and was about to leave for his room when Totten had asked him to wait in the alcove.

Wake wanted to get this over with. "Well, I'm glad to be of help, Mr. de Lesseps, but I'm not sure what you want of me."

"I want the truth, Commander. I want to know what you know about the canal route and Panama and the people in this room."

"Why me, Mr. de Lesseps? You've got all kinds of experts in that room out there just waiting to be asked."

De Lesseps loudly let out a breath. "Ha! *That* is exactly why, Commander. They are all just waiting to tell me their opinion of this and of that. And most of them want money to go along with the opinion. Directly, indirectly, they have a . . . Oh, how do you say this in English . . . *arrièrre-pensée?*"

"Ulterior motive?"

"*Oui,* that is it! Money is the motivation for those people out there. I cannot trust everything that is said to me by them." De Lesseps leaned forward in his chair. "But you, you are different."

"Me? How am I different?"

"You have no motive, Commander. You will have no agenda. You will make no money. But there is something far more important—something we have in common. I saw it today. You wear *that* and so do I." He pointed to one of the two medals on Wake's chest. It was a five-pointed white star on a green wreath, suspended from a red ribbon.

De Lesseps touched the similar medal on his chest. "The *Légion d'honneur.* I received mine for building the canal at Suez in Africa. You received yours for what you did in Africa. Oh, yes, I know of your name, Commander. And of your bravery in rescuing my countrymen in the desert of *Maroc.* With that medal we have a bond, you and I. Now, please stay here and help me for a while. I appreciate the time you give to me."

Wake didn't know what to say. He had always thought himself merely lucky that his attempt to save the missionary hostages, and himself, in Morocco had turned out well. Images came into his mind. Frightening images. Thinking about it all made the chest wound gained during that rescue start to throb. Still, it felt good to know that Ferdinand de Lesseps, of all people, had heard of him and understood what that medal stood for. Oh Lord, he wondered, maybe I'm getting narcissistic.

"I was lucky in Morocco, Mr. de Lesseps. Very lucky. But I'll help you with all that I know about Panama. Ask away."

De Lesseps smiled and rubbed his hands. "Good! Now please tell me which route you prefer."

"Of the five, two in Nicaragua and three in Panama, I think the Chagres–Rio Grande route is the best. The one you chose."

"Do you believe it can be done without locks. A sea level canal?"

Wake shook his head. "No. The elevation of the continental divide is too high and too broad, even for the most modern of steam equipment, to reduce down to sea level. I've been there. The rock formations are loose and unstable so you'd have to excavate a huge swath for the right width and proper slopes to eliminate sliding and filling in. With locks you can eliminate about ninety—maybe a hundred—feet of elevation. That means less digging, less time, fewer problems." He saw de Lesseps' face tighten. "But I'm not an engineer, sir. Your engineers might have a way to accomplish that. I don't know."

"But the commanding officer of your survey expedition, Commander Selfridge, recommended a sea level canal. I heard him say so at a conference on the canal I attended in the United States."

"Yes, he did believe in a sea level canal, sir. He recommended it be done on the Atrato River far to the east of here, on the Gulf of Urabá. But I disagree with him on that. It can't be done there either. For the same reasons—the mountains."

"Hmm. We shall see. And the climate?"

Wake winced, remembering the heat and insects. "Deadly. Disease is the worst, but floods, insects, predators, and the heat will kill just as many men. Make sure you have good hospitals. But I'm sure Gaston Blanchet must have reported all this after his last inspection tour."

De Lesseps was on the edge of his seat now, eyes boring into Wake. An aide entered abruptly and he brusquely waved him away. "I've seen information to that effect, but described differently. What about the labor force here?"

"In Panama?" Wake shook his head. "You'll need tens of thousands of real laborers that are desperate for the work, have the strength to do the work, and can still survive in the jungle. Panamanians are afraid of the jungle and aren't strong enough for this kind of thing. They stay on the coasts."

"The Indians of the interior, perhaps?"

"No. Not enough of them, they don't understand our concepts of work, and they wouldn't help you destroy their land anyway. You'll have to import workers."

"But several local businessmen have assured me they can supply laborers."

"Not in the numbers you need, Mr. de Lesseps."

"I do not understand. Our projections—"

"I've heard your projections. They're wrong. You'll need at least three to four times the number of men, far more than your staff thinks is required to build the canal."

"That is preposterous, Commander. We have precisely calculated the number of men needed in each facet of the operation."

Wake held up a hand, stopping de Lesseps, then said flatly, "You didn't calculate the most important factor. Death. For every man needed to actually build the canal—two more will die."

Wake saw the man's reaction and continued. "Did you see Matachin today? Where the Chinese laborers building the railroad years ago committed mass suicide?"

"Yes, someone spoke of it as we passed, but the car was full of people talking. I did not hear what exactly was said."

"They were driven to that act by this hellish place. This country is full of death, Mr. de Lesseps. It damned near killed me with malaria. And you have to accept that fact and plan for it."

Wake could see that de Lesseps was having trouble understanding it all, that this was new to him. No one, neither staff or local officials, had told him the extent of the labor and disease problem. Obviously, they didn't want to scare him, and his money, away.

"Mr. de Lesseps, when you built the Suez Canal it took you nearly eleven years. You had hundreds of thousands of slaves furnished to you by the Egyptian Khedive in the early years before the British protested. Those were local inhabitants who were acclimated to the heat and diseases, but you still lost many of them. In Panama the locals won't do the work in the middle of the Isthmus, and your imported laborers will drop by the thousands. No one told you, did they? It happened in the fifties when they built the railroad. Everyone here knows that. Matachin is just a small example."

De Lesseps was clearly upset. His cheery public face had changed to a mixture of fright and anger. "You are very negative, Commander Wake."

"I am realistic."

"So you think this cannot be done?"

"I'm not sure, sir. But I think there is a possiblity, if done *well*."

"Then we will do it *well*, Commander. Thank you for your time this evening."

De Lesseps stood, his confident manner returned as he straightened his tunic. "I must not ignore the others any further, Commander Wake. It is a new year coming in just a few minutes. A new year with new possibilities and new hopes. And new strength of purpose."

"I wish you all kinds of good luck in this endeavor, sir. There'll be enough bad luck around already."

"Luck?" De Lesseps said with disdain. "There is an old Spanish proverb—stout hearts break bad luck. My men have stout hearts, Commander. Even this place you dread so much cannot diminish that. We will *build* this canal. You will see!"

He was warming to his subject, as if a crowd were gathered instead of a lone American naval officer who had just poured cold water on his dream. A finger pointed skyward for emphasis. "And I want you to be there tomorrow, on the first day of a new decade, as we cast the first shovel of dirt for this canal that will span the oceans.

You will be my personal guest at this momentous ceremony."

Wake dared not refuse. Instead, he took a breath and gave the age-old weary reply of a sailor. "Aye, aye, sir."

De Lesseps patted Wake on the shoulder and slid between the curtains to a room of applauding admirers. Wake started to follow but was blocked by a small man in crimson and white robes who deftly stepped inside the alcove. Wake recognized him as the bishop of Panama. He grinned at Wake's surprise and offered a thin hand. His bony fingers were cold when Wake shook them, but the English was startlingly fluent.

"We met on the train yesterday, I believe, Commander Wake. I am José Teleforo Paúl Vargas, Bishop of Panama. I see you have just had a conversation—a rather long one—with Monsiuer de Lesseps. Perhaps you administered a dose of plain talk, so rare for the famous man to hear these days?

Wake ignored the comment. "How can I assist you, Your Excellency?"

The bishop sat and beckoned Wake to take the other chair. "By indulging me for merely a few minutes, for it is I who have something for you. Two somethings actually. The first is pleasant for me—a hello from a friend of yours who is a Jesuit brother and a friend of mine, Bishop Ferro of Genoa. I remembered your name in a story he told me when I last saw him in Rome a year ago." Vargas laughed softly. "Oh, Commander, do not worry, it was a *good* story. You know, we bishops like to tell a juicy story as much as anyone, and he told one involving you at a castle in Italy—when the French and the Germans almost went to war again. Very humorous."

Wake winced at the memory. Five years earlier, while an admiral's flag lieutenant stationed in Europe, he'd managed to say some impolitic things to a senior German diplomat during a social event at a British diplomat's castle. The German had been rudely treating the French envoy and the two had threatened a duel. In addition to insulting the German, Wake caused a further stir by his close friendship with the French diplomat's wife. Tongues had wagged and Wake was in a bad spot for a while. Ferro knew the whole story. Wake wondered how much he'd told Vargas.

"I remember Bishop Ferro fondly, sir. He was a kind and charming man."

Vargas laughed. "Yes, sometimes he is. But back to the point. Ferro told me he admired you, an unusual thing for him. He said, though you are not of the faith, you are the kind of man whom the Church should assist if possible, should the opportunity arise. Said to say hello if I ever saw you. I found it interesting that he thought I might."

Wake tried not to show his impatience. "Very nice of him, but what's the second point you wanted to make, sir?"

The mirth left Vargas's face. "It is not pleasant for me, but crucial for you. I am going to assist you by passing along some information involving your life, Commander Wake. It appears that you have angered certain powers in authority in Chile. They think you had something to do with the murder of a man in Lima who was very valuable to them, and that you are going to tell your government to abandon its neutrality in the sad war raging south of here and support the Peruvians."

Wake's mind raced. Egglestone? But he didn't do anything to the man. "I don't understand, Bishop. I didn't kill anyone in Lima. You must have some wrong information, or the wrong man."

"No, it is *you*. It doesn't matter what you did or didn't do, my son. It only matters what they think and what they do. The Chileans are very suspicious of you. Be careful."

That got Wake mad. "That's ridiculous. I'm an American naval officer and I don't go around murdering people. And I don't like the inferred threat at all. How in the world do you even know this?"

"I hear many things from many sources in many places, Commander. I have now fulfilled the duty to my friend Ferro. What you do with that information is your decision." He stood, parted the curtain and looked at de Lesseps standing before the assemblage. The bishop gestured toward de Lesseps. "So, let us join *Le Grand Français* for the moment of rejoicing, shall we? It is almost midnight, Commander. A new year awaits."

Wake was shaken, still baffled by the bishop's warning. He had followed the line of neutrality very closely—except for that one moment in Lima with Egglestone. Questions filled his thoughts—did the Brits still think he was involved in Egglestone's murder? Is the rumor widespread? Have the American consuls in Latin America heard that rumor? The ominous question—has Washington? He suddenly noticed Vargas had just said something. "What did you say, sir? '*Le*' what?"

Vargas flashed the grin again as he held the curtain open for Wake. "*Le Grand Français.* The great Frenchman! That's what they called him after Suez."

As Wake emerged into the celebration he heard the bishop mutter to himself. "And I wonder what they will call him after *Panama?*"

The next morning saw de Lesseps and entourage—including Wake—attending the inauguration of President Cervera at the Cabildo. The ceremony and subsequent cathedral mass took so long the party missed the tide and were late for the big heralded event—the one everyone really wanted to see. While still in Paris months earlier, de Lesseps had proclaimed that the first symbolic shovelful to build the canal would occur on the first day of the first month of the new year.

The afternoon was sunlit, with a sea breeze providing some relief from the heat. Following de Lesseps' flag-bedecked steam tug on small craft, hundreds of well-wishers, full of complimentary champagne and cognac, traveled three miles west through azure waters glittering in the sunlight to the mouth of the Rio Grande, Pacific terminus of the future canal. French and Colombian flags fluttered.

Wake quietly watched from the bridge deck, scanning the

people to discern anyone intently watching him. Could the Chileans want to kill him and try to steal his report and recommendations? Were they that desperate? He checked the crowd again, but found no one who looked like an assassin. Then he realized he had nothing really to go on. There was a Chilean consul in the city, but he didn't know the man or his description. No matter, he reasoned—a killer would probably be some hired local criminal, hungry for money, who might be dressed up for the job and in the crowd. Frustrated, Wake decided to not worry. Besides, the bishop probably misunderstood what he'd heard.

Unable to get to the proper location because of the falling tide, the vessels drifted around out on the bay off a brown and black rocky beach exposed by the low tide. Behind the beach rose hills blanketed with different shades of green forest. After waiting for a while, the celebrants on the tug and other vessels grew quiet, wondering when the moment would happen now that the grand plan had been thwarted. All eyes were on the afterdeck of the tug, where the guest of honor and his close intimates were gathered.

De Lesseps literally rose to the occasion by climbing on a seat and standing on the pitching vessel as two men held him, calling for all to lend their attention. He proclaimed they would still have a symbolic first blow—he pointed to a champagne crate he'd had filled with sand on the deck. Then his beautiful young wife, decades his junior, helped their little daughter swing a small shiny pickaxe specially made for the occasion. The floating audience erupted with applause.

De Lesseps beamed as the crowd cheered him in Spanish, French, and English. It was the fulfillment of his dream. After all the years of preparation, of convincing skeptics, of personal financial sacrifice, it was about to happen. Acknowledging the shouted compliments and kisses from his adoring fans, de Lesseps appeared ten years younger to the American naval officer standing next to the tug captain.

Wake silently lifted up a prayer. Not for de Lesseps or the surrounding throng, but for the thousands of men who would soon find themselves in the middle of that jungle hellhole. No champagne for those poor souls, Wake thought ruefully.

The next day Wake was walking to the train station when a two-horse cart came careening around a corner, the driver a scraggy-looking Indio who locked his crazed eyes with Wake's and steered straight for him. The cart never swerved away, the wheels missing him by inches as Wake jumped to the side. As the cart rattled away down the street, Wake regained his breath and scanned the passersby. None reacted—it was just another near miss on the streets of Panama City. Wake made sure to walk along the sides of the streets after that, constantly looking at the people around him, hoping it was just an unfounded paranoia.

He made it to the train to Colón. Aboard, he stayed alert for any sign of surveillance or assault. Halfway across he saw one man in business suit watching him, then another. Both were Latino. Both walked away when he stared at them. Wake decided it wasn't paranoia.

Exhausted by the time he reached the Atlantic end of the rail line, he sat at the back corner table in a barroom in Colón drinking rum-laced coffee and trying to stay awake until the steam packet began boarding passengers. One of the men from the train was in the *taverna* across the street, sipping a mug of something, occasionally glancing at the American naval officer, the only one in the town. Wake fingered the large revolver under his coat. If the man approached him, he would find a .45-caliber muzzle jammed in his face.

He concentrated on imagining his homecoming with Linda and the children, blocking out the man across the street, the stench of Colón's open sewers, the cackling whores at the table next to him, and the heat rash in his crotch that made every step painful.

At six in the evening, Wake walked along Front Street toward the steamer dock. Out of the corner of his eye he saw that the man followed. It was better to do this here and now, Wake told himself, before they got to the dock and the crowd hid the man's approach. He whirled around, revolver in hand at waist height, looking for the man. There was a teenaged boy, an old derelict, and two hookers. But no man in a suit.

The others stood still, saying nothing. Wake lowered the pistol but kept it in his hand and turned back to walking toward the dock. The others gave him a wide berth and though he spun around twice more, Wake never saw the man again. Ten minutes later he was ascending the gangway.

Standing at the railing while the steamer backed away, he looked out over the shacks of Colón. He was just about to go below to his cabin when he saw him. A block away, leaning on a telegraph pole and looking at the ship was the man in the suit. Wake wished he had a telescope to see the face clearly, to memorize it. Then he realized there was no need. He wouldn't be back. His mission was over.

That evening as a blood-red sun lowered in the west, Wake stood on the stern of the French steamer *Lafayette* looking south. He let the cool sea air flow over his skin and breathed a huge sigh of relief as those fetid green-clad hills of Panama, and the strange men in suits, receded below the dark horizon.

Wake was going home.

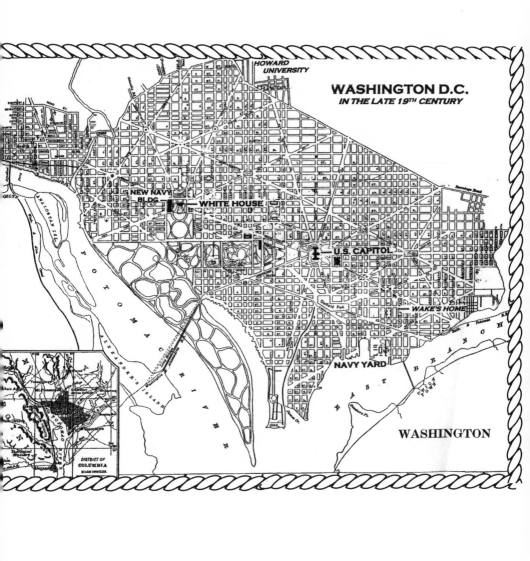

WASHINGTON D.C.
IN THE LATE 19TH CENTURY

HOWARD UNIVERSITY

NEW NAVY BLDG.

WHITE HOUSE

U.S. CAPITOL

WAKE'S HOME

NAVY YARD

WASHINGTON

POTOMAC RIVER

EAST BRANCH

DISTRICT OF COLUMBIA

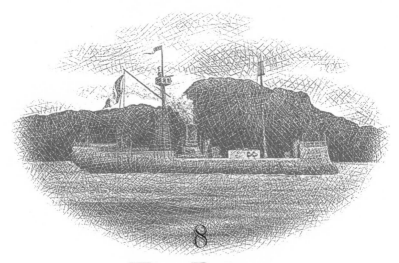

# 8

# The Palace

## January 1880

It was cold, very cold, after Panama, and Wake bundled tighter into his great coat, watching the rows of apartment buildings go by the grimy window dripping with condensation. He caught a glimpse of his family's apartment as the crowded train rumbled up Virginia Avenue between the Marine Barracks and the Washington Navy Yard. Smoke was everywhere, home chimneys and factory stacks making a black cloud over the city, with wafting soot speckling the freshly fallen January snow. The slush in the streets was already turning into brownish-black sludge. Inside the train car, it smelled of unwashed bodies, greasy food, and cigars. Wake sighed. The scene certainly wasn't inspiring, but it was home.

*Lafayette* had docked in New York late the previous night and Wake had taken the first train to Washington available—the six A.M. express—right after telegraphing the department that he was now back in the country. First, he had to check into the Navy Department's duty officer, submit his travel vouchers to the fourth auditor's office, present his assessment document of the War of the Pacific to the navy secretary's clerk, and later see his bureau commanding officer. Only after that could he go home to his wife and children. It had been seven and a half long months, and twelve thousand rough miles since Wake had last held Linda.

He got off with a herd of humanity in the Baltimore and Potomac's chaotic main station on Sixth Street, just down from Pennsylvania Avenue. Lugging his sea bag and valise out into the street, Wake turned north and started walking. He was one of the few naval officers he knew who actually liked Washington. Ambling about among the legendary monuments and buildings, seeing the myriad kinds of people that inhabited the place, always intrigued him. Washington wasn't *dull.*

The cold bothered him, but he took a deep breath and decided a walk would be good for him, get him back in touch with the thriving city that ran the United States. Besides, he admitted with a moan, he had no money left for a cab ride or even the trolley. The walkways were icy in some spots and he slowed his gait, shifting the sea bag to the other shoulder.

Wake had left Washington in May on a beautiful day, warm and breezy, with flowers everywhere. That day he had walked the reverse of his present course, filled with anticipation and excitement. Now, he thought it ironic that instead of joy at being home, he felt a sense of trepidation. He trudged along, brooding over what his personal reception would be, how they would react to his assessment report. A muddy splash from a passing wagon wheel followed by a vulgar shout brought him back to his surroundings.

Wake circumvented the growing crowd of gawking pedestrians at an accident scene, avoided a landau swerving along the sidewalk, and forged onward. At Pennsylvania Avenue he angled left and headed northwest toward the White House, nine blocks up the broad avenue, hidden behind the Treasury Building that dominated the skyline. Striding along the south side of the street on a dry patch of pavement, Wake passed the well-known hotels on Pennsylvania that he would never be able to afford: the

National, Metropolitan, St. Marc, and St. James. Dodging carriages and wagons, he made his way across the dangerous intersection of Louisiana and Pennsylvania and saw Ford's Theater and Opera House ahead on the right. At that time of the morning no one was around the infamous place of Lincoln's assassination and it looked drab and desolate.

Wake was always saddened when he passed by that building, a melancholy based upon what he had hoped could have been a peaceful future for the country if Lincoln had only been allowed to reunify the North and South after the war ended. Instead, bitter partisan acrimony had tainted almost all debate and paralyzed most progress since that day in April. Had it really been fifteen years?

The Willard Hotel, its bar a gathering spot for political types—both in and out of uniform—for three decades, loomed up on the right. Like most experienced naval officers, Wake couldn't stand the place and the people in it. He walked across Fifteenth Street to the imposing Ionic columns along the front of the Treasury Building. Clerks were unloading something from a box-wagon, surrounded by armed policemen who looked out at the passersby warily, fingering shotguns cradled in their arms.

Cutting away from the street and along the south side of the building, Wake entered the grounds of the Presidential Park. Once past the Treasury, the White House came into sight through the park's bare-limbed trees. Even in the dead of winter, the sight cheered him up a bit. The stately old mansion, in which he and Linda had attended a few military balls during his tour of duty in Washington, always seemed a wonderful link with the past. He got strength from its longevity, its symbolism, its survival in desperate times. They would go to balls there again, he hoped, and enjoy evenings of romance and gaiety. Linda loved that sort of thing. Wake thought all girls imagined themselves princesses in their dreams, and a ball at the White House was the closest thing to a royal gathering America had.

He continued west through the park grounds toward the Washington's newest edifice-to-be, the future State, War, and

Navy Building. A grandiose French Second Empire design that took up an entire block, it reminded Wake of royal palaces he'd seen in Italy. Many said it was too ornate, too European—that it was distinctly un-American in appearance. Derricks and scaffolding and piles of material hid most of the structure from sight. Men crawled around and in it. Shouted commands echoed and steam whistled from machinery doing the heavy lifting—the whole affair disconcerting to the eye and ear so close to the park around the president's mansion.

The building had been a typical bureaucratic project: needed for the last thirty years, it was talked about for fifteen years and had been under construction for nine years. Allegations of corruption, incompetence, and outright theft had been in the newspapers for the life of the venture and pundits predicted it would be under construction for another ten years. Various offices of the State Department had been using part of the building since 1875 and the navy and army were scheduled to move into their sections soon, but Wake didn't think that could've happened in his absence. He figured that would have been far too efficient for the government.

He got to Seventeenth Street and turned right. Nestled in the midst of the massive new building's construction chaos stood the old L-shaped Navy Department. Wake noticed that there weren't many carriages parked and that most of the chimneys weren't smoking. Another ridiculous economy proclamation, he assumed with a weary shake of his head. One quick appearance at headquarters was necessary to drop off the paperwork—he could maybe get away with seeing Commodore Jeffers the next day over at his office in the Navy Yard—so Wake entered the foyer with a smile of anticipation. With any kind of luck he'd be out and on his way home in five minutes.

The laconic man at the front desk told him the staff, including the Fourth Auditor's Office, wasn't there. They had moved into their offices at the new building. The old one was going to be demolished to make room for the western sections of the massive construction project. The last of the navy staff was moving the coming week. The man pulled out a watch. "It's now thirty minutes past eleven o'clock on a Thursday morn. Hmm . . . I think there'll be someone there to receive your paperwork, Commander. But you'd better hurry. Lunch waits for no man, not in the District of Columbia."

Frustrated at the attitude and the news, Wake stalked out and walked around the block to the east side of the new building that faced the White House. Sure enough, he saw a sign that announced the Navy Department was located on the first and second floors. Looking up at the massive façade of the building, with hundreds of columns along the main floor and perhaps thousands of windows in the five stories above it, it was obvious why it took so long to construct, and why it generated so much debate along the way. There was nothing like it in Washington. It was beyond ornate. To Wake it looked almost cathedral-like. A cathedral of bureaucracy, he mused.

Walking up a huge set of wide granite steps, slippery in the slush, Wake passed through double columns outside the main doors and entered the main hall. He stopped and took it all in.

"Well, times have certainly changed in the United States Navy," he muttered aloud to himself. When he'd left six months ago headquarters was an old run-down office with faded curtains, dingy halls, and dirty floors.

"May I assist you, Commander?" came a young voice from behind. Wake turned. An ensign was standing before him, having come out from behind the reception desk. Wake realized he'd been caught standing there gape-jawed like a hick in the city for the first time.

"Duty officer?"

"At the desk right there, sir, but he stepped out for a minute. I'm the assistant duty officer, Ensign Robert Wells. May I help you, sir?"

"Perhaps, Mr. Wells. I'm just back from special assignment in South America. I need to check in with the duty officer, present my field report, and turn in my vouchers at the Office of the Fourth Auditor. Can you help me accomplish all that, Ensign?" Wake saw the young man's face go pale.

"You're Commander Wake, sir? *The* Lieutenant Commander Peter Wake?"

"That would be me, son. Now where do I go to get this done as fast as possible? I want to get home to my family and not waste any time here."

"Oh, sir. We've been waiting for you. You're supposed to report in to the boss's office right away—weeks ago, sir!"

Wake sighed. It was January fifteenth, the day he had predicted in the Panama City telegram he'd arrive. But of course, the leadership, used to having people run at their beck and call, hadn't realized it took time to travel thousands of miles at sea. They'd probably been hounding the staff for sign of him, some commodore in the Bureau of Navigation, where officer assignments were made, making noises about the missing lieutenant commander. Wake had been expecting an assignment change. He was due one awhile ago. And of course it would be, no doubt, to some hell-hole.

"And what boss would that be, son?"

"The secretary, sir!"

"Whose secretary? And calm down, Ensign Wells. Get ahold of yourself."

Wells blurted out, "The secretary of the whole friggin' navy, sir!" Realizing he had just sworn while referring to a superior, in front of a superior, the ensign melted. "Oh, beg pardon, sir. Please beg pardon for my swearing."

Oh, this is just wonderful, thought Wake. Now it'll be hours before I get home. "All right, it looks like I'm going to be here awhile, Mr. Wells. Where do I find the secretary's office?"

"I'll take you there, sir, but first I have to let them know we're coming. One moment, please, sir."

Wake watched, fascinated as the ensign darted behind the desk, reached down and lifted from a shelf a two-foot-tall black wooden statue. A cord, like a reef point lashing, connected it to the wall. The youngster pulled the whole contraption apart and put a small piece to his ear, the two connected with smaller cord, then he spoke into the bell-shaped top of the statue.

Has the kid gone daft? was Wake's silent reaction. Wells appeared to be talking to the statue, which stayed mute. Wake looked around to see if anyone else was noticing this bizarre behavior. Officers and messengers walked through the entry hall without a break in stride. Maybe they've all gone daft, Wake thought.

The ensign put the statue away and said, "They're expecting you, Commander."

Wake couldn't stand it. "What the hell were you just doing, Ensign, talking into a wood statue? And what's that a statue of, anyway? Never seen one like that."

"The telephone, sir? Just using it to call them upstairs. This new building has them. First in government service, sir. We're even connected directly to the president's office in the White House."

It suddenly dawned on Wake. The gadget was a telephone. He'd heard of them but had never seen one. And now they were here, in his navy. The ensign was staring at him oddly.

"Lead on, Ensign."

"Yes, sir. It's on the second floor. Please follow me."

Wake glanced up as he followed Wells across the floor of black and white granite tiles. Fifty feet above them was a magnificent elliptical rotunda, the blue and white stained glass of which was done in a nautical motif. The gold leaf molding around the edges and on the ceiling was also done in naval theme. Under the rotunda they passed a winding stairway with stone steps and a beautifully carved mahogany railing supported by polished bronze balusters. The stairs ascended in a gentle free-standing curve, making Wake marvel at the design that could keep it up. The whole thing was palatial, he decided. It even *smelled* new.

"We'll go over here, sir, to the new Otis lifting elevator."

"The *what?*" Wake asked, his mind speculating that possibly he'd just entered a Jules Verne novel, conjecturing what innovative item would be next.

"In here, sir." Wells showed him through two small doors with windows into a tiny room with a miniature gas chandelier and a wall bench cushioned in navy blue velvet. A diminutive man in bellboy garb stood patiently in the corner. Wells closed the doors and took position in the middle, looking at the doors. Wake stood slightly to the side, watching the ensign and mystified as to why the three of them were standing in a closet. The bellboy shoved a lever down, then clicked something somewhere behind him. With a sickening groan the room lurched. Unprepared, Wake almost fell down and, hearing a snicker behind him, glared at the bellboy as the room lifted up.

"Here we are, sir. Second floor," announced Wells as the room stopped its ascent.

"Good Lord!" exclaimed Wake, all pretense at dignity gone, as he emerged. "I've heard of these things and now I've damn well seen it. All that commotion just to go up one deck."

"Modernity, sir! Only the best for the navy," Wells quipped, leading the way down the hall and into an anteroom with several doors. Officers sat nervously in chairs while they waited to be called for audiences with oral promotion examination boards or to receive word on their new tours of duty. Wells, looking slightly puffed up by this time, grandly breezed past them and showed Wake into a private office where a spectacled man in a somber black suit contemplated the mound of papers on his desk.

"I'll leave you here, sir, if I may," said Wells, already heading for the doorway. "This is Mr. Conner, administrative assistant to the chief of staff, and he'll take you from here."

"The chief isn't here, you're going directly into the admiral," said Conner, who then looked over his spectacles at Wake. "He's been waiting for you."

Wake didn't like the sound of that. "Yes, so I've heard, Mr. Conner."

Conner opened the far door and announced, "Lieutenant

Commander Wake reporting, sir."

A gruff command to enter was the reply, and Wake marched in, stood three feet in front of a desk at attention and echoed Conner's announcement. Admiral Porter waved to a chair and rocked back in his own, chin on hand, watching Wake, who sat at attention and waited.

Porter perched forward. His face had deep-set furrows, the kind you get from years at sea squinting at the far-off horizon in the glare of the sun. "So you're the man we sent down to the bottom of the world to find out what the devil is going on down there?"

Wake had received his orders in an envelope and had never gotten verbal instructions. He also had never met the famous Porter.

"Yes, sir."

"And when was it you were to return by?"

So it's going to be this way, Wake groaned inwardly. "September or October, sir."

Porter's furrows deepened even more. "And the date today is?"

"January fifteenth, sir."

"I'm sure you have a good reason for being three months late?"

"Yes, sir."

"And that is in your report as well?"

"Yes, sir."

"You will see the secretary momentarily, Commander Wake. I hope you're ready."

"I am, sir."

Porter looked intrigued. "Then good luck, Wake. I'm curious as to what is so sensitive in your report that it can't be telegraphed. This should be quite interesting—and it'd better be damned good."

# 9

# Room 274

Seconds later Wake walked behind Porter through a side doorway with arched transom, "Room 274" lettered in brass on the wall next to the doorknob. The flash of those Chilean guns filled his mind and he wished he was facing them again instead of this egocentric political snake pit.

He followed Admiral Porter into a room that made the rest of the building look Spartan. Wake was stunned.

Room 274 was fully fifty feet long and twenty wide, with four sets of doors along the interior wall and windows all along the exterior wall, allowing a glorious natural illumination of the space that highlighted the floor's inlaid parquet with red, brown, and black woods. Three large gas chandeliers descended from a pale blue scalloped ceiling, the concave lines marching athwart the length of the room, each one delicately engraved with nautical themes. The corners, ceiling, chair rails—every prominent design line in the room—were all ornately carved with ropes and ships and seahorses. At either end, set between two doors, was a black marble fireplace over which a wall-sized mirror reflected the room before it, giving the impression the area was even larger. One of the doors at either end, and one in the middle of the windows, led to a balcony as long as the room. The whole affair had a panorama of the White House, just a few hundred feet to the east across the manicured lawn.

Porter walked past a conference table designed for a dozen, the largest globe Wake had ever seen—fully five feet in diameter—and three large tables topped with models of famous American warships. The admiral stopped in front of a massive desk, at which sat a plainly dressed but assertive-looking man in his early seventies, his average appearance incongruous with the royal surroundings.

"Here's our man back from South America, Mr. Secretary. The one we've been waiting for. Lieutenant Commander Wake," Porter said with subdued tone as he sat in a chair. Wake stood at attention, willing himself not to appear awed by the grandeur around him. Having never been in a Secretary of the Navy's office before, he didn't know the protocol, so did what he thought best.

"Lieutenant Commander Wake reporting in from special assignment to the War of the Pacific, sir."

Porter sighed. Thompson said nothing as his large eyes took in Wake from head to toe. Finally he spoke. "Ah yes, the navy's wayward son. Is your report ready?"

"Yes, sir. I have it here." Wake tried to sound confident as he patted the valise.

"I'll read that later. But I want to hear a summary of it while you're here." Thompson paused while Wake wondered where to start in his summary.

"Ah, you may proceed *now*, Commander Wake."

Wake realized the man was waiting for him to speak. "Aye, aye, sir." He started to open the valise, but Thompson held up a hand. "Extemporaneously, Commander. I've no time for long lectures and documents today. Just give me a brief and candid summary and leave out the fluff."

Wake went back to attention. "Yes, sir. I'll start with the political overview. The war is economic in origin. It's over who gets to harvest bird droppings used for fertilizers and desert nitrate-filled sands used in explosives. Ten of millions of dollars are at stake. The Chileans started it in reaction to arrogant Bolivian demands for tax fees. The Peruvians got dragged into it by a defense treaty with Bolivia.

"The Chileans are European-centered, the Andean wall sealing them off from the rest of South America. The British and Germans have heavy influence there. The Bolivians are a completely backward conglomeration of tribes, run by self-centered ignorant warlords, with few relations to other nations. The Peruvians are continentally centered—maintaining cultural, political, and economic interaction with their neighbors. They are moderately developed and trying to become more so."

"What is the military situation?" asked Porter.

"Militarily, the Chileans have an overwhelming advantage. They have overrun the narrow coastal plain from their border northward, through the Bolivian coastline, to the Peruvian coast. They now have the most valuable lands—the ones they always wanted. The Bolivians are a joke, have run from every fight, and will negotiate a settlement. They never did settle their coast and for years allowed the Chileans to work and export the resources there. It's not that important to them other than income."

"And the Peruvians?" asked Porter.

"Peruvians are desperately trying to defend their national ground, sir. They had some minor successes in the beginning, but in the main have lost land engagements. Their navy has been the force holding off the invasion of their country."

"I heard they've lost most of that now. Their big ironclad was captured," interrupted Thompson.

"Yes, sir. The *Huascar.* I was there when it happened—"

"Really? It was out at sea." Porter's tone lowered. "How were you there?"

"*Huascar* captured the merchant ship I was traveling aboard—which is why I am late in getting to Washington, sir. Just before the battle, Admiral Grau had me transferred to the corvette that was escorting *Huascar.* He knew the battle would be one-sided and wanted me to get word to Washington about what was going on down there. He was right—*Huascar* was lost to Chile in the battle. Grau was killed."

"Hmm . . . so you were aboard a combatant? Doesn't sound very neutral, Commander. I believe your orders were clear on that."

Wake started to explain, but Thompson waved his hand. "Never mind that now, this battle of the ironclads—describe it."

"Peruvians were outnumbered more than three to one. Only had one ironclad and one small corvette. Their ships needed an overhaul, sir. Chilean gunnery was much better—hundreds of shots, dozens of hits. But the important thing is that the Peruvians *never gave up.* The Chileans pounded them. Hell, Admiral, *I* would've given up. But they didn't. And the Chileans could *not* sink that ship. Even at close range."

"Heard in the news reports that there was ramming involved in the battle," said Porter.

"Attempted ramming—no impacts, sir. The Chileans finally swarmed and boarded the *Huascar,* capturing her."

"So the ramming was not decisive? We've heard it was," asked the admiral.

"No, sir. It was not. And I believe that if the Peruvians had a more experienced crew their gunnery would've been better and there would've been a chance for their survival."

Thompson looked at his watch. "Anything else?"

"Yes, sir. The Peruvians have something that is a naval novelty and just may prove important, if not decisive."

"Go ahead and get it out," said Thompson as he drummed his fingers on the desk."

"A submarine, sir. A real one, not like the Confederate's *Hunley* or the French navy's *Plonguer* or Spain's *Icteneu.* Those crafts went down a few feet, the deepest was *Plonguer* at thirty feet and that was uncontrolled. The Peruvians have one that goes down beyond seventy feet." Thompson and Porter reacted the way Wake thought they would. "Yes, sir, I said deeper than seventy feet. And it's mobile under water. Uses an array of towed torpedo mines. They call it the *Toro*."

"We've heard nothing about it!" exclaimed Porter, an early and consistent advocate of the U.S. Navy's torpedo station at Newport.

Thompson was suspicious. "Just where did you hear about this wonder weapon, Commander? Sounds like a tale that Twain would dream up."

"*Toro* is very real, Mr. Secretary. I inadvertently saw her hauled out at Callao and later heard more about her sea trials from various people. I've kept that knowledge secret. I'm sure they are getting ready to use her against the Chileans. The Chileans probably know something about her since I know the Brits do. I heard a bit about her from the Brits, who are friends of the Chileans and have a vested interested in their victory. The Brits think her a joke. I don't."

"Why not," asked Thompson.

"Because it's about striking fear into the enemy, sir. She has to sink only one Chilean ship blockading off the port Callao and panic ensues—remember what happened after *Hunley* sank *Housatonic* at Charleston? This vessel is far beyond the capability of *Hunley*. I think we should find out all we can about this vessel and see about replicating her for our navy. It'd be invaluable for harbor and coastal defense."

"Very interesting, Commander. Anything else of salient import to include in this summary?" asked Porter.

"Ah, yes, sir. It's political in nature."

Porter glanced at Thompson, then nodded.

"Well, sir. It has to do with our national position on the conflict. The consul's office in Santiago wants us to be pro-Chilean since they are favored to win this and we should get on their good side—which is true. Everyone in Latin America thinks they are going to win. In fact, everyone thought they were going to win this before now. Thought they would compel the Peruvians to surrender at the outset."

"But that didn't happen . . ." offered Thompson.

"No, sir. Quite the opposite, in fact. The Peruvians—outnumbered, out-equipped and out-led—held on against all odds. They have something, gentlemen. Something almost indefinable, but that gives them a power out of proportion to their numbers. I personally saw it aboard *Huascar.* The reason I am here and not dead is because Admiral Grau wanted you to hear of it from me. They have guts. They are defending their homeland now. They remind me of the Rebs under Lee. And it took another two years *after* Gettysburg to vanquish *them.*"

Porter's head bobbed thoughtfully.

"In addition, sir, the Chileans are nearing the end of their supply line capabilities. I also believe, due to their relatively small population and army, they will have difficulty in garrisoning what they capture. It may become a quagmire for them, bogging down their forward momentum. It takes double or triple the number of men used in an attack to occupy a hostile country."

Wake held up a warning finger. "Look, I know there is considerable pressure to join the Chileans, or at least ignore the Peruvians' cries for help." He shook his head. "But I wouldn't do that. Instead, my counsel is for the American leadership not to enter the war on the Chilean side, because this isn't over by a long shot. Especially once the Peruvians get that submarine operational. The Chileans are not close with the rest of Latin America. The Peruvians are. The other countries are all watching.

"At the very least, stay neutral and try to end this with some semblance of Peru's border intact. Do we really want a victorious Chile controlling most of the eastern South Pacific? That's where most of our whaling fleet goes—"

"You sound anti-Chilean, Commander. Why should I not think you are biased?" interrupted Thompson. Wake heard the chill in the secretary's voice.

"I respect the Chileans greatly, sir. I'm not anti-Chilean. I'm for either a neutral stance or for backing Peru to regain her lost territory. I'm looking at this from the perspective of what's best for the United States, her image, and her future in the region."

Thompson leveled his eyes at Wake. "I'm afraid that's not what William Evarts thinks, Commander. The secretary of state told me he's heard reports the Chileans consider you pro-Peruvian. Yes, *you* have become the topic of conversations. There's even a rumor about that you were involved in the death of a British diplomat in Lima who'd had some friends among the Chileans. Are you aware of these attitudes toward you?"

"I didn't know that the secretary of state had heard anything about me, sir, but was made aware while in Panama of the rumor about being involved in the man's death, which is patently false. There always lots of rumors in Latin America. I didn't worry about that one—it's too absurd." He decided not to tell of Vargas' warning or the surveillance in Panama. It would be too inflammatory without real proof.

"However, I actually did meet the man, a Mr. Egglestone, the British cultural attaché in Lima, and persuaded him to get me aboard a Royal Navy ship that was leaving Callao so I could get home to deliver this report, but I had nothing to do with his subsequent death, which I think was done by Peruvian nationalists. I do believe he was more than merely friends with some Chileans, though. I think he was a British political operative for the Foreign Office that was assisting the Chileans with information about the Peruvian defenses."

"Hmm. I'm a former judge from Indiana, Commander. I like to see *proof* before lending credence to an accusation. Can you prove what you just alleged?"

Wake felt his face flush. "No, sir. Just an opinion based on circumstantial information."

Thompson eased back in his chair and folded his hands. "Very well. Interesting points, Commander. There *have* been recommendations to ally with the Chileans and side with the winners. But you've presented some very interesting points that I haven't heard before." He glanced at a large clock on the wall, then stood abruptly. "Oh, I'm late! Got to get over to Willard's for a luncheon. Tonight I'll read that assessment report with great attention, Commander Wake."

"Mr. Secretary, one more question, if I may impose?" queried Porter. "You just came through from Panama, Commander, and were there on Selfridge's Isthmus survey back in seventy, I believe. On a scale of one to ten, what is your impression of the chances for success on that French canal project?"

"Probably three out of ten. The only reason I give them three is because of the amount of money they have available. I met with Mr. de Lesseps when he was in Panama, sir. Because of my familiarity with Panama he asked me my opinion on various facets of the project."

"Really, you met the great man himself? You *do* get around, don't you?" said Thompson, stopped in mid-stride toward the coat rack. "And, pray tell, what happened?"

"I gave him my opinion, sir. It's all in my report. I don't think they are prepared at all for this. They are treating it as another Suez type of engineering situation, and the two are completely different in every way. Not only will they fail, but thousands will die."

Thompson frowned. "Well, that sounds a bit gloomy, Commander, don't you think? I've met him too and am impressed with his *élan.*"

"It's not gloomy, it's *realistic,* Mr. Secretary. I've been in that jungle. They haven't."

"Very interesting, Commander. I'll remember that."

Then Porter told Wake he was dismissed. Wake gave the admiral the envelope containing his report and departed the room, using the door at the end through which he'd entered. Once past all the offices and in the hallway outside, he breathed a lungful of air and sat in a chair for a moment to calm down. His hands were trembling.

Inside the office Thompson was putting on his overcoat. "Quite a sharp fellow, Admiral. Gets things done. Concise rendition and not afraid to speak plain talk. I like that, but I do wonder about his assessment, at odds as it is with Evarts' people's opinions."

"He was asked his opinion, sir. He gave it."

"Yes, he did, Admiral. And that is exactly why I think you need to keep an eye on that man."

"Yes, Mr. Secretary," said Porter, his mind already churning with thoughts regarding Wake's future. "I think I will be doing just that."

Thompson paused in the doorway. "So tell me, Admiral, do you think Wake killed the Brit diplomat in Lima?"

Porter ruminated for several seconds. "I think not, Mr. Secretary. But after meeting him today there's no doubt in my mind that he could—if he thought it necessary."

In the hall, Wake took the stairs down to the main floor, stopped at the front desk for his sea bag, and before anyone else could divert him, walked out the grand entry for the three-mile hike to his home. After what he'd been through, the frigid air outside felt good.

He headed south across the parkland toward the Fourteenth Street Bridge over the drainage ditch along northern edge of the Mall. The red-bricked Smithsonian Institution came into sight on the left and Wake angled southeast on Virginia Avenue, bypassing the worst of the seedy area of brothels and bars in the area between the Smithsonian and the Capitol building known as Reservation C. A few street toughs and trollops eyed him as he walked by, one of the girls brazen enough to call out to him.

Wake wasn't in the mood for people, especially the kind of people around Mary Hall's high-class house of entertainment for gentlemen—which meant politicians—on Maryland Avenue. Mary had retired but the clients still hung around the neighboring establishments.

It had been an exhausting day. Wake was tired and let the long walk work out the tenseness built up within him as he imagined his home. Linda was up there, just ahead. He could already smell the jasmine perfume, feel her soft hair, see those green eyes. Only two miles to go.

# 10

# Homeport

Linda Wake heard a pounding on the apartment's front door, then her daughter calling from the parlor. "Mama, somebody's at the door! Do you want me to get it?"

Linda suppressed a rude reply, her frustration caused by a recalcitrant stovepipe that had been leaking fumes for several days. Linda had spent the afternoon trying to reconnect the exhaust pipes—unsuccessfully—after disassembling and cleaning them. Covered in grime, she looked like a chimney sweep and felt she was no sight for a visitor to see. "Useppa, dear, you've got to. I'm absolutely filthy from trying to fix this stove."

A shriek came from the parlor, followed by, "Daddy! Mama, come quick, it's *Daddy!*"

Linda never made it around the corner to the parlor, her husband was faster and arrived in the tiny kitchen first. They stood facing each other for a moment, then silently folded into each other's arms, Linda crying and Wake trying to keep composed and failing.

Sean and Useppa hugged them both until Useppa pulled Sean away. With a stern tone she told him to "go to the Navy

Yard and tell Uncle Sean the news and invite him to supper, then to go by the butcher's shop and get five decent sirloins, those new Delmonico cuts." Then she announced to her parents that she was going to prepare a dinner party and they didn't have to do a thing except relax in their room and come out at six o'clock. She further declared she was going to the vegetable market while Sean did his errands and that they'd both be back at the apartment in not less than an hour. Useppa repeated the last part for Sean.

Wake looked at his suddenly grown-up daughter, appearing so assertive and serious. He hugged her again. "Thank you, dear. That's just wonderful of you."

"Thank you, Useppa," echoed Linda with a mischievous smile as she led her husband by the hand to their bedroom.

"You're doing what!" exclaimed an amazed Wake as he passed the carrots.

Rork laughed. It did seem impossible. "I said that I'll be a gettin' married, proud an' proper, Peter. I found the right woman at last. 'Twas a long an' weary search, I admit."

Rork had been a bachelor all forty-nine years of his life. It had been a long running joke between them, but Wake had always known Rork was envious of Wake's marriage and family. "Well, who's the lucky lady, Sean?"

"Lass named Sheila. Sheila O'Toole. Met her when I reported in five months ago. Her father's a gunner's mate at the foundry. Lovely lass, she is, Peter. An' Irish as a misty day. Family's from Wexford, too."

"Sounds like she's perfect. So when's the big day, Sean?"

"Well, there's the rub, me friend. Bit o' a dilemma. I've no family left since me sister passed away years ago, but Sheila does. An' her family is not fancyin' this betrothal a'tall."

"Wait a minute. Her father's a navy man. I'll bet he is probably happy she's marrying a fellow sailor. Plus you're Irish. You'd be a good catch for anyone, especially an Irish girl."

"Not for a *Protestant* Irish girl, Peter. They're Anglican. Orange Irish, not Green Irish. I even said the children could be raised Anglican, no worries there for me, but they wouldn't hear o' the thing a'tall. May be a while till a church sees our weddin'."

"Oh. Hmm . . . Well, remember that Linda and I had a similar problem during the war? As you well know, our marriage was frowned upon by both sides." He reached for Linda's hand. "A forbidden love. I think that made it even spicier, didn't it darling?"

The mischievous smile returned to her face. "I think it did indeed, Peter Wake. And we've two lovely children as a result."

"I'm not lovely. That's for girls!" muttered young Sean, making everyone laugh.

"It certainly looks like a lot's happened since I left in May," said Wake.

"More than you, know, Peter," said Linda. "In addition to Sean being transferred to the Navy Yard here, some of our other friends have moved to the area too. Mary Alice Pickett and her husband are living down near Fredericksburg, and Martha Boltz and her new husband are running an inn on Chain Bridge Road north of Fairfax."

"I'd heard that somewhere about Mary Alice. Martha's remarried? Now that's good to hear."

"Yes, they're doing quite well. He was her first husband's brother, the one that fought for the South. Virginia regiment. We see them over there at the inn occasionally on Sundays or when they come into the city. Martha loves the children and loves to tell them stories of Key West and the islands." Linda raised her eyebrows. "Although sometimes those stories are a bit too mature for young ears, if you know what I mean."

"Martha knew real *pirates* down in the islands, Daddy," said young Sean.

"Aye, that she did, lad," agreed Rork. "Why ol' Martha could spin a tale, tempt a saint, or cudgel the biggest brute in the tavern of her inn on Duval Street. An' I've seen her do all three in a single evenin'."

"Oh Sean Rork, you are incorrigible! He's not serious, dear. That's just a sailor's yarn," Linda said to her son as Rork grinned and winked at him.

Wake cleared his throat and stood. "And now that dinner is over, there comes my pleasant duty of presenting the gifts I collected for you on my journey. I have two for each of you—one for Christmas and one for my sailor's return." He left the room and returned with his sea bag. His family loved this part of his homecomings from sea, when he would hand out presents to each of them and tell the story of where they were from, what they meant, and how he found them.

"For my pretty princess Useppa, I have this Spanish fan from the ladies of Panama. The ladies of Panama are very beautiful and they have a special language of thoughts they convey with the way they hold these fans." He pulled another item from the bag.

"Here is a pamphlet explaining them in English—very difficult to obtain, by the way. They can tell a man that they like him or dislike him. Whether he can approach them or should go away. Whether he can kiss them or not." He caught Linda's look and ended the fan language explanation there. "And for Christmas, I brought you a shawl of Spanish lace, princess. I've seen princesses with them and knew it would look perfect on you."

He spread the shawl around her shoulders as she teared up. "Oh, Daddy, they're both absolutely beautiful. I've seen pictures in *Harpers* of these. Oh Daddy, I do feel like a princess. I really do."

That got Wake teary-eyed himself. He walked around the table to young Sean. "And as for you, young sailor, I have a very unique item from the Indian tribes deep in heart of the jungles of Panama." He pulled out a long stick and handed it to his son. "A native blow dart gun. The native use poisoned darts." Wake quickly held up a hand to Linda. "It's without darts, dear."

"And son, for Christmas you get a real Royal Navy bosun's whistle."

"Wow, Daddy. Wait till the fellas see these!"

"An' I'll teach you how to sound a call on that, Sean," offered Rork.

Wake went to Linda and pulled her to her feet. "And for the queen of the family I have this for Christmas." He produced a small plain wooden box, which she opened slowly. Linda gasped softly as she lifted an emerald and black onyx pendant on a gold chain out of the box. The emerald glinted in the candlelight. "Oh Peter, it's magnificent. Simply magnificent."

"Ah, but there's more, my dear. For being my wife and my lover and a wonderful mother to our children, there is this. For our next formal naval ball." He handed her another box and said, "I love you, Linda."

She started crying as she opened it. There were two emerald and onyx earrings, suspended with filigreed gold, that matched the pendant. "Oh, Peter. I don't know what to say. I got so scared when I didn't hear . . ."

Wake took her in his arms and kissed her, stroking her hair. "I'm home now, dear. I'm home . . ."

Rork turned to the children. "Come bear a hand, you two. We've got to get these dishes to the galley and everything washed up ship-shape. Those two are wantin' some time alone."

"Aw, they just wanna kiss and stuff," said young Sean.

"Then we'll let 'em, Sean. They deserve it, lad. They deserve it."

With the sunrise came a much shorter journey by foot for Wake. Three blocks south on Eighth Street took him to the Latrobe Gate—main entrance to Washington Navy Yard, the most prestigious station in the United States Navy. It was also the home of the Bureau of Ordnance, his nominal unit.

A chilling wind blew off the Anacostia River East Branch as Wake returned the Marine guard's salute and entered the Greek Revival structure of the gate—its Doric columns, pilaster friezes, and perched eagle grasping an anchor, all giving a false impression of American naval strength to visitors.

Strolling down Dahlgren Avenue, Wake saw that the renovations were still under way on many of the officers quarters—one of the reasons his family lived off station—but noticed repairs to the commandant's house were completed. He'd heard that Alex Semmes, cousin of the famous Rebel sailor and Wake's friend from their days as officers in the East Gulf Blockading Squadron, was about to transfer from Pensacola to take command of the Navy Yard in Washington. That was considered to be a plum assignment in a naval career and the commandant's two-story home with wrap-around verandahs was one of the most comfortable in the navy.

Due to Admiral Dahlgren's influence, the yard had been primarily an ordnance facility since the war, building only one ship lately, the gunboat *Nipsic* the year before. Now the two immense ship construction buildings were used as gun factories, with numerous outbuildings working as powder and shot magazines, boiler shops, iron shops, carpenter shops. The giant Quadrangle, a four-hundred by three-hundred-foot brick building containing the main foundry, was the center of the operations at the navy yard, always busy with workmen and the blaring noise and acrid odors of mechanical commotion. That was where Wake found Commodore Jeffers, standing next to a nine-inch Parrot rifled gun tube and discussing metallurgy with a civil engineer.

William Jeffers, a year younger and three ranks higher than Wake, was a large jovial balding man with a reputation for being an expert in gunnery. He also knew ironclads well, having been *Monitor*'s second commanding officer. Jeffers looked up and exclaimed, "Peter Wake! By God, you really are back. Heard a rumor you were returning. Successful down there?"

"Yes, sir, it was. Found out what was happening and have reported in to the senior leadership. I got in yesterday, sir, and stopped at the department to drop off my vouchers and report in, and Admiral Porter summoned me to see the secretary. I had planned to see you first, sir, but I got shanghaied."

"Not to worry, Peter. I've got enough to keep me busy. You were assigned to work for them, anyway. Did you see any of those ironclads down in the Pacific? What about that fight I've heard about down there?"

"Yep, I saw the ships and was there at the fight, Commodore. First ever fight between ocean-going ironclads that I know of."

"Peter, I don't have time right now, but you and I are definitely having dinner today. I want to hear all about that battle—and about their armor and gunnery."

"Yes, sir. I'll be by your office at eleven-thirty."

Wake went by the communal office he shared with a dozen other officers. Most were working on testing practical applications of new ordnance designs or quality inspections at the gun foundry. Several were members of the new United States Naval Institute, which some of the old entrenched elite in the navy viewed as a group of brash upstarts. Actually, it was an intellectual association of naval officers founded in 1873 to promote the advancement of professional and scientific knowledge, and Wake was an early member, having joined in seventy-five. The navy may be backward in funding and ships, he thought as he looked around, but we'll be ready for expansion and modernization if it ever does come.

The office was full with every desk occupied. Papers were piled on tables with two harried yeomen bringing in more. One of the officers welcomed him back from his "holiday leave down south." Another asked him if he was next headed to Monte Carlo. Heading for the mailboxes, he saw a lieutenant sitting at a small table pecking at the keys of a device that appeared to be a miniature piano. "Remington" was embossed in gilt lettering across the front. Wake was mystified. It didn't look like a firearm, but of course, this was the place they tested guns. He stopped to look at it. It did have a barrel across the top.

The lieutenant paused and noticed Wake's puzzlement. "Typewriter machine, Commander. I'm typewriting my report on the latest test torpedo runs of the *Alarm* yesterday. Commodore Jeffers wants them ready by noon."

"Oh! So that's what one of those looks like. It looks like typewriting is slower than hand writing the report."

"Well, I guess it is. For me, anyway. But at least you can read my report when I get done." He grinned. "Can't say that'd be the case if I wrote it out in cursive."

"When did we get these things?" asked Wake.

"June, right after you left the last time."

Shaking his head in amazement, he checked for inter-office mail and found a note that the Bureau of Navigation's Office of Detail, the unit that handled assignments of naval officers, wanted to talk with him. That was at the big building downtown, so he decided to head over to the navy department, stop by that office and also make sure his travel and expense vouchers were being processed by the Fourth Auditor's Office. He told his friend Commander Montgomery Sicard, one of the more well-known gunnery wizards in the navy, that he was heading to headquarters.

"Peter, hold up," said Sicard. "Don't make that long trip, just use the telephone." He pointed to a black apparatus on the far desk. "We're connected now. Saves time."

"Right. Thanks Monte. I guess I'll try that." Wake approached the telephone, embarrassed that he didn't know how to operate it. He picked it up, put the top of it to his ear and a part fell off, dangling by a cord and rattling on the desk. That got everyone's attention.

Wake was about to offer some humor to cover his blunder while he figured out how to talk on the gadget when he saw everyone stand. He heard footsteps in the doorway behind him. A gruff voice said, "Commander, you'd better learn how to use that thing. Times are changing and naval officers have to keep up! The modern navy's got no room for dunderheads."

It was Captain Stephen Luce, commanding officer of the training squadron, one of the leaders of the naval professional revolution, and one of the most visually intimidating senior officers in the navy. With enormous side-whiskers jutting out like an old tomcat and moving every time he spoke, the man strode into the center of the room and demanded to know where precisely Commodore Jeffers was located. Ten hands pointed toward the Quadrangle and a junior lieutenant croaked out that the commodore was probably at the rifled gun section, near the south end of the building. Luce nodded violently and walked through the room and out the other door.

For ten seconds it was silent, until Lieutenant Billy Kimball, a machine gun expert, broke the tension and slapped Wake on the back. "Very impressive performance, Peter Wake, *sir.* Welcome back home to the *modern* navy!"

"And by God, all of you had better remember—there's no room for dunderhead lieutenant commanders around here!" added Sicard.

They all roared with laughter, Wake joining them while quietly pondering what his future looked like in the "modern navy." Five minutes later, after learning from Sicard how to operate the telephone, he marveled at the fact he was talking with a clerk in the Office of Detail, three miles away. The clerk said that a month ago they had wanted to talk with him about his next tour of duty. But that had changed.

Now it was Admiral Porter who wanted to see him about his assignment.

This time Wake was seated in the admiral's office. He was still nervous though, and Porter's demeanor was anything but reassuring. The admiral was squinting through those sun-crinkled eyes.

"All right, now. Do you want to stay at headquarters, Commander, with special assignments for the senior staff? Or do you want a sea billet? You're due one. No guarantees of a command. We're far too short of ships."

Porter had asked a loaded question. Any reply could be wrong, but a decision had to be made right then and there. He wanted the second option but in deference to Linda he picked number one. Porter looked askance for a moment—most naval officers wanted a sea billet. He asked why Wake decided on that preference.

"Because I've been at sea for the last seven, almost eight, months, Admiral. My family would like to have me around for a while."

"Very well, Commander. You know the academy graduates are already passing you by in promotions. I presume that doesn't bother you?"

Wake had heard that one before. "I've been up against that since my first day in the navy back in the war, Admiral. I produce results whatever my assignment, and still think that counts the most. I don't worry about the competition for promotion."

Porter's brow furrowed. "You seem pretty sure of yourself, Commander Wake. Do you think you produced results on your last assignment? Please tell me what they were."

"Yes, sir. You now know in detail from my written report about the military, economic, and civil state of each party in the conflict; about the naval actions and how modern weaponry fared; about the new Peruvian submarine; and about the inaugural efforts and attitudes at the French canal project. All of which is new information."

"And does violating department neutrality orders by participating in naval battles, and getting involved in assassinations, fall into the category of producing results also?"

"In the first instance I had no choice, sir. In the second

instance, that is a false rumor. Neither instance altered the results of my mission."

"Good defense, Commander Wake. Spirited, brief, and factual." Porter waited for a moment, standing up but gesturing for Wake to remain seated. The admiral paced the floor, then spun around and faced Wake. "You are transferred to the Bureau of Navigation, effective immediately. You officially will be assigned to the Board of Inspection and assigned to an office one deck down on the main floor here. Room one-seven-four. I am the president of the board and you will report to me. Your duty will be to travel occasionally and conduct seaworthiness and efficiency inspections of vessels. I will have other assignments for you, some of which may be unusual."

Porter glanced at a ship's chronometer mounted on the wall. "It is now four bells in the forewatch. Get ready for action in that office in two hours."

Wake stood, answered, "Aye, aye, sir," and marched out, his mind reeling. He had done the odd job for various seniors at headquarters for the last few years. But now, it looked like he was going to work full-time for the most important, and sometimes the most despised, man in the navy.

He knew it wouldn't be easy. Porter did not suffer fools. Wake also knew it wouldn't be dull.

"And how did it go today, dear? Your first day back at the yard—was the same group there? And how is Commodore Jeffers?" Linda was still enjoying the freshness of having him home. Of having someone adult in the house to talk with. She'd met him at the door with a warm toddy of rum and it was delicious after the cold outside. They had stood in an embrace for a long time, then sat in the chairs by the bay window, relaxing as Useppa got supper ready.

"It was an interesting first day, Linda. I'm no longer at the yard, I'm now at the new building downtown—working directly for Admiral Porter. Board of Inspection."

"Oh dear. I don't know what to make of that. Is that good?"

"Not sure myself, darling. Won't be bored, that's for sure."

"Board of Inspection. Sally's husband served on that, I think. She said he went around and looked at ships. Said he recommended if they be sold out of the navy for being too old or leaky or something."

"Yes, that's pretty much it. A little travel. A lot of paperwork. By the way, I have one of those new typewriter machines. Have to use that to do reports."

"Oh, I've read in *Scribner's* that those machines are just the thing in business nowadays" Linda lowered her voice. "Hmm, speaking of reading, you should know that your daughter has taken to reading the *Washington Post* lately. I don't approve, but didn't say anything for fear of stifling her curiosity. I think reading is good for her, even if it is anti-Republican."

Wake laughed. His wife looked so worried. "Darling, we wanted her to grow up to be confident and independent. Sounds like she's well on her way."

"It's just that the *Post* is so, so positively vulgar in its descriptions of the White House and the president. And their views on rights for black people, well! Peter, they castigated the president on his veto of that bill to extend the voting rights act. Now, I don't mind differing views, dear, but they should at least show a minimum of respect to the president and not be so racist."

Wake could see she was just starting to warm up to the subject and though he agreed with her, he didn't feel like discussing the *Post*'s well-known pro-Democrat editorials. "Linda, reading the *Post* may show her the folly of the other side better than any other argument. I think we ought to just let her read what she wants."

As Useppa called out that the meal was ready, a double knock sounded at the door. "Messenger for Lieutenant Commander Wake."

Sean raced to the door and flung it open. "Dad, it's a Marine!"

"Show him in, son"

Lance Corporal Pestle stood at attention, announced himself, and handed Wake an envelope. It was pale blue and small, not official department issue. His name was lettered in calligraphy on the front. Wake turned it over to see the sender. The Executive Mansion of the President. With a wary smile he gave it to Linda to open.

"Oh my, Peter. This is an invitation to the Valentine's Day Ball at the White House and it's signed by Mrs. Hayes herself. Well, of course it's so very wonderful we've been invited and all, but really, I don't know, Peter. I just don't know if I have anything to wear. Oh, I think my dress from last year may not fit, but then again Mrs. Wenz can do alterations."

Out of the corner of his eye Wake saw the corporal suppressing a grin. "Yes, dear, we'll go. And you'll look beautiful. Is there a reply card?"

"Yes, of course, it's the White House, for goodness sakes. Mrs. Hayes is a very refined lady and would follow the proper—"

Even Linda, his stalwart anchor in life, could get flustered by this sort of thing, which made Wake love her all the more. He filled out the reply and thanked the corporal. Afterward, he interrupted Linda and Useppa's excited discussion of bustles and petticoats and ruffled hems. "Do you suppose the two hungry men of the house could prevail upon our lovely ladies to postpone the fashion conference long enough to join us for supper?"

"Thanks, Dad," said Sean, with mock exasperation. "I've had a really *long* day and I'm hungry. It looked like they'd never stop."

# 11

# An Officer and a Gentleman

## February 1880

The winter months always dragged in Washington, with the inhospitable weather dominating discussions even more than politics. Snowstorms and gray skies infected inhabitants with a general gloom that made true Yankee visitors shake their heads. Washington was in the South, after all, they would say incredulously, and the tiny amounts of snow were laughable.

Wake, though born and raised in Massachusetts, wasn't laughing, however. His blood had thinned out over seventeen long years of tropical duty and even though he'd been in Washington for a couple of years, his body had never regained its resistance to low temperatures. It was *cold* to him. The family's apartment was located near his former assignment at the Navy Yard, and it had been no great hardship to walk the three blocks to work there. But his new office was across town, and every day's journey in the frigid air of January and February took its toll on his forty-year-old bones and muscles. To save money he only rode the trolley two days a week, but each of those days it felt almost decadently luxurious to ride warmly in fifteen minutes the route he normally trudged for an hour or more.

Fortunately, once he got to the new building, which he kept thinking of as "the palace," he would be nicely heated for the day. Along with the other innovative appliances he had discovered there, Wake was pleased to learn the building had one of those new-fangled systems to circulate heat in the winter and cool air in the summer. The heat was spread through piping and emerged in the rooms by way of decorative fireplaces. In fact, he found to his amazement, most of the fireplaces were not meant to burn fires at all—they were heating vents.

Room 174 was one of the rooms with a heat vent, and Wake could work in shirtsleeves as he sat for hours at his desk, meeting with ship constructors, marine surveyors, ship captains, and engineering officers. He compiled hundreds of pages of ship inspection forms, captains' repair requests, and contractor estimations. Then, working with officers and civilian experts at the Bureau of Construction and Repair, the Bureau of Steam Engineering, and the Bureau of Equipment, he acted as the composer of recommendations regarding the subject vessels. Most of them were distressingly negative. The fleet was old.

The Board of Inspection, presided over by Admiral Porter in his usual dour manner, would grimly read the reports and attendant recommendations and decide on whether to repair the problem, ignore the problem, or scrap the ship. Each decision had considerable financial repercussions on the budget, civilian government contracts, and operational abilities of the navy. The assignment gave him an unusual insight into the real condition of the navy and the budgetary politics of Washington. It was not a reassuring impression.

The special assignments Porter had alluded to never materialized. Even journeys for inspections of ships on squadron duty never came up. Wake, sensing scrutiny by the admiral, hadn't inquired into either possibility. Instead, he plunged into the desk assignment, tackling three piles of incoming papers on his desk each morning and amalgamating them into one pile of finished recommendation reports by the end of the day.

Within a week he'd become proficient with a telephone, comfortable with an elevator, and was even acquiring some competence with the typewriting machine. By the middle of February, though he loved being with Linda and the children, he hated his job. The tour of duty was for two more years. He thought of the sea billet Porter offered and wondered how he was going to last in the bizarre world of staff duty in Washington, with its sycophantic distortion of reality and the incredible hypocrisy of the political leadership. The previous several years of staff duty had been difficult, but he had been working apart from the center of the bureaucratic cortex. Now that he was in the midst of it all Wake was starting to feel that the coming years would be almost impossible to get through without speaking his mind and thereby getting in trouble.

Lieutenant Commander John Williams, an old friend and shipmate from the war, stopped by on a Saturday for a home-cooked supper on his way to the European Squadron. Sean Rork joined them at Wake's house and the three of them relived the good times of the war—Williams reminding them of the establishments they frequented in Key West, Rork recalling the Wakes' beautiful wedding by the sea, and Wake himself describing his adventures in Havana. Toasts were drunk to absent comrades, good ships, and friendly taverns. Jokes were told and scoundrels cursed. Old shipmates were remembered.

The story of battling the crazed pirate in Haiti in sixty-nine was retold, the three of them wishing that Durling, who had made the shots count that day, was there with them. Almost fifty-five, the irascible gunner's mate was still working up at Newport Torpedo Station and Wake hadn't seen him in four years.

Linda sent Sean and Useppa off to bed early that evening, disappearing herself to let the men have a night to themselves. She could see the signs of his restlessness and was worried about her husband. As Linda lay curled up in bed under the covers, listening to the men relaxing and laughing late into the night, she decided not to tell Peter about that pain that kept bothering her. In the same area but far more stabbing than the usual menstrual cramping, it was returning more frequently lately. Maybe later, she told herself, if it gets any worse, I'll tell him and go see the navy doctor.

The next day a queasy Wake bid an unsteady Williams good luck in Europe and saw him off at the train depot. Then the Wake family took the trolley to the Sunday service at the Foundry Methodist Church on G Street by Fourteenth. The Metropolitan Methodist Church at Judiciary Square was closer and more fashionable, but Linda liked the Foundry Church better, mainly because President and Mrs. Hayes and their children attended each week. Abraham Lincoln had been a member, as had many other presidents over the years. It was only a block and a half from the White House.

The pastor's sermon that day was on Christian endurance of pain and suffering. Wake felt like the man was speaking directly at him, chastising him for being so weak in the face of miniscule tribulations, not to mention the drinking the night before. He resolved to be more steadfast in his devotion to work and family.

As they were leaving the church Linda saw Mrs. Hayes and reminded her husband the Valentine's Ball was the coming Saturday. The presidential social season had started in January and the Hayeses were known to have at least two events a month. Normally lieutenant commanders were not on the regular list of invitees, their rank being too junior, but Linda was hoping that with his new responsibilities he would get noticed and they would receive more invitations.

He remembered her explaining to him two years earlier. "Peter, I work hard to keep this family strong. Attending the social functions of the city is my only form of recreation and relaxation. And I don't mind saying I'm proud that I, a shopkeeper's daughter from far-off Key West, have attended the highest social affairs of the nation. I think that's what America is all about. Even somebody like me gets invited."

Wake thought it all a chore instead of a pleasure. As if reading his mind, Linda squeezed his arm and said, "Oh Peter, it's nothing to fret over. It'll be positively grand to go to the White House again."

"Yes, dear. Quite grand indeed."

Linda wouldn't hear of them going by trolley. The hansom cab cost a pretty penny and meant that the quality of a meal would suffer in the near future, but it all was worth the look on her face as they climbed in and the horse clomped off from the apartments toward the president's mansion. The neighbor ladies duly noticed, several waving their good wishes while a few others glumly watched. Linda glowed with delight with the elegant departure, her eyes more lively than he'd seen in a long time.

Linda had been naturally attractive all her life, a plain unaffected allure that needed no paint or powder. But Wake had pleasantly noticed that in the last few years she had become a stunning beauty. It had more to do with her carriage and confidence, a look in her eyes, the way she walked, talked. Wake found it very enticing, especially this evening, when she was gowned in patterned green silk, trimmed in gold lace, with a low cut that complimented her still-impressive figure.

The dress, along with a beaver fur stole, was borrowed from Mrs. Sampson, neighbor just below them and wife of a commander in the Bureau of Construction. The loan was done after much consultation about alterations and comparative measurements, which Wake had thought amusing until set straight by his wife. This was serious business, she admonished him, and her attire and manners would reflect upon him and his career. It was, she reminded him, *the White House,* and not some gathering of the locals at the corner tavern.

Linda wore the emerald and gold earrings and pendant. He was awed by how she brought out the colors in them and thought they gave her appearance a grace and sophistication the equal of Paris. He couldn't remember when she'd looked lovelier. His eyes lingered on the pendant.

By the light of a tiny interior lamp she caught him leering at her cleavage and gave him that naughty wink that promised so much, later in the evening. He leaned over, moaned in her ear and was rewarded with a giggle. Linda deflected his wandering hand and murmured, "Later, sailor. Don't worry, it'll be worth the wait. Right now I need to look unmussed."

Wake moaned again and she laughed. "I tell you what, Peter the Great. You don't make me look disheveled now and I won't get you in trouble for being out of uniform when we arrive. And whatever would your mean old admiral say if you arrived in a state like that?" Her eyes twinkled with that look he adored. "Though I do admit that you look very handsome and I am very tempted."

With an exaggerated sigh he reluctantly agreed and withdrew his hands. "You win, Linda. But remember this—a promise made . . . *is a debt unpaid.*"

She got in the last laugh. "Now how could I fail to pay off that debt to a naval officer in that magnificent uniform, especially when I'll be sleeping with him tonight?"

Wake grinned appreciatively. He was in his newly cleaned and pressed full dress uniform, the accoutrements of which had been shined that very afternoon. The navy blue was studded with gold buttons, the gold belt sash, and his fringed epaulettes with the gold oak leaves of his rank. He was thankful that naval and military officers had permission to forgo the wearing of dress swords at official social functions at the White House. Swords were a huge encumbrance—making even sitting down an ordeal. Besides, Wake thought, they looked silly in the modern day, along with the cocked hat, the "fore and aft," that he was obliged to wear.

One of Sean Rork's sayings flashed through his mind. "Aye, never take a cutlass to a gun fight, sir. You'd look damned ridiculous as you die." How true. Nobody used swords anymore.

The most conspicuous part of his dress uniform were the two medals on his chest—the Lion of the Atlas, presented by the Sultan of Morocco, and the famous Legion of Honor from France. Both bestowed in appreciation for Wake's courage and accomplishment in Africa five years earlier. He remembered de Lesseps' comment that they had a bond because of the French award. Medals could also cause animosity born of jealousy, as Wake well knew. Especially in Washington. Especially foreign medals. Few American naval officers had medals and usually those were admirals who received them as political gifts from governments during overseas assignments.

Slightly graying hair hinted at his age, but Wake still stood at six feet even and maintained his trim frame, though after seeing himself in the mirror that morning he'd admitted it was getting more difficult all the time. At his rank he was allowed to cultivate facial hair but hadn't, feeling that too many had done so rather too flamboyantly. He didn't want to be thought of as flamboyant in the least.

As the cab rounded the corner at Seventeenth and Pennsylvania Avenue and passed the red-stoned Corcoran Gallery he steeled himself for the trial about to unfold. Linda was enjoying this and he would do nothing to spoil that for her, though he revolted inwardly against the false frivolity of upper-class soirées. The cab stopped in front of the north lawn behind a line of other vehicles. Lanterns lit the sidewalk and entry all the way to the mansion's portico, casting a golden light reflected in the shinier accessories of the assembling guests. Marines in dress blues, white cross belts standing out in the gloom of the dusk, snapped to attention and saluted each officer as they and their ladies entered the grounds.

Looking out the cab window, Wake tried to sound enthused. "Well, here we are, darling. And you, my little island girl from

Key West, will be the most beautiful woman in the house."

"Why, thank you, Peter. Dear, it's not that far, why don't we just walk to the gate from here instead of waiting for the line to move up?" Linda said as she adjusted the beaver fur around her shoulders.

"Your wish is my command."

The Marine sergeant at the northwest gate clicked to attention and rendered the regulation salute. That elicited the required counter-salute from Wake and a quiet, "How lovely," from Linda in appreciation for the first pageantry of the evening.

They entered the tiled vestibule, brightly lit by a huge gas chandelier reflected by enormous wall mirrors, from the portico through a ceremonial guard of more Marines. An ancient black usher sauntered out from the Ushers Cloak Room on the right, took their outer garments and led the Wakes through the glass doors that separated the foyer from main hall. There he bid them a smiling good evening and suggested they join the line of black-tied and -tailed gentlemen and gowned ladies across the more sedately lit hall. Seated on the grand stairs at the western end of the hallway, the Marine Band played light background airs that Wake vaguely identified as probably French, since they were high-pitched and frilly.

The Wakes stood behind an aloof congressman and his bored wife, who spoke to no one in the line. Following Linda stood the president of an Ohio furniture-making company and his wide-eyed spouse, the two couples making small talk as the line slowly progressed toward the door leading into the Red Room. The Wakes had been to these sort of affairs before, but the Ohioans, Mr. and Mrs. Hunter, were Republican supporters on their first visit to Washington. Linda filled the time by explaining the protocol and the locales they would see within the mansion.

"First we will go into the Red Room and present our calling cards, then we'll enter the Blue Room and be introduced to President and Mrs. Hayes, and then we'll go into the Green Room until the president has met everyone. At that point they will open the East Room and the grand soirée will begin."

The Red Room looked the same as the last time Wake had been there. Gray walls decorated with red trim, crimson carpet and furniture, with the most notable features being an upright piano against the south wall and a desk. Wake liked the dark oak desk best. Massive, with intricate paneling and trim, it had a wonderful story which he narrated to the Hunters.

"This desk is very special to naval officers in the American and Royal Navies. The tale starts with a ship named HMS *Resolute,* which was sent with three other British warships back in eighteen-fifty-two to search for Sir John Franklin, who'd been lost in the Canadian Arctic while looking for the Northwest Passage. *Resolute* and another vessel were stuck in the ice for *two years,* the crews barely surviving, so the commander of the expedition finally decided to abandon those two ships, transfer the men to the floating ships and sail home." Wake paused for effect. "Now the story gets really interesting . . ."

"Good Lord, I thought it was already!" said Mrs. Hunter, fanning her chest with a pudgy hand.

"Oh, no, Mrs. Hunter. Just starting. After they left, *Resolute* broke free of the ice on her own, drifted out to sea and was found by an American whaler, then towed into Boston. She was purchased by Congress, refitted, and afterward presented as a gift of peace to Great Britain."

"My goodness, I never heard that story before," said Mr. Hunter. "A gift of peace, you say?"

"Yes, but even there's more, Mr. Hunter. The commander of the expedition was subsequently court-martialed for abandoning a seaworthy vessel and the returned *Resolute* was recommissioned into the Royal Navy. She went on to serve another twenty years and was finally broken up just four years ago. Last year Queen Victoria had two desks made from the lumber of the ship. One is in her office at Buckingham Palace. You're looking at the other one—a return gift of peace from Her Majesty to President Hayes."

"Oh, sir, what a wonderful story!" gushed Mrs. Hunter, pulling on her husband's sleeve. "Thadeus, you must remember this story to tell at the commerce club next month."

The four of them stood in line admiring the desk when a well-dressed young man walked up to Wake. "Commander, I couldn't help hearing that you know the origin of our famous desk and tell the story well. Allow me to introduce myself. I'm George Gustin, personal secretary to President Hayes. You and Mrs. Wake have been asked to come immediately into the Blue Room by Admiral Porter and Navy Secretary Thompson. Would you please follow me?"

Wake heard a guttural sound from the congressman as he and Linda made their way past the line into the oval Blue Room with its blue and gold trim and large doors opening to the piazza along the south face of the mansion. Gustin took them around the awaiting throng and directly to President and Mrs. Hayes, greeting guests by the central circular divan. Thompson and Porter were standing there too, all smiles and joviality. It was the first time Wake had seen Thompson since his interrogation in the secretary's office. He began feeling very nervous.

Secretary of the Navy Thompson waved them over and turned to the Hayes. "Ah, yes, here they are, sir. Mr. President, Mrs. Hayes—may I present Lieutenant Commander Peter Wake and Mrs. Wake?"

Hayes smiled at Linda, then studied Wake while gripping his hand. The president's hair and beard were gray, and his frame had gone heavy, but he had a boyish glint in those deep-set eyes. Wake knew that—unlike many politicians in Washington—Hayes had been in battle with an Ohio infantry regiment during the war. The president had seen danger and death. Wake also knew that the boyish glimmer was not naïveté, it was energy. As president, Hayes had been a decisive leader in a turbulent time, fighting against Democrats trying to curtail the progress for black freedmen's civil rights the Republicans had made over the previous nineteen years.

Wake thought the president also a man of Constitutional principal, who had let it be known he was only going to serve one term, and indeed, that he favored a term limit for presidents of one six-year term. Hayes was a man of honor and definitely *not* a man to underestimate.

The president spoke quietly. "So you are the man who wrote that report about the Peruvians and Chileans? I found it interesting. If you would indulge me, son, I'd like to speak with you later in the evening about that situation."

The president had read the report? And wanted to speak with *him?* Wake was astonished but tried not to show it. "Yes, sir. Of course, sir."

Thompson moved between the President and Wake. "The president is interested in your observations and opinions, Commander."

Hayes nodded. "Quite so, Mr. Secretary. I need to comprehend the real situation there in order to make the best decision." He looked at Wake. "Commander, I'll call for you tonight after my official departure from the reception. We'll talk somewhere private."

Then he was facing the other direction, smiling at a woman sparkling with diamonds and saying something humorous about tariffs with her husband. Wake turned to see Mrs. Hayes speaking with an army general and Linda being introduced to a distinguished-looking gentleman down the row of dignitaries, who he realized was Vice President Wheeler. Thompson and Porter had left the room.

Moments later Wake was holding Linda's hand as they entered the Green Room to await word that the main reception would begin. She sat in a black and green satin chair and remarked on the presidential busts arranged around the room. Fruits and cookies, along with punch and sparkling waters, were brought around by liveried servants and eagerly consumed by the attendees, who chattered away in a buzz that grew as more people entered the room to wait.

When a stir was heard in the hall and trumpets flared, Linda stood and curtsied to Wake. In the Southern accent she sometimes used for the effect she said, "Would you kindly escort me into the grand soirée, sir?

"Why of course, my dear," he answered with a flourish. "I am an officer and a gentleman, and therefore but a hopeless devotee to your beauty, madam, as well as a servant to your wishes. A duty that is an honor and privilege to perform."

# 12

# Perceptions

It turned out that Secretary Thompson and Admiral Porter had not left the building. Wake saw them in the far corner of the East Room when he entered with the crowd. Linda had gone to speak with some naval wives she knew, leaving him standing there, wondering what to do next. Along the far wall, the president was speaking intently with a diplomat and close by the vice president was suffering through a long-winded monologue by a huge woman in bright blue.

Wake glanced at Thompson and Porter again. The naval leaders were talking with a man in the bemedalled uniform of a Royal Navy captain. Porter looked up and saw Wake, then leaned over and said something to the British officer. The man turned around, his haughty stare transforming into a huge grin as he recognized Wake.

It was none other than Jacky Fisher, Wake's old acquaintance from the Mediterranean who saved Wake from a pirate attack in the Straights of Gibraltar and subsequently transported him to Morocco, where he gained fame and the medals on his chest. A dynamo of innovative change, Fisher was a torpedo and gunnery expert, and a modernizing force in the Royal Navy, insisting on progress when others were content to keep the status quo.

"Sir! I had heard you were promoted shortly after I last saw you. A belated heart-felt congratulations," offered Wake as he and Fisher met in the middle of the vast room.

"Thank you, my Yankee friend. I've good news, Peter. As of last September, I am flag captain of the squadron on the North American Station. Vice Admiral McClintock, commanding."

"Congratulations again, sir. That's a prestigious assignment in the Royal Navy. What ship did they give you?"

"*Northampton!* She's a beauty, Peter, simply brilliant, with all the modern features. I'll have you aboard so you can be properly awed. I may well let you have some of our decent rum as well."

Fisher noticed a tall naval officer approaching. "Ah, well, speak of the Irish. Here's the admiral now."

He gestured to Wake. "Admiral, may I present Lieutenant Commander Peter Wake, a man who knows not only how to get into trouble, but how to emerge from it smelling of success."

The admiral replied, his words tinged with a Gaelic accent. "A rare ability! Perhaps we could all learn a thing or two from you, Commander. And how is it that you know my energetic young flag captain?"

Wake instantly liked the man, whose fame as a seaman and polar explorer was internationally known. Ironically, McClintock had been on the expedition to find Franklin in the Arctic, and his ship—HMS *Intrepid*—was the other vessel abandoned in the ice with *Resolute*. Wake wondered if McClintock knew about the desk in the room close by.

"Your flag captain saved my life from some homicidally unpleasant locals back in seventy-four, sir."

"I see. Yes, that sort of thing does cement a friendship, doesn't it? But does he have you doing these infernal dances too? My Jacky has grown quite the fearsome reputation in our navy for insisting upon constant exercise by dancing."

McClintock's eyes filled with mirth as he cocked an eyebrow

at Fisher. "See here, Jacky. I've heard there may be dance music tonight and in the interest of Anglo-American amity must beg you not to exhaust these American ladies. They may not be as enthusiastic or skilled as you for leaping and sashaying about. Someone might get hurt."

"Whatever you wish, Admiral," Fisher drew himself up straight. "I promise to leave the colonial women alone, sir."

The Marine Band had set up in the corner and started performing waltzes. Wake struggled through three with his wife, managing not to trip or step on her feet. He had no prowess at formal dancing, preferring far more to hold Linda closely and move very slowly to the music, but that was something that would never do at this kind of affair. Afterward, Linda thanked him for the effort and suggested they mingle and meet back at the refreshment tables in thirty minutes.

It was a long thirty minutes. Fisher twirled by, waltzing madly with the wife of the Italian chargé d'affaires. Wake laughed at Fisher's shrug—the man had a force of personality that could not be ignored. He was your best friend or worst enemy. Many thought he was destined for the top in the Royal Navy. And he was two years younger and two ranks higher than Wake.

It was boring watching the milling crowd, listening to the inane chatter, the pasted-on smiles of the dancers as they looked at anything but the face of their partner. Wake could swear that damned uniform collar was getting tighter since he'd been back in Washington. It choked him whenever he bent forward at all, making him feel like he was in a straightjacket. He wanted to get the thing off. Plus, unlike most naval gatherings, there was nothing interesting to drink.

Wake had no problem with the First Lady's rule of temperance at the White House, but wished for just a *little* rum in the punch to make the evening more tolerable. He was headed to the refreshments table to meet Linda when the Marine Band abruptly stood and a deep voice called out, "Ladies and Gentlemen, the President of the United States of America and Mrs. Hayes!"

"Hail to the Chief" thundered throughout the room. Wake joined the guests applauding as a hand touched his shoulder from behind. Gustin said, "This is the presidential promenade, Commander. It signifies the beginning of the end of the reception. Once he's gone all the way around the room, President Hayes will leave through the main doors and ascend the formal staircase at the end of the hall. Wait five minutes, then follow. I'll meet you at the top of the stairs."

Wake turned around but Gustin was already over by the President and Mrs. Hayes, clearing a way for them. Hayes caught his eye and nodded while shaking hands with one person and speaking to another. Wake swung his gaze around and found Linda over at the table. She was chatting with a tall artillery officer with bold sideburns who was far too handsome for Wake's liking. Linda had just accepted a glass of punch from the major when Wake arrived at her side.

Following brief introductions with the "gun jockey," as sailors called army artillerymen, he said to Linda, "Dear, I'm afraid I have to stay for a while after the reception starts to wind down. I'm wanted for a private conference."

"Tonight? Here? At this hour? Why it must be ten o'clock already, Peter. Who in the world would want to have a conference now? It's very rude."

Wake didn't want to name the requestor in front of the major, but his face must've given it away. "The president?" she exclaimed as he hushed her to be quieter and the major looked politely away before excusing himself and leaving.

Linda asked, "The president wants to see you *personally?*"

"Yes, and I think it may be for a while."

"No offense, dear, but why *you?*"

"South America. He wants my opinion, evidently."

Linda's face changed from amazed to coy. She turned and looked over her shoulder at him. "You know, a sailor once told me that a promise made, is a debt unpaid." She shook her head slowly as a sly grin spread. "So what's it gonna be, sailor? The

President of the United States—or me?"

Wake couldn't help himself, he laughed out loud. If only the president could've seen that performance he would've ordered them both immediately home to bed. God, he loved that girl's sense of humor.

Not to be outdone in the theatrical department, he countered with, "Well, my dear, here is the situation. I'm a United States naval officer, and that means that I—unlike most mortal men— have the unique capacity to accomplish both tasks tonight. I have every intention of assisting the supreme leader of our nation *and* seeing that that most anticipated of debts be satisfied." He winked. "Probably with accrued interest."

"I will wait for my man like a good wife. But try not to keep the president up too late. You're not getting any younger, you know."

"Aye, aye, ma'am."

Ten minutes later Peter Wake was on the eastern end of the second floor of the White House—just over the East Room below— waiting in the private study of the president. At the far end of the family's floor, it was the opposite of the official public rooms on the first floor: plain plaster walls with few decorations, one painting of an Ohio pastoral scene, a wartime sepia photograph of army officers by a tent, three cane chairs for visitors, and a desk with swivel chair. He noted that the papers on the desk were neatly arranged and every pigeonhole above, each labeled, was filled. A photograph of Hayes, his wife Lucy, and their six children, was propped up next to a telephone.

Wake stood when Hayes walked in alone. Wake had expected Porter or Thompson to be present but no one else was there. The president was in his shirtsleeves, cuffs undone and rolled back. He looked tired.

"Thank you for staying over, Commander. I'm sorry for keeping you from the lovely Mrs. Wake, but I can assure you this is important. I asked to see you alone because, though I know you've been told to be candid, I want to make sure you're candid."

"Yes, sir." Wake felt a surge of electricity flow through him as his gut tightened.

"Your report is self explanatory. My interest is not necessarily in the past, but in the future. Question one: do you believe each party wants to have a cease-fire truce and negotiate a peace treaty right now?"

Wake took a breath, thinking. "No, sir. Two of them do and one doesn't. I believe the Bolivians have written off their coastal province and will parley for any money they can get. The Chileans will offer them inducements to forget claims and also to forge a union with Chile. The Peruvians will accept a truce *in situ,* with the hope of realignment to their original national boundaries. They haven't lost much of their territory yet, but know that's merely a matter of time, something that's not on their side. The Peruvians are scared, but not defeatist, Mr. President. They can and will fight if negotiations fail." As Wake paused, he felt the president's intent concentration on him. Trying not to sound nervous, he continued.

"The Chileans, on the other hand, know that time is on their side. Their armies are advancing up toward the Peruvian heartland, Bolivia is out of the fight so their eastern flank is secure, and their navy now dominates the Pacific Ocean flank. I anticipate more Chilean landings along the Peru coast, behind the Peruvian front lines, to out-flank them. I think they'll be successful. So why should they give any of this away? They won't, sir. I think they smell blood and want to take the Peruvian coast too. It wouldn't surprise me if they tried to take the whole country."

"Do you think the British want negotiations to succeed at this point in time?"

"Yes, sir. Their commercial interests have achieved what they want—those guano and nitrate deposits on the Bolivian coast."

"Hmm. I see. Do you think the United States has enough influence with all parties to bring them together and create a real peace treaty?"

"No, sir. We can bring them together, but I doubt it will be successful. The U.S. does have influence with Peru. But we have very little influence with the Bolivians, and the Chileans are Eurocentric. The Chileans have no incentive or pressure to stop their invasion."

Wake could see the president didn't like that answer. "So there's no reason to try. We'd just end up failing."

"No, sir. I think we have to try. All of Latin America is watching us, waiting to see what we do. Now is the time to do the right thing and try to end the fighting. That will gain us good will with the more enlightened elements and increase influence with the pragmatic politicians in the region. Most of them are wary of Chile."

"And this is also about British versus American commercial and political influence, and which will be ascendant in the years to come?"

Wake suddenly realized Hayes wasn't interested what he answered, but how he answered. The president was testing *him,* his ability to think and reply quickly and convincingly. And that wasn't good. "Yes, Mr. President. It's also about that. There's an opportunity here for us, though—if we provide some leadership in breaking the deadlock. Or at least try."

"So, Commander, I understand you support Peru in this. Why?"

"Sir, that's not really true. I support a policy of strict neutrality, as opposed to the implicit lean toward Chile that I've heard other American officials suggest—mainly for economic gain. I think that is a short-sighted position to take. In addition, the Peruvians are the victims in this ridiculous war, and I think they deserve a bit of compassion, if nothing else, because of that."

"And how exactly are they victims?"

"They are victims of Bolivian political maneuvering that got them involved in the first place and Chilean military aggression that took advantage of the situation to expand the war into Peru. Good God, Mr. President, the war is over bird dung. Pretty damn shameful, if you ask me, sir."

Hayes's facial expression went cold. "You seem passionate about this, Commander. Is the rumor about you and the Brit diplomat in Lima true?"

Wake locked eyes with the president. He'd wondered if the man had heard that rumor, probably from the State Department. "No, sir. I never did anything to harm the man. He was killed after I left him in his office at the British legation in Lima. Someone started that rumor to cast aspersions against my mission to the area, or against my country's influence."

The president leaned back in his chair and relaxed. "Glad to hear that, Commander. I didn't give it any credence. Nobody, including the Brits, does. Well, maybe some of the Chileans, but they could be just posturing. Now, if we do try to set up a cease-fire commission where should that be held? Ecuador? Brazil?"

Wake was relieved the president had backed him regarding the rumor. He switched his thought process and pondered about a location for truce talks. Brazil was too far away. Even Ecuador was a quite distance removed from the scene. The Peruvians would want it near their southern border, to draw attention to their claims. But it had to be a safe, neutral place. . . .

"One of *our* ships, sir. A neutral U.S. warship, anchored off the Peruvian coast."

Hayes rubbed his chin. "Well, I must admit—that didn't occur to me. Yes, I think we could do that. Good idea, Commander."

"I've heard that *Lackawanna* is heading for that squadron, Mr. President. Might be there by now, not sure. She could be the neutral parley place for all parties. Anchored off Arica, Peru, would be most convenient for them."

"Yes, quite." Hayes paused while looking out the window. "And there's another positive factor arguing for it."

"Sir?"

A presidential eyebrow rose deviously, showing that boyish glint. "No Europeans in attendance there or hovering nearby. The French are running things in Panama and have a strong squadron on that Pacific coast, the Brits are all over Chile and also have a strong squadron down there, the Germans are in Argentina and Venezuela, and the Spanish are displaying their usual barbaric idiocy in Cuba." He sighed. "I am getting mightily tired of them all, Commander. Monroe's concept of hemispheric unity and protection from Old World intrigues has unfortunately been forgotten. And it's about time we led from the front again on that subject. Or at least looked like we were."

"Yes, sir. It surely is. Perceptions are important."

"Son, perceptions are *everything* in politics—be it local in Zanesville, Ohio, or international in South America."

The president scratched some notes on a pad, then returned his gaze to Wake. "And now, Commander, about Panama and that French canal. I read in the report of your interesting conversation with de Lesseps. You seem to think they'll fail. Disease and engineering, right?"

"Yes, sir. That's it, basically."

"That's not what experts are saying in New York and Washington. A bunch of them are saying it will work. But if de Lesseps does fail, what is your opinion of what will happen subsequently?"

Wake had considered that very issue while in Panama. It was a thorny one, with some unpleasant potential consequences.

"Well, sir, since technically it's a private company, French civil law has jurisdiction and it would go bankrupt when the capital runs out and the loans default. Lawsuits, perhaps? But also at that point the Colombian government has legal authority to take over the local assets and the project itself, bidding it out to someone else.

"Or the French government could try to financially revive the project with public money out of national pride. We all know about their pride. But that would, of course, be a violation of the Bidlack-Mallarino Treaty of eighteen-forty-six that was supposed to keep foreign *governmental* powers out of the Isthmus, as well as the Monroe Doctrine prohibiting any new European colonization in the Americas."

Hayes kept his eyes on Wake. "You didn't tell me what you think will happen—which of those two scenarios, Commander?"

"I think the French government will try to get involved, sir—absent any preemptive proclamation from the United States to reiterate that the canal is vital to our nation and our concerns that this canal be kept neutral."

The president exhaled loudly. "All right, I can see that, but I don't like it one bit. The global rush for colonies is on in Europe. They can have the whole of Africa and Asia for all I care, but I worry that they're eyeing our hemisphere too. And that canal in particular. Of course, in the long run, all we've got is our navy to dissuade them."

Wake wasn't sure what to say to that. He felt like saying "Then we're in deep trouble," but he didn't. Hayes looked stressed. Wake imagined this would be a political hot potato domestically, too. Finally, he said, "We'll do our best, Mr. President, if called upon."

President Hayes didn't reply, instead he unexpectedly got up from the desk swivel chair. "Goodness, I see it's well past eleven, Commander. We've kept your bride far longer than I planned, but you've helped me immensely. Thank you for your candor. Perhaps we'll see each other again on this subject."

Hayes spoke into the telephone, then bid Wake goodnight and departed for his bedroom down the hall. Seconds later Gustin appeared and showed Wake downstairs to Linda in the vestibule. She was having a fine time conversing with the ushers and chefs, listening to stories about the parties of various presidents and first ladies. The pastry chef who had created the confectionery centerpiece for the reception, for which the White House had become famous, was explaining the secrets of his work of art when Wake entered. By their faces it was obvious all were enjoying his wife's company and recognition of their efforts.

Wake interrupted. "I'm sorry, gentlemen, but I must take your beautiful guest away and whisk her home. Forgive me, but somehow I'm sure you *understand*."

That got a laugh from the assembled men. Linda blushed. When they were in the back of a cab she asked, "How did your talk with the president go?"

"Not sure, really. He looked like he valued my opinion. Who knows?"

"Well, I'm sure he did." She snuggled close to him. "Peter, it's been a wonderful evening, but I think the time for talking is over. It's Valentine's night. Time to pay off that debt, don't you think?"

"My dear, that is precisely what I've been thinking about for the last four hours."

# 13

# Politics

## April 1880

Spring was always beautiful in Washington. The trees and flowers were in bloom everywhere and though Wake wasn't versed in their names and details, he appreciated their role in improving the spirits of the city's inhabitants. Even the most morose of the winter's survivors smiled wider and stepped lighter.

It was now late April and Wake looked back over the months gone by. They were busy months, but with little to call tangible accomplishment. But he knew such was the way of life at head-quarters for a naval officer, where time was measured by paper-work created or organized, and success was described by the social status of one's invitations. It was the price a naval man paid to have a normal home life. Wake endured.

For the previous two months he had been inundated with work at the Board of Inspection and, curiously, was never approached by Porter about the presidential conversation. Nor did he see Thompson or the president, except in passing. Hayes nodded knowingly to him across the room at a reception once, but never spoke with him again. Resigning himself to be content and successful at his mundane assignment, Wake realized his report and recommendations had been forgotten, a mere momentary briefing of busy men, and his days of important special missions were over.

The War of the Pacific may have become part of the past for Wake, but not for the newspaper writers. Headlines proclaimed doom for the Peruvians after the defeat at Pacocha Bay in late February when twelve thousand Chilean soldiers under General Baquedano were landed by their navy and subsequently severed the supply lines of the Peruvians in Arica to the south. The defenders of Arica, under General Buendía, were down to four thousand men, cut off from reinforcements and starving throughout March. It was exactly as Wake had predicted, the Chileans were effectively using their navy as an offensive factor along the watery flank in the land campaign. By April the Peruvian lines were teetering and the question was how much longer it would be until total collapse.

President Hayes maintained his official neutrality regarding the Chilean-Peruvian-Bolivian war, but political momentum was quietly building in Washington for a de facto recognition of Chile's successes. Some were calling for American mediation, however. That still seemed the best idea to Wake.

The French canal in Panama was front and center on the American scene during the spring also. Ferdinand de Lesseps departed Panama bound for New York and a campaign across the nation, seeking good will and stock buyers for his canal building company. On the voyage north he'd slashed his projected cost for the project from $240 million dollars to $131 million dollars, indicating to the press that now that he'd seen the area he could confidently say it would be easier.

His tour went on for a month, from New York to Philadelphia, Chicago, and San Francisco, making headlines each week with his charm, his assertiveness. He overcame technical concerns, political worries, and financial wariness with his personality. People flocked to hear him speak and came away wishing him well, amazed at the audacity and scale of the construction operation.

However, for all the time and money spent in his effort to woo America, he didn't sell a single share of stock to an American capitalist. And when he reached Washington there was a cordial reception from the government, but no huge banquets, no grand assemblies of fawning masses. Instead, emerging from a committee meeting on Capitol Hill, he was greeted by the press who had a copy of a proclamation just issued by the president regarding the canal across Panama.

President Hayes' declaration was concise. The Unites States had a vital interest in any canal built in Panama and would defend its neutrality. No European governmental power, or combination of powers, would ever be allowed to control the canal, since it was vital to internal shipping transport between the coasts of America. And no corporation or private person investing in the enterprise should expect any protection for the project from any European power. Any canal would always remain under *American* control and protection.

De Lesseps, an expert at promoting and presenting the best possible face on things, didn't flinch when confronted by Hayes' cold announcement. Quite the contrary, he welcomed the presidential statement, saying it guaranteed the political security of the canal.

Wake smiled when Useppa read it all to him from the newspaper. De Lesseps reminded him of lawyers he had known who could conform to any position they encountered, and Hayes had carried through on his conviction from their conversation, even more strongly than Wake had anticipated. He privately wondered how the United States was going to defend a Panamanian canal, now that the president had drawn that line in the sand.

But Hayes' bluff worked. Within days the French minister in Washington sent an official note to Secretary of State Evarts explaining that the French government was not involved in the project and had no intentions of giving it any support. Wake breathed a bit easier, proud that he had perhaps influenced American foreign policy just a little and glad that his navy wouldn't have to face the French navy because of it. For he knew that, in reality, America's army and navy were in no shape to defend her vital interests against Europe, or anyone else.

Europe that spring, however, passed over the canal commotion. The frightening specter of anarchy that had riveted the continent thirty years earlier during the revolutions of the forties was still a real possibility. Rather than dwelling on a construction project in the Panamanian swamps, the powers were more concerned with the assassination attempt on Tsar Alexander's life when terrorists blew up his dining room in the Winter Palace in St. Petersburg just after St. Valentine's Day. Though Alexander was known as an enlightened monarch who had instituted many reforms, including some in the imperial navy, Wake wondered how long he could dodge killers from within his own people— this was the third attempt on his life.

In Great Britain the indefatigable William Gladstone was once again back in power. The man amazed Wake with his many political comebacks. The effect on the enthusiastic expansion of the empire had yet to be seen, but Wake predicted it would no doubt slow down a bit, since Gladstone was known to be hesitant about further foreign adventures, especially with the war in Afghanistan still raging.

Wake heard good news about an old friend. Wake had become close with Lieutenant Peter Allen, Royal Marine Light Infantry, during his last tour in the Caribbean, which was followed by a hair-raising time the two had ashore in Spain back in seventy-four. Wake read a newspaper account describing the Royal Navy's assaults on several pirate strongholds along the Malay Peninsula. Allen had been with the landing force from HMS *Kestrel* and HMS *Encounter* that tried to put an end to kidnappings and piracy by the Balinini and Illanuan tribes in the Straights of Malacca. Many American, Dutch, and British ships had been attacked by the pirates, with some of the crews sold as slaves in Borneo. According to the article, Allen's next duty station was said to be with the Royal Navy's North American squadron.

But bad news came from the Royal Navy, too. Wake learned that Phillip Fisher, the twenty-two-year-old brother of Jacky Fisher, had perished in the North Atlantic aboard the training ship *Atalanta* when she was lost with all hands. The reason was a mystery and even the offer of a substantial reward for information hadn't resolved it. Wake's friend Jacky had been despondent when he'd last seen him at a social function at the British minister's home.

Useppa loved to read him the news in the morning from the paper, especially developments of a positive scientific nature, like Mr. Edison's never-ending search for feasible uses of electricity. One morning she enthusiastically read to him about Edison's new electric horseshoe lamp and the inventor's prediction that in the near future every home in American cities would be lit by electric lamps. Wake marveled at that and thought it probably true. So many things were changing with technical advances—many unheard of merely ten years earlier—being touted in the papers as accomplished practically every day. It seemed to Wake that the incredibly imaginative tales of one of his favorite writers, Jules Verne, were turning into reality.

Closer to home, in early March, Sean Rork and Sheila O'Toole announced a date for their wedding, having overcome the protestations of her family, or at least worn them down a bit. Pretty and twenty-five years younger, Sheila wàs Rork's opposite—petite, quiet, pensive. But Wake noticed that the planning for the ceremony brought out a strong-willed streak in her. Nothing was left to chance, everything was to be done perfectly. Wake had seen military operations with less preparation.

He remembered his marriage ceremony with Linda sixteen years earlier, during a gorgeous sunset at the African beach in Key West. It was simple, with just a few navy friends, and no frills. A forbidden marriage between supposed enemies performed in a former slave cemetery by a black Bahamian minister, it was still the most beautiful wedding Wake had ever seen.

Sheila's big day was to be June first, with a full church wedding. Rork was bewildered by the event's arrangements but content with his decision. After a long and hard life it was time to settle down. Wake was happy to say yes to his friend's request to be best man and Linda and Useppa were thrilled when asked by Sheila to be bridesmaids.

Wake's home life was the happiest he had ever known. He enjoyed being around Useppa and Sean, seeing them growing up in mind and body—particularly his daughter, who had turned fifteen on April tenth. It was a grand celebration, with many navy people, other children in the neighborhood, and adult friends gathered at the patch of lawn behind their apartment building for an afternoon dinner. Best of all, it was a surprise carried off perfectly. His daughter was astounded when she came home from working at the church and saw the crowd assembled in her honor. He'd always loved watching Useppa and her mother do things together around the house, but had thought of Useppa as a little girl. Seeing his daughter that afternoon, he realized suddenly that she was growing up.

Useppa's limp was still there, but she had managed over the years to compensate for it until it appeared to be nothing more than a minor nuisance for her. Lately the doctors had said there was nothing more they could do but let nature take its course. Most of the pain had left, or so she'd told them, and the strong-willed girl was determined to do anything she wished, even if that defied social convention. He'd been very proud when Useppa announced she was going to help with the church's poor mission, something usually left to older people. It was a noble endeavor, and when she'd hesitantly told him and her mother, he hugged her and wished her well. He wanted her to be confident and able in the modern world that was changing around them.

Sean was another matter. The boy seemed disposed to getting into trouble. It wasn't malicious trouble, mainly just curiosity and exuberance. It was distressing and dangerous nonetheless. In mid-March he'd been sent home with a note from the principal stating that he had climbed to the roof of the three-story building on a dare, then jumped down onto an awning, ripping it in two but escaping unhurt. Now Wake had to pay for the awning to be restored.

Rork suggested that a navy sail-maker could repair it on off-duty time—he had a friend that wouldn't mind at all. But Wake decided that young Sean should do it himself, stitch by stitch, every afternoon and inspected each evening by his father. When the boy protested that it sounded like girl's work, Wake suggested he say that to the grizzled old sail-makers at the Navy Yard, that his father could take him there right then. Sean sheepishly apologized and an hour later was lugging the canvas home.

Young Sean's Irish namesake helped him by teaching him the looping overhand sailor's stitch in the evenings. The project was coming along nicely until one night Rork informed the boy he wouldn't be available to help anymore, he was going off to sea. When Wake inquired about the unusual abruptness of the sailing orders, Rork grimly bobbed his head toward the door and they went outside for a quiet talk alone.

"'Tis the famine in Ireland, Peter. They're sendin' *Constellation* with food an' supplies an' I've been asked to go as the ol' girl's senior bosun. Asked, mind ya—never ordered. 'Tis an honor. All the Irish bosuns in Uncle Sam's navy would jump at the chance to help on that mission. But they chose *me* an' I'm a-goin'."

Wake had read about the potato crop failing again in Ireland. It was in all the papers and Wake had seen commentaries accusing the British of doing nothing while the Irish peasants died by the thousands. Across the United States tempers flared and old anti-British feelings had surfaced. Bowing to the pressure, the president was sending *Constellation* with food, just as they had sent her back in forty-eight during the first famine.

"Well, I understand that, Sean. She's used for training now, so it'll probably be a few months and she'll return to that duty. You'll be home by mid-summer and back to duty at the yard. So why the glum looks, my friend?"

"Because though *you* understand, there's one that don't. Sheila's been a bloody fright about it. Accused me o' dodgin' the weddin' by takin' off. Said *she* was Irish an' felt no urge to head off yonder with spuds to the ol' isle. Said her mum'd lived without a real husban' an' she'd be damned if she'd live the same way. I never seen her this way, Peter. As bitter as thick milk, she is. Nasty side to her. An' I don't mind sayin' it scares me. Bad portent o' things to come."

Wake knew that feeling completely. He and Linda had been through some very tough times. The sailor's life made wives live alone for long periods. "Well, she's the daughter of a petty officer so she knows ships and the sea. Surely she knows you'll be back in four or five months, or maybe sooner? Just postpone the wedding a bit."

"No matter. 'Tis that weddin' date that gets her. Ironclad, it is. Won't postpone it even a wee bit an' doesn't think I should make her. Doesn't think I should go a'tall, an' faults me for sayin' yes to the offer."

Wake saw the anguish in his friend. "Perhaps she'll calm down with time?"

"Don't matter now, Peter. Weddin's called off. Said she has second thoughts on me suitability. Me own *suitability*, can ya imagine that? Actually used that word! Who the devil did she think she was marryin'?"

"Maybe when you get back she'll have a change of heart, Sean."

Rork sighed. "Nay, she won't an' I'm a-startin' to see it all clearer now, anyways. Sheila's not the lass I thought she was.

Wants more than poor Sean Rork can give. Ya know, Peter, 'twas gonna take all her dad's money, an' that o' me too, to pay for that weddin' the way she wanted it. Grandiose, it was. Too bloody grandiose for the likes of an Irish bosun named Sean Rork."

"I'm sorry, Sean. Maybe things will change for the better, but I agree with you going and wish you luck on the voyage. When do you leave?"

"Tomorrow on the train for New York, where I join the ship. They reconfigured her berthing deck up there an' put in twenty-five hundred barrels o' flour an' potatoes. Should take a few months to get her over an' back. Maybe I'll find a *true* Irish girl back in the ol' isle. One not so fancy with me money."

And with that said and a farewell handshake Rork was off down the street, back to his barracks at the Navy Yard to pack. That had been on March twenty-sixth. *Constellation* set sail for Ireland from New York on the twenty-eighth.

By April thirtieth the spring was getting warm. The vaunted cooling system of the building struggled to keep it comfortable, and Wake guessed that when the notorious Washington summer arrived it would be stifling in the building.

Taking a break from his office, Wake read the well-worn April issue of *Atlantic Monthly* in the officer's head near his office in the Navy Department. The restrooms of the new building were state-of-the-art, with modern plumbing and patented toilets, marbled sinks, and even bathtubs for officers to refresh themselves prior to reporting to the senior-most above them. With the new facilities had come stringent regulations, sadly necessary since there had already been a few transgressions by junior officers and clerical types, like cleaning ink pens, spittoons, and boots in the sinks and bathtubs. Still, the restrooms were magnificent, almost decadent, hideaways for an officer, giving him time and privacy to think about something other than the mindless bureaucracy in which he found himself a cog.

An article caught Wake's eye. It illuminated the reader about the Republican front-runners in the race for the nomination to the presidential election later that year. There was a strict rule in the navy that politics and religion were never discussed—naval officers were above that sort of thing and the recent civil war had provided a bloody lesson in why wardrooms and clubs were not the places to air one's partisan views. But Wake noticed the article was the most dog-eared in the issue, making it obvious that naval officers were still interested in such subjects, even if they couldn't converse about them publicly.

The article's pundit had it that Grant was on the comeback trail and the man to beat, though Secretary of the Treasury John Sherman was a close second. It was Sherman, after all, who had pulled the country out of the depression that started in 1873, or at least so the public thought. Senator Blaine of Maine was a substantial contender also. Vice President Wheeler was mentioned as having little hope of victory. President Hayes had declared at the beginning of his term that he would not seek re-election, so he was out of the running. James Garfield of Ohio, a former general, made the long-shot list for the Republican nomination, but few thought him likely to win. No, it looked to the article's writer, and to Wake, that Grant would be the party's nominee for president.

Wake anticipated the Democrats would probably nominate Winfield Scott Hancock, also a former general. Wake thought him a good man, better than Tilden, who had lost the disputed close election of seventy-six. Hancock had served in southwestern Florida during the Seminole Wars, a jungled place Wake got to know only too well while fighting Confederates there. Wake had never subscribed to the notion of voting on party lines; he voted for the man best suited, Democrat or Republican.

Though he respected Hancock for his military success and identified with him because of common experiences in Florida, he worried about him. The problem with Hancock wasn't the man, it was his party. The Democrats were gaining control throughout the South and reversing progress for black citizens. Wake worried that Hancock, who had no political experience, would be merely a figurehead for the party's backroom boys who were determined to eliminate all vestiges of racial equality.

Grant, who'd had no experience himself when first taking office, had learned a tremendous amount since 1868—the hard way. His recent two-year triumphant world tour had revived his reputation after the scandal disasters of his presidential years, which had provided him with vivid lessons on what *not* to do. Plus, Wake knew Grant would not allow regression on black civil rights. So for all of that, sitting there in the officers' restroom, Wake decided he was a Grant man once again.

The irony of the location of his decision was not lost on him. With a rueful frown, he hoped it wouldn't be prophetic. Time would tell what the future would bring. That future would affect the navy. And now that Wake was in Washington, he understood only too well that the outcome of that upcoming election might affect him too.

An hour after emerging from the men's room he was summoned by a flustered clerk to go immediately to the office of Secretary Thompson. There was no further explanation—just get there now, the secretary wants you. Wake's mind ran through his recent work, trying to discern which case file might have gotten the attention of the head of the navy. Hell, he finally decided in the elevator, it could be any of them. Probably a congressional inquiry into a ship disposition.

When Wake arrived at the office, Porter and Thompson were there, looking as if they'd just had an unpleasant conversation, along with a third man out on the balcony. Wake stood at attention, waiting while Thompson went to confer with the man outside. He noticed Porter watching him solemnly until Thompson and the other entered. Then the admiral stood. Wake glanced quickly out of the corner of his eye to see who could get the famous Porter to rise in respect.

It was President Hayes. He motioned everyone to sit, then lounged in a big wingback. Wake took the small chair farthest away and tried to look professional. His heart was pounding.

Hayes nodded to Thompson, who said, "Commander, you seem to have a grasp on the situation in Panama and down in Peru. Your report was well done and your advice valuable. I told you before that there might be further call for your services on a special mission. That time has come. You're heading back down there, by order of the president."

Porter's eyes were hooded, as if asleep, but suddenly he growled, "This'll be dicey, Commander Wake. Do *not* give any wrong impressions this time. No trouble. Understood?"

"Yes, sir," replied Wake, not understanding anything. He was stunned.

Hayes waved a hand. "He'll do just fine, Admiral. I've no fear of that. Commander Wake, you will go down to Panama, see what's going on there, then go to Peru and report back the situation. I'm getting information from the consuls down there, and others, but I want an independent assessment."

He paused, roguish grin crinkling his face. "By the way, what did you think of my canal declaration when de Lesseps was in town? You have permission to be blunt, son."

Looking at Hayes, Wake had the urge to grin himself, but contained it. "Right on target, Mr. President. Got the point to the French."

"Yes, that's what I thought, too. Made a few folks in this town nervous, but after what you told me and some pondering on the issue, I thought it had to be said. Make it plain to all."

"Well, gentlemen, I've got to mosey on back over to the mansion." The president stood, with the three others rising until he waved them down. "Mrs. Hayes has got some darned thing for me to do. Ladies Temperance Club of Dayton, I think, meeting in the conservatory among the roses. I'm needed to go look presidential—which is not, for your information, easy while balancing a teacup on a lace doily atop your knee."

He shook Wake's hand. "Your reports will be read by only three people, Commander. The men in this room. Good luck."

Wake straightened. "Yes, sir. Thank you, sir."

After Hayes left, Thompson leaned forward on his desk. "Commander, you'll leave in three days. Admiral Porter will give you the details of your assignment."

"Aye, aye, sir," said Wake, puzzled at the abrupt turn of events in his life.

As he and Porter were leaving, Thompson called out. "Remember this, Commander Wake. Steer clear of politics on this trip."

"Aye, aye, sir," replied Wake again, knowing *that* would be hard to do in Latin America.

# 14

# The Man with Two First Names

"You're what?" Linda stared at him, not believing what he'd just said. She looked out their bedroom window, seeing little Sean playing stickball on the street below with his friends. Useppa was at her friend's house for dinner. It was their Friday evening routine.

"I'm heading south again. Panama and then Peru. Official naval observer."

"No warning? At least in regular duty you know when changes are and can get prepared. This is so sudden. When do you leave?" she asked coldly.

"Three days. Train down to New Orleans, then passenger steamer to Panama."

"When will you be back?" She set her jaw and added, "Really back."

Wake didn't know exactly. "Maybe in September or October, if everyone agrees on negotiating. Maybe longer if they don't."

"You'll miss Sean's birthday. July fifth—"

"I know when my son's birthday is, Linda. I didn't ask for this. The president asked for me. That makes it important. There's a lot riding on this."

"More important than your family?" She regretted it the moment she said that. "I'm sorry, Peter, that was cruel. Look, I know you didn't suggest or ask for this. It's just that after the last time you were down there in that war—it's not even our war, for God's sake—you nearly got killed. No, you never told me and I never told you I knew, but I read it in the papers even before you got home. That Peruvian ship you were on had almost everyone killed aboard her."

"That I was aboard her was a freak happenstance, dear. And they took care to get me off before the battle. This time I'll be in a much safer situation." He held her. "And the minute I can get out of there and back here in bed with you—I'll be northbound. I hate sleeping without you."

He nuzzled her neck. She felt so tired and now this. "I know how that feels, Peter. I hate it too, but I'm used to it after all these long years."

"I'll be back as soon as I can. I have to for my sanity too, Linda." His hand reached around her waist. "Useppa's over at Mrs. Nyland's, right?"

"Oh, Peter, you're so predictable. Yes, she's over there for supper and Sean's playing in the street." She took in his expectant eyes, caressed his face. "I suppose we have time to—"

The pain knifed into her. Linda doubled over, clutching her abdomen, tears streaming from the agony, unable to speak. Her husband stood there for several seconds, terrified at what he was seeing, then helped her to the bed, where she curled up in a fetal position.

"Linda? What is it? What's the matter?"

The searing pain subsided to a throbbing ache and she took a breath, exhaling loudly. "I'm all right, Peter. Not anything major, just a pain I sometimes get. Probably have an ulcer or some sort of inflammation of my digestive tract."

He curled up next to her and held her. "That seemed pretty bad, Linda. How long's it been going on?"

"Oh, a little while, off and on. It's gone now, though." She forced a smile. "Seriously, Peter, I am all right now. It's just a temporary ache that sometimes happens."

"How long?" He turned her face to him. "Tell me straight, Linda."

"Maybe six months, eight months. Since last summer."

"You've hidden it all this time? I've been back for months and you haven't told me? Linda—"

"Peter, don't make this a major event. It's only a stomach pain. Embarrassing, that's all."

"What's the doctor said about it?"

"Well, of course I haven't bothered a doctor about a case of the collywobbles, dear. It's just an indigestion episode. I'm not going to see a doctor for indigestion."

He couldn't believe she said that. It certainly wasn't indigestion. Wake'd had malaria and dysentery. Her pain reminded him of what he'd seen and felt himself.

"Tomorrow morning I am taking you to the doctor at the naval hospital, period. No mutiny on this. For once follow my orders. Now lie back and rest. I'll bring supper up to you when it's ready."

He kissed her forehead, then pulled the window shade down.

"Peter, I'll have a rest after I make supper."

"No. You will stay in that bed. I am not completely incompetent in the area of cooking. I won't promise it'll be anywhere as good as yours, but supper will be ready in just a little while. I mean it, Linda. Stay in the damn bed."

She could tell he was scared so she decided to stay in bed to calm him down. He closed the door behind him as she called out. "Yes, dear. But try to keep it simple, Peter. And please don't make a big mess!"

She knew, like most navy wives, that her husband needed to feel like he could protect her. Linda gazed up at the ceiling after he went downstairs. She had this feeling the problem wasn't her stomach, but was afraid to even consider the other possibilities. She'd heard other ladies speaking of those, in hushed tones.

"Mrs. Wake, you may have a distended or inflamed colon that has caused the pains," said Dr. Magg after the patient interview and cursory examination, consisting of running his hand over her lower abdomen outside of her dress. His diagnosis prompted Linda to give her husband an I-told-you-so look.

"Or," he continued, "they may be a symptom of certain female problems. I'll give you some medicine for colic disorders and if that doesn't subside your symptoms, then we'll send you to the doctors at the university. They've started some very interesting work over there on female problems."

"Thank you, doctor, for your time," said Linda. "Come on dear, let's go home."

Wake wasn't mollified in his apprehensions. He thought Linda was being too glib and the doctor too superficial in his investigation.

"Peter, come on. Let's leave the doctor to his other patients, the ones that have serious problems." She was at the door.

The doctor looked at him with a wan smile. Wake went with his wife.

That evening in bed she rolled over and kissed him, gently waking him. The moonlight seeped in around the shades, casting a silvery glow throughout the room, softening shadows and light. He held her to his chest.

"Peter, don't worry. It's just a touch of dyspepsia. I'm getting older now and I have to expect that sort of thing. I don't want that to spoil our last nights together before you leave."

"I'm thinking of not going, dear. I can tell them to get someone else."

Linda sat up on one elbow. She didn't want him to go, desperately wanted him to stay, to have a normal life like other married couples. A life they'd never had but she'd always dreamed of. But not this way. Not out of pity or misplaced concern. "Because I've got some heartburn from a bad stomach? It's an embarrassment, but not serious. Really, darling, you're blowing this way out of proportion."

"No, I'm worried about leaving you like this."

"Stop it, Peter. You're going. Discussion's over. I'm not on my deathbed and I'll not have you make career decisions based upon my minor medical maladies."

"Nice alliteration, Linda," he said, trying to lighten the mood.

"Alliteration? I didn't know you were aware of that word, Peter Wake," she said while tickling him. "There must be parts of you I don't know about."

"Hmm. Looks like you're not feeling badly now, island girl."

She tickled him again, then touched him in that special place. "And I see *you're* not ill at all, Lieutenant Commander Peter Wake, United States Navy."

"Linda, maybe we shouldn't. It might aggravate the problem."

She mocked his quarterdeck command voice. "I outrank you here in this room, *Mister* Wake. Besides, wives have needs too. Do as I say. *Now.*"

At that point, he couldn't help but do what she wanted.

His travel orders changed at the last minute. He was to leave from New York—the bean counters at the navy department deemed it cheaper. Normally, the fast steam packet from New York could get a passenger to the Caribbean side of Panama in ten days. But the packet was in refit, the relief packet was broken down in

Nassau, and the French steamer *Lafayette* that also sailed that route was crossing the Atlantic. He telegraphed the department from New York and asked for further orders.

They took three days to figure it out and reply. He was to go to New Orleans by rail after all. From there he would go to Havana, switch ships, and head to Kingston in Jamaica, then take a small steamer to Colón. All of which meant that Wake arrived in Panama in late May—the start of the sickly season in Panama, when the heavens opened up each afternoon unloading tons of water onto the land, making life miserable for everyone.

Colón was exactly the same as it had been the two dozen other times Wake had been there—dirty, noisy, crowded. The air of Colón had a rancid stench from the open sewer ditches that made first-time visitors gag and returnees wonder why they came back. The steamer got in on a Friday night, far too late to catch the train, and Wake needed a room, so in the dark he walked up Front Street from the dock, crossed the main and side tracks of the railroad, and made his way along the boarded sidewalk. Checking at the most decent place in town, the Washington House, he found they were full—of French engineers and supply contractors. The clerk said most of the rooms in Colón were taken by contractors, and suggested that perhaps he'd find a room by looking at the "more affordable inns."

He headed back out onto the street. Even at ten in the evening it was humid. Passing the 4th of July Saloon, complete with large U.S. flag outside indolently draped from a bamboo pole, he edged around a volatile crowd at the door urging on two men squared-off against each other. One man dressed in sweat-stained brown vest and coat yelled the other was "nothing more than a white trash cracker." His young opponent, shining eyes reflecting the rum he'd drunk all day, countered by accusing the first of being, "a no-account frog-lovin' Yankee dog." Above it all, a barely-clad pubescent Latina with garish face paint hung her tiny bosom over the third-floor railing, inviting "strong sailor man" Wake to climb up the stairs for some "good *amor,* no much money."

Next door was the brightly lit office of Silva & Kern, whose placard promised successful legal results with any civil or criminal problems, and also land transactions. Inside, Wake saw a lone well-dressed man with oiled-down hair sipping from a glass while relaxed with his feet atop a desk, silently watching the front door. The man's wary eyes followed him as he passed by the doorway.

Beside the lawyer's office was the Gran Hotel Roma, a three-story boarding house whose large sign board belied the peeling paint and broken chairs in the diminutive lobby. Wake trudged inside and dropped his sea bag, exhausted by the exertion of walking in the steaming dampness, though he'd been ashore for less than an hour. An emaciated young black man emerged from a back room coughed and with a bored look stared at the naval officer standing before him.

"You have a vacant room?" asked Wake.

"By the hour or the night, *señor?*" Outside, the crowded roared encouragement to the fight and a woman shrieked with laughter. Up above, the prostitute called out to another sailor with the same offer she'd made to Wake.

"The night. I'll be gone at sunrise."

The man tossed Wake a crude iron key and said, "Three oh two. Floor number three. Twenty five cents—now."

Welcome back to Panama, Wake thought wearily, as he put a quarter on the desk and plodded up the rickety stairs to a room that reeked of urine. The sleepless night was spent listening to the mob's ebb and flow thirty feet below his room.

The following day Wake was aboard the morning train, swaying and jerking across the Isthmus as he tried unsuccessfully to catch up on his rest. At Barbacoas he was shocked to see the bridge repaired and functioning, concluding the French must have pushed the effort. By that evening he was far more comfortable—

back in his original room at the Grand Hotel in Panama City. The French canal company had taken over the hotel that spring, establishing its headquarters there as well as guest lodgings. Wake was lucky to get a room.

For the next week he checked with the American consulate for telegraph messages each day and generally relaxed in the hotel as he waited for a southbound ship to Callao—there weren't many putting in at that wartime port these days. Talk about the docks said a French or Spanish merchant ship might be coming through heading for Peru. No naval vessels were allowed inside the harbor there anymore.

On a Saturday night in the smoky hotel bar he met some British naval officers ashore from HMS *Gannet*. They mentioned that a humorous Royal Marine in transit was with the ship, due to cross the Isthmus the next day on his way to a new duty with the North American station. Wake asked his name. How many Royal Marine lieutenants could there be passing through toward Fisher's squadron?

"Well, speak of the devil and he shall appear. There he is now, Commander," the officer said, gesturing toward a red-coated figure entering the barroom. "Lieutenant Peter Allen, RMLI, meet Lieutenant Commander Peter Wake, American Navy."

Allen stopped, gaping. "I damn well don't believe it. Peter Wake!"

"I'm as shocked as you. What're the odds we'd meet here?"

Allen looked around the bar quickly, then turned to the bewildered naval officers. "My God, should I go and fetch my sidearm? With Peter Wake about there's bound to be trouble, and probably a fair amount of spilled blood."

"Nice to see you too, Pete," said Wake, grinning as he stood and grasped the Marine's hand. "Never let it be said that I reneged on a promise, so your first rum's on me."

"You two know each other?" asked the puzzled officer who'd introduced the Marine. Wake summoned a waiter as Allen sat down in the American's chair.

Draining Wake's glass, Allen replied. "Yes, we do. Back in seventy-four, when this man was a mere lieutenant, he managed to embroil me in a stew of trouble in *Spain,* of all places. I was young and impressionable in those days, of course. Now I'm wiser. And if this American chap should try to tell you of certain misbehavior on my part, I expect that Anglo solidarity will repel such notions from your heads."

The naval officers laughed and everyone settled in for an evening that was starting to look like fun. Allen slapped Wake's shoulder when he sat down next to him. "So how are the lovely Linda and the children?

"Fine. Linda is as pretty as ever and the kids are growing up fast."

"And that notorious Irish bosun?"

"Rork is fine also. Almost got married."

"No! The Gaelic Don Juan of the seas?"

"Yep. Ol' Rork was bound full and by in that direction. But the fog cleared away and he saw reefs ahead and altered course."

Allen raised his glass. "Gentlemen, here's to fog getting cleared, when on a lee shore or with the gentler sex, either place is deadly to a sailor. . . ."

Everyone's glass was clinked and Allen asked Wake, "And why are you here? I thought you had some posh ticket in Washington."

"I did, but they sent me here as a naval observer on the war. I was here last year and they figured I knew the situation so I'm back. Temporary duty staff assignment with our Pacific Squadron."

"That sounds sufficiently vague enough to be intriguing, but I'll be good and let it go."

When the others started talking among themselves, Wake asked Allen, "Just come up from Callao?"

"Yes, depressing place. No runs ashore, dreary skies, and a bunch of randy sailors, not to mention *me.* I'd been afloat for eight endless months in the farthest reaches of Her Majesty's empire teaching the locals to behave and appreciate us—not an easy task, mind you, Wake. I joined Admiral Stirling's squadron temporarily on my passage east to my new duty station." He flashed a beaming smile. "But no worries now! In two days I'll be bound out of these horrific tropics, heading north to the squadron at Halifax. I'll be quite happy not to see a palm tree for a while." He glanced skyward and tented his hands in solemnity. "Thank you, God."

The Royal Navy officers interrupted and said their goodbyes, explaining that they were heading to cheaper watering-holes in the city. When they'd gone Allen leaned closer to his friend. "Heard some odd rumors about you among the officers on the ships of this squadron."

"Regarding a certain Brit diplo's death in Lima last year?"

"Yes. Most unseemly, Peter."

"And most *untrue.*"

"As I thought. Bloody rumors are raised to an art form in these latitudes. I think it has to do with the heat. And possibly the rather unrefined hooch they drink. Actually, the navy lads didn't believe that gossip—in fact, they thought it all rather silly. You colonials are well known to be that barbaric, of course, but not that Machiavellian."

"Gee, how very British of you, Peter. I guess I'll take that as a compliment," said Wake. "So what *is* going on at Callao now?"

"And how very unsubtle of *you,* Yank. You really should disguise your fishing for intelligence with a bit more finesse. Didn't I teach you better than that in Barbados?" Allen winked at a raven-haired girl in the print dress by the bar as he waved to the waiter for more rum and a cigar. Wake realized it was going to be a very long evening.

"Oh, all right, Yank. I'll give you a briefing on Peru, Chile, et al. The things I do for Anglo-American fraternity."

Allen settled back in his chair. "It's really very short and simple. The Peruvians are buggered. The Chilean army's operations have made Colonel what's-his-name's rabble down at Arica irrelevant to the whole war and the Chilean navy has cut off most outside supplies to the main Peruvian army defending their homeland. The Chileans' landings along the coast have been executed brilliantly so far. Lots of senior what's-its in my service are paying close attention. They were very surprised at the capabilities the Chileans have shown."

Allen knocked back a rum and signaled for another. "As far as the naval situation goes, the bulk of the Chilean naval heavy weights are blockading Callao. They appear pretty well drilled, accurate gunfire, et cetera, Peter. Not much is getting through. I think a neutral French packet steamer occasionally. Peruvians won't let us in anymore. They think we're *biased,* can you believe that?"

Wake didn't comment. "Anything big happened lately, or is it status quo?"

"Nothing lately, but I would expect rather decisive news from Arica any day now. What with the Chileans building up their forces, it's a matter of time. Probably not much time. Once Arica goes and the Chileans can throw all their forces at the main Peruvian lines, I'd say Lima would be wrapped up shortly thereafter. War'll be over and your little naval observer job will be finished."

"Thanks for the update," said Wake. "I guess we should make the most of the evening. Might not see each other for another few years."

Allen's attention swung around to the doorway to the bar where a demurely beautiful female entered. "Uh oh, quite the rig on that dear girl. Impressive artillery. Oh damn, she's with some chap. And bloody confounded hell, they've got a God-botherer along, too. Oh well, no joy."

Wake laughed. Peter Allen, the Royal Marine ladies' man, would never change. The woman he referred to was the new wife of the French chief engineer, Gaston Blanchet, who was escorting her. The other man Allen described in sailor slang was the head of the Catholic Church in Panama, Bishop Vargas. The three were looking for a table in the rapidly filling room. When de Lesseps was in the city six months earlier Blanchet had fallen hopelessly in love with the daughter of the Grand Hotel's owner. The bishop married them that week.

During the week Wake had been back in Panama he'd heard stories about how Blanchet had been trying to get things started on the canal. It wasn't going well.

"That, my not-so-couth English friend, is the bishop, the head French engineer, and his new wife."

Allen shrugged, took a pull from the new drink and leered peripherally at Mrs. Blanchet. Bishop Vargas noticed Wake, waved and made his way to the table. He and Wake had spoken briefly at lunch two days earlier.

"Such a big table for only two gentlemen, Commander Wake! It is a shame you do not have some beautiful companions, no? I am surprised."

"Our companions were some sailors, Bishop, and most definitely not beautiful. They just left. Would you and your party care to sit here with us? This is Lieutenant Peter Allen of the Royal Marines, sir. Lieutenant, may I present José Teleforo Paúl Vargas, Bishop of Panama."

Allen drained his fourth rum glass and leaped to his feet. "At your service, sir."

"And it is a unique experience to meet a real Royal Marine of Her Majesty Queen Victoria. You must be very busy, Lieutenant."

"Quite so, shur," slurred Allen. "But itsh's always an honor to serve my queen."

"Thank you for the invitation. We accept with pleasure." The bishop called for his friends to come over. Wake was pleased he could get a chance to talk with the canal project's head engineer—maybe he could find out the real story of what was going on—but worried about Allen, who was pantomiming a bottle of rum to the head waiter. A bottle soon appeared at the table.

Introductions were made around the table and everyone sat

down to have dinner. The conversation was light, mainly about the music and crafts of Panama. No one brought up the canal. Allen was still surreptitiously ogling the lady. Wake caught Allen's eye and tried to convey a momentary stern glare of reproach, but was met with innocently raised eyebrows. He knew that look. The last time he'd seen that was in Palma de Majorca. In a tavern.

Wake was mentally adding up his portion of the bill as they finished the main course, when Blanchet inquired, "Were you not here in seventy during the American canal survey?"

"Yes, I was."

"And what do you think of our chances, Commander?"

Wake liked Blanchet. The man was energetic but not arrogant. He also sounded sincere in his question. Perhaps Wake could find out what the real story was on the French canal. He phrased his answer carefully. "It will be very difficult, *monsieur.* I'm not sure you have taken into account the huge amounts of rain that create the hydrological forces that are so distinctive to Panama. The rainfall in Panama is measured in feet per year. On the Caribbean side it is approximately ten feet or more. On the Pacific side it is at least five and sometimes six feet. That enormous volume of water is dangerous to work with but can be used, if engineered properly. In fact, it is essential for a lock canal. You have excellent engineers, sir. They can handle that part."

"Our canal will not have locks, so we have no need for that water."

"But you will still have to fight that water, sir—every step of the way. I fear that few in your project understand that, particularly Mr. de Lesseps, since he was here in the short dry season. You are now here in the rainy season."

"Yes, the water is a large factor in our efforts. But, of course, right now we are in the beginning phases of the project."

"I understand you are cutting away the jungle for a width of four hundred feet along the path of the new canal all the way across from Colón to Panama City?"

"No. Paris decided to make it only fifty feet wide. But it is still a helpful . . . how do you say in English? . . . a helpful *swath* to let us know what we will face when we start to dig."

"And what did you learn, sir?"

Blanchet shrugged and swirled the wine in his glass. "That it is exceedingly hard to cut a fifty-foot swath through fifty miles of Panamanian jungle." He looked at the American with sad eyes and was about to say something when an English accent cut in.

"Thatsh right, ol' Blanchy. But remember this—don't you dare eat the bloody frogs around this part of the world, monshur, 'cause they'll bloody well *kill* you. They will, won't they Peter?" Allen nodded sagely. "And Peter friggin' Wake knows, 'cause the silly sod damn near died here. I heard the story."

Blanchet frowned, put his arm around Mrs. Blanchet and said, "It is late. We must go. *Bonne nuit.*"

Wake stifled a retort to Allen. He wanted Blanchet to stay. The Frenchman was ready to open up with the inside truth about how the canal was progressing. Bishop Vargas bid good night also, stopping next to Wake long enough to whisper, "What I told you on New Year's Eve is still valid. The Chileans don't like you. Be careful."

Not that again, Wake thought. He looked at Vargas. "Just how precisely do you know that information, sir?"

Vargas was stepping away, his eyes on the Brit who was holding onto a chair as he stood. The bishop smiled. "I know. That is sufficient. And now I think it is very late, and you should take care of your *compadre* here, the man with two first names." He paused again, obviously bemused. "Oh, by the way, your old friends Bishop Ferro in Italy and Father Muñosa in Sevilla both say hello. You know, for a Methodist you are developing quite the following among the Jesuits, Peter Wake. *Buenas noches, mi amigo.*"

The bishop left Wake standing there holding up his drunken friend, one of Rork's Irish witticisms going through his mind— "Never trust a man with two first names. You'll never know if they're coming or going."

Allen abruptly raised a bony finger upward and pondered aloud the question, "And why in bloody hell do those people even *want* to eat frogs?"

Wake sighed. He completely understood Rork's saying.

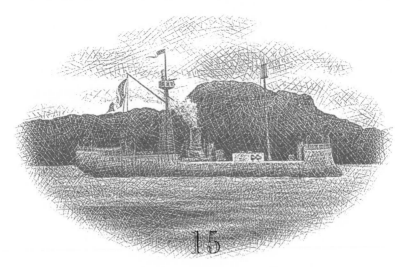

# 15

# Southbound

## June 1880

Wake sat in the shade of a café reading the latest news in the *Panama Star & Herald*'s English edition as he enjoyed a breakfast of juice, coffee, and croissant. Since the arrival of the French, the pastry situation in Panama had improved considerably, with several restaurants even changing their names to sound more Gallic.

The War of the Pacific was headline news with the situation in Peru changed, just as Allen had predicted a week earlier. On June seventh, just three days earlier, seven thousand Chilean soldiers and marines, supported by naval gunfire, had charged up the slope of Morro de Arica, a seaside hill guarding the ocean flank of Arica's defenses. The Peruvians had thought it too steep for a successful attack.

They were wrong. Led by Colonel Pedro Lagos, the Chileans endured a withering fire that killed five hundred and wounded thousands as they climbed upward toward the two thousand Peruvians under Colonel Bolognesi. In the end, Bolognesi and almost a thousand of his men were killed, the main defensive position of Arica was captured and the city occupied shortly thereafter. All Peruvian defenses south of the main line outside Lima were now gone. The article, written by a freelance journalist and full of praises for the Chilean bravery, said that the end of Peru was near.

Well, it *was* brave, Wake admitted. And successful. He drank more orange juice and decided the Chilean armed forces were the best he'd seen in Latin America. Could the Peruvians hold out by sheer willpower against overwhelming odds and technological might? The Confederates had for years. But they eventually collapsed completely. Or would the enormous cost of the war—the newspaper writer quoted experts as saying it was costing Chile millions—force the regime in Santiago to seek an end short of total Peruvian capitulation? That was a thought, Wake said to the coffee cup. Could we persuade the Chileans it was economically detrimental to spend the time and effort to crush the Peruvians? I'm getting ahead of myself, he chided inwardly as he called for more coffee and perused the section devoted to American news.

"Well, I'll be . . ." he said out loud. It turned out that Wake had misread the Republican Party's mood completely. Their national convention had met in the Exposition Hall in Chicago and gone through thirty-four separate ballots without a clear nominee. Wake was amazed, and wondered what Grant thought of *that!* He could just see the man chewing his cigar to bits, waiting while the politicos did their arm-twisting and deal making.

And in the end most of the delegates voted for a likeable Ohioan they heard give a speech the day before. Wake couldn't believe it—on the *thirty-fifth* ballot Wisconsin switched its sixteen votes, starting a momentum until the whole convention picked a fellow no one had previously thought a real contender: James Garfield. Garfield chose another long shot, Chester Arthur of New York, as his running mate. Suddenly former president Grant was out—lock, stock, and barrel, and the other front runners were beaten. Wake wondered what the deals were with

Senator Blaine and Treasury Secretary John Sherman. Apparently, President Hayes had stayed above the fray, though that was hard to believe.

The paper went on to explain that the Democrats were about to have their convention in St. Louis. Hancock, hero of the war, was certain to be their candidate since Tilden, their man in seventy-six, was like Grant—out of political action.

Wake tried to remember what Hancock's position was on the South American mess and couldn't come up with it. Then he tried to recall Garfield's. No luck. The election was in November, with five months of campaigning ahead and the only thing Wake knew was that Hancock was against tariffs and Garfield was for them. Wake pondered how the election would affect the navy, and his own career. Garfield and Hancock were former army, but Chester Arthur was from New York, and New Yorkers understood the need for a strong navy.

Putting down the newspaper, he again read the letter from Linda that had arrived the day before. In it she wished him happy birthday in advance, reminding him that he turned forty-one on June twenty-sixth. Also that Sean would turn into a teenager on July fifth. Linda wrote that her pains were less frequent and she hoped the stomach medicine was working, that Useppa was going to write for the school paper, and that Sheila O'Toole was despondent over her estrangement from Sean Rork.

Linda had received his telegram from New Orleans on the way southbound and was looking forward to others as his travels progressed. She wondered about how the canal was doing and was praying the war would end before he arrived in that region. She admonished him not to get involved in anything dangerous and to stay on the sidelines as an observer, reminding him of Spain, where he and Peter Allen had inadvertently ended up embroiled in the civil war raging at the time. The letter was from early May, and she concluded it with a description of the trees and bushes flowering everywhere, but the heat of a Washington summer was beginning to be felt and life was starting to slow down in the city.

If they think it's hot in Washington, they should try here, he opined. He wished she was there right then. She always woke up looking lovely, unlike some women he'd heard of, who were shrewish until they had "put on their faces." Not so Linda, he thought with a sigh. She would enjoy being right there in that café in the mornings, sitting and watching the diverse people go by. They'd hold hands and maybe more . . .

Wake's daydream was interrupted by the waiter. "*Señor,* a messenger from the steamship company is here for you. He said you told them you'd be here."

A little boy came forward and handed him a note from the Pacific Mail Steamship Company's local office. The note apologized that service to Peru was not reopened yet as they had hoped, but announced a Mexican-registered steamer was in port and headed south, including a port call in Callao. Wake called for the bill, tipped the boy, and headed for the hotel—it was time to move fast.

The fact that the *Estrellita* provided the sole transportation to Callao was the only thing in her favor. Otherwise she was an unseaworthy, vermin-infested deathtrap. To begin with, she was a thirty-year-old schooner with an auxiliary steam engine. Certainly not a steamer in the correct sense. The engine was an ancient, cantankerous affair with long crankshaft rods that protruded up through the deck—the whole contraption taken from a shipwreck off Nicaragua. The engine was only used to enter and leave harbors at upwards of two knots on a good day, if it ran at all. The *Estrellita's* spars and rigging were worn down; the sails a patchwork of cotton sackcloth, woven jute, and threadbare canvas.

Capitan Roberto Verde didn't admit, to himself or anyone else, that his ship was a joke. That balding, pot-bellied worthy maintained himself in grimy splendor in his cabin, receiving port agents, contractors, and customs officials with bon vivant flair, a role made easier by the copious quantities of rotgut rum he consumed each morning. He drank nothing past two in the afternoon, since he was usually passed out by then.

Wake knew the type, had seen them in every port in the world, and knew the best thing was for him to be quiet and unseen, a typical *gringo* passenger. He was wearing civilian clothes, his uniform packed in the sea bag. He dealt with the mate, known to all as *Jefe*, upon walking up the gangway, and concluded the passage contract to Callao—ten dollars and they'd be there in two weeks, if all went well.

Wake had no choice and paid the exorbitant price, then was shown to the fetid communal cabin for the six "first-class" passengers, which meant they ate at a table and had individual hammocks. It was the same life as the lowest seaman in the navy, except they were not expected to work the deck or sails. The ten "second-class" passengers slept and ate on the foredeck amidst the cargo, no matter what the weather.

It obviously was going to be a miserable voyage. Wake lashed his sea bag into the assigned hammock with several carrick-bends and hitches that would take a veteran seaman a fair amount of time to undo, then he went out on the main deck where at least there was some air moving. He stood at the heel of the bowsprit and watched the show unfold.

The mate grunted out an order and the dock lines were taken in. Another shout and a blast of smoke exploded from the skinny stack, followed by a cloud of carbon and cinders that fell unnoticed on the deck. There was a slow shudder as the shaft turned over. Wake could feel the misalignment of the shaft from his position and couldn't see how it could function at any speed. Kerr . . . thunk . . . kerr . . . thunk, then the clutch was engaged and it actually did speed up. Kerr, thunk, kerr, thunk, kerr, thunk, kerr, thunk. The schooner moved forward slowly as the crew glumly cast off furling lines, eased fore and main sheets, and hauled away on the halyards. None of them appeared enthused, most looked badly hung over.

*Jefe* ordered all sail set, an evolution taking almost half an hour, during which the fore-staysail ripped and the foresail gaff peak dropped like a guillotine when its halyard chafed through. A few minutes later the shaft stopped thumping and the wheeze of the stack ceased. *Jefe* swore. The engine was no longer steaming. *Estrellita* drifted forward, not even out of the harbor and barely making way through the water. Captain Verde shrugged and went below. The voyage was beginning badly.

The crew didn't seem surprised.

Their first port of call was the misnamed Buenaventura, on the coast of mainland Colombia. Riding the flood tide, the schooner sailed up the sound, through a puzzle of mangrove islands and bays, to a morbid shanty village that was the sole deep-water port for the region. The inhabitants were vacant-eyed sticklike figures who moved and spoke slowly. It reminded Wake of some of the pestilent scum-holes he'd seen in Africa. They'd been worse, but not by much.

After surveying the shacks ashore, Wake didn't leave the schooner when she tied up at the bamboo dock, third vessel outboard. Sharp-eyed youngsters were flitting around everywhere, trying to cajole money from passengers or work their way onto the deck to steal anything of value. Captain Verde maintained a twenty-four-hour guard with two armed crewmen who had orders to shoot first and not bother with questions later.

They did. On the second morning Wake saw them shoot a teen who had an old rigging block from the foredeck in his hand as he prepared to dive from the anchor cathead. The body drifted away on the tide. Verde sent a boat to retrieve the block.

It took two days to unload her cargo of tinned goods and farm equipment and to load Colombian coffee and animal hides.

The hides were barely cured and tanned and stank up the ship even worse. After two days at Buenaventura, Wake re-evaluated his opinion of the port—it was the very *worst* place he'd ever seen, and that included a lot of places.

As usual, the engine wasn't working despite the oaths and assaults by the chief and only machinist, so *Estrellita* sailed out on the ebb, slowly. Their next stop would be Esmeraldas in Ecuador, then Callao.

Esmeraldas was a better version of Buenaventura. Sprawled around the curving mouth of the Esmeraldas River, it had more colonial vestiges and government control. There was a semblance of civilization. Wake walked around the town and found the Ecuadorians to be friendly, the food good, and the local *aguardiente* a deadly drink. While he saw the town, copra, coffee, and some unrecognizable plant were loaded for transport south. The next day they were back at sea, sailing the land breeze on a broad reach along the coast, the growth-fouled hull making a snail's progress at four knots. It was all he could do not to scream with frustration.

Wake's anxiety grew the closer they got to Callao. His orders were verbal from Porter, which meant they were deniable, and they called for him to enter Peru and ascertain the real situation within the government, the armed forces, and civil society, then report it. Afterward, he was to stand by for the planned warship to arrive and act as a negotiating location. It all sounded simple sitting there in an ornate office in Washington, but the reality of Latin America, where nothing was simple, had set in.

Getting into Peru was going to be difficult, but the rest of the mission might well be impossible.

~~

"You want go on land, yes?" asked *Estrellita's* skipper, looking remarkably sober for eleven in the morning. The schooner was heeled over on a broad reach a few miles off the coast. It was a sunny day and the dark green mountains were stark against the powder-blue sky. A faded Mexican flag streamed from her main mast to proclaim her neutrality as she neared the danger zone. There had been no sign of Chilean warships yet.

"Yes. I have business there," replied Wake slowly. He'd already reminded Verde several times during the voyage about disembarking at Callao. Now they were off the coast of Peru twenty miles north of the port and the man was balking. Wake went into Spanish and tried to sound insistent. "*Yo tengo que ir a la terra.*"

Verde regretfully shook his head. "*Problemas a la puerta. La armada de Chile, señor.* Navy *de* Chile no want us there."

Wake recognized that it was time to be innovative. With pantomime, he communicated his idea. "In the dark, *en la noche,* before the sun rises, *antes del sol, Capitan* Verde, you take this ship close to shore at Chanca, *norte de* Callao. We row in dinghy to beach, *barca pequeña a la playa.* Dinghy comes back to *Estrellita.* You sail away before sun rises. Chile warship no see you—*invisible en la noche.*"

"*Muy peligroso, señor.* Danger. I no like."

Wake rotated his head and stretched his tensed neck muscles. This was typical. The drunkard of a captain had no problem in Panama taking Wake's money to get to Callao. Now he had a memory loss regarding the deal and didn't want the danger.

"Capitan Verde, there is a ten-dollar gold piece in it for you." He pulled out the coin and flipped it up in the air, the sun glinting off it as it landed back in his palm. Verde's eyes followed it through the air. "Your man gets it when I reach the beach at Chanca. Then he takes it back to you. No beach, no gold. *No playa—no oro.*"

Several of the crew saw it also and were watching Wake with new interest, their faces giving away their thoughts—the disheveled *pasajero gringo* was not what he seemed, and he had serious money. Wake saw it was obviously time to deter any ill-thoughts, so he nonchalantly pulled back his coat six inches to reveal the new army Colt .45 in his belt, a special gift from Henry

Nettleton, the ordinance inspector at the Springfield Armory. That got their attention immediately. A buzz started among crew and passengers. The *gringo* had money and a big gun.

Verde gazed at Wake, his hooded eyes revealing no fear to the sight of the pistol. "I . . . *capitan*. Only I have *pistolo* on ship. I take *pistolo*."

Wake figured Verde had a gun aboard, probably for protection from his own crew. He imagined the captain wanted the Colt because it was better than his firearm. Plus, it would be worth a fair amount in these parts.

"*No, capitan, con respecto total*. But after I get to beach, yes. *Pero, cuando estoy en la playa, sí*."

The talk stopped. Everyone on deck watched what would happen. The *gringo* had said no to the captain. Verde was a drunk, but he was a mean drunk and had killed before. Verde studied Wake, then allowed a lopsided leer. The words came out in a hiss. "Yes, you give me *mas tarde*. On beach." He wagged a fat finger. "No shoot on ship. Only I shoot on ship."

"*Sí, señor. Claro. Claro.* Wouldn't think of it, Captain," said Wake, who knew he couldn't dare risk sleep now. He also knew that he wasn't going to give that gun to anyone on the beach.

They'd been lucky so far—no Chilean warship had seen them along the coast. But that just made everyone even more agitated. Luck like that was sure to end soon.

The night was bright with moonlight. Verde was beyond nervous, he seethed as he prowled the deck, glancing at the moon and kicking a sailor here and there for perceived infractions. *Estrellita* was no more than a quarter mile off the beach, hove to in the night land breeze, with fully half the crew on lookout. The captain spoke to Wake as he climbed down the side to the dinghy bobbing in the waves.

"*Pistolo y oro a la playa.*"

Wake looked up, trying to appear sincere. "*Por supuesto, Capitan. Pistolo y oro a la playa.*"

The moonlight scared Wake too. He'd forgotten it when he'd made the bargain. *Estrellita* was lit up as effectively as by one of those new spotlights Wake had seen on a British warship. No one could miss her.

It wasn't only the Chileans who might take exception to his entering Peru this way. A Peruvian beach patrol might think he was a Chilean spy. Either way he was dead, or worse—a prisoner. He'd heard tales of what that was like in this war, had experienced a sample of it himself back in Africa. Wake had the sickening vision of getting shot by a sixteen-year-old conscript, with Admiral Porter reading the Peruvian account six months later, after complaining to Thompson that Wake was late with his situation reports yet again. It would be an inglorious way to end his career, to put it mildly.

The man silently rowing him to the beach was half-Indian, a badly stitched scar crossing his cheek from nose to ear. His yellowish eyes were eerie as he stared at Wake while pulling at the oars. For the three weeks of the voyage Wake had never heard him talk or seen him smile.

They reached the diminutive surf line and without looking ahead the man aligned the dinghy to the waves and rode them shoreward, spinning the boat just before hitting the sand so that the stern touched the beach. It was a neat bit of seamanship and Wake nodded his appreciation. The man warily nodded back, then held out one palm while keeping position with the other oar.

Wake put the gold piece in the hand and drew out the revolver as he stepped over the gunwale into the ankle-deep water. Throwing his sea bag higher up on the beach, he backed up to the dry sand, keeping an eye on the man in the boat who had pocketed the gold and was watching him. Glancing quickly around, Wake saw no one nearby, then picked up the sea bag. He explained to the man that he was very sorry, but the pistol was needed in such a dangerous place.

The man grunted something masked by the sound of the waves, but Wake didn't stick around to continue the conversation. He said, "*Adios, amigo,*" and was off running into the forest. Ten feet in he briefly turned as he ran, expecting to see an irate piratical type chasing him, but instead catching a glimpse of the boat heading out through the surf line, the schooner silhouetted beyond. Then the jungle closed in around him. Running due east for another five minutes, he stopped and took a break, squatting on the matted floor of the forest, already soaked with sweat from his exertion. Wake struck a match and checked his pocket compass, calculated he'd made maybe a hundred yards through the thick tangle and estimated the coast road must be another two or three hundred yards inland—most coastal roads were.

As he willed himself to calm down and control his breathing, Wake surveyed his surroundings, listening for anyone who might be looking for him. All he heard was the drone of insects. Any sounds of the sea were gone. Something crawled near his ear and he slapped it. The sickly sweet aroma of rotting death replaced the clean salt air of the beach. The smell of the jungle—a smell he knew only too well and a world completely separate from the sea.

He got up and pushed his way through the creepers and sawtooth fronds to the east, concentrating on the area just in front of him, dimly discernible in the diffused light. Once he got to the road he would head south past Chanca toward Callao and Lima, but for now he had to focus on getting through the jungle without injury.

Wake knew that from this point on, he would be in mortal danger all the time. Then, with a start, he also realized that it was Saturday, June twenty-sixth—his forty-first birthday.

# 16

# Desperation

## July 1880

A week later, Wake still couldn't believe it. He'd come out of the jungle intact and managed to find a ride with a pig farmer driving his cart into the market at Chanca, a small town north of Callao. Once there, now smelling strongly of pig, he'd had the good fortune to get a seat on the train to Callao, where he'd gone to the Navy Yard and met with Lieutenant Roberto Perez, an English-speaking naval officer that had been detailed to him briefly as a guide the previous year. As Perez dryly noted when Wake expressed gratitude for finding an old friend, there weren't a lot of ships for Peruvian naval officers to serve aboard anymore, so what else could he do but stay at the base?

Wake sent a note to the American legation in Lima that he had arrived and was staying temporarily at the Peruvian naval station, to please notify Washington. The next day a reply note reached Wake asking how he had managed to enter Peru. American ships, indeed no ships, were allowed to pass the Chilean blockade. Wake declined to say in writing. He would tell them later when he went the six miles to Lima.

On the third day in Callao Perez said something that intrigued Wake. The submarine Wake had glimpsed eight months earlier was now operational and no longer a real secret. Everyone in Callao knew of it, and the Chileans were so worried that they periodically withdrew their blockading fleet in front of the harbor three miles offshore each night. Perez asked his friend if he'd like to see it.

"Does this thing *really* work, Roberto? Or is it only an engineer's dream?"

Wake was standing in the hot sun in front of the boiler tube submarine hanging suspended from a derrick, ready for launching. Looking like a large iron cigar with rivets and metal straps to hold it together, it had six-foot-high ventilation stacks rising from just aft of the bow and forward of the stern, where a broad-pitched two-bladed propeller was affixed just over a large rudder. A shorter tower with hatch was amidship. Perez called it the conning tower, where the helmsman stood. The body of the thing was only five and a half feet in diameter at the widest point, tapering down to points at both ends. It appeared claustrophobic inside.

"Yes, *Toro* does work," replied Perez, a touch of resentment showing. "An engineer with the railroad up at Piura designed it and tested it."

"Well, I did hear something about a test run awhile ago. But still, Roberto, does it *consistently* work under water? Can it be used against the Chileans?"

Perez hesitated. The *norteamericano* was asking difficult questions. "Yes, on both questions. But I think, Commander, that you should meet with Captain Miguel Gonzalez, my superior. I will seek an audience for you. He is well versed in this craft and can answer you better than I. But it might take awhile to get permission."

Wake's interest was piqued. No navy in the world had an operational submarine that could dive as deep as *Toro* was reputed to go, or for as long a time under water. He needed all the information he could get.

"Thank you. I'd like that, Lieutenant."

The next week Wake attended a dinner at naval headquarters. The conversation centered on the latest news from the front in southern Peru. The Chileans had consolidated their forces after the victory at Arica and were marching north up the coast road, assisted by naval gunfire. Arica was six hundred miles away but the main Chilean armies were now only two hundred miles away with the defenses of Lima being built at a feverish pace. Stories of Chilean atrocities were rampant and civilians were fleeing before the advancing enemy, adding to the confusion.

Captain Gonzalez was the senior officer attending. He rose after the dinner, the traditional signal for the junior men to depart, then asked Lieutenant Perez and Wake to join him in his office. Once there he brought up the subject that had dominated Wake's mind all evening. Gonzalez had no English, so Perez translated.

"I understand you are interested in *Toro?*"

"Yes, sir. I am." Wake wanted to be careful. His goal was to see the inside the submarine. But he didn't want to set off alarms by being too pushy, so he put his curiosity in general terms. "I find it fascinating to think of the concept of underwater travel. I think the navy of Peru may have made history here."

Gonzalez nodded pensively. "I think you are right, Commander Wake. We have. Do you wish to see the submarine closely?"

Wake waited a moment, then said, "Why yes, sir. That would be educational for me."

"Then it will be done, Commander. You will realize your wish. Lieutenant Perez will bring you to the *Toro* tomorrow at five o'clock in the afternoon. You will see our little bull that so many have ridiculed."

Gonzalez's tone was odd, setting Wake on edge. "Thank you very much, sir. When I go back to Washington I can tell them how advanced your navy has become. They will be impressed."

Gonzalez muttered his answer, "Time will tell. Good night, Commander."

"The hatchway is tight, be careful when you enter, sir."

Wake's frame squeezed down into the interior of the *Toro*—barely. "Thank you, Roberto. I'm making it."

*Toro* was tied up alongside a tug at the navy wharf in Callao harbor. A small assembly of civilians and naval officers was on the deck of the tug, examining the submarine. One was the minister of war, listening to a short middle-aged man with German-accented Spanish explain how the craft functioned. Wake had been introduced to the speaker moments before. He was Frederico Blume Othon, the bespectacled railroad civil engineer who had designed *Toro* years earlier and finished building the submarine the previous fall. His son was part of the crew.

Inside, three dim lanterns showed condensation glistening on the overhead. Half a dozen curious faces peered out from the gloom in the after section, startling Wake as his eyes adjusted. He didn't think anyone was in the craft, much less this many, and wondered why they were there. Dockyard workmen installing some apparatus?

He concentrated on memorizing the interior, starting with the three gauges labeled in English—pressure, depth, and ballast tank water level. Down in the bilge he saw a hose and pump and at either end of the tube two small fans, evidently to circulate air. Neither fan was turning. Where he stood beneath the hatch was a crude steering staff at the helmsman station. Taut lines led from the staff through turning blocks on either side of the hull and aft to a rudder quadrant in the stern. Along both sides of the craft a bench sat lengthwise, from midship aft to the stern. Down the centerline was a large crankshaft with handles spaced at intervals. The propulsion source, realized Wake. Just like the *Hunley.*

Someone else was descending the ladder, so Wake sat on the bench on the port side, observing that the men were just sitting on the benches, not installing or adjusting anything. They were waiting for something or someone. It was damp and musty, smelling of foul bilge water and rusting iron. Wake felt his chest tighten and his heart begin to pound as it got more crowded. Was it getting warmer? He'd seen the inside, now it was time to leave the coffinlike iron tube. He rose from the bench, but a hand reached for him.

"*Bienvenidos a Toro, señor,*" said a young voice from the dark. "*Usted . . .* work . . . *con nosotros . . .* make *Toro* go?" The submarine suddenly swayed as more people stepped aboard.

"What?" said Wake as another pair of shoes came down the ladder. It was Othon, with the minister, followed by Gonzalez. Wake was pushed aft by the new bodies filling the cramped space in front of him. He ended up back on the bench as an involved discussion in Spanish began that he didn't understand. Perez wasn't inside to translate. He looked longingly at the hatchway, then braced himself against the curved side of the submarine when someone bumped into him. His hand recoiled from the iron—it was wet.

Gonzalez sat down, his back to Wake, forcing him even farther aft. The farther back he was pushed the narrower the tube got until he was hunched over like the others. Now it was definitely warm inside, the body heat filling the submarine. The smell of sweating men soon overwhelmed the bilge odor. Wake felt his throat constrict. All right, now we know what it's like inside. Time to go.

"Uh . . . So, we're seeing how many men she can hold—at the dock?" Wake croaked to Othon, the only man inside who spoke English well. The inventor ignored him as he explained something to the minister.

Wake tugged on Gonzalez's sleeve, wanting to ask to leave but forgot the words in Spanish at that moment. "Oh God, how the hell do you say, 'I am leaving?'" he muttered aloud, but no one understood. He ended up asking, "*¿Que pasa?*"

Gonzalez turned to him, rancid garlic odor spewing from his mouth just inches away. "*No problemas, Señor Wake. Será un viaje muy interesante.*"

Wake understood that—the man told him it would be a very interesting trip. "What! Good God above, man, I don't want to go on a *trip* on this damned thing. I thought we were going to stay at the dock!"

"*De nada, señor.*"

"What the hell do you mean, 'you're welcome?' Get me out of here! *¡Yo quiero que ir—ahora!*"

He considered making a rush for the hatchway. To hell with his dignity and the image of the United States Navy. There was just enough room, if he could get past Gonzalez quickly, then elbow the minister of war to the side. . . .

All of a sudden Othon announced something definitive in Spanish, the words hard to understand with the sound of the men's breathing. The men behind Wake started to turn the crank. Someone closed the hatch, the clang sounding like doom itself. Then Wake caught the words, "*¡Vamonos!*" and realized it was too late to escape.

A hand slapped Wake on the shoulder, someone said, "*Ayuda, por favor, señor,*" and everyone, including the war minister, was pulling the crankshaft around. Othon stood at the helm and steered, peering out glass ports set into the conning tower. Wake felt a faint waft of air and saw the fans turning, obviously connected to the crankshaft in some fashion.

Gonzalez grinned and joked, *"¡Buen viaje!"*—which only aggravated Wake's anger. Reluctantly, he joined the others and grabbed a handle, taking out his rage on the shaft while uttering every foul oath learned in twenty-six years at sea.

Othon told them to slow down a few minutes later. The shaft slowed to about twenty revolutions a minute, the momentum of the centrifugal force easing the strain on the men. Still, everyone was dripping with sweat and gasping for breath, the ventilation tubes overhead not providing any noticeable new draft and the fans just circulating the existing pungent air. Wake wondered how long it took a man to suffocate in a submarine as he pushed and pulled the crankshaft.

Othon described their progress across the harbor, giving course and speed. They were now near the outer side of the anchorage, approaching San Lorenzo Island where the Chilean fleet loitered and occasionally exchanged gunfire with the Peruvian batteries ashore. He ordered the man in the stern to pull a lever as he did the same forward.

Wake felt the deck cant downward. The pump below him gushed water through the canvas hose line. They were sinking by the bow, but no one looked concerned. Everyone continued cranking. The submarine kept on sinking and the light inside got dimmer as Wake looked up and saw with horror that outside, the water was covering the conning tower ports. The seams in the hull started to drip. Big drops. It was as if he were watching himself drown. Intentionally. Like suicide. He struggled not to scream.

Othon steadily called out the depth as they sank faster. Two meters. Five meters. The seam leaks became thin streams of water. Ten meters. Fifteen meters. Twenty meters. More seams leaking, the streams now gushing continually. Above the gasps Wake heard one man softly mutter an oath in the back. Another called on God. Twenty-five meters. Othon's monotone voice gave their progress. Turning to starboard, course due north. Othon called for the stern man to push the lever, the deck leveled.

Thud. The sound came from outside the hull, echoing through the water. Othon shook his head, then laughed.

Thud again, a shock wave rolled against them under water. Another thud, this one on the other side of the craft. Two more thuds, distant, muffled.

Othon made a comment to the war minister who chuckled, then laughed out loud. The others in the submarine joined him. The Chileans were firing at the spot where they had last seen *Toro* near the surface. They clearly had no idea where she was now. It was surreal for Wake. There was mortal danger just seventy-five feet away—*above* them. But here he was safe from the Chilean cannons.

Othon got them back to work cranking the shaft and swimming the metal coffin across the harbor underwater on a course based upon an estimate of their position and the tidal current. Half an hour later *Toro* was on the surface and the hatch opened. Wake never knew air could smell so sweet. He, and every other man aboard, drank it in.

On the dock Perez asked Wake what he thought of his experience. His limbs were throbbing with pain and he still was out of breath. Othon and the others were close enough to hear his answer, which Perez translated into Spanish.

"Well, no one told me we were actually going out on the damned thing, Perez. And that I'd be going *under* the friggin' water!" Wake remembered his mind-numbing panic, knowing the others saw it. He was embarrassed. "And I admit that I was feeling pretty desperate there for a while."

Gonzalez walked over to Wake and shook his hand, then spoke quietly, intently. Wake couldn't understand it all, so Perez put it in English.

"Desperation? We in Peru know that emotion very well these days. Remember this though: desperation can win battles."

# 17

# The Striped-Pants Crowd

The street outside the U.S. legation offices in Lima was echoing with the stamp of boots and shouted orders as an infantry regiment marched by. It was one of the elite regular army regiments and once again they were heading south, toward the front. Relaxing in an upholstered chair, Wake studied them through the window as a clerk handed him an envelope. The soldiers were tired and grim, but not crestfallen. They still had fight left in them. He'd seen far worse during the Civil War.

He opened the envelope. The telegram from the navy department was terse: Send report by telegram now. Wake thanked the clerk and sighed. Porter was impatient and didn't want to wait for a secure report by courier, but demanded he use the open telegraph lines. Wake wondered if Admiral David Dixon Porter, the press's American Hero and World-Renowned Sailor Extraordinaire, ever had harassment like this on a foreign assignment? He did the math. No, Porter didn't, because underwater ocean telegraph lines didn't exist when he was Wake's rank. Everything was by mail aboard a ship.

Now, with the advent of ocean-transiting telegraph cables, a telegram sent from Lima could be read in Washington a few minutes later. And Washington expected a constant stream of up-to-the-minute information daily. They got it from the State Department officials. They expected it from Wake.

Wake had heard stories of the army field commanders during the Civil War constantly being badgered by Washington for the latest intelligence on what was happening, even when no one at the front really knew. Traditionally, the navy wasn't as bothered because telegraph communiqués weren't available at the far-flung places where naval officers were sent. Ah, but now they were, Wake lamented. Cables spanned the bottoms of the oceans linking continents so that superiors could plague subordinates with questions.

Taking a message pad, he wrote a brief update, using the abbreviated style common to naval telegrams—every letter increased the cost—couching the description of *Toro* in vague words to evade the inevitable eavesdroppers on the cable along the way in Peru, Panama, Jamaica, Cuba, and Florida.

TO ADM D.PORTER, NVY DPT, WASH DC
FROM LTCMDR P.WAKE, LIMA, PERU

CANAL WRK MUCH SLWR THAN EXPCTDxxxLABR DISEAS WATR PROBLMSxxxBLANCHET SMRT BUT PLANS BADxxxSIT CHANGED IN PERUxxxCHILE ARMY HDG UP CST TO LIMAxxxETA THIS AREA 30 DYSxxxLIMA MOBILIZED STRONG LAND DEFNS 4 EXPCTD ATTKxxxAUTHORITIES AND PEOPLE DETERMINEDxxxNO SIGN OF SURRNDRxxxGERMN MADE CALLAO BATTERIES EFFCTVE REPELLING ENMY IRONCLADS SO FARxxxENMY BLCKAD EFFCTVE AT CALLAO PRT CLSD TO ALL SHIPPINGxxxOTH PLACES ON CST STILL OPNxxxBOVINE LOOKS VERY STRONG BUT NO PLOWING YETxxxWISH WE HAD ONExxxANGLO-FRANCO WRSHPS WATNG OFF

CALLAOxxxFRNCH CORTNG PERU BRITS PRO
CHILExxxLOCALS WONDER ABT USN?xxxMANY HOPE
FOR USA INTRVENTNxxxMTG LDRS TONITExxxMORE
DETLS IN LATER COMMxxxP WAKE

Once the communiqué was registered in the legation clerk's
office and then taken by messenger to the Pacific Mail and
Telegraph office for transmission, Wake went back to the window
seat and thought about how he would handle the diplomatic function that evening. It would be a venue where he hoped to obtain
more intelligence about what was happening currently on the
front lines and in the government. He also intended to fulfill one
of the primary goals of his mission—deliver a confidential verbal
message from President Hayes to the president of Peru, Nicolás
Piérola, which Wake had memorized. The back-channel route was
for a simple reason—it had to be kept quiet and deniable.

The obnoxious chargé d'affaires that had been at the U.S.
legation the previous year when Wake was trying to leave Peru
was gone, having transferred to Paraguay. The position hadn't
been filled—few people were volunteering to be posted in Lima
at this point—and the position's duties were being handled by the
chief clerk, a serious pinched-faced young man named Austin
Kronburg. Wake had dealt with him on his last visit and briefly
this time. He thought the man officious and incompetent, a
younger version of his departed boss.

It was obvious that Kronburg was trying to impress someone,
anyone, so that he too could get another posting, preferably in
Europe. Peru in wartime just didn't have the prestige and social
opportunities to further an ambitious career. Nobody wanted to
be with the losers.

An hour earlier, Kronburg had cast a disapproving eye over
Wake, then informed him he should be at the Foreign Ministry
of Peru that night promptly at seven o'clock, in a *neatly* made-up
full-dress uniform. Kronburg went on to say that the occasion
was the annual ball in celebration of Peruvian Independence Day,

and that as an American naval officer he should therefore be prepared to compliment his hosts accordingly. Wake, in return, repressed the urge to twist the skinny bureaucrat's neck and replied that he would be delighted to attend—nonchalantly adding that it would remind him of his duty in Washington and many evenings with President Hayes at the White House. Kronburg harrumphed, spun on his heel and went back to his tiny office. Wake wandered off toward his hotel.

The legation itself had no rooms for visiting naval officers, but they did have a relationship with a hotel close by, the Posada del Liberator. Wake had been there for three days now and, knowing that he'd need it, already had his dress uniform cleaned and pressed. He was as ready as he could be, except for one rather important factor. The leadership of Peru had changed completely since last fall and he didn't know the new man in charge. He also didn't really know the American in charge of the legation—that had changed too. Walking down Avenida Cuzco he reviewed the complicated political situation.

The new American minister to Peru was Isaac Christiancy, who'd replaced Richard Gibbs late in 1879. Christiancy was a sixty-eight-year-old Republican from Michigan with a receding hairline and a white Lincolnesque beard. He had never been to South America before being appointed to the post in Lima by President Hayes. That much was apparent to most people in Peru. But Wake had found out some interesting things from the office staff in the legation. Things most people in Peru did not know.

First of all, Christiancy was brilliant. At age thirteen he had taught school in his hometown of Johnstown, New York, in order to support his family. When he was twenty-four he moved to rural Michigan, set up a law practice and later became an elected official. A vehement abolitionist, he helped to found the Republican Party in the state and worked for Lincoln's election several years later. At age forty-six he was elected to the Michigan Supreme Court and served in that capacity during the war. After the war he went to Washington as a U.S. senator from Michigan, and that, Wake's informant said, was where Christiancy's life turned sour.

A lonely widower far from home, Christiancy attracted the attention of a predatory young woman, who accepted compliments from him as a promise of marriage, then threatened to sue him for breach of promise when he protested the point. A public humiliation was more than the proud man could endure, so he acquiesced and married her, spending the next several years in a miserable marriage that became the talk of Washington. Wake vaguely remembered hearing some of that, but thought it just rumor at the time. The place was perversely full of them.

Finally, in an act of despair, Christiancy resigned his senatorial position and petitioned his old friend Rutherford Hayes for an appointment overseas. And so, sadly, Christiancy ended up fleeing to a war zone to represent the United States in a swirling political mess that tested his wits and stamina—but at least he was *sans* wife.

Wake liked the man and appreciated his sense of honor, though it had served him false indeed. But honor was a concept central to perceptions and negotiations in Latin America, and Christiancy understood that. Perhaps he could make a difference in the rapidly unfolding events by using that innate sense. Wake crossed the street and continued east as he thought of the other part of the equation for the evening—Peru's new supreme leader. He had seen him just once, for five minutes at the Callao naval station. But that, and Perez's description of the man's history, formed a working assumption for Wake.

Forty-one-year-old Nicolás de Piérola was short, thin and nervous, with intense eyes that alternated between sad and angry. He had been a lawyer turned national finance minister at twenty-nine. However, within a year of his taking office in the late eighteen-sixties, Piérola was caught up in a controversial government contract with the French Dreyfus company. Dreyfus ended up with a monopoly on mining Peruvian guano. During the ensuing finger-pointing in Lima, Piérola was accused of embezzling government funds and forced into exile in Bolivia. Undaunted, in the mid-seventies he tried to overthrow the Peruvian government by revolution several times but failed.

At the beginning of the War of the Pacific, Piérola was allowed to return to Peru and fight for his country, which he did in non-combatant roles around the capital until the elected president, Mariano Prado, decided in late December 1879 to leave Peru for Europe, ostensibly to seek money with which to fight the Chilean invaders. He left Vice President La Puerta in charge, but the public outcry over Prado's obvious desertion left an opening that Piérola quickly filled. On December 23, Piérola declared himself commander-in-chief while Prado wisely stayed out of the way in Europe. All of that had happened after Wake's last brief visit in Lima, and it hadn't gone well for the Peruvians since then.

What a cast of characters, Wake decided as he entered his hotel room and lay on the bed to rest. *Can I work around the egos and accomplish my mission?* The bells of nearby Iglesia de San Pedro rang out five times. *Two hours to go.*

The Peruvian government had pulled out all the stops to impress the foreign legations with the legitimacy and solidity of the current administration, decided Wake as he surveyed the main ballroom of the Foreign Ministry Building at the magnificent Plaza de Armas, in the center of the ancient city of Lima. It was across from the cathedral and next to the presidential palace, the whole area swarming with troops to keep out any saboteurs or riffraff. Inside the columned edifice, built in the previous century to demonstrate the longevity of the Spanish Empire, staff in red and blue livery glided to and fro with trays of hors d'oeuvres and champagne, smiling but never talking, their eyes seeing everything but betraying nothing. Perfumed ladies in expensive gowns mingled with gallant gentlemen in handsome uniforms.

In the far corner, a ten-man string ensemble soothed the air with French and Italian pieces, while along one entire gold-damask-draped wall a table tempted the guests with delicate pastries and beautifully carved confectionary works depicting the flag of Peru; the national cathedral of Peru; the liberator of Peru, Don José San Martin; and the liberator of South America, Simon Bolívar. The red and white flag of Peru was displayed everywhere, and the room was filled with older officers of the army and navy. The young ones were off fighting.

It was as gay a scene as Wake had ever witnessed. He shook his head in wonder of it all—you'd never know the place was the capital of a country being overrun by the enemy. An enemy that at that moment was heading for that very city and building.

"Commander Wake, good to see you again," offered Minister Christiancy with a bland smile.

Wake had met him for less than thirty seconds in the hallway four days earlier. "Thank you, sir. It's nice to be invited."

"I presume my staff has been of assistance to your naval observation work? How's that going?"

Wake had no intention of lying to Christiancy. He also had no intention of telling him everything. "Oh, the usual, sir. Meetings, evaluations, interviews."

"I'm still amazed at how you arrived here. Mexican schooner that rowed you ashore through the blockade? Incredible danger. The bizarre stuff of novels, Commander."

Not nearly as bizarre as your personal life, Wake thought. "Just the way things are done down here, sir. Not that unusual."

"Well, this is a big celebration for the Peruvians, son. They've worked hard to impress everyone, so I hope you have a good time tonight."

"I'm sure I will, sir."

Christiancy spotted someone across the room, then discreetly pointed him out to Wake. "Well, well, the French navy has come ashore. That's their admiral. I wonder how he talked the

Peruvians into letting them do that. I'll have to ask. Come along and I'll introduce you—sailor to sailor."

Abel Nicolas Bergasse Dupetit-Thouars was a tall and balding forty-eight-year-old with enormous mutton chop sideburns, the whole effect presenting a comical image—until one looked at those deadpan eyes and expressionless mouth. The celebrated French admiral, who had just returned from quelling a revolt in Polynesia, reminded Wake of an undertaker.

Christiancy attempted to be suave. "*Bon soir, Amiral.* May I present Lieutenant Commander Peter Wake, of our navy? He's here on a naval observation mission. Commander, I have the honor to introduce you to Rear Admiral Abel Nicolas Bergasse Dupetit-Thouars, Knight of the Legion of Honor, commanding officer of the French Naval Observation Mission."

Both naval officers bowed slightly, the admiral saying nothing and Wake, as expected from a junior, presenting a compliment. "*C'est un honneur, Amiral. Enchanté. Bonne chance avec le travail en Peru.*"

Christiancy's jaw gaped while the admiral scrutinized Wake's medals, especially the one with the white star. "*Merci, Commandant. Et bonne chance à vous, aussi.*"

"Why, I had no idea you spoke French, Commander," stammered Christiancy.

"I'm very sorry to admit that don't speak it very well, sir. It is a beautiful language and I hope to do it justice some day."

Dupetit-Thouars nodded appreciatively. "You speak it quite well enough, Commander. In fact, I know that you did more than speaking well to receive that particular decoration." He turned to Christiancy. "Do you know that award, sir?"

The French admiral explained the significance of the *Légion d'honneur* started in 1802 by Napoleon, that very few foreigners had the award, and that he and Wake were both *chevaliers,* or knights of the Legion of Honor. He said that Wake's award had become well known in the French navy and briefly related the story to a wide-eyed Christiancy, who then turned to his countryman.

"Commander, I must say you continually surprise me."

The admiral leaned forward, "Should you require the assistance of the navy of France in this troubled place, Commander, it will be an honor to render it."

"*Merci beaucoup, Amiral.*"

Christiancy asked how the Frenchman convinced the Peruvians to let him ashore—they'd been shooting at anything approaching the harbor.

Dupetit-Thouars shrugged. "They needed some decent cognac for the evening." Then he clicked his heels and announced he had to meet other guests and was off.

"Damned odd fellow, that one. Know anything about him?" said Christiancy.

"Only that he has a reputation in the profession for being smart and ruthless, sir. And I wouldn't be surprised by anything he may do."

"He seems to like *you.*"

"Well, I suppose it's the medal, sir."

Wake excused himself and moved toward the refreshment table. The tension of mingling with the elite, and of carrying off his mission that evening, made him nervous. He needed a stiff drink, something cooling, with strength. As Wake picked up a glass of chilled fruit juice with rum, he heard a deep voice rumble behind him.

"Now I know this hellhole's getting desperate. They're letting in do-gooder *gringo* sailor squids who manage to attract trouble like flies to a turd."

Wake almost dropped the glass. He turned around and faced someone he hadn't seen in years. The middle-aged man standing before him was a shade taller than Wake, tanned and clearly muscular, with close-cropped gray hair and eyes that could go from mirth to mania instantly. He was wearing a plain black suit with no adornments and appeared to be just another government functionary. A minor one at that.

It was Michael Woodgerd, former U.S. Army colonel discharged under a very dark cloud near the end of the Civil War, and since then a mercenary. They had first met at a train station in Genoa, Italy, six years earlier, where Wake saw Woodgerd kill a street thug who had kicked a dog. They last met in North Africa four months later, when Woodgerd had served as the commander of the Royal Guard for the Sultan of Morocco. He'd been there when Wake had earned those medals. Both had nearly died. They'd started out as wary allies back then and ended up as grudging friends. Each owed his life to the other. Neither thought he'd ever see the other again.

Wake shook his head in disbelief. "Well, if it isn't the man who believes in nothing and will fight for anything. How are you, Mike? You here as a tourist or are you working?"

"Working, of course. I don't go to war zones unless I get paid for it."

"So which side are you on in this one?"

Woodgerd grinned. "The one who paid the best, of course—the Peruvians. Piérola doesn't know crap about real war, just palace coups. He needed somebody to advise him on what to do. And that, my old friend, would be me."

"Well, I don't think this one will look good on the résumé, Mike. Doesn't seem to be going too well lately for the Peruvians."

Woodgerd frowned. "Hey, don't blame me, squid. I just got here two months ago."

"So where are you stationed?"

"Officially? Consultant on the general staff. Unofficially, I wander around all over, give advice, report back to the president what's really going on. But enough of me, what are *you* doing here?"

"Neutral naval observer."

Woodgerd cocked an eyebrow. "Now Peter, that's not what I hear. Little birdies have informed me that you haven't been very neutral and have been doing far more than merely observing. Word has it that you're on *our* side. That you actually like Peru. You always were a believer." He gestured around the room. "I suppose you believe in this cause?"

Wake held up both hands. "No, I'm down the middle on this one, Mike. Seriously down the middle. Straight arrow neutral. The Unites States just hopes the bloodshed will stop."

"Never play poker, squid. Don't have the face for it. You're about as neutral as that frog admiral over there. Let me tell you, my sailor friend, he's here because of the loans the Peruvians have with the Paris banks. If the Chilis," Woodgerd used the slang term for Chileans, "conquer the place, the loans get defaulted and a bunch of upper class French people lose a lot of money. Paris is nervous, so their navy gets diverted here. He was on his way home from killing naked savages over in the South Sea islands when he got word to sit off the harbor here for a while. And he ain't thrilled about it from what we hear. Neither are the Brits. Hell, the Limeys aren't even allowed ashore here. That was one of my suggestions the Peruvies followed, by the way. Rather proud of that one."

"Yes, well so much for the French and the British. What's your outlook for the Peruvians' future?"

"Now why in the world should I tell you, Peter? I only give advice for money."

"Because you shouldn't play poker either, buddy. I can see in your eyes that you don't like this job at all. You're losing and you don't like to lose. You need to talk to somebody, get it off your chest, and I'm probably the only man on this continent you can trust. Or that trusts you."

"Does it stay with *you?*"

Wake passed him a rum and fruit juice. "Probably not. It just might go way up the chain. But your name won't be attached."

"Ah, what the hell. You're right. I hate losing." He looked around. "My outlook for the Peruvies? I think they've probably got another six months. Maybe less. They're ignoring my suggestions, of course, and even if they followed my advice, I'm not sure there's enough time to rearm and train the foot soldiers. Many of the officers are pretty good actually, but the soldiers need a lot of work. They've got guts, lots of guts. But they need more than that.

"Problem is that most of them are Indians from the middle of nowhere and have never even fired a rifle, for God's sake. Don't know basic sanitation. Can't even speak or understand Spanish. You've got to first teach 'em how to *live* in a modern society— then how to fight with a modern army. Hell, Peter, it took the Army of the Potomac a year to come together and another year to start winning. And those boys were from an up-to-date sophisticated culture. Down here we're dealing with conscripted aboriginal people from the mountains. Ridiculous, really."

"Six months? That's all?"

"At the most. And it's gonna get real messy when the Chilis do come in here. Revenge is too nice a word for it. They've got spies everywhere here. Hell, half the Chinese coolies used for labor in Peru are on the Chilean payroll. Where do you think they came from? Up from the desert coast where they worked the guano mines."

Wake had seen the coolies working on the city's defenses. And in the Navy Yard. The Chileans must know all about *Toro*. "What are the plans to defend the heartland of the country? Do they have any?"

Woodgerd reached for another glass and drained it. "Defense plans? You must be joking. This place didn't even have an army before this thing started. The only defense plan they have is to look confident while they hope the U.S. comes to their aid with warships and artillery before the Chilis overrun them. That's their *plan.*"

"Damn, Mike, I don't think that's going to happen."

"Neither do I, *amigo.* So, do you want to meet the headman himself? He's quite the politician. An absolute picture of confidence. Speaks English, too. Fancies himself as the sophisticated leader of the striped-pants diplomatic crowd. And here he is on Peru's Independence Day in a ballroom full of striped-pants boys. He'll be in heaven. I'll introduce you."

Wake couldn't help but laugh. "Ah, Mike . . . you're wearing striped pants yourself tonight."

Woodgerd cast a rueful glance over his attire. "Yeah, tells you just how far I'll sink for money, don't it?"

Wake had wondered how he'd get close enough to Piérola to get time alone so he could deliver the message. The help had come in the unexpected person of a mercenary friend from his past. What were the odds?

"Lead onward and upward, Mike. I'm in your hands."

## 18

# The Messenger

Wake hadn't seen Woodgerd this serious even in front of the Sultan of Morocco—and *that* man was known to behead people. The soldier-for-hire looked grimly respectful when he intoned, "Your Excellency, may I introduce Lieutenant Commander Peter Wake, a neutral naval observer from the United States Navy."

Piérola nodded imperiously as Woodgerd droned on. "Commander Wake, I have the esteemed honor of presenting His Excellency Nicolás de Piérola, President of the People, and Commander-in-Chief of the Armed Forces of the Great Republic of Peru."

Not to be outdone, Wake straightened up to attention, then bowed as impressively as he could. "*Encantado de conocer el Presidente de la Republica, Su Excelencia. Con respetos muchos de la armada de los Estados Unidos. Español es una lingua muy hermosa. Pero, por favor, Su Excelencia, dispenseme, porque mi español es pobre. Necesito que practicar mi gramática.*"

Piérola reacted the way Wake hoped, surprised that a *gringo* could speak Spanish, including the expected respects and regrets.

A presidential assistant hovering nearby saw the president's obvious interest in the American and shooed approaching people away. The Americans remained in the corner with Piérola.

"Commander, your Spanish is very good and I appreciate your description of our language. Yes, it *is* beautiful, is it not? So musical, so passionate. I wish you well with your practice. And how is my English?"

"Perfect, Your Excellency."

"Thank you, Commander. The instructors at the Seminario de Santo Toribio would be happy to know that. They took great *pains* to make it so. In fact, I still bear the marks." Piérola chuckled at his pun. "In their honor, I suggest we speak in English. How is your visit to our land?"

"Very interesting, Your Excellency. You have a fascinating land and people."

Woodgerd interrupted. "Commander Wake was here last year also, sir."

"Several times, sir," added Wake. "I've since been back to Washington, where I reported my observations on the naval war to my superiors."

Now Piérola was intently scrutinizing Wake. "Really? Yes, I remember hearing of your name now. You were with Admiral Grau before his death. And who are those superiors in Washington, Commander?"

Wake had no doubt that Piérola knew all about his observer mission and the rumors about the British diplomat the previous year. But he was sure the man didn't know exactly why he was there now. He struggled to sound bland—it was time for the *pièce de résistance.*

"The Secretary of the Navy and the President of the United States, sir. They are greatly interested in the situation here."

There was a momentary lull in the music. Wake thought he heard Woodgerd mutter something, then cough. Piérola was better at concealing his reaction. "President Hayes? How very intriguing. You suddenly appear to be something more than a mere 'neutral naval observer,' Commander Wake."

"I am strictly neutral in this war, sir, as is my country. But yes, I do have another reason to be here besides observing developments."

Piérola shot Woodgerd a questioning look, then bored his eyes into Wake's. "And what is that, Commander?"

"A personal message from President Hayes, to be delivered in private to you, sir."

"Ah? Very well. This gets more interesting as we go along. Colonel Woodgerd, excuse yourself for five minutes and see that we are not disturbed."

When they were alone in the corner, with hundreds of people now watching them from sixty feet away, Piérola said, "Tell me exactly what he said."

Wake had imagined the conversation would be in a private office, but the expression on Piérola's face told him not to dawdle.

"Here is the message from President Hayes to you: The United States will act as the official mediator for peace talks aboard the American warship *Lackawanna*, to be anchored off the harbor at Arica. The talks will go on for no more than one month, starting on September thirtieth, during which time all three nations at war must come to terms and stop the bloodshed. The Unites States urges Peru to realize it cannot win this war and to negotiate to the best of her ability to save her people from further slaughter and destruction."

"And if we do not do what the United States wants us to do?"

"The message is as I stated it, sir. It does not go further."

"But you know the attitude in Washington, Commander. And I know they want me to hear what happens if I refuse to negotiate away my country's freedom."

"The message says it all, sir. Absolutely *nothing* will happen. Fate will be allowed to have its way. Peru will disappear as an independent entity and become a province of Chile. We won't raise a finger, just as we aren't in the Argentinean war right now."

Piérola's face drained of color, haughty demeanor evaporated. "So this is it? We will be defeated and you will not help at all."

Wake stared back into those black eyes. "Yes, it certainly would appear so, sir. Unites States neutrality and assistance in negotiating peace is the very best you can hope for. Unless you can defeat the Chileans by force of arms."

Piérola gazed out at the crowd, which was busy conjecturing about the dialogue they saw unfolding but couldn't hear. He sighed and briefly rubbed a temple. "That is all, Commander. You may return to the gathering now."

"Thank you, sir."

"And Commander Wake . . ."

"Yes, sir?"

Piérola words were sarcastically light-hearted, his eyes full of anger. "I want you to particularly enjoy tonight's festivities in honor of Peruvian Independence Day—the twenty-eighth day of July, in eighteen twenty-one, when we declared our sovereignty as a people and nation. This may well be our last celebration of that accomplishment."

Wake stood speechless, as Piérola wandered off mingling with the guests, smiling and laughing as if the somber conversation hadn't occurred. The musicians started a waltz and Piérola was the first gentleman to ask a lady to dance—the wife of the French minister to Peru. As Wake got to the bar table he noticed Christiancy studying him from across the room. The diplomat wasn't smiling.

Woodgerd bumped him at the bar. "Neutral naval observer— but also a personal messenger from the president of the United States? You've come up in the world, Peter. Way the hell up. You know, when I was pouring out my little demented heart about future predictions, I don't quite remember you mentioning the special messenger from the U.S. president part of your assignment."

"You didn't ask and I didn't volunteer. It's supposed to be secret, Mike."

"Well, whatever the secret message was, it sure didn't appear positive by the look on *el supremo*'s face when you told him. The whole place is buzzing about what you said. Half of them were trying to read your lips. Hell, I tried too."

Woodgerd tossed down a straight rum. Wake saw they were serving Ron Pampero, a fine sipping rum from Venezuela. He ordered one and downed it too, then said, "I guess Peru's president shouldn't play poker, Colonel. Even an old squid like me could see he was upset."

Wake ordered two more drinks for them, noticing that no one would stand near them, though several army officers were watching the two Americans.

"So, what was the message?"

"Can't say, Mike."

"Come on. I leveled with you, Wake."

"But I work for my country, Mike. My loyalty's a little more deeply ingrained. Sorry, I can't say. Besides, you just gave me your opinion, not state secrets."

Woodgerd voice dropped low. "Should I make plans to exit the country, *quietly?*"

Another round dropped down their throats. Woodgerd gestured for two more.

"Not at this time, Mike. But when and if it gets really dicey around here, we both better have plans to exit quietly. And rapidly."

Christiancy walked up. "Sorry to intrude, gentlemen, but I wonder if I might have a word with my fellow countryman, Colonel?"

Woodgerd turned his eyes to the man. There was an uncomfortable pause, then the mercenary exhaled and walked off. The diplomat spoke softly to Wake. "As the American representative here, I think I should know what was the content of your private conversation with Peru's president, Commander. It seems to have created quite a stir and people are expecting me to know what is going on."

Admiral Porter had covered this eventuality in his verbal

instructions, which had really come from Secretary Thompson. The message from Hayes was to remain secret, even from Christiancy.

"It was a message of American hopes for an end to the war, sir."

"Hmm. How odd that it didn't come through regular channels. Who was it from?"

"The leadership of the U.S. Navy, sir." *Technically,* Wake reminded himself, his explanation was not a lie. The president was the head of the navy. And everything else.

"Oh! Is that all?" The man perked up. "Well, I must say I thought it was something considerably more substantial. Very good, Commander."

"Yes, sir."

Christiancy departed the table, bound for the French representative who'd been trying to eavesdrop from thirty feet away. No one yet had come to the refreshment table near Wake until a tall gaunt man in the robes of a Catholic bishop approached. He asked the barman in Spanish for a glass of champagne, then switched to English.

"Good evening, Commander Wake. Please forgive my intrusion, but you appeared alone. I am Mario Mocenni, the Vatican apostolic delegate to Peru. In other words, the personal envoy of the Holy Father in Rome." He held out a thin hand, cold to Wake's touch.

"Very nice to meet you, sir."

"I understand you are an observer of the war for your country. What is your opinion of the near future here, if an old priest might be so bold as to ask? I have no skill in such martial things, of course."

Lima, Peru, was getting curiouser and curiouser, thought Wake. Mocenni didn't wander up for a social discussion while having a drink. The way the man was looking at him made Wake wonder if there was something else the bishop wanted to say. Was the question, which was the topic on everyone's minds lately, just a polite entré?

"I'm afraid no one has much skill at predicting the future in war, sir."

"Then many people in this room tonight are mistaken, for they assume by the reaction of President Piérola to your conversation awhile ago that you have some knowledge of important events yet to transpire. Unfortunate events. Please indulge my rambling a moment longer, Commander."

Wake couldn't believe this. He was being pumped for information by a Catholic bishop, albeit nicely. Mocenni continued.

"Were such events likely to come to fruition, could old friends count on each other to provide a modicum of cautionary notification? I have this feeling that you might possibly become the possessor of such knowledge, which would be very useful for me. Lives could hang in the balance, my son."

Wake stuck to his role, parroting the line he said so many times to so many people. "I am only a neutral naval observer, Bishop Mocenni. I have no inside knowledge of Peruvian or Chilean military operations."

"Yes, of course, Commander. But if you ever should find yourself in a position to help save lives, please consider me an old friend. You and I have mutual friends in Spain and Italy and Panama that would want you to know that.

"Really, Commander, do not look so surprised. You have far more friends than you know. And if I can ever assist you, please let me know. I live very close by here, at the Monastario de San Francisco. I will always be at your service. You should come by sometime."

Wake tried to think fast as the old man waited for a reply. Mocenni knew Vargas? And Ferro in Genoa? Muñosa in Spain? Did the Catholic Church actually care about Peter Wake, a Protestant? It was true that Muñosa had helped him escape Carlist forces in Sevilla back in seventy-four. He'd always wondered if Ferro had helped defuse that ugly situation he found himself in at Porto Fino, Italy, that same year. And lately Vargas had passed along the information to him in Panama. But what was their motivation? Why him?

"Ah, thank you, sir. I'm a Methodist, though, not Catholic."

Mocenni's tired eyes crinkled in amusement. "Oh yes, I know that, my son. And a good one, I imagine. But we are all the children of God and as such, welcome in the Church. And the invitation was not only for your soul. The monastery also has a very good cook."

Wake decided a meal with the bishop might prove to be enlightening. "Yes, well thank you again, sir. If time permits, I might very well do that."

"I hope you do, my son. I hope you do."

Woodgerd crossed paths with Wake outside the entrance. They walked together across the plaza, Woodgerd headed to the presidential palace, Wake to his hotel.

"What did the Vatican's man want?" asked Woodgerd.

"The same as everyone else. He wanted to know if I know what's happening."

"Well, for a squid that didn't even attend the navy's charm school at Annapolis, it's amazing how sought after you've become in the space of a single evening, Peter."

"I was just delivering a message."

"Ah, yes. And that makes you a very popular messenger."

Thinking about Woodgerd's assessment, he thought about Vargas's warning about the Chileans and the shadowy men in Panama. Hoping he wasn't getting too fearful, Wake opted not to continue walking the six blocks back to his hotel in the dark. Lima wasn't a safe place in the best of times. He'd hail a taxi on the other side of the plaza.

"Popular might not be the right word, Mike. I just hope no one around here decides to *shoot* the messenger."

## 19

# No Time to Be Sick

### August 1880
### Washington, D.C.

Drying a dish from breakfast, Linda Wake wiped the rivulet of sweat from her eyes with her sleeve. It was hot. Very hot. Even the children in the neighborhood were moving slow. There was no breeze, no rain. At night, according to the *Washington Star,* the temperatures would go down into the eighties, and in the afternoons it was over one hundred degrees. It felt hotter than that. Even growing up in the South, she had never endured heat like this. Linda thought the air itself seemed to have weight and mass, pushing down on her, crushing the energy out of her.

Fruit and greens rotted overnight, ice was only for the rich, and alcohol-fueled arguments roiled through the listless nights from other apartments. The family wore as little as decency permitted, but it was still too much, and clothing became soaked with perspiration within minutes. No one she knew was baking or ironing—it heated up an apartment even more. Besides, few were really hungry and clothes were wrinkling anyway. It was almost as if God was reminding people that in spite of all their modern machines and innovations—nature remained in charge of their daily lives.

Linda thought of the old Florida witticism that Southern ladies never sweat—oh no, Southern ladies *glistened.* Well, we're not glistening now. She sniffed an unpleasant odor and made a mental note to try and find some clean fresh water for a bath.

The children were napping, the chores were done, and she was exhausted, so she stretched out on her bed, unbuttoned her blouse and ran a wet cloth over her skin. For a fleeting moment she felt slightly cooler, then she was covered in perspiration again. It was hopeless.

Lately the pains had visited more often and were combined with bowel problems. She just wanted it all to go away—all the pain and the heat and the irritable people. As if on cue, a woman yelled an obscenity in an apartment across the street and the pain throbbed in her abdomen. Linda looked around the room for something to focus on to try to quell the ache. Peter's last letter was on the bedside table. With a shaking hand she read it once again.

*Darling Linda,*                                                  *27 July 1880*

*A quick note, since I hear there is mail out today and that's rare indeed in this place, so I've got to get this note over to the legation to put with their post.*

*I made it through the Isthmus. Panama was the same, of course—nothing ever changes there. The French will soon find that out. I wish them well, but fear they haven't planned or funded for the realities in that terrible place. But on the brighter side, at least the Panamanians are happy with the new money in the area!*

*Finally made it to Peru after a bit of a circuitous route, politics and bureaucrats making the trip far more difficult than it needed to be. Bureaucrats in this part of the world have raised incompetence to an art form. Their inertia colors everything here—the war effort, civil society, helping the refugees, everything.*

*My mission is rather mundane and boring, but I do get to meet some intriguing types, mostly European. There is little in the way of social activity here in Lima. What with the war and all they're usually not in the mood, but tomorrow will be a big celebration for their independence, which I'm probably to attend. Find out at the last minute with my luck. I imagine it won't be anything like our nights at the White House, though.*

*Not sure when I'll be home, but after October for sure and hopefully by Christmas. That's my dream each night—Christmas with you and the children.*

*Don't worry about me. Other than the odd paper cut I haven't seen any danger. The fighting is still well south of here. I suppose I'm too old for that sort of thing now. I'll do my fighting with a pen. Unfortunately, for right now I'll also have to do my loving with one, in the form of this letter and others.*

*Write me often and know that you are in my mind and heart constantly—that's what happens when a man is hopelessly in love with the island girl of his dreams. Until we can make the dream a reality in a few months, that will have to do. Please give Useppa and Sean a hug and kiss from their Daddy.*

*With lots of love from your husband,*
*Peter*

The pain departed and Linda dozed off, imagining her husband in an office south of the Equator reading documents and writing reports. And dreaming of her.

"The Nicaraguan project isn't doing very well, is it? What are you hearing from your people?" Secretary Thompson asked Secretary of State William Evarts, referring to a canal project begun there by an American company. There had been bad press lately about design problems and foreign influence. Politicians were getting questions about the viability of the Nicaraguan venture—the only real competition to the French in Panama.

Thompson was in the secretary of state's office on the south side of the State, Navy and War Building, about three hundred feet down the hall from his own quarters. He liked his office better—it overlooked the president's mansion. Evarts's office was in Room 208 and far less opulent than Thompson's, but impressive in its own right. Three windows and a portico overlooked the Potomac River in the distance, and the interior was done in a gray chocolate motif accented by gilt trim. Greco-patterned stencils decorated the walls and an enormous oriental rug was spread in front of the large mahogany mantelpiece. The focus of all entering the office, however, was the display of the Great Seal of the United States of America, of which the Secretary of State was the legal guardian.

Evarts was a tall, handsome, sophisticated lawyer who still turned women's heads at age sixty-two. Born in Boston, educated at Boston Latin School, Yale, and Harvard Law, he was the grandson of a signer of the Declaration of Independence, the confidant and legal counselor of several presidents, and known as the consummate power broker in Washington.

"From what I've heard, financial problems are influencing it. People are jittery about throwing good money away on a ditch that might not get dug," said Evarts as he rocked back in his executive chair and studied the gasolier above them. "Not to mention the engineering problems. I'm hearing that even the British are having second thoughts about investing in it."

"Thank you. That's what I'm hearing too. I'm thinking the French in Panama have the right route anyway. Plus, they have de Lesseps's experience. The man sounds like he knows what he's doing. Got that canal done in Egypt. Knows how to get things accomplished with native people in far-off places. Man has solid credibility."

"Yes, that he does, Richard. De Lesseps was quite the showman on that tour last winter. And I think *eventually* he'll pull it off. But it'll be tougher than he told folks. And he'll need a lot more money."

"Well, of course, with some American money infused into the project—private investments, of course—he'll have enough to accomplish it."

"That would do it. But he's not getting any from the U.S. I'm hearing some of the French investment people are starting to slow down. Dutch too. They're taking a beating in Peru and Argentina. Getting a little wary of Latin America, I'd say."

"Very interesting. That opens it up to us. I think the French need some American know-how, both on the construction project and in stock sales. With Americans involved the sky's the limit." Thompson spread his hands. "What an opportunity! If an American leader that people trust would stand up and lend his support, de Lesseps could get those investors. The people who got in this early on would do well. Very well, indeed."

"They'd also incur the wrath of President Hayes, who's made it pretty clear that any American who gets involved does so at their own risk and shouldn't count on this or any other government rescuing their investment."

"And that is as it should be, Bill. The president was right. But he didn't *prohibit* American investment, he only cautioned people to be careful."

Evarts wondered why Thompson, who had been lukewarm about the French effort and wasn't an admirer of Latin America, was suddenly interested, even supportive. Evarts knew Thompson had his own channels of information and wondered what he knew. In Washington, knowledge was power and not something to be given away lightly.

"Why all this interest, Richard? You starting to like the navy or what? They've been calling for a canal for years."

"Everyone west of the Mississippi has, Bill. The whole country is interested in this canal in Panama. The economic benefits are immense."

"What's your man down there say?"

"What man would that be, Bill? Admiral Stevens?"

"No, not the admiral, he's always on his boat. I mean that officer I keep hearing about from my consuls and ministers. I seem to have forgotten his name. You know, the fellow with that nasty rumor about the British diplomat's death." Evarts rubbed his chin. "Now what the devil *was* that man's name?"

Thompson rose from his chair. "Not sure of who you're talking about, Bill. Let me know who when you remember. Say, is it time to leave for the reception yet? Garfield'll be there and we're supposed to be on time."

Then it struck Evarts. Thompson, as well as Evarts himself and all the cabinet, would be out of a job in a few months when Hayes stepped down. Was Thompson laying the groundwork for a lucrative post-government position with the French canal company? In Panama? That sounded beyond ridiculous. Thompson didn't even like Latin America. Wrote that absurd book. No, after Washington Richard Thompson would go back to Indiana and be a retired gentleman corn farmer, or whatever those people did out there, and forget all about Panama. Evarts was sure of that, at least.

Still, as he got up to follow Thompson out, he made a mental note to inquire about that naval officer down there. Something was going on. Evarts could smell political intrigue a mile away, and he was getting a whiff of it now.

It had been a long walk in the oppressive heat, almost four miles to the northern outskirts of the city, by Le Droit Park. Linda had walked it both ways twice in the last week. She wished she could have gone to a doctor closer to her home, but the navy physicians made it clear they weren't well versed in women's illnesses and she should go to a doctor that was.

The problem, as in so many areas, was money. Linda had none, except her husband's pay and what little she made on the side sewing for neighborhood ladies. She was the wife of an officer and was embarrassed to let anyone know of her financial woes. She knew she couldn't afford a civilian doctor, at least not one that specialized in ladies' ailments. That left her with one choice, the black hospital at Howard University. She'd read in the *Washington Star* how highly regarded it had become, including a medical college that provided clinical care for the surrounding neighborhood. Started to help newly freed blacks after the war gain an education, the university was named after its founder, Oliver Otis Howard, a war hero general who had lost his right arm in combat in 1862. After the war he was in charge of the Freedmen's Bureau and had been instrumental in improving educational and medical care throughout the South for blacks. Devoted to assisting them, the university had started a medical school with a faculty of former black and white former army surgeons. Howard was still in the army, now fighting Indians out West.

The newspaper described one of its course specialties as "Obstetrics and Diseases of Women and Children." Linda walked there and met Dr. Charles Purvis, a black doctor who got his experience as a surgeon during the war in the black regiments. He now taught and treated civilians of all colors.

Born a free man in Norfolk, Virginia, twenty years before the war, Purvis was light-skinned, with sorrowful eyes and a tremendous set of whiskers that made him appear older than his thirty-eight years. After he listened to her complaint on the first visit, three days earlier, he asked gently, "Ah, well, you do know that I need to examine you, Mrs. Wake, right?"

"Of course, you're a doctor. We need to find out what is wrong."

"Very well, madam. It's just that it's unusual that a lady of your standing would be here and I didn't want any misunderstanding. I'm sorry that your circumstances force you to use this facility, Mrs. Wake, but I want you to know I'll do the very best in my ability. We'll work out a payment scheme, but that's not the most important thing. Making you feel better is our primary concern. And we have a very good staff here to assist me in that endeavor."

"Doctor Purvis, I'm aware of your concern about a white lady being seen by a black doctor, but I'm past all that. I just want some help. I'm desperate to end this pain."

The examination was brief, checking for masses, tenderness, or discoloration. In contrast, the interview about her symptoms and habits was extensive. Purvis's thoroughness gave her hope for an answer to this thing that was making her miserable. He gave her some mild medicine for pain and told her to come back in three days, during which he would consult with his colleagues.

Now she was back at the university, exhausted after the walk and soaked with sweat. When she walked into the room, Purvis stood and held out a chair.

"Mrs. Wake, we're not exactly sure what is causing your pains, but there are several possibilities. We're going to find out and take care of you."

"What exactly are the possible problems, doctor?"

"Digestive difficulties may be it, but I doubt it." Purvis didn't know how to say the rest of it except bluntly. "Or it *may* be a type of tumor or cancer. I will require a more in-depth examination, then if we are still uncertain, possibly surgery to survey the area internally. In the event that you do have a cancerous growth, there are treatments and surgeries to address it."

Linda's face flushed and her pulse began pounding in her ears. She'd heard of cancer, usually with older people. It was one of those illnesses one heard of but did not know much about. It was an illness the very mention of which scared people. She took a breath and exhaled slowly.

"I see. Do you know what the procedure is from here, Doctor?"

Purvis was relieved to see this woman was strong-willed. "Yes.

Many physicians are not trained or equipped for this type of examination and diagnosis, but here at the university we are. We can get started whenever you are ready, Mrs. Wake. I suggest we begin immediately. Cancerous tumors can sometimes grow rapidly, so if you have one, I'd like to know now while it's hopefully small and more easily taken care of. We'll do an operation, explore the area, and remove the tumor if one is found. The concept is simple."

"Yes, I can understand that. Then we'll start today, Doctor. I need to know myself what is happening and how to deal with it. Keep me *informed*, Doctor Purvis."

"Very well, madam."

Linda's face hardened. "One crucial thing, though, Doctor."

"Yes, madam?"

"No one other than the staff here is to know about this if I do have a tumor. *No* one. No idle gossip, no chat with other physicians with my name used. I don't want people looking at me with pity. Understood?"

Purvis nodded. "I understand, madam. We take confidentiality very seriously. I will not betray your trust."

"Good. Now let's get started. I've no time to be sick, Doctor."

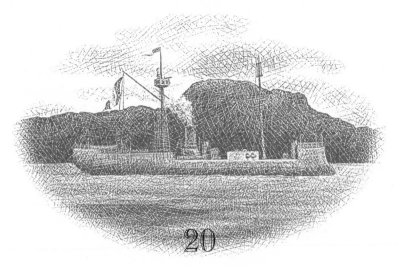

## 20

# Unwritten Worries

## October 1880

The day after the conversation with Piérola, Wake cryptically telegrammed his superiors that the presidential message had been sent. The reply arrived three days later—wait for developments and report. For two months Wake had done just that.

One of those developments almost turned deadly for Wake. He'd been invited to visit *Toro* again one evening in early September to witness a test dive. Making sure they knew he wasn't traveling under water this time, he agreed and with Perez arrived at the dock after sunset. Only a few lamps were lit, apparently out of fear of the Chilean naval gunners offshore, who had been getting more aggressive lately. This time the place was vastly different. No politicians, no senior officers, no entourage. Just the commander Othon, the crew, and a few men to handle the lines from the wharf were present.

Wake noticed new gear aboard also. Coiled on the afterdeck were two long lines, each attached to a buoylike contraption. Captain Gonzalez loomed up in the dark, hands rubbing together in anticipation of something, his grinning teeth a flash of white in the night. He pointed to the stern as Perez converted his words into English.

"Ah, Commander Wake! Thank you for coming. Now you can see our *Toro's* stinger. You have been given the honor of seeing her first combat—from the shore. Unless you would like to accompany *Toro* on her mission of destiny? We are happy to oblige that request. It would, of course, be a tremendous experience for a professional such as yourself."

Yes, thought Wake, I imagine you would be happy to get me aboard that iron coffin in combat. He remembered what happened to every single man in three separate crews aboard the Rebel boat *Hunley* during the war—all of them ended up dead. It would make a fine mess for the United States if an American naval officer was in a Peruvian submarine warship—a weapon a lot of the world considered inhuman and cowardly—during an attack on a Chilean warship. And if the American should die? The Peruvians would make much of fraternal blood shed for liberty, trying to drag the U.S. into the war. Yes, that would get Secretary Thompson's attention all right. Wake speculated on whether this was Piérola's idea. Probably, he decided.

"No, thank you, sir. I must decline that esteemed honor as I am a neutral and it would violate my orders." Besides, he said to himself, I'd have to be a moronic fool to get in that thing again. "Though I am envious of these brave warriors, I will have to be content watching from shore. Orders can be so frustrating."

"Very well. I offered." Gonzalez shrugged and swept an arm to the west. "They are out there. *Cochrane* and *Blanco Escalada*— two of the enemy's strongest ships. Until tonight, when they meet little *Toro*. The submarine will tow the two torpedo explosives that will float just below the surface, then *Toro* will dive under one of the ships and go past it, pulling the explosives into its hull. The other enemy ship will flee after they see the destruction. By tomorrow's sun, Commander, the blockade will be lifted and our nation will start to repel the invaders. And you will see it all start here with your own eyes."

Gonzalez stepped closer and said with a flourish, "This opportunity is a gesture of goodwill from Peru to the United States, my naval friend."

Now Wake was certain this was all Piérola's idea. "Thank you for the opportunity, sir. It will be extremely interesting to observe."

In the moonless night the submarine was towed by a tiny steam launch away from the dock and cast loose in the harbor. By starlight Wake last saw it—he had a hard time thinking of the submarine as a "her"—heading west toward San Lorenzo Island, where the Chileans waited aboard their darkened warships.

"We will go to the promenade and watch the explosions there," said Gonzalez. A ride of five minutes by carriage took them around to the breakwater, where they stood expectantly. Perez suddenly pointed just beyond the breakwater. It was the conning tower of the submarine, visible only as a black mass against the lighter background of the rippled water. The thin white line of a small wave vee'd out from the submarine. Wake wondered if the other side could see that as well.

Then the wave disappeared. *Toro* was diving under water. Wake's memory immediately filled him with that sensation of dread he'd had seeing the water covering the portholes as that iron "thing" sank below the surface. He shivered.

Gonzalez peered through binoculars. Wake heard him swearing under his breath, Perez explaining that the Chilean ships were not where they usually patrolled inshore at night. For some reason they were farther out. Then Gonzalez let out a furious oath, growling to Perez that he could see the enemy slowly heading southwest—away from where the submarine had planned to attack them.

Just then two flashes lit up the western sky and Wake heard the deep-throated reports of the guns. Boom, boom. Geysers erupted in the channel a quarter mile away, faint gray fountains in the black background. More flashes. A series of booms. Geysers erupted all along the channel, some rounds landing in the water close to the promenade. Spray splattered the officers and Wake heard someone laugh nervously at a muttered joke about Chilean accuracy.

Suddenly there was a blinding flash close by to the left. Thunder filled Wake's ears as he felt the air forced out of his lungs. His body twisted around, flung down onto the rough stone decking of the breakwater. He landed on his right shoulder, just above the gunshot wound he received in Africa, sending waves of pain through his chest. Chunks of cement and stone rained down on Wake as he rolled onto his stomach, curling up to protect his face.

He heard a man groan far away, a long muffled moan, then realized it was himself. Everything hurt. Wake assessed his situation—legs functioned, arms functioned, no blood from the shoulder, he could see and hear somewhat. Wake felt around his body. No, there wasn't any obvious blood. He sat up on his left elbow with an effort and surveyed the scene.

Perez was on his back, gashed on the face, shaking his head. Gonzalez was still standing and growling out oaths, his uniform splotched with dark stains. The young officer who'd accompanied them, ensign somebody, staggered around at the foot of the breakwater promenade, asking for help. Soldiers from the nearby artillery battery were running their way. Orders were shouted. In the harbor another geyser erupted.

Perez's face didn't look good. Using his left arm and both legs, Wake crawled over to him. "Roberto, sit up. Get your head above your heart, *amigo. Cabeza mas arriba del corazon.* It will help slow the bleeding. *Despacio el sangre.*"

Using his good arm, Wake helped Perez up to a kneeling position. Wiping away the blood flow with his own hand as Perez swayed, he examined the gash. It ran across the bridge of the man's nose and down into the cheek. Something blunt, probably stone debris, had smashed into the face. Even in the night Wake could see the wound was jagged and deep, exposing the bone. He quickly took off the Peruvian's coat and tore his shirt-sleeve apart for a bandage, which he wound tight around Perez's head, covering his face.

"Hold this tight to help stop the flow, Roberto. Hold it tight!"

Two soldiers picked up Perez, carrying him to the artillery position where a doctor was being summoned. Others ran to Gonzalez. One soldier was saying something to Wake, concerned, questioning. He waved the soldier to the ensign, forty feet away still wandering with hands in the air.

Gonzalez, obviously in pain, stumbled over to where Wake knelt. "*Herido?*"

Wake could barely understand the one-word question. His ears were still ringing. Then he got it and shook his head. "No, Captain. I'm not wounded. *No herido. Estoy bien, Capitan Gonzalez.*"

Wake looked out to sea. All gunfire had stopped. He couldn't see anything. "*¿Pero, que pasa con los enemigos?*"

Gonzalez's eyes were focused on the ground, his words hardly audible. "*Desaparecido . . .*"

Wake's mind was dulled. He tried to remember that word. It came to him a moment later. "Disappeared."

With a grunt, Wake ignored the throbbing in his right shoulder and raised up on a knee. Slowly, he stood unsteadily. His head swirled and he swayed to the right, then overcorrected to the left. A moment later Wake saw soldiers running toward him, just as he started to fall back onto the stone surface. The back of his head hit with a thud. Oddly, Wake registered that it didn't hurt. Then everything went blank.

*◡◡*

The doctor pronounced Wake concussed, with a strained and contused shoulder. There were no major wounds. The prescription was for rum and coffee over the next two days, starting right then. He was further told to use the shoulder and arm, not to let them atrophy. Feeling better after his initial "medicine," Wake was taken to his hotel room and told to rest. The massive headache and caffeine nixed that idea.

After two days of lying in bed Wake actually did begin to feel better, until he tried to walk down the street. The piercing pain of his shoulder made every movement hurt, sometimes taking his breath. Forcing himself to exercise his right arm by lifting small things, Wake focused on regaining his strength and mobility. Gradually, he felt his range of movement increase, until the arm worked for most normal uses. He prayed his thanks to God, for Wake knew how close he'd come with the shell burst.

Wake reported in at the legation on the fifth day, where Kronburg shook his head in admonition, having already heard from the Peruvians about Wake's experience. He said that when he'd informed Minister Christiancy of Wake's situation, the diplomat suggested that American naval observers not be allowed to go near combat areas—the political consequences were just too serious. Wake then commented that he didn't come under the minister's command and, "would continue to do my job, which is to observe this new type of war."

In answer to his inquiry, he was informed that the *Toro* had not gone down in the attempted attack. When the Chileans left the scene it was on the bottom and the furious shelling never harmed it. When asked if anything new was occurring among the diplomatic endeavors, Kronburg laconically replied no, locally nothing had happened but that Washington was sending a warship and inviting the warring parties to have talks aboard her. Kronburg thought that was "some fool's idea. Diplomats don't negotiate on boats."

Saying nothing in reply, Wake smiled inwardly and wondered what Kronburg would say if he found exactly who the fools were. He was tempted to tell him but resisted. He found it interesting that during the five-minute conversation Kronburg never asked about his injury. So much for American brotherhood—I guess

I'm more of an embarrassment to the State Department, Wake decided.

Wake worked at rebuilding strength as he waited for the *Lackawanna* to arrive, exercising, walking. The days were spent chatting with locals in taverns, visiting Perez in the hospital, and meeting with officers at the Callao naval station, including the indomitable Gonzalez. The captain, swathed in bandages, said *Toro* was ready for another attack but the Chileans were not obliging them—they were staying farther offshore in fear of the little craft.

Perez was blind in one eye, his once-handsome face permanently marred by the badly healing gash, which showed persistent infection. With his career over, depression had taken hold of the young officer. Morose ramblings turned into hostility toward everyone in the ward. The visits became increasingly strained. After two weeks Wake stopped going.

Nights were taken up by the occasional diplomatic or military social function, having a drink with Woodgerd once every couple weeks, or just sitting alone in his room. The mercenary offered a typical response to Wake's bout with death. "See what being a nice fellow gets you, squid? Dead. Next time tell 'em you'll watch from *beyond* gun range."

That he was under a sort of loose surveillance was obvious to Wake—by whom was the question. Footsteps echoing in the dark, fleeting forms darting into shadows, once a dark face peering through a curtain at him from across the street. Not enough to form a definite idea or suspect, but Vargas's warning was always in the back of his mind. He'd broached it to Woodgerd once, but was met with, "Hell, Wake, everybody watches everybody down here. Could be Piérola's boys, or some Chinese working for the Chileans—we know they are using them for spies, maybe even your own legation keeping an eye on their wayward squid. Who knows? It's probably just your guilty conscience getting the best of you."

One evening he took the bishop up on the offer of dinner at

the monastery of San Francisco. It was an oasis of tranquility in wartime Lima. Their table was in a cool tiled courtyard, shaded by fragrant orange trees, serenaded by a distant choir practicing, and surrounded by a two-story church and religious community of monks and priests. Dinner was pompano fish sautéed in wine butter with rice, grilled carrots, and green beans, and then custard, served by two silent old women. Bent over as they shuffled along, their watery eyes watched Wake constantly.

Afterward, the two men retired to an airy library set back from the corridor encompassing the courtyard. There were no doors. Mocenni explained that the books on the dusty shelves were three hundred years old, some were four hundred. Wake was astounded. The volumes he saw everywhere were priceless originals documenting the conquest of South America.

Over fine cognac they spoke of their mutual friends and their own lives, the bishop telling of his adventures and Wake describing his family. The bishop related his duties in Lima as envoy of the Pope and his love for the place in which he lived. At that point Mocenni made a comment Wake found odd. "This monastery has many secrets, many treasures. Someday, perhaps you may find them useful, Peter."

The conversation steered to politics and the war, neither man really able to predict the future and both fearful of the consequences. Wake left that night still wondering about Mocenni and the Church's interest in a junior American naval officer. One thing was certain to him. None of it was coincidental.

The waiting for orders was getting to Wake. Linda's letters only added to his disquiet. Something was wrong back in Washington, he could sense it from the absence of negative news. Her letters were just too light-hearted.

Sitting in his musty room, Wake unfolded the one on his

desk table. Lately he'd noticed that he was squinting more and more when reading. Getting old, he realized with a scowl. He focused on the letter.

*Dearest Husband,*        *August 21ˢᵗ, 1880*
*All is well here, if you discount the summer heat, which seems slightly worse this year. They say we need more rain too. The rivers are down and navigation more difficult.*

 *Useppa's church work takes up almost all her time—when she's not reading newspapers. Your daughter is becoming quite knowledgeable about the political condition of the country and now she wants to know why women can't vote. With our luck she'll probably turn into one of those suffragette women and get arrested for inciting a riot. I insist she inherited that part of her character from you! Her leg is the same, but she says it doesn't hurt as much. I can't tell. But she seems happy in general.*

 *Sean is spending the summer loitering with his friends among the old petty officers down at the docks. I suppose that is relatively good, but they fill him with the most outrageous sea stories that he then repeats to one and all. One was not fit for a little boy to tell and he won't repeat that one again in my presence. He is growing like a weed and now as tall as me. Just wait until you see him. Now I know what you looked like as a boy.*

 *The big news is that Sean Rork isn't coming back to duty at the Navy Yard here. He returned to New York from Ireland aboard* Constellation *a few weeks ago, then right away volunteered for more sea duty in the South Atlantic. He shipped out as a bosun in transit on a warship bound to the East Indies squadron. When they pass by Brazil he's supposed to join Admiral Bryson's flagship* Shenandoah *in the South Atlantic Squadron. So I guess he'll be on one side of South America while you're on the other. Pity the South Americans!*

 *It's probably good for Sean but devastated poor Sheila, who is heart-broken that she scared him off. She comes by and pours out her woes, which sound rather hollow to me. She's pretty and smart (too smart for her own good?) and will soon get another man.*

*I miss you more than I can convey in a letter, Peter. I miss your smell, your skin, your hands, your eyes. I miss you in bed with me, the way we snuggle together when we sleep. I miss having someone to talk to, someone I trust. It's now late August though, and I know that in a few weeks the heat will be gone, that autumn will start to color the trees, and in a few months my sailor man will be home. I can't wait. You may have more than you can handle, sailor.*

*Loving you more than ever, your wife*
*Linda*

Over seventeen years of reading Linda's letters had given Wake the ability to discern what was unwritten—the concerns she didn't want to bother him with. This time he detected something but couldn't put his finger on it. From the pile of letters he took the newest and read it again.

*Dear Peter,*                                                  *September 16th, 1880*
*Autumn isn't here yet, in spite of the yearning for cool weather. It's not as hot, but still quite warm. The children are back in school. Useppa is doing well, though I worry her opinions may cause friction. Sean is doing better this year and is fond of reading histories.*

*Mrs. Galen's son just was promoted to gunner's mate. Mrs. Washburn's husband John is now a lieutenant commander at the Navy Yard. I think he'll be assigned to Boston soon. Got a short letter from Sean Rork on the* Shenandoah *in the South Atlantic Squadron—only took three weeks, which is faster than yours. Is that because he's closer? Sean says he is senior bosun's mate aboard and that she's a good ship and crew. Said maybe they'll round the Horn and see the squadron where you are.*

*The election is at "full speed ahead," as you say. Useppa predicts Garfield will win, with all kinds of reasoning why, but the Washington Post says Hancock will be president. I hope it's not close like last time. That got so contentious that I think it poisoned people's outlooks. I'm ready for a "nice" election.*

*Missing you even more now. Sometimes I wake up smelling you, but you're not here. I hope that doesn't make me a candidate for lunacy, but I think that does show me hopelessly in love. Loneliness is part of loving a sailor. So are the reunions!*

*Until then, with all my love,*
*Linda*

Wake realized the one thing she hadn't mentioned in any of the ten letters was the abdominal pain that had bothered her so much. He'd asked in two letters how she was feeling, but received no update. That was it, he was sure now. She would've included that in her news had it disappeared.

He never wrote her about the shell explosion because he didn't want her worried about him. Now he realized she was probably doing the same with him. That worried Wake even more.

## 21

# Better than Nothing

The arrival of the American Pacific Squadron was not heralded with much fanfare. Wake got a note at his room one day of the second week in October.

*Wake,*
*Your navy boats just showed up at Callao. You and Minister Christiancy are required by the admiral—something to do with the proposed talks? Keep us adv of what is happening—especially political.*
*Kronburg*

Annoyed by Kronburg's continuing arrogance but glad to get away and do something useful, Wake packed quickly, settled his account and paid extra for a two-horse cab to Callao.

At the naval station he saw three wooden warships anchored off the docks, huge United States ensigns fluttering from their mastheads to proclaim they were neutral ships: *Lackawanna, Richmond,* and *Pensacola.* The entire naval might, as antiquated as it was, of his country in the South Pacific, was assembled before him. Wake sighed. The twenty-year-old ships that had seen their prime during the war fifteen years earlier weren't impressive anymore. The British, French, even the Chileans had ironclads drifting off the harbor, any single one of which could take on and sink all three American vessels.

He walked past the saluting guards—by this time everyone knew the *norteamericano*—into the headquarters building. Gonzalez hailed him with a smile.

"Ah, *mi compadre norteamericano. Su armada magnifica está en la puerta.*"

Wake replied haltingly in Gonzalez's language. "How did they get permission to anchor inside the harbor?"

Gonzalez spoke slowly so Wake could understand his Spanish. "They are here for some very important passengers—you and *Señor* Christiancy. Permission to enter came from President Piérola himself. We sent word to your diplomats to tell you. *Señor* Christiancy is already on the warship."

"Captain, can you have a boat take me out to the ship, and also have a messenger take a letter to Lima?"

"For my brother-in-battle, anything."

Wake wrote the note with a bit of *yanqui* code.

*Woodgerd,*
*Off to an Uncle Sam squid bucket. Later on, I may be like a bad penny. Remember, amigo, a stitch in time saves nine and those rolling stones don't gather any moss, especially when under a heavy enfilade.*

*Wake*

As he walked out, Wake stopped and motioned for another piece of paper, remembering the bishop. One never knew when contacts in the Catholic Church might prove helpful. Especially when things went bad.

*Bishop Mocenni,*
*Gone out of town for a while. Thank you again for the dinner. Perhaps when I return I can reciprocate.*

*Wake*

The Marine sentry knocked three times on the cabin door and opened it, calling out Wake's presence as he entered the admiral's quarters. Taking a deep breath, Wake tried to project confidence as he strode inside. He was about to meet some of the men, all of whom outranked him, who were assembled to implement an effort he had suggested months earlier in an office ten thousand miles away in Washington. While coming to attention in the center of the cabin, Wake quickly surveyed his superiors.

Sixty-one-year-old Rear Admiral Thomas Holdup Stevens lounged on the transom seat beneath *Lackawanna's* great cabin stern window. He was a sailor of the old school—a midshipman three years before Wake was born, he'd served at every station and aboard most of the major ships in the United States Navy. The war against the South had given him several opportunities to distinguish himself and he became known as one of Farragut's boys—officers who had the appreciation of the great man and who did well because of it over the ensuing years.

Unlike many of his contemporaries, Stevens was without prominent fuzzy facial adornments. Wake thought that just as well. Too many older officers had disheveled whiskers that detracted from their presence and made them the butt of jokes in the fleet. Stevens, however, was still tall and handsome, his hairline receding graciously over trimmed sideburns and moustache, the jaw and eyes as firm as ever. He was a man you knew at once was not to be trifled with, by word or deed. He glanced at Wake, then went back to studying a paper in his hand.

The flag captain of the squadron was Commander Edward Terry, who sat on the starboard bunk, holding a glass of orange juice. Wake's age, Terry was young and junior in rank for the assignment, which he had held for two years. Another of

Farragut's boys—he and Stevens had fought at Mobile Bay with Farragut and emerged heroes—Terry was an up and comer in the navy with a good reputation as a thinker. Wake had met him at an ordnance meeting three years earlier when Terry was commandant of midshipmen at Annapolis.

Terry nodded to Wake and smiled, gesturing for him to sit on the ladder-back chair by the front of the admiral's desk. Wake remained at attention and made the time-honored announcement, "Lieutenant Commander Peter Wake, on special assignment as neutral naval observer, reporting as ordered, sir." Then he sat in the chair, at attention.

Christiancy was in a leather and cane rocker beside the desk. He, in contrast to the others, looked distinctly unhappy, a frown dominating his face. Wake thought he heard some mumbling come from the diplomat, but wasn't sure.

Stevens put down the paper. "Commander Wake, you are ordered to assist us in this mission to hopefully end this silly war. Mr. Christiancy will lead the effort and you and I, with Commander Terry here, will provide support. Edward, do you have his orders?"

Terry handed over the dark blue envelope to Wake. Stevens went on.

"I understand you have some idea of this mission?"

"Well, sir, I know what it was conceived as, many months ago in Washington: the use of the U.S. Navy to provide a neutral platform for peace talks between the countries at war. Should also boost our stature in the region."

"Yes, that's it in a nutshell—"

Christiancy interrupted, the frown turning to a glare. "Has this got to do with that private talk you had with the president, Wake?"

Stevens and Terry leaned forward, the admiral with a bemused look. Wake was mightily tired of the State Department types and replied as nonchalantly as he could. "Which president are you referring to, sir?"

"Which president! Good God above, man, how many are there? I was referring to your *tête-à-tête* with Piérola at that soirée, Wake. Who were you talking about?"

"Oh, that talk. Yes, it does have something to do with that, sir. I thought you might be speaking of President Hayes, though. It has something to do with my conversation with him, also. Earlier in the year, at President Hayes' request, I gave him my opinion of the situation here. That was before your arrival here, sir. The talk with Piérola was a private message from Hayes concerning mediation."

Christiancy's face went red. Looking like he was about to have a heart attack, he managed to stammer out, "The navy is transmitting presidential messages. That is *not* the province of the navy at all. It's the duty of the State Department to see to our foreign affairs and maintain diplomatic relations!"

Stevens interjected. "Now, Mr. Christiancy, let's not have a conniption about this. In the envelope I gave you, which was in Washington a few weeks ago, it'll explain the foundations of this endeavor and how it's to unfold. We are here to help *you* on this. And for your information, sir, the United States Navy has, does, and will continue to, frequently represent the nation in foreign affairs. Of course, I know you are new to all this, and new to a distant overseas assignment, but your duties . . ."

Christiancy wagged a slim finger at Stevens, the jerking of his jaw-line beard accentuating his anger. "I am a former justice of the Michigan Supreme Court! Do not even start to lecture me about the legal duties of my current office. I am also a former United States senator with considerable influence in Washington and I will not stand by and play second fiddle to a . . ." he glared again at Wake, "to a *sailor*, of all things, meddling in international law. This will be protested to the highest authority in Washington—to the president himself. He personally sent me here last year!"

Stevens shrugged. "Open the envelope, Mr. Christiancy. *It came from the president.* Wake's message was secret because your telegraph traffic was and is being read. It came through the navy because that very peculiarity would impress Piérola. Tell him what you said to the Peruvian president, Commander."

Wake spoke calmly. "Sir, I told him to take our offer of mediation and negotiate the best deal he could, because the U.S. wasn't going to back Peru. We're staying neutral, even if Peru goes under. This will be Peru's last chance at limited survival."

Through clenched lips Christiancy muttered, "Everyone knows but *me?* You told me that night it was a greeting from our navy's leadership."

"The president *is* the head of our navy, sir. It wasn't a lie and I was forbidden by the president from telling anyone else the actual message at the time."

"I see. And now I am to take this convoluted *fait accompli* of a diplomatic initiative and make something of it?"

Stevens chuckled. "Yes, that's about it, wouldn't you say, Edward?"

Terry raised his glass. "Yes, sir. I do believe it is."

Christiancy drummed his fingers on the desk. "And just who, might I ask, dreamed up this idea in the first place?"

Stevens titled his head with a grin toward Wake. "Commander, would you care to elucidate Mr. Christiancy on that matter?"

"Ah, yes, sir. That would be me, sir. I was asked for my opinion by the president on what to do and gave it. And here we are now, sir."

Christiancy deflated. "Well, that beats all. We've got some uneducated junior sailor formulating foreign policy . . ."

Wake thought of Grau's last words a year earlier and retorted. "Nobody else was *doing* anything, sir. Thousands of men were dying for bird guano. I thought this was better than nothing."

Stevens stood, signifying the meeting was over. "And that, gentlemen, is that. Let's get to work."

## 22

# Good News and Bad News

*Lackawanna's* great cabin was crowded. The body heat of the assembled men couldn't be dissipated by the few ports that opened and protocol dictated that full suits and uniforms be worn. A dozen men were crammed around an elliptical table elbow to elbow, papers and files piled in front of each. Two stewards stood at the door, waiting for orders from Commander Terry, who sat on his accustomed perch at the day bunk in the forward starboard corner.

The picture-perfect view through the stern window was lost on the morose attendees, but not on Wake. Not a sign of war could be discerned in the view. Arica's colorful harbor front floated serenely in the distance, pastel buildings rising out of the gun-metal-blue calm water, as the ship rose and fell with the low swells coming in from the vast Pacific. Golden rays from a late afternoon sun highlighted the church steeple and the municipal building. The heavy dong, dong . . . dong, dong . . . dong, dong . . . of the church bells announced the hour as El Morro fortress's western-facing walls glowed amber from a shaft of sunlight. The hills beyond the town were charcoal-colored with scattered greenery, all shrouded in a shimmering mist that didn't quite reach out to the coast.

It was the 27th of October and the last session—the last opportunity to beg, coerce, or induce the parties to agree. Everyone in the cabin was exhausted after enduring a week inside a swaying cabin listening to fruitless postulating: the Bolivians quietly bewildered by it all, the Peruvians alternating between depression and anger, and the Chileans guardedly optimistic.

The smiling American diplomatic representatives included the U.S. ministers to each country, who shuffled papers into neat piles as they spoke among themselves, waiting for the session to start. Wake, standing by Terry and sweating profusely, wondered how so much paperwork could've been generated in a peace convention that was an utter failure—papers no one would ever read about an event that never came off. Would some future historian peruse them and wonder what it was all about? Why did so many die? Why didn't someone stop it? Wake took a deep breath and let it out slowly. The inane paperwork symbolized the whole effort. Talking but not listening. Writing but not reading. Peace wasn't to be, but appearances must still be kept up.

Christiancy was in charge, seated with his back to the great window, Admiral Stevens by his right side not even trying to conceal his boredom. On that side of the table were the other Americans: Kansan politico Thomas Andrew Osborn, minister to Chile; and young German-born Charles Adams, minister to poor Bolivia, a country looted from without and within.

Across from them sat the somber Latin American negotiators. Peru was represented by an older, thoughtful diplomat named Antonio Arenas and by Wake's old naval acquaintance, the stern Captain Aurelio Garcia of the *Union*. Mariano Baptista, a government functionary with a permanently sad expression, had the bad luck to represent dictator Hilarión Daza of Bolivia. Eulogio Altamirano, an official of the interior ministry, put forth the demands of Chile. None of them seemed to like the representatives of the other countries, though all were cordial with Wake and the other Americans—except Altamirano of Chile. Wake caught the man giving him sharp glances, and when they spoke, the Chilean locked eyes, as if memorizing his minutest features. Garcia told Wake one evening that Altamirano had great influence in Santiago and was once the head of the police services. He said that he too noticed the Chilean's attitude toward Wake, adding that it appeared the man was studying him for some reason.

The session opened with Christiancy giving the floor to Osborn, which had happened quite often during the talks. Osborn asked for all to state their position one more time for the clerk-stenographer. A deadpan Altamirano went first, summarizing for the tenth time that Chile regretted having to go to war against Bolivia to uphold the pre-existing commercial agreements that had been in effect, that as a result of her being forced to do so she was demanding remuneration in the form of either territory or funds, and that she was in a position to maintain the status quo or improve upon it. At the end, he let his spectacles fall on the table for dramatic effect, then sat and turned inquiringly to Baptista of Bolivia.

Baptista took a moment to fiddle with his papers. Wake noticed the hands shaking and felt sorry for the man. Humiliation in front of foreigners was nothing compared to what his supreme dictator back in La Paz would inflict when he learned that there was no negotiated end to this running sore of a war. Baptista again called for an adjustment of the previous boundaries and agreements, then glanced at the Peruvians and said no territory could be permanently lost by the allies.

Garcia stood up and spoke for Peru in his typically blunt style. Peru did not start the war. Peru came to the aid of her neighbor that was invaded. Peru had made good faith overtures for peace that had been rejected by Chile. Chile may be dominant militarily, but Peru would never surrender her land, people, or treasure to an aggressor. Then he sat down with a harrumph and joined the others in gazing expectantly at Osborn.

Osborn waited for a few seconds before standing slowly. He

said that the people of the three warring countries, and of the United States, were desperate for an end to the bloodshed. Perhaps they could not arrive at a perfect solution, but at least some kind of *ending*. He lamented the failure and predicted negative consequences for all the men in the room. Osborn then slumped down into his seat and sighed.

Wake thought Osborn's effort lame. The man clearly had no influence with the Chileans, who made it obvious that they were not there to negotiate, but to dictate. Wake thought Osborn could've been more blunt, should have used the only threat the U.S. had—sanctions and public opinion. It might not have produced any leverage, but now they would never know. Osborn would return to Santiago with the Chileans comfortably, having not alienated them. It all bore out what Wake had long thought—in-country envoys took on the views of their hosts.

Christiancy, not even rising, pronounced the peace convention over and wished everyone a safe return home. No one replied beyond a mumble, instead stuffing their papers in valises as quickly as they could and leaving the cabin. Admiral Stevens got Wake's attention and gestured for him to stay.

When the others had left, there was only the admiral, Terry, Wake and Christiancy in the cabin. Stevens lost no time.

"All right, we tried. It was a foregone conclusion but, as Commander Wake said when we started, somebody had try something to stop this stupid war." He saw Christiancy about to speak and waved him down. "Now . . . the important point is what do we do from here out? I don't know what *you* will do, Mr. Christiancy, but here is what *we* will do.

"The navy will stay on the Peruvian coast. *Pensacola* will stay at Callao, *Lackawanna* down here at Arica. *Richmond* will stay on the northern coast and also transit between Peru and Panama. Commander Terry and I will be aboard *Pensacola*. Lieutenant Commander Wake will be the U.S. naval liaison officer ashore in the Callao-Lima area.

"By my view, there will be action—lots of action—in the near future, and we need to be close by to assist Americans caught in the war and protect our national commercial interests. It goes without saying that if you need us, we'll be there, Mr. Christiancy. Any questions, gentlemen?"

There weren't any. Each man knew things would get far more difficult for them, and for Americans in Peru, in the next several months. Christancy muttered his thanks for the hospitality and retired from the cabin. Wake made his way up to the main deck and leaned against the port rail, gazing at the brown coast a mile away. Two of the ship's boats, flying large U.S. flags, were being rowed from *Lackawanna* toward the docks—one with the Chilean envoys and the other with the Bolivian. The Peruvians were riding back to Lima aboard the ship. It promised to be a gloomy passage.

Wake was certain he'd been right in suggesting this effort, even as he knew if would most probably fail. Still, he felt deflated and closed his eyes for a moment. The face of Admiral Grau swam into mental focus and he jerked awake with a shudder. The time for talking was over.

"Nothing doing, eh?" said Woodgerd, downing his lukewarm beer. It was two days after *Lackawanna* had returned from the peace talks. He and Wake were the only *gringos* in the dimly lit stone-walled tavern outside the central barracks in Lima. Named the "San Sebastian" for the patron saint of soldiers, the building must have been at least three centuries old, Wake guessed. The colonel ignored the stares of the other patrons, most of whom were tradesmen, and pounded his empty on the table.

"Unfortunately, no joy on the *Lackawanna*," Wake said as he called for two more bottles. "No one came to the damn thing to compromise, just give a statement and sit there. They had a chance to end this whole friggin' tragedy, but just sat there and watched it slip away."

"Aw hell, cheer up, buddy. You tried. At least you got 'em together. That's more than the fancy pants boys ever managed to do. Besides, amigo, you're not the one who just was told he's headed to the front with a regiment in the last of the special reserves. Piérola's idea. Thinks my *stalwart* demeanor will rally the troops."

Wake looked askance at him. "Special reserves? That sounds pretty 'fancy pants' to me."

"Yeah, it does. Officially part of the Fifth Special Reserve Division, under General Cáceres. *He's* not too bad. Got some guts. But the force itself sounds a helluva lot more grandiose than what it actually is—the dregs of the army. Deserters, thieves, new conscripts, busted-down NCOs, old militiamen, wet-eared officer cadets, and elderly officers that last saw combat half a century ago. Very impressive against Chilean Gatling guns and Armstrong artillery, don't you think?"

"Ah yes, a glorious charge into the abyss . . ."

"You've got it. Just the thing to create another legend for future school children."

Wake nodded sympathetically. "Hmm—that does sound damned glorious. Ya know, they do *glorious* pretty well down here. But the only problem, amigo, is that *you'll* be there with them."

"Yeah, precisely. I am rather good at killing, Peter, but I really don't do stupid suicidal gestures particularly well." Woodgerd paused, his brows pensively raised as he downed another gulp. "At least it should be damned interesting."

Wake saw Woodgerd's face tighten as the colonel finished the latest bottle and put it in the line of empties on the table. Word had it that the defensive lines were collapsing everywhere, with the Chileans advancing not just up the coast but even inland. The mercenary was being sent on an impossible mission, and he knew it.

"What're you going to do, Mike?"

Woodgerd tilted his head back and studied the roughly hewn beams.

"Hell if I know, squid. But I'll think of something brilliant. I usually do." He signaled for more beer. "You'll be outta here soon, right?"

"Supposed to leave sometime soon. The naval end of this is over."

Woodgerd lost his sarcasm. "Can you take a letter and get it to my wife?"

Commander Terry's cabin was far less spacious than the admiral's. Having a flag officer aboard meant the captain lost his regal domain and took the executive officer's cabin, less than a quarter the size of the one farther aft. Wake entered it not knowing the reason for the summons. Terry sat at the small desk built into the bulkhead.

"Hello, Peter. Anything new ashore?"

"No, sir. Same as in my report on Tuesday—continuation of the same general military theme. The Peruvian defensive lines are shrinking on the southern front, with the Third Division extending to the left inland. The Fifth Reserves just got to the front and are already being used as mobile reinforcements or rearguards. Most of the Peruvian army is falling back toward the prepared positions at San Juan and Miraflores, where it looks like the main battle will be fought. General Baquedano's Chilean forces are only about twenty or thirty miles away from the main city. They appear to be taking their time, keeping the retreating Peruvian units under pressure, and bringing up their supply trains in good order with them. Baquedano's doing it right by the book."

"Political situation in Lima?"

"Government is intact, sir. No sign of a coup d'état. Piérola is still in charge and showing confidence, but the civil situation is grim. People are scared. Many are leaving or getting ready to. Refugees are clogging the roads north out of the city. Money value is inflating and bartering is taking over. Been some banditry in the city. Martial law has helped a bit, but still there is a lack of security since most troops are at the front."

"Thank you. It's a mess no matter what happens." Terry indicated the lone other chair. "Sit down, Peter. I've got good news and bad for you. Which do you want first?"

Wake had worried about this. It was the last day of October and he'd had no news, either family or naval, from Washington for weeks. The telegraph lines were down but there should've been orders via ship by now for his return to headquarters. And at least two letters from Linda.

"Bad, sir."

"All right. *Richmond* just arrived from Panama with mail. You have orders finally, and I've received command copies of them. You're to stay here, ashore, and monitor events. Your contacts in the Peruvian military and government are providing the best information we're getting. You've made yourself indispensable, Peter. My impression is that your reports are being read at the highest level. I don't quite understand who your acquaintances are in Washington, but whoever the hell they are, they want you to stay here and keep writing those reports."

Wake had been afraid of this. *Richmond* was making nonstop transits to and from Panama, carrying Americans fleeing Peru and Wake's reports since the telegraph lines had gotten unreliable. "How long, sir?"

"Until this is over."

Wake struggled not to show his dismay. "Ah . . . yes, sir. Aye, aye, sir." He was trying to figure out how to write Linda he wouldn't be home for Christmas. He suddenly saw that Terry was saying something.

" . . . Peter. Well?"

"I'm very sorry, sir. My mind was on my wife and family.

What did you say, sir?"

"I said do you want the good news?"

Wake couldn't imagine any good news. "Ah, yes, sir."

"Here are two letters from your wife." He handed the envelopes over. "And you've got a visitor. An old friend and shipmate. Came aboard yesterday before you got back from the front."

"A visitor, sir?"

"A rather determined bosun's mate named Rork. Wrangled a transfer to this squadron from *Shenandoah* off Argentina, transited the Horn with a merchant ship and ended up here. Insisted to his new division officer that he be allowed to say hello to you whenever you arrived aboard. Officer of the deck has him standing by now."

Wake jumped to his feet, forgetting naval courtesy. "Sean Rork is here? Well, I'll be damned . . ."

Five minutes later he and Rork were on the foredeck; petty officers, even senior ones like Rork, did not have nonnaval conversations with commissioned officers aft of the main mast. Grinning as they exchanged greetings and caught up on what all had happened to them since the spring, the two men were a rare sight in the disciplined world of the navy. Commander Terry looked on from the quarterdeck, remembering Wake's reputation among the lower ranks, pondering if that kind of relationship with enlisted men was good or bad for good naval order.

## 23

# Fish out of Water

## December 1880

An ominous feeling he couldn't define and wasn't able to shake had settled over Wake. On the face of it—things were the same and he was doing his job well. Each week, Wake would spend three days at Peruvian army headquarters, then travel to the ship to report personal observations of the land war. It was laborious, but at least kept his mind occupied. Admiral Stevens and Commander Terry appreciated the intelligence, which was shuttled north to Panama by ship and thence onto Washington by submarine telegraph cable. Stevens even indicated that the reports were being read at the highest levels. However, Wake noticed signs that things were changing politically. The inevitable outcome was certain and American interest was waning.

In mid-November *Richmond* departed to join *Ticonderoga* in the Asiatic Squadron. *Lackawanna* was rumored to be the next to go to the Orient, leaving only *Pensacola* on the station. Relations were tensing up with the Hermit Kingdom of Korea again, this time with Japan more actively involved. Consequently, the

American presence at the South American conflict was diminishing. In addition, Wake received fewer return communiqués from Washington about his reports and no requests for further specific information beyond his usual accounts. It seemed that his presidential message to Piérola four months earlier was being realized. Peru's imminent fall was a foregone conclusion in Washington. And no one cared anymore.

Then Garfield won the election. By early December he started setting the scene for a new foreign policy toward Latin America once he would be inaugurated in March. The whispered secretary of state–to-be, one-time presidential rival Blaine, favored a slightly more pro-Peruvian stance. Wake thought it too little too late. By the time the new administration took office it would all be over. Still, it was enough to buoy spirits in Lima and trigger scowls in Santiago.

So Wake played the game, as he thought of it at that point, sending the best intelligence he could to the decision-makers. On his trips ashore he saw Woodgerd frequently now. The glorious charge hadn't materialized but the mercenary colonel was busy drilling his ragtag troops for the Armageddon he was sure would come.

Wake also spoke with Rork aboard *Pensacola*. In a late-night session by the bowsprit, the bosun told him that yes, he did flee Sheila by volunteering for a distant station, and he was "damned happy about it. 'Twas a near thing, too near." Rork settled into the monotonous routine of a senior petty officer aboard a warship at anchor for long periods, but soon he was bored and asked Wake to go ashore as his aide and bodyguard. Glad to have him along, Wake arranged it with Commander Terry, suggesting that the ship didn't really need Rork while at anchor. Like most ship captains, the commander was reluctant to lose experienced men, but he grudgingly went along with it.

The real concern in Wake's mind was Linda. The last letter finally hinted at the problem she wouldn't write about in earlier letters. Wake was sure she was not telling him everything, even though he had asked pointedly about her pains in his letters home.

*Dear Peter,*                   *November 10th, 1880*
*All are well here. Useppa is in high excitement about Garfield winning the election, with predictions about all it means. Sean is engaged in sports, including that new one called football that looks far too dangerous to me. He has your love of adventure, I fear, and I hope he doesn't get hurt. They play frightfully rough.*

*Sheila is over Sean Rork now, she has a new civilian beau who works in the treasury. Says he will be the head of something or other someday and they will live famously well. Evidently the man in question doesn't know her plans for him.*

*Dearest darling, I understand by now, after all these years as a navy wife, that duty comes first and that situations change, but that doesn't make my desolation over another Christmas without you any less. I worry about you—your jokes about "paper cuts" being the most dangerous part of your assignment notwithstanding. Be careful. I also miss you terribly, as only a wife can miss a husband.*

*You've asked in your letters how I am doing with the stomach pains. Well, I've found out with no surprise that navy doctors don't have much experience with ladies' ailments, but the doctors at Howard University are very knowledgeable about such things and have set up a regimen to make me better. Won't take up space on this page with details, but I hope to be cured of the pains and good as new (remember that far back?) by the time you get home. But you, of course, will be the very best medicine for this lonely island girl.*

*Dreaming of you here beside me,*
*Linda*

Wake put the letter away with the others and concentrated on the issue at hand. He and Rork were going ashore to army headquarters with the quest of determining how much longer the Peruvian army could hold out. For the previous year, he had observed the war unfold with professional interest. Now it was different. The fall of Lima, and therefore Peru, would have personal consequences for Wake. He could go home to Linda.

A two-hour downpour, unusual for that time of year, had turned the road from powdered sand into chocolate slime, kneaded ankle-deep from thousands of Peruvian feet, hooves, and wheels heading north after the latest defeat at Cañete. One glance at the column told the story.

It was a drab collection of mostly Indians and half-Indians, faces downcast as they plodded through the sucking ooze, pressed into service for a country they could not comprehend, led by officers whose Spanish they did not understand, and clothed in torn remnants of uncomfortable new uniforms they chafed at wearing. Only one of three had retained his weapon, fewer than that had stayed with their assigned unit. Officers rode on emaciated horses. The dazed wounded walked or died where they fell.

Wake heard no orders given, no shouts, no curses from the men—no human sounds at all. Only the clinking of wagon tongues and traces, and the slopping plop of booted feet in and out of the mud. The retreating men trudged north, knowing only that north was the direction away from the enemy's modern killing machines that had eaten them man by man for the past four months—killing machines that could not be stopped, that kept coming north. The hollow look in their eyes showed they had seen more than they would ever be able to convey.

Heading south along the edge of the road, Wake rode on an old sway-backed mare. Rork followed on a nearly dead mule by the name of Pepe that stumbled constantly but somehow kept going. Neither of them was a skilled rider. The bosun, who distrusted anything like a horse, swore creatively in Gaelic and English about Pepe's ancestry, making Wake smile. Rork could always be relied upon to relieve a tense or maudlin moment.

They couldn't find the headquarters of General Cáceres, or anyone who knew exactly where it was. One major said there was a rumor it was in the town of Barranco, a few kilometers back up the road to the north. The man seemed confused and unsteady on his feet, so Wake ignored him and pressed on to the south. But gradually, as they rode against the ebb tide of demoralized soldiers, he considered turning around. He didn't like at all what was he was seeing.

He talked it over with Rork. In the end, curiosity prevailed. Very well, he reasoned, just one more hill where they could see out to the south and then they'd head west to the beach and north along the coast. He wasn't going to get caught in the column of men crawling up the road if the Chilean cavalry swept down on them. There was little quarter given in this war so far, and he doubted if anyone on either side cared that he and Rork were officially neutral. Anyway, he and Rork could go faster along the shoreline and, as sailors, would naturally feel more comfortable near the sea.

They rounded a bend in the road near a farm and heard heavy thuds ahead. Cannon fire—heavier than the usual field artillery twelve-pounders, Rork opined. Then came the lighter staccato burst of a Gatling. The mud-covered column heading north showed no reaction and continued wading through the mire. Rork caught Wake's eye and pointed to the southeast, in the hills away from the coast. Another line of men was heading south down a path toward the road. Peruvian soldiers, heading *toward* the enemy. It would intersect half a mile to the south. Wake immediately saw it hadn't been involved in the disaster at Cañete—it was marching in regimental formation, weapons were held at the ready, bayonets fixed.

It was useless to try to get the mounts to speed up, they weren't physically able, so the Americans kept their steady pace. Wake studied the approaching regiment closely and guessed whose it was. At the road intersection he was proven right.

"Well, I do declare," roared Woodgerd with a huge grin,

incongruous with the surroundings. "You show up at the damnedest places, squid. Is that Rork I see? The two of you in the middle of nowhere? All right, *now* I'm worried."

Behind him the regiment marched by, looking serious and disciplined, completely the opposite of the column of broken men retreating up the road to the rear. The end of the line was coming up, the fright on their faces stark and unnerving to Wake. Beyond them there was no one else in sight, but the sound of hooves could be heard.

"Enchanted, as always, to see you too, Mike," answered Wake, submerging his fear in the same light vein. Rork and Woodgerd nodded hello and shook hands. They'd last seen each other in Africa.

Wake swept his arm around the scene. "I see the war is going along quite nicely for you. Headed for the victory parade in Santiago? Or possibly a glorious infantry charge someplace?"

"No, not quite either. Gonna provide rear-guard for the army and keep the Chilis at bay for a while. What are *you* doing here?"

"Oh, the same old thing. Observing the action, providing quality reports to the leadership that they'll ignore."

"My, my, Peter—that sounded positively sarcastic. Well, the *action* is about to happen right here and now, my friend. The Chilis'll have cavalry heading over that crest any minute. You might want to skedaddle outta here. Can't make the report if you're dead."

Shots banged out in the direction of the hill he had indicated. The Gatling went off again down the road. Wake thought it sounded closer. He realized Woodgerd was right.

"Good point, Mike. Think we'll head back to Barranco. Go back with a report tomorrow. Where's your army headquarters?"

"Last I heard General Cáceres set up shop around Barranco, but he may have withdrawn by now."

"Where the hell's your artillery and cavalry, Mike? How're you going to stop anyone with just infantry?"

"Carefully. Very carefully. The arty and horsy boys are gone.

All headed back to the trenches at Miraflores and Chorillos." The Gatling rattled again, now joined by another on the eastern flank. "Look, you'd better get going *now*, Peter. I'm not sure how long we can hold them up. And we are the last of the last. This ain't no place for a squid."

He suddenly looked tired to Wake. "Right. We're off. Good luck, Mike."

Woodgerd didn't reply. He'd already turned and was giving orders in his badly accented Spanish, deploying the regiment by companies in line abreast. They were to dig in just below the crest on the other side of the rise.

Wake and Rork didn't hesitate, they left the road and cut west across the fields, toward the sea four miles distant. They'd gotten about a mile when they heard volleys of rifle fire.

"Them'd be Springfields, sir," said Rork. "That seventy-three model with the big powder charge. Big bang, even bigger hole. Same as what our army lads use."

"Then that's Woodgerd's men. The Chileans are using British Enfields," Wake said. Both knew Custer had used Springfields in his last infamous battle, but neither brought that subject up.

"He'll do well, sir. He's a right tough bird, the colonel is."

Wake saw smoke behind them. He couldn't see any details because of the distance. Sporadic rifle fire popped. Several Gatlings sounded from different directions, the concentrated fusillades of gunfire terrifying even at that distance. Wake's mind visualized the men dying back there. His hands trembled. He forced himself to think. This wasn't neutral observing anymore. This was survival.

"All right, Rork, there're rocky headlands jutting out from the beaches in this area. If we went up the beach, one of them could cut off our course, so on second thought let's stay just inland from the beach and find a path going north."

"Very good, sir. Lead on an' I'll get this ol' nag to follow." Rork looked around the landscape and wearily shook his head. "Say, I don't suppose they'll be a bit o' ale back in Barranco for a couple o' thirsty fish out o' water, do ye think?"

"The hell with ale, Rork. I could use some decent rum at this point."

"Aye, then rum it is, sir. An' first tumbler's on you, of course." He gave Wake the devilish grin he was famous for. "You bein' the *officer* an' all . . ."

## 24

# Divine Providence

Wake had never seen Kronburg agitated, instead the man always appeared unruffled and superior. But now the bureaucrat was absolutely frantic with questions as the naval officer walked through the legation's front door into the anteroom. Where was the front located? How long could it hold? Would the *Pensacola* send Marines into Lima to rescue the diplomatic community and American citizens? Where in the world was the navy! Oh my God, should the reception be cancelled for that evening?

As Rork stood stoically at parade rest by the door, Wake responded.

"First of all, Kronburg, gather yourself together and stop whining like a little girl. Act like a professional and do your job, whatever the hell that is. Now, I don't have much time and I need to brief the minister, but here are the short answers: the battle lines are just south of the city near San Juan and Chorrillos; they can hold for maybe ten or twelve days at the most or they could fall apart at any minute; *Pensacola* doesn't have enough men to rescue anybody; Congress never voted us the budget to build an adequate fleet, so no—the navy isn't here in strength. And I don't give one iota of damn what *you* do tonight."

Wake then strode out of the room, past the empty clerks' desks and up the stairs to Christiancy's office, where he walked into the envoy's office. Christiancy sat staring out the window. Seeing Wake enter he absentmindedly greeted him, then apologized for forgetting his manners and not rising. In that instant, Wake felt a surge of sympathy for the dignified old politician from Indiana, wondering if Christiancy regretted his decision to flee Washington and end up in this tiny office in a strange culture. The man appeared suddenly far older than even his advanced years, aged by being thrust into representing the United States in a modern war zone of swirling political machinations and frightful military devastation.

The Chilean juggernaut had come twelve hundred miles across some of the most hostile terrain in the world. The deserts and mountains that Lima had counted on to gradually weaken the enemy were bypassed in naval landings leapfrogging up the coast. It was a war unlike anything anyone had seen, but now it had faded on the American political agenda, and men like Christiancy were left to salvage what they could, literally.

Wake had no time to waste. "Sir, the final stage had arrived. The Chileans are surrounding Lima. Enemy infantry has extended their flanks to the east and north, cavalry just cut off the mountain road to Pasco in the interior, and the last road out of the capital, to Huaras in the north by way of the coastal road through Chanca, is in danger of falling at any moment."

"What—so soon? But just yesterday President Piérola said—"

Wake cut him off. "Piérola's not at the front. I was. I recommend the foreign legations get out, right now, if they're going by way of that last road. By tonight it might be too late. Of course, the French and British diplomatic staffs can go out to their warships. The people in our legation can do the same. But I urge you to make plans for that now, sir."

"What about Cáceres? Is he—'

"General Cáceres is doing his best but he's overwhelmed. If

you're going by the land route, get out now, sir. If you want to get out to our ship, likewise."

Christiancy couldn't grasp the suddenness of the collapse. He looked back out the window as Kronburg came in, ignoring Wake to speak to his boss. "Sir, due to the unpleasantness of the current news, I've cancelled the reception for tonight. Just so you know, sir, the Italian, Colombian, and Spanish legations are talking about possibly relocating in another city. I'm also hearing that the Piérola government is thinking of doing the same. I imagine the British and probably the French will go out to their ships."

Wake stood. "Well, sir, there's nothing more to report. We've all done everything we could. It's out of our hands now. I wish you luck. *Pensacola* will keep a boat in the harbor near the commercial dock as long as possible to carry you off, but don't wait too long. Once the lines break it will only be hours before the Chileans are in the city."

"Commander, really now, you're acting like they are uncivilized barbarians. I'm sure they wouldn't behave contrary to international law."

Wake was at the doorway, but paused long enough to say, "Their generals and senior people are gentlemen. The common soldiers, no. They view this place as a rich city full of plunder ripe for the taking. Look what happened down at Arica and other places on the coast. Discipline will disappear, a mob mentality takes over, and anyone who gets in their way gets killed. And I wonder about the local Chinese, too. I'm hearing that many are pro-Chilean. Yes, sir, this city will be looted and once that starts, Mr. Christiancy, diplomatic immunity is just a word. Doesn't mean much for a dead body."

"Yes . . . well, thank you, Commander."

Wake left the two men discussing how to pack the office. He and Rork walked out of the building, hailed a cab and paid four times the usual rate to get to Callao naval station, the driver insisting on American money. Hysteria was evident everywhere around them as they slowly made their way through the city—

streets jammed with vehicles, drivers screaming epithets; worried policemen trying to make sense out of the snarled traffic; frightened mothers with their children walking toward the outskirts, carrying everything they owned; imperious upper class *caballeros* leaning out of their carriages, scowling at their drivers; crazed renegades, obviously drunk, running to or from something.

As they clopped through the bricked streets, Rork's right hand rested on the butt of the revolver in his belt as he scanned back and forth watching for robbery threats. Wake noticed without comment that his friend's eyes were sad. The bosun let out his breath as he looked out over the scene, "Saw the same thing in China durin' one o' their local wars few years back, sir. Bad times comin' for these folks."

Back aboard the warship, anchored even farther off the harbor in an effort to stay out of the immediate battle zone, as were the British and French, Wake presented his report to Admiral Stevens and Commander Terry. Both were stone-faced as he described the situation at the front and in the city. *Pensacola* had only a handful of Marines and sailors to spare for a landing party if it came to rescuing the legation. Stevens folded his hands as he leaned back in his chair.

"Hmm. I don't like this at all. Seems these damned politicos will probably dither until it's too damned late. Then we'll have to send in an armed landing party and have to fight our way through to rescue them, then fight our way back. Edward, how many can you send?"

"Twenty, sir," said Terry. "Can't take the gun crews or steam gang and I need enough to work the ship and weigh anchor."

"Well, that won't do. I'm not sending twenty men in against thousands. Commander Wake, you're going back ashore tonight with a message from me to Christiancy that tomorrow at sunrise he and his staff are getting out, whether they want to or not. I'll write it out while you get something to eat. Then you'll go."

All Wake wanted was a bunk for four hours. He was exhausted. "Aye, aye, sir."

~~

Callao was more chaotic in the dark. The few lanterns that were lit—people were saving candles and oil—dimly illuminated a well-dressed crowd of desperate people crowding the commercial piers. Ignoring shouts and curses, the Americans elbowed their way through the mob, most of whom were begging for passage out of Peru on the few tiny fishing smacks still around.

Outside the gate, Rork found a man with a small empty vegetable cart ready to leave to go to Lima. For a considerable sum, the Americans jumped on the back. Inflation had doubled again since the afternoon ride and Wake suddenly worried about the ship's account money he was spending—at this rate they'd run out quickly. Rork, as usual, tried to make light of their basic mode of transport.

"Jus' the thing, this cart is, sir. Small an' inconspicuous."

It jarred over a bump, almost tossing Wake off the back. "Next time, please look to see if it has springs, Rork."

The cart man took them by a different route into Lima, saying the main route was clogged with traffic. The night cold could really be felt and Wake pulled his coat collar tight and rubbed his arms. They went up a winding path, bouncing all the way, close to the Rimac River that led inland. Slowly the lights and sounds of the city fell behind and they were in the countryside. Wake watched for bandits and tried to navigate by the few stars visible while Rork got some much-needed rest. Like most foredeck men, the bosun could sleep anywhere, an asset Wake envied.

The path led across a rickety bamboo bridge over a canal

243

reeking of sewage. They entered a cluster of high-peaked Chinese laborer shacks—quiet at that hour, in contrast to the panic of Callao and Lima. Just then Wake noticed movement in the shadows of the huts on the right and elbowed Rork. Something was wrong. He whispered in Spanish to the driver, "Where are we?" but got no answer as the cart slowed to a stop. Three men stepped out from behind a hut, one carrying a torch. Two more materialized in the dark behind the cart. Others could be heard speaking, their language different from Spanish.

The driver jumped to the ground, turned to the Americans and took off the woolen Inca cap that had been jammed over his head. In the torchlight Wake saw the man was Oriental, presumably Chinese. He was leering at them, his face a twisted picture of hatred. Wake's mind rapidly went through the possibilities—was this an assassination? Robbery? Kidnapping? Were they working for the Chileans? Were they after *him?*

Rork stood up from the cart, hand nearing the inside of his coat. So far Wake didn't see any weapons among the Chinese. He hoped this could be defused without anyone, especially him and Rork, getting hurt.

The bosun edged closer to Wake. "Very sorry for picking this driver, sir. Couldn't see the little bugger properly when I parleyed the ride. Didn't know he was a Chinaman. One o' the pro-Chili ones, I imagine now."

"Not your fault, Rork. But please keep smiling and do *not* reach for your revolver. Let's get out of this peaceably. I think we can talk our way out."

"Aye, aye, sir. Jus' hope these lads share your optimism on that account."

The villagers closed in until they formed a circle fifty feet in diameter. Wake counted eleven against two. Several brandished clubs now. None of them spoke to the Americans. Apparently they were waiting for someone, a leader.

Wake tried Spanish. "*Vamos en paz. Norteamericanos. No estamos en la guerra.*" No response, though he knew they understood him.

Rork muttered his assessment. "Ah, it's lookin' like they don't care a damn that we came in peace an' aren't in the war, sir. By the glint in them eyes, me thinks there's a financial angle to all this. The point of the matter is whether they'll steal us blind while we're alive, or after we're dead."

The cart driver, who until then had been silent, grinned and grunted out an order. Two of the villagers swung old shotguns up from concealed positions. The muzzles seemed huge. One was pointed at Wake, the other at Rork. The gunmen smiled, enjoying the reactions of the Americans.

Wake made a decision, knowing Rork would understand and follow instantly. He whispered "port and starboard," then fell off the cart to the left, drawing his revolver. Rork dove to the right. Two blasts simultaneously roared in the night, the tongues of flame lashing three feet out from the shotguns and lighting up a tableau of shocked faces around the circle.

Wake got off three rounds toward his assailant. Rork fired two toward his. Both then fired around the circle as the cart mule screamed in pain from the shotgun pellets that ripped into his body. Wake yelled, "reloading," and Rork fired again to cover his friend. Someone cried out in Chinese, obviously hit. Then Wake fired two times at the cart driver's face and Rork reloaded and fired twice at the fleeing crowd. Each had carried eighteen rounds going ashore. They were now down to about ten each as they huddled under the cart, facing out either side. The shotgun men lay crumpled twenty feet away. One moaned frightfully, muttering in Chinese. Another man was on the ground closer to them, not moving, his head at an odd angle. It was the cart driver.

In the commotion the torch fell on the ground, dousing the light. Complete darkness covered the scene; the only sense left was sound. Angry threats in sing-song Chinese pierced the night as Wake thought about putting the screaming mule out of his misery. He made his way by sound to the mule and fired a round, then reloaded with his last spare ammunition. In the near distance he could hear feet running away. His night vision started to return and he whispered to Rork, "What do you see?"

"Buggers're gone, sir. Headman's dead. I suggest we weigh anchor an' get the hell out of here, posthaste like. Their friends'll be arrivin' soon."

"All right, we'll get back to the river and follow it east, then come around the village and back to the path. That should take us into Lima."

They ran back down the pathway to the bridge, cut to the right and skirted the canal to the river, swinging wide around the village and moving deliberately, alert for any further ambush. Other than occasional shouts in the village they heard nothing and saw nothing suspicious. A mile to the east they were back on the path, walking fast toward the loom of the city. Behind them on the coast, the thump, thump, thump of heavy guns could be heard—the Chilean fleet at work.

The path entered Lima from a different direction than Wake was accustomed to, running along a dual railroad track and ending up near the big railroad depot at Santa Rosa—the place empty since the rail lines had been sealed off by the enemy. Leaving the foul stench of the river and traversing the tracks, Wake and Rork made their way carefully into the central area of the city on Calle Amazonas. Hooves and squealing wheels echoed in the streets as a constant stream of traffic passed by bound for the Tacna Bridge, but the pedestrian crowds in the city center were noticeably thinned out. As they crossed to Avenida Lampas, Rork pointed out uniformed figures a block away watching them.

Wake heard the distant thunder increase—even more guns of the Chilean fleet at Callao—and wondered if the final attack had begun. There was no time to dawdle, they needed to press on. He was about to say as much to Rork when a voice came softly from the shadows of an alley near them.

"Well, I do say, such a lone pleasant surprise in this time of tribulation. Thank you, my Lord, for bringing a friend by when I needed one. Especially this one."

The Americans turned to see Bishop Mocenni standing on the sidewalk, hands on hips, obviously surprised.

Wake showed his own shock at seeing the Papal envoy in the dark. "Bishop . . . hello, sir, but what are you doing out on the street at ten o'clock at night?"

"Taking my evening stroll, my son. But why, pray tell, are *you* out, tonight of all nights? And who is your friend?"

"We're delivering a message to the legation. Forgive my manners, sir, this is Sean Rork, Bosun's Mate, United States Navy. Sean, this is Bishop Mario Mocenni."

Rork stepped forward and bowed slightly, something Wake had never seen him do. Then Rork said, "Commander Wake mentioned to me he had met the Papal delegate to Peru, sir. 'Tis an honor to meet Your Excellency."

Mocenni smiled. "Well, well. I hear by your accent that you must be a son of that sainted isle in the Atlantic Ocean. And a faithful son of the mother Church as well, might I conclude, sir?"

"Aye, that I am—on both accounts, Your Excellency."

"Good! Then I shall invoke Catholic loyalty. Truly, divine providence has led you both to me, particularly *tonight* of all nights. Perhaps I can enlist your support in an endeavor that may require the assistance of two brave young Americans. I would not ask lightly, but it is a matter of some importance, possibly of life and death. And then this evening, with all that is happening, of all people, I see you gentlemen. Well, I think you will soon understand why."

Wake was amazed when Rork bowed again—his friend was acting positively courtly. "Of course, sir. Just let us know how we can help, an' it'll be done."

Mocenni clapped his hands in delight. "Wonderful. Thank you so very much, my son."

Wake stood there watching the conversation, amazed as Rork

pledged them to some unexplained commitment. He was nervous and exhausted, with no sense of patience left in him. It was time to regain control of the situation and bring Rork back to his senses. "Bishop, I'm sorry, but we're both already busy with a serious duty. Maybe we can help later."

Mocenni's smile faded. "Oh dear, I really needed you now, my son. Time is of the essence. It won't take long, I promise."

Rork intervened. "We will help you *now,* Your Excellency."

He touched Wake's shoulder. "Commander, it's late an' the legation staff is probably asleep. The message can be delivered *after* we help the bishop, sir."

"Now Rork—"

The bosun held up a hand. He wasn't smiling anymore. "Peter, we cannot say no to the bishop. Not tonight. Not now."

"And why exactly is that, Bosun Rork!" Wake growled.

Rork turned to Mocenni. "He's been under a lot of strain, Your Excellency. Had a wee bit o' trouble this evenin' with some o' the local lads, so he probably forgot the date. Please forgive him." Then he looked at Wake.

"Because tonight is Christmas Eve, Peter."

# 25

# All in the Same Boat

Mocenni led them around the corner, down an alley, through a gate set into a wall, across a courtyard and into the Monastery of San Francisco. Inside, Wake couldn't see anyone in the gloom, but could hear footsteps echoing in different directions. Somewhere back in the cavernous interior a high-pitched chant provided an otherworldly sense, an eerie incongruousness to the chaos outside, which under the circumstances made Wake uneasy.

The old bishop walked fast, taking them through the building and out to the tranquil plaza where he and Wake had shared dinner weeks before. They followed the frescoed mezzanine around the plaza and entered an anteroom with walls covered in priceless Spanish art, Rork's head swiveling as he took it all in, then strode through the monastery's ancient library where long tapered candles cast a yellow glow around the stacks and shelves of books. An ancient Jesuit priest, bent over from age and the huge leather-bound volume in his arms, looked up angrily, muttering something as they breezed past.

Leaving the library, the three of them clattered down several sets of broad marble stairs, until they were two levels below the street and in a broad hall. Running steps echoed above them, the flopping of sandals showing it to be a priest, and they stopped. The young priest ran down the stairs, slid on the floor and breathlessly stopped in front of Mocenni. He blurted out something in rapid Latin to the bishop, who frowned and gave an order of some sort. The priest bounded back up the stairs. Mocenni glanced at the two Americans. "Complications, always complications. We live in exciting times, gentlemen."

He didn't wait for a reply, but marched across the hall and into a meeting room with long tables but no chairs, only benches set into paneled walls. At one end was an altar. Two candle sconces provided minimal light, but Wake could see the paneling contained intricate carvings of various saints. He could feel the sanctity of the room and wondered its purpose, but kept on walking fast, for the bishop never slacked his pace. Glancing back to make sure they were close behind him, Mocenni made his way around the tables and then abruptly stopped in the farthest dark corner.

Reaching up for a stout piece of the wood molding trim in the wall, he pulled one end out and downward—an unseen lever, camouflaged into the paneling. The five-foot-high panel section of the wall jolted free, hinged on one side as a door. Mocenni pushed one side open and motioned for the others to follow him. They entered a rough-hewn passage that was curiously brighter than the paneled room—an ancient oil lantern hung from a hook on the whitewashed wall, the whole effect illuminating by reflection the tunnel for some distance, perhaps sixty feet. The bishop carefully replaced the panel from the inside.

Wake began to ask where they were, but was hushed by the cleric, whose face was now grim, his eyes glittering in the dim light. Mocenni took the lantern and marched onward down the tunnel, went to the apparent end and turned sharply right, disappearing from sight. Their heads bowed beneath the dripping rock ceiling, the wary Americans followed and found the bishop making his way down a sloping passage, which narrowed until it was barely the width of a man. After a hundred feet he held up a hand and stopped, facing a crude plank door. Wake calculated they were almost forty feet below street level. Mocenni took a ring of huge keys from his inside pocket and fitted one into the iron lock, then twisted it. The door creaked with an almost human wail as he slowly opened it.

The bishop stepped inside with the lantern, illuminating the dark space. There was no whitewash on the walls here, only a slimy narrow tunnel with shoulder-height alcoves forming shelves along the sides.

Wake paused, peering into the void and smelling a sweetly rancid stench that instantly emanated from the space and filled the passageway. Then his eyes adjusted and he recoiled, at the same time identifying the odor—decomposed bodies. Rork caught the smell and reeled back. "Oh, Lord Jesus and Mother Mary, where in the world are we?"

From the shelves, discolored skulls stared at them. Wake had heard of this place during his first visit to Lima the year before, but had discounted it as an old myth, or maybe a nightmare. Now he knew it was only too real. Far below the city of Lima they had entered a place few had ever seen in four centuries—the Catacombs of the Dead.

Rork and Wake exchanged horrified glances as Mocenni's hand emerged from the lantern's dimming glow and beckoned them urgently to step inside. "Hurry, gentlemen. I've not much time." They reluctantly obliged, Wake about to protest but keeping silent as the bishop closed the plank door behind them and locked it, encasing them in blackness aside from the tiny circle of light.

Mocenni walked down the tunnel for twenty feet, stopping in a small room with rudimentary brick half walls subdividing it. Facing the Americans he looked ghoulish, stooped over with his gaunt face and bony fingers protruding from the black robes. His usually soft voice had gained strength.

"My sons, we are now with the remains of thousands of the

departed, in the legendary Catacombs of the Dead. But there are living souls here also. Do not fear what you are about to see. God is with us. And soon you will know why I need your help."

Wake was scared, lost, and exhausted. His normal courtesy had vanished. He glared at Rork, then turned to the clergyman. "Bishop Mocenni—I need an explanation and I need it right now. This long walk had better be worth it. I don't care if it is Christmas Eve. We've got very serious things to do tonight and traipsing around down here isn't included."

Suddenly Rork gripped his elbow and pointed down, then around the room. In the large areas formed by the half walls were intricate mosaics composed of thousands of—Wake's mind registered the materials with horror—bones. All kinds of bones, some of children, arranged in patterns with long bones emanating out from skulls and pelvises. Some complex, some simple. They were everywhere he looked.

Rork swallowed hard, his eyes wide as he stammered out. "Your Excellency, what *is* it you need us for? 'Cause I'm not a fan-cyin' this one wee bit. An' the commander is sorely right. We've got to be gettin' our work done tonight." He looked pleadingly overhead. "Up there. Topside, where we belong."

Mocenni spread his arms. "I know you are both apprehensive of the surroundings, my dear sons. But fear not these mere remains of past mortals. They will not, cannot, hurt you. And the point of all this will be absolutely clear in a moment."

He gestured into the murkiness, then raised his lantern to show another door set into the far wall, crudely planked like the first. He went over and knocked two times, then once more. A moaning sound rose from a man on the other side. Wake realized it was a chant elongating the Latin words. "*Tempus fugit.*"

Rork leaned over to Wake and whispered, "What's the cater-waulin,' sir?"

"Latin for 'time flies,' " Wake whispered back, remembering Mr. Stonegall's classics classes from his childhood. At the time he'd hated Mr. Stonegall and his confounding Latin.

Mocenni knocked again, singing his own chant to the man beyond the door, "*Sic transit gloria mundi.*"

Wake struggled with that one. "*So goes earthly glory?*"

"Very good, my son," said Mocenni. "You understand our passwords. The correct translation would be 'So *passes* earthly glory.' Rather apropos, given the current political situation, yes?"

Wake nodded warily as a heavy bolt slid across the inside of the door and it squeaked open, showing a robed and hooded figure in a lamp-lit cavern. The figure's arms were folded in front, one hand clutching a long thin dagger. Mocenni ducked down and passed through the door, his two companions taking deep breaths and following.

The bishop introduced the menacing man. "This is Brother Damian. He is guarding the flock."

Damian's face was barely seen inside the hood, bushy facial hair concealing his features and giving a fierce appearance for a man of the cloth. Mocenni went on. "He is a former colleague of your profession, gentlemen—a warrior. Damian was an officer in Bismarck's army until he decided to devote his life to more peaceful endeavors, but in dire times there are still uses for his skills."

Wake was weary of the theatrics and wanted this over. "I'm tired of the games and we're leaving."

Mocenni simply pointed behind Wake and Rork and said, "*There* is the reason for the complicated journey and subterfuge tonight."

Wake scowled, about to utter an oath in anger, but Rork turned him around. The bosun shook his head and gasped, "Oh, Lord, what have I gotten us into now?"

Staring back at the men were a hundred tiny faces reflected in the lamps' glow. Chinese faces with pleading eyes. Wake saw that many of the children were sitting on bone mosaics that covered the floor. Leg and arm bones were arranged on shelf alcoves around the walls. It was a ghastly scene.

Mocenni stepped forward and spoke softly in Spanish.

"My children, remember what tonight is?" He took out a

pocket watch and held it up to the light. "Ah, and now it is almost midnight, so I think we can sing the song for our guests you have been practicing with Brother Damian. These men are friends of mine and they are here to help us. You will be safe with them. Ready? Now, let us sing this special song for them. . . ."

A hundred little bodies squirmed, then their voices lilted up in chorus, filling the room with a gentle rendition of "*Noche de Paz,*" the Spanish version of "Silent Night." A vision of his wife and children came to Wake and he felt the tears come. Rork looked away and dabbed his own eyes.

When it ended, Mocenni thanked the children in Spanish. Then in English he told Wake and Rork, "Brother Damian taught them that song from his youth. It was written sixty years ago near his hometown of Salzburg."

The bishop's frail hand rested on Wake's shoulder. "Commander, these children, these one hundred and seven little Chinese-Peruvian girls and boys, can be your family tonight. They need you and I think that in no small way, tonight you need them."

Wake sighed, already certain of the request and calculating how much food he could get to the children. The bishop had him and he knew it.

"All right, sir. How can I help?"

"It is simple, but not easy. Allow me to explain. These children's parents were Chinese laborers who emigrated to Peru two generations ago. Their families lived in the south, near Arica and worked in the mines. Over the years some Chinese, like the families of these children, converted to Christianity. When the Chileans invaded, these Chinese, unlike so many, stayed loyal to Peru. Their parents were killed by pro-Chilean Chinese gangs and in the ensuing confusion these children—the only *living witnesses* to that tragedy—were smuggled out of that area by priests and brought here. They have lived here, in this ancient sepulcher of the dead, this place no child should ever have to see, for three months.

"We kept them secret, knowing they are in danger even here in the capital, from enemy Chinese spies or from Chilean military forces should they occupy the city. When the Chileans' Chinese gangsters do find these children, they will probably be killed to prevent the atrocity from coming out in a court, no doubt *ostensibly* killed by a regrettable accident of war. Now, sadly, that fear is coming to reality. The city is surrounded and gangs are days or hours away from finding this hiding place. The children need to get out."

Wake started to feel his knees buckle. Mocenni smiled. "*You* will get them out."

Rork whistled in amazement. Wake took in a breath. "Look Bishop, that's impossible. I can't take them on a warship. They won't be allowed aboard."

"Yes, I know that," said Mocenni. "But I have faith that you will find a way for them to escape. They can't go by land now, it is closed, the sea is the only route."

The enormity of it hit Wake. The bishop didn't understand. Wake couldn't get them out. "Bishop, I appreciate their plight, but I can't do anything for them. No naval vessels will take them."

"Yes, I know that. It is because of their race, Commander. I know that too. If they were American or European children the naval ships would take them. But they are merely Orientals, and no one will lift a finger to help them escape their impending death. Except you."

Wake saw that the children were following the conversation, understanding the facial expressions, the gestures, knowing their fate was in the hands of this stranger in uniform. He felt the walls closing in.

"Why me, Bishop? If you know I can't get them aboard a warship, then why me?"

"Because my brothers in Christ have told me you are a man who does the right thing, even when it is inconvenient, or dangerous. Yes, yes, we know you are not of our Holy Church, but we also know you are a Christian and will not fail these children."

"Who is this *we*? You mean Bishop Vargas of Panama? He's in on this?"

Mocenni shrugged. "Of course. And Bishop Ferro of Genoa and Father Muñosa of Sevilla. You have friends among the Jesuits, Peter. When I needed help, they suggested you in their letters."

"But I met Bishop Vargas back in Panama. That was months ago. The others were *years* ago."

"Peter, I have been aware of you for more than a year, ever since your first visit here as a naval observer. How, my friend, do you think Bishop Vargas up in Panama knew to warn you about the Chilean threat to your life? I learned of it and passed it along to him."

Wake saw Rork looking at him oddly and said, "It's long story. I'll tell you later."

Mocenni went on, "And it is not just recently, here in Latin America. Remember six years ago, that little incident at the castle in Porto Fino when you found yourself in a very compromising position—who do you think got you out of it? Yes, Bishop Ferro. Of course, I suppose I don't have to tell you about how Father Muñosa saved you in Sevilla."

"I had no idea you were all in correspondence about me. Me . . ."

"Not just you, Peter Wake. We have many friends, all over the world, who have special skills that come in very useful at the most ominous times. This is your time."

Wake struggled to keep it in professional perspective. There must be a way. "You said the sea is the only way. Is the road north to Chanca closed?"

"A report from one of our parishes north of the city says it closed a few hours ago, around sunset. Chilean forces arrived on the scene and forced the refugees back into the city."

"Well, then you're right. The sea is the only way. There aren't any commercial steamers left and no warship will take them—that leaves the small fishing boats, but with so many children you'd need a large fishing vessel. I saw two at the north dock."

Rork chimed in. "Aye, sir. They're lookin' a bit worse for wear, but they're floatin' sure enough."

The bishop nodded. "Yes, we thought of chartering those months ago, but our sources at the docks said the crews were untrustworthy, especially with these children. Chinese are among the crews—possibly ones allied with the Chileans.

"We dared not engage a captain and crew to sail our precious cargo away, for once they saw the cargo they might alert the gangs that the children were aboard. That way they would get twice the profit—our money and the gangs' also."

Wake growled inwardly in frustration. Rork raised an eyebrow in optimism. "Not to worry, just find a new captain an' crew. Have some *trustworthy* lads sail her out. I suppose that—"

Mocenni replied quickly. "Precisely what I was thinking, my son. Thank you for volunteering!" He ignored Wake's rising protest and went on. "We didn't engage a captain and crew, but we did pay the owner of a certain vessel a retainer to stay ready at the dock. A sizable retainer. That is why it is still at Callao. Now we can sail the children away in her."

Wake glared at Rork. "Did you know about this ahead of time?"

"No, he most certainly did not, Peter," said Mocenni. "But I am gratified for his offer."

Rork's shoulders sagged. "What're we supposed to do, Peter? Leave them here, sitting in bone dust an' fearin' a gang o' cutthroats that'll kill 'em? Nay, we can't do that an' you know it, plain as day."

"Yeah, I know, Sean. But we can't just leave our assignment and do it right now. Maybe we can raise some volunteers among our crew, if the admiral gives us permission. There are political factors to be considered, not to mention naval discipline. The admiral has to be asked before we can do anything. And all of that will come *after* we do what we came ashore to do tonight. We've got to pass the message to the legation first."

Rork turned angry. "Well, there's no politics for these wee ones, Commander. I'll volunteer straight away. Me an' a few stout lads could have these children in Panama afore long. The navigatin's easy, jes' keep the land to starboard on your way north. No need for an officer for that."

The bishop grimaced. "I'm afraid that asking permission of your admiral will not be an option, gentlemen. Your ship has left. The priest who spoke to me earlier in the sanctum reported that the Chileans started bombarding the port. You heard the gunfire when we were up on the street. It is reported that the American warship, regrettably but understandably, had to go away." The bishop continued in a lighter vein. "So it appears that you and I and the children are now—as I believe they say in America—*all in the same boat.*"

An exasperated Wake pounded a fist into his hand. "Damn it all!"

Some of the children gasped at Wake's expression. Rork looked horrified. "Oh, we're terribly sorry for that curse, Your Excellency, it bein' sort o' a church an' all."

Mocenni gently shook his head. "God forgives us all, my son. These are trying times. Actions are far more important than mere words, anyway."

Wake growled. "Rork, remind me to gag your mouth the next time we go ashore, so you can't get us involved in any other hair-brained schemes. Assuming we live through this one."

"Aye, aye, sir," replied Rork, grudgingly. "An' I'm supposin' at this point our official courier mission to the legation is ended— a bit o' a moot point with the ship gone."

"Yeah, Rork. The message is moot and the mission is ended . . . along with our careers."

## 26

# A Moment in Time

"Thanks for the Yuletide nip, Bill," said Attorney General Charles Devens as he leaned back in a chair appreciating Secretary of State Evarts's bourbon. He was known as a feisty plain-speaker, but that evening he looked older than his sixty years. They were sitting in Evarts's elegant office, along with Thompson of the navy, Secretary of War Alexander Ramsey, and Treasury Secretary John Sherman. The building was deserted of staff and the men were sharing their last Christmas as Cabinet members. In half an hour each man was expected to join his wife at the White House for a Christmas Eve celebration, *sans* alcohol.

"Yes, thank you greatly for the pick-me-up, Bill. Mighty nice of you," agreed Ramsey, savoring a cloud of cigar smoke. A Minnesota politician, he had never served in the army he oversaw. "Got to have something enjoyable before we visit Lemonade Lucy and the dour dames of the White House, though yes, I love and respect the good lady."

He stretched his neck and groaned. "Besides, running the army has been taking a lot out of me lately. I wish those boys'd fight the Indians as connivingly as they fight among themselves.

Your older brother excepted of course, John. By God, now *he* knows how to get things done."

"That he does. Always did," said Sherman.

"Well, look, it'll all soon be over, gentlemen," offered Thompson. "And we'll be free to go about our ways and live our lives. Four months until Garfield gets what he wished for, Lord help him."

Evarts laughed. "Quite right, there, Richard. And you're all quite welcome for the whiskey. I thought we should taste a bit of our unofficial national spirits before heading over next door to the chief's house. But boys, I'm sensing a deplorable lack of enthusiasm in the room. You gents don't seem to be enjoying this Washington game anymore, do you? I myself still find it genuinely exhilarating. Gets the heart pumping!"

"Bill, my heart stopped pumping back in June at that convention when ol' Gar got nominated," Sherman countered. Heads bobbed in sympathy. Garfield had been Sherman's campaign manager, but ended up the convention's nominee and went on to win the election. "That got Sam Grant's attention, too. Remember the look on his face?"

"Bet he was drinking that night," offered Ramsey.

Thompson waved a hand toward the Great Seal of the United States. "Yes, Bill, I'll admit it. I'm tired of it here. Be glad to go home to Indiana, away from all this."

Devens sighed, "Richard, I'm in considerable agreement with you there. Heading home to Massachusetts. Done my duty for this country and my duty almost did me in."

As he took another drink, Ramsey wagged a finger at Devens, who'd been wounded badly in the war. "Charlie, you're right. You've done your duty, and darn well. Very good attorney general—much better than me at war. Oh! Fellas, I think that was a pun, and it calls for another round before we face the ladies. Mr. Secretary of State?"

Evarts poured more for each, stopping in front of Thompson. "Just in case the president asks, have you heard anything more from Peru, Richard?"

"No. Lines are cut, as you know. Last we heard was the Chileans were about to overrun Lima. It's all over down there."

Evarts nodded. "Same thing I heard. Our legation's incommunicado. Of course, once the smoke clears and the Chileans establish themselves, the lines will go back on. Then everybody'll adjust to the new masters. Until the next war."

"Yep, get 'em all the time down there."

The others were conversing about the tariff issue. They didn't care about South America. Evarts leaned over to Thompson. "Except in Panama. Too much money to be made *without* a war now. French still moving forward on the canal work?"

"Now Bill, I know you've got your own sources there, so we probably hear the same things. From what I am getting, yes, they are. Slowly, but surely. I think they'll do it."

"What about your navy man down there? What's he say?"

Thompson leveled his eyes at Evarts. "Hasn't been there in six months. He's in Peru now. But last report was that he thinks they've learned a lot and will get it done."

"Really?" Evarts knew that wasn't what the man had told President Hayes the previous year.

Thompson took out his pocket watch and stood. "Oh yes. In fact, I think the canal's a capital idea. But now, Mr. Secretary, I think it's time to go put in our appearance at the boss's last big hurrah and wish a Merry Christmas to all."

"I wish Daddy were here. He's never seen me in a real lady's dress, like this one," said Useppa to her mother as they and Sean walked down the aisle for the Christmas Eve service. It was a festive scene in the sanctuary—families dressed in their best chatting and laughing, candles and ladies' perfume filling the air, the choir incanting a soft hymn, and boughs of holly and pine hung with red ribbons everywhere.

"I wish he were here, too, dear. He would love to see you. I know it's hard, but we need to be thankful for what we have," said Linda as she steered Sean into the pew. He was dressed in a suit for the first time in his life and looked it.

Linda had worked on her part-time seamstress job for many hours making the money to get the material for the dress and suit. Many more hours were spent, with Useppa's help, sewing them just for this event. She wanted her family to look presentable, respectable. They were getting older and it was important to learn how to handle themselves in social situations.

The parishioners stood as President and Mrs. Hayes, with their children, entered from the side door. Several cabinet secretaries arrived with them and sat in the second pew. They must've come from the social gathering for the city's elite that Linda remembered seeing in the newspaper's social agenda. The last Christmas party of the Hayes' administration was the social topic of the press that week, along with the news that New York's Broadway Avenue and its theaters were illuminated by that modern phenomenon, electricity.

The president nodded solemnly to the congregation as he and his family took their place at the front. That's the man who personally sent my husband into harm's way in another hemisphere, Linda said to herself. It didn't anger her, she had accepted her life long ago, but it still awed her that men like Peter subjugated themselves to the will of strangers. She could never fully understand that.

Sean stretched up on his toes to see the president. He was fascinated with presidents—not from a political point of view, but from the possibilities for adventure a presidential order could bring. He pointed out the secretary of the navy, sitting behind the president. Warned to be on his best behavior for the evening, Sean still couldn't help blurting out, "Do you suppose the president's heard from Daddy lately? I bet Daddy's fighting nasty pirates down there right now, this very minute, Mama."

"Well I hope not, dear. I hope that right now he's in a church and thinking of us."

Useppa patted her mother's hand. "I'm sure he is, Mama." She glared at her brother. "And Sean Wake, you are an insensitive and crude boy."

Sean glared back, then put his arm around his mother, his brow seriously furrowed. "Yeah, you're right, Mama. He probably killed 'em off this morning and right now he's in church, just like us."

Oh, he's so much like his father, but without the polished edges, Linda thought for the hundredth time. "Well thank you, dear, for making me feel so much more comfortable. But let's hope that he's not fighting anyone, anywhere, and pray that he comes home soon."

Then her face tightened suddenly. Oh no, not here, not now, she begged God quietly. The pain clenched her lower abdomen and tears formed as she struggled to hold her composure. Useppa noticed it first, nudging her little brother, who stopped the wisecrack he was about to make.

He reached for her hand. "Mama, can I do something to help?"

"Yes, Sean, you can. Say a prayer for God's help in making me feel better. This is a good place to do that."

He immediately bowed his head and softly mouthed out a prayer as his sister moved over next to her mother and took the other hand. "Mama, we can all leave if you need to get home and rest. Maybe this is too much for you."

"No, dear. It's Christmas Eve and we should be here. It's important to me that we're all here together, here in church. This pain will pass."

Useppa racked her mind for something positive to say. The choir was singing louder now, their voices uniting in a rising tone that consumed the attention of everyone inside the church. It was "O come, all ye Faithful," and soon everyone was joining in. Useppa hugged her mother and whispered in her ear. "Think of Daddy, Mama. Think of him right here next to us. That might help make the pain go away."

"Oh Useppa, that's a wonderful idea, dear. You hold me and

I'll think of him and it won't hurt as much. And when I have the operation it'll all be better. You'll see."

The choir changed directly into another hymn, slower, more soulful. The tears came and Linda didn't try to stop them. The three of them sang "Silent night, Holy night" and thought of their father and husband, so far away. Weeping gently, Linda sang louder than she usually did, her voice straining at times, almost as if she were trying to reach out to Peter through the hymn. As it faded away in a long plaintive note she felt the pain subside too. A shiver, cold and crisp, went through her and Linda suddenly had a fleeting image of her husband with Sean Rork and a clergyman in a darkened church. They were laughing.

"Daddy's all right, my darlings," she said as she held her children tightly. "It's all right now."

The elderly pastor in white robes slowly mounted the steps to the pulpit. In a voice far louder than his stature would indicate, he welcomed the president and his family, the distinguished attendees, and "the faithful, who had come from the toils of their lives" to spend the evening in special celebration. After the greeting he reminded all to thank God the nation was in a state of tranquility, with no American threatened by the horrors of war. Linda noticed that her son shook his head at that, grimly staring ahead. She prayed for God to move Sean toward another direction in life, away from becoming a naval officer.

One warrior in the family was all the worry she could take, Linda admitted as she held her babies close to her. Savoring the respite from pain and the ancient beauty of the Christmas Eve liturgy, she vowed to always remember this moment, when her family was around her and safe, even though Peter was there only in spirit.

## 27

# A Notorious Irish Trait

## January 1881

Wake, amazed and more than a little dismayed by Bishop Mocenni's machinations that had somehow orchestrated the Americans' presence in Lima just when he needed them, went to Callao at dawn hoping to see his ship. Instead, he confirmed *Pensacola* had departed the harbor. He saw British and French ships offshore, but couldn't determine if the American warship was out there. Later that day he reported in to the legation, explained the *Pensacola* had left and that all of them were on their own.

Kronburg was stunned, his eyes clearly reflecting fear, but Christiancy greeted the news with equanimity and stated that he was certain the Chileans would behave as gentlemen ought when they did finally arrive in the city. After all, they had German and British advisors, didn't they? Wake didn't comment on that and left the legation without word on his own particular plans for the future. He noticed also that no one asked. He was a messenger to them, nothing more and nothing less.

With nowhere to go and no mission to accomplish, Wake

realized his excuses for not assisting the bishop had disappeared. He also knew that from the moment he'd seen those children, his heart was bound to them and he and Rork would do what they could to save them. So after leaving the legation, the two Americans made their way through the chaotic streets of Lima toward the bishop's monastery. Mocenni showered him and Rork with admiration for being "decent Christians and good men." At the same time, he suggested that the two stay down in the catacombs, hidden with the children, saying, "It certainly wouldn't do to have it known that Peter Wake was in the monastery, would it? Someone might tell the Chileans when they occupy the city. And by now you know what the Chileans think of you."

They waited a week for the Chilean bombardment to let up. It didn't. The new year arrived but the situation stayed the same—the Chileans were building up their forces methodically, professionally, remaining in their trenches until all was ready.

On the coast at Callao the Peruvian monitor gunboat *Atahualpa,* the former USS *Catawba* purchased from the United States in 1868, slugged it out with the Chilean fleet, which was mainly targeting the fortifications. *Atahualpa's* Civil War–era engines were so decrepit that she couldn't move from her berth, but the twin fifteen-inch guns in her single turret kept the enemy out of the harbor. On land Chilean artillery concentrated on the main Peruvian defenses south of the city, a few stray shells landing inside the old quarter but causing little damage.

January of 1881 found Wake and Rork living below ground in perpetual semi-darkness, bone dust in their lungs, and helping Damian tend to the children while they waited for word from above the time was right to make good their escape. Since it was judged too incautious for him to personally inspect the fishing boat, Wake talked to Mocenni about the vessel that was waiting, writing down questions as to seaworthiness, equipment, and provisions. The bishop dispatched plain-clothed monks to follow up on the questions. For a week the vessel was surreptitiously provisioned and equipped, Wake realizing he was trusting all their lives on third parties accomplishing unaccustomed tasks—people who had no idea of the dangers of the sea, or of modern naval war.

He also got to know the children, who seemed to have adapted to life fifty feet underground with the dead of the catacombs. Somehow they stayed children, playing and laughing and crying, thankful for the slightest affection and capable of giving a hug for the least reason. Damian said they had seen so much, too much, in their lives. Wake also noticed they were devoutly, almost desperately, religious, not merely going along as did so many youngsters in churches he had attended—as he himself had done when younger. Mocenni explained the church was all they had left and they clung to it in mortal fear of the world outside.

Wake was surprised that Rork, the life-long bachelor raised in the hard world of the gundeck, was so good with the boys and girls. He would regale them, through Brother Oswaldo's translations, with hilarious sea stories of storms and faroff lands and exotic peoples—but never of war. He tenderly told them of his visit to their cultural homeland in China, a place none of them had seen, and of how much he loved the art and food and music. Little almond-shaped eyes would light up when he described his first visions of the South Sea islands, or the cold Arctic north, or the mountainous waves of Cape Horn.

Rork had been to them all, was far better traveled than Wake, and using gestures and facial expressions, could act out a scene as if it were yesterday—having the kids duck as an imaginary boom swung above a deck, or hold their noses against the smell of rotting fish, or get them all swaying with the foretopmast of a ship in a storm. They would laugh as he pranced about describing American sailors dancing to a hornpipe jig, and ooh and aah when he showed them the way whales would come up out of the water and flop back down.

All his stories had good endings with no one hurt and everyone happy, even though there were some scary times to get through. It was delightful to watch and Wake found he enjoyed it as much as the little ones. Even the monks and Bishop

Mocenni could be found in a dark back corner, spellbound and grinning as they swayed and laughed with everyone else through the sea stories.

When asked later about the veracity of the stories, Rork shrugged. "Well, I suppose that *maybe* part o' them are not particularly the *whole* truth. Methinks perhaps some o' the more frightenin' things in the stories got left out. But 'tis all jus' a wee bit o' trainin' afore they go to sea, anyway, sir. Get the little tykes used to things at sea an' make it all a grand adventure. Like a yachtin' trip, don't ya know. That way, whatever we come across, they'll know we'll get through it with nary a worry."

Wake thought it brilliant. Mocenni said it was angelic. Damian announced, "*Ist sehr gut . . .*"

Even with the comic relief of Rork's antics, and the laughter of the children, life in the catacombs took its toll on Wake. The constant damp air, laden with the sweet rancidity of death, and the lack of sunlight made him irritable. But the worst was being dependent on Mocenni and his staff for everything. Wake was like a caged animal, pacing for hours a day, his mind going over possible obstacles on the escape route, courses at sea, alternative plans in case of discovery. He was physically charged with energy and fought the urge to shout and swear and pound the walls while waiting for the chance to get out of the caves, out of Peru, and home to Linda and their own children.

As the first two weeks passed, he grew more and more restless within, though more calm and quiet toward everyone else. Rork saw the change and knew what it meant. He'd seen it during the Confederate rebellion, in those times when his friend had decided on action that would mean danger and probable death. The bosun knew Wake's frustration had evolved into an intense, visceral hatred for the catacombs and the Chileans who had driven these children into them. The conflict was no longer the object of his friend's neutral professional observation. The Americans had crossed a perilous line while hiding with the dead of Lima.

Wake was at war.

On the Americans' twenty-fourth day in the catacombs Mocenni appeared out of the gloom, his face a study in controlled fear. He motioned Wake and Rork into the side chamber where they slept on cots, then intoned the words everyone had known was coming.

"It has happened."

"What are the details?" asked Wake.

"The Chileans are attacking the Peruvian defenses at Miraflores Hill as I speak. The front line has broken and General Cáceres is falling back to the trench lines at Surquillo, but no one expects him to hold. It will not be long now before the Chileans come here. My lookouts have seen Chinese keeping watch on government and church buildings in the city center, so we must assume we are under surveillance."

Wake nodded. "All right, we expected all that. But how are things looking in the port at Callao. Have they invaded there?"

"No, they have not invaded, but last night they did silence *Atahualpa's* guns. I've been told she is flooded and sitting on the bottom with her deck out of water. The Peruvian navy officers told my man they think perhaps the coastal bombardment was a feint and the main attack will come on land."

"Why, that's great news, sir," offered Rork. "In the confusion of the land battle we can get away as long as they're not invading the port with troops too."

The bishop shook his head and swallowed hard. "There may be another problem. A Chilean shell hit near the fishing boat and put many holes in it from the exploding metal. I do not know the word in English."

"Shrapnel . . ." muttered Wake. "How bad?"

Mocenni continued. "My man looked at the boat and counted fourteen holes in the hull. He said the mast was intact, but he is not of the sea and does not know if she is able to sail. He did say that the cabin door was still locked so our food and water supplies should be untouched."

"Was she listing?" asked Rork.

"What is that?"

"Was she leaning over? From water coming inside the hull."

"I did not ask and he did not say, my son. He is gone now. I sent him on another chore."

Wake looked at the bosun. "What do you think?"

"Well, sir, I think it's our only chance. They're after the children, that we know. An' they may well fancy you dead too. Oh, not a murder or anything so nasty as that. No, no—methinks maybe jus' an *accidental* death so you won't make it back to Washington this time. So I say we seize the chance an' go with it."

"That's what I was thinking too." Wake pulled out his watch and held it to the light. "Four o'clock. Is it afternoon or morning outside? Afternoon, right?"

"Yes, it is the afternoon now, my son," Mocenni answered.

"Good. Then we wait until nightfall and go to Callao just the way we've planned, Bishop. Once we get to the dock, we load the children and get under way. Four men can handle her, even if two aren't sailors. With any luck we'll sail past the Chileans in the dark. Hopefully they'll be occupied with other matters and won't be able to see us."

Mocenni cleared his throat. "Ah-hhhmm. Unfortunately, there is another factor, gentlemen. Last night I noticed that there is a moon. A rather bright moon. I checked our almanac in the library. It will be full tonight."

"Oh damn it all to *hell,*" growled Wake, then glanced at Mocenni. "Oh, please pardon my French, sir."

The bishop waved away the concern, "Sometimes the situation even makes *me* speak French, my son. You simply said what I was thinking."

"We've still gotta go tonight, Peter," said Rork. "Now or never for these little ones."

Wake held up a hand. "Diversion. We need a diversion. I've got an idea. Bishop, can you get a message to Captain Gonzalez at the naval station in Callao? Do you know him?"

"Miguel Gonzalez? Yes, I know him. I allowed him to win at cards a year ago." He mused for a moment, one eyebrow ruefully raised. "One never knows when a well-placed defeat in a game of chance can become the foundation of a future favor. I believe, as you Americans say, 'he owes me one.' Now, what is the message?"

Wake wondered how many other favors Mocenni had out there waiting to be called in. The man was positively Machiavellian. "The message is simple: *Send the bull into the northern pasture when the moon is over the yardarm. The owner will get a reward.* Make it from me."

Mocenni repeated it in English, then in Spanish. "It will be sent immediately by my personal courier, Commander. It sounds deliciously ominous."

"Hopefully it'll do more than just *sound* ominous. It might provide our chance to get around the Chilean ships."

After the bishop departed Rork said, "Nicely done, indeed, sir. Gonzalez knows you have influence in Washington an' will do it to curry favor for Peru, thinkin' you're on your way out to report on the war. So when the moon starts to set low in the west, probably around three or four in the morn', they'll take the submarine out of the harbor on a obvious sortie to the north, as if to escape, an' draw the Chilean fleet away from the harbor entrance in chase. An' in the confusion, cute as a bride in Derry, we go out of the harbor an' head south, toward the enemy's homeland an' away from freedom in Panama. Nary a one would guess that direction."

"Yes, Sean, you've got it exactly. We sail south along the coast for a couple of hours, then head west for a day, then sail north to Panama. Adds time and distance, but we might evade their fleet. They won't anticipate someone escaping to the *south*. That's just sheer craziness."

"A rather notorious Irish trait, I might add, sir."

"Yeah, well, I guess I'm getting it from you—God help me. But we've still got to get to the docks in the first place, so we'll need a little Irish *luck* tonight too."

Rork grinned. "Ah, now that'd be my specialty, sir. An' if it don't come o' its own accord, I'll provide some wee boostin' o' my own."

## 28

# Para los Niños

"The wagons are coming back from the front, Peter," reported Mocenni. "The children have been told about the cargo and why. They are as ready as they can be. I suppose what they've seen, followed by four months in the catacombs, has numbed them to almost any horror."

Wake nodded his reply. The children might be numbed, but he wasn't. When Mocenni first had proposed the plan he had immediately said no. It was too ghastly. Further reflection proved that the bishop's idea was the only way to get one hundred and seven death-targeted Chinese-Peruvian children; several clerics, only one of whom spoke English; and two formerly neutral American sailors out of Lima, down the eight miles to the harbor at Callao, and aboard a shot-up fishing boat.

Mocenni's plan was simple. Take all ten carts and wagons from the cathedral and the monastery and build a false floor over the cargo bed of each one. Under the false floor build a space where fugitives could hide. On top of the false floor, load the dead bodies of Peruvian soldiers from the front lines. It was, he said, a last duty to their country. The caravan would travel from the front lines to Lima, hide the children inside the wagons and drive down to Callao, ostensibly for burial of the soldiers' bodies. If the Chilean invaders stopped them, it wouldn't be for long. The stench was overwhelming.

The "front" was a fluid concept. It had dissolved earlier in the day until there were scattered pockets of Peruvian resistance in a sea of Chilean soldiers. Mocenni knew the wagoneers driving the specially modified vehicles were headed for the battle area near Surquillo, six miles away. He knew they should be back by eight o'clock, just after dark.

He didn't know that most of them were dead.

"I hear voices," said Brother Oswaldo. He cocked his head to hear better. Wake and Rork did the same and soon heard it too. A faint rumble echoed down the tunnel. Many people. Men. Angry words. It wasn't monks or priests.

Damian was on guard in the passageway from the sanctum. He closed the final door to the chambers where the children huddled, their eyes betraying the quiet horror that even this most dismal of places might not be safe. The door thudded shut and Oswaldo lowered a thick plank across it, barring entry. Damian would stay outside in the passageway to kill and die if necessary.

Oswaldo raised a finger to his lips, calling for silence. The lanterns were doused, only a thin corona of light coming from the edges of the door. Wake and Rork fingered the revolvers hidden by their coats and stared at the entryway, ready to kill any figure coming through it not in religious robes. Echoing sounds clarified into individual boots now, military boots. Separate male voices in Spanish could be distinguished out in the sanctum at the end of the passageway. They must be near the hidden panel in the corner, Wake realized as he recognized one voice as Mocenni commanding the others to go away, that they were defiling the house of God. Laughter was the response.

In the chamber no one moved or even seemed to breathe. The smallest child understood. All waited, eyes were riveted on the plank door. Gradually the voices faded. Wake breathed again.

A barely perceptible knock, followed by three more slow knocks, sounded on the door. Oswaldo slowly unbarred the door. Wake raised his pistol for the potential center mass of an intruder as Oswaldo pulled open the planks.

Damian leaned into the chamber and whispered something to his brother monk. Oswaldo gave the thumbs up sign to Wake. Suddenly, he dropped his hand as rapid footsteps clumped down the passageway, getting louder quickly. Damian spun around and crouched. In an instant he withdrew the long dagger in his right hand, holding it like a street fighter at waist level, his left hand outstretched for balance. Wake felt Rork beside him, revolver pointing at the doorway too. A tall shadow filled the dim light of the passageway.

It was Mocenni. Damian nonchalantly flourished the dagger and slid it neatly into its sheath as Wake nearly collapsed with relief. He heard a Gaelic oath softly uttered beside him in the dark. Oswaldo, middle-aged and overweight, held a hand on his chest calming himself as the bishop entered to report what had occurred.

"Chilean army officers. They are spreading throughout the city. I hear gunfire in the streets and there are large fires south of the center of the city. It has begun. They are sacking Lima."

Rork stood up and holstered his pistol. "What did they say to you, sir?"

"They said they had heard of the catacombs and thought we might have treasures from the church hidden away in them. I told them that our valuables were in plain sight in the sanctuary and chapel, that we do not hide our precious service in the house of God."

"Did they leave?" asked Wake.

"For now, but they will be back. I could see it in their eyes.

And when they do, they will tear everything apart looking for the entrance into the catacombs. It will be fruitless. There have been rumors of treasure down in here for centuries. But in reality there are only bones. Of course, they might not be looking for *treasure*."

"What about the wagons? Are they here? It's past time for them to arrive."

"No, my son. There are not here. I do not know why, but I fear the worst."

"What about the pro-Chilean Chinese? Have you seen them?"

"Yes, they are strutting around with the Chilean army. There is word from the southern part of the city that there are mobs of Chinese and Chileans looting there and heading here."

Wake's shoulder throbbed and a headache pounded. He rubbed his temples, trying to think. "Our plan is moot now. We've got to go by foot through the streets."

Mocenni sighed. In the dim light he looked even more gaunt, like a dead man's apparition standing and talking. "No. We will go *under* the streets, my son. You only know a small part of the catacombs. There is more. It is a large network of interconnecting tunnels. Secret tunnels."

"Can we get out of the city *underground?*"

"No, not all the way out, but most of the way to the edge of the city."

Wake was suddenly angry. "Why didn't you tell us before!"

Oswaldo recoiled from the violence in Wake's tone. The bishop held out both skeletal hands. "Because they were built over two centuries ago by slaves so that the clergy might have secret escape routes in the event of a rebellion against the Church. No one except the religious was to know of them. They've always been the last escape to refuge for us."

"So what do we do now?" said Wake, astonished at Mocenni's ability to deceive. Again, he had the feeling the bishop was ten steps ahead of him, that he and Rork were pawns in a plan of which he was ignorant.

"I will send some of the faithful out to find the wagons with the message to meet us at another location. We will go to that location—it is the church of Santo Domingo—through the catacombs and meet the wagons there. Then follow the same back road to Callao we spoke of earlier."

Mocenni paused. "But I must warn you. This is our final chance. It is this or nothing."

The way he said it bothered Wake. "Anything else we should know?"

The frail bishop's hand disappeared inside his robes and emerged with a scroll of some sort. Even in the dim light Wake could see that it was old. Very old.

Mocenni's voice quavered slightly as he looked at the parchment. "This is the only map of the entire network of catacombs. It was drawn in the seventeenth century and kept safe all these years. I have never traveled this route."

The bishop looked up at them. "No one ever has—for two hundred years."

Wake felt his stomach twist and glanced at his friend. The bosun was shaking his head in shock and spoke first. "Your Excellency, how do you know these tunnels even still exist? Or ever did?"

"I do not *know*, my son. But I do believe with my faith that two hundred years ago God in His greatness foresaw this future situation and provided a way out for these children. That is enough for me. Besides, what other option is there?"

Wake felt a hundred pairs of eyes on him. "None. We'd better go . . ."

Seconds later they heard more sounds from the sanctum beyond the passageway. Voices again. And soldiers' boots.

They escaped through a hatch hidden twenty feet away, under a pattern of bones the children had been sitting on for months. Wake never knew it was there. The bishop consulted the map for the location and closed his hands in a prayer of thanks when he found it. The sounds in the sanctum grew in volume. The bishop motioned for everyone to follow him down into the hole. There was no time to gather provisions or belongings, he said as he dropped down with a grunt.

The planked door was closed and barred from the inside. Damian was not staying behind. He was to be the rear guard in the line, but not to fight. This time he was to cover their trail by replacing the bone-covered hatch as carefully as he could. Lowering themselves down almost six feet, they crawled fifty feet along a tunnel hewn into the rock—Mocenni with a lantern in the lead, followed by the Americans—and came out in a space so low they could not even stand. The bishop, knowing the tail end of the line must still be in the bones chamber, kept on going into another tunnel. In another fifty feet, by Wake's reckoning, they emerged into a slightly larger chamber where at least they could stand. There were two tunnels at the other end of the room.

Oswaldo held the lantern as Mocenni deciphered the ancient map, shriveled and blanched with time. It was in Latin, more a diagram than a scaled plan, with the swirled lettering faded and difficult to even see. The bishop's eyes squinted as he mouthed the words and tried to conjure the meanings.

By the glow Rork pointed toward a rat scurrying off toward the darkness as the chamber filled with murmuring children. This section of the catacombs was different. Wake noticed no smell of death, saw no bones. The air was dank. The dripping walls, floor and ceiling were crudely mined out, with sharp edges everywhere. He'd already been cut several times on his arms and head. Looking around he saw blood on all of them as they crowded in.

It took all of his self-discipline not to scream in the close space. He willed himself to slow his breathing and concentrate on what they would do once they got to the boat. Next to him, Rork was helping the children gather around him, smiling and winking at them. He appeared completely at ease. Wake couldn't imagine anyone not being terrified in this tomb. He tried to figure out their location or direction of travel and couldn't. It made him even more claustrophobic.

Damian passed the word forward from the end of the line that everyone was down in the tunnel and the hatch closed. He didn't know if the enemy had found their hiding place yet, but suggested they keep moving. Rork heard the translation, then checked his friend.

"Peter, are you all right? You're not looking well."

"Actually, Sean, I'm not." He ran a hand through his bloodied hair. "This must finally be getting to me. Don't know why now, after all this time, but I can't stand this confinement down here. Having trouble breathing . . ."

Rork spoke with the voice of a petty officer to a superior. "Won't be long now, Commander." He saw it had the expected result. Wake tightened his jaw and nodded. Rork continued in the same tone. "Then we'll be out of here, sir, an' you'll be in command of the escape route to Callao."

"*Ah ha!*" blurted out Mocenni to Oswaldo. "Of course, now I see it. We go to the cathedral, and when we get there we enter the tunnel that goes off to the right, then follow it under the Plaza de Armas and onto Santo Domingo. Let me see, that would mean we take the left tunnel in this room and that should take us to the cathedral."

He turned to the others, smiling for the first time since they started out. "Gentlemen, if you would care to follow me?"

"It's locked, sir," said Rork as he rattled the doorway by the light of Oswaldo's lantern. They thought they were near or under the cathedral, but instead of an open passageway the tunnel was barricaded by a door not shown on the map. This one was a substantial affair of heavy paneling and iron straps. The monk pointed to a massive lock mechanism connected to a sliding bolt.

"Maybe they added this door after the map was made?" offered Mocenni, adding, "I have three keys from the box in the vault at the monastery where the scrolled map was kept. Perhaps one is for this door."

His attempts with all three keys didn't work. Rork edged over and examined the lock with the lantern close by, trying the keys one at a time. He ended his efforts and frowned. "The lock, 'tis rusted shut. One o' these may be the one, but we'll never know."

Damian sent word up from the rear end of the line that he heard thudding sounds behind them, but couldn't identify how close or who they were. The bishop's hands started shaking. "We have to get through this door, gentlemen. We cannot go back." He knelt in silent prayer.

Rork shook his head and growled, "Then I guess 'tis time for old skills learned in me misspent youth. Stand aside an' let an Irishman at it."

With that said, he took out a pocketknife, positioning it inside the keyhole at an angle. Then, to the amazement of the bishop, he rapidly hit it with the butt of his pistol four times. Nothing happened.

"Aye, no joy," he grumbled. "Now 'tis made me vexed for sure." Rork reared his arm back and smashed the pistol butt with all his might into the knife handle. The blade broke off, gouging his hand and making the bosun go immediately into Gaelic curses, some of which needed no translation.

Wake looked at Mocenni, who raised an eyebrow and said, "It's all right my son, I am about to use some French phrases myself."

The tittering of the children ended abruptly when Rork swung around, aiming the revolver at the lock, and thundered, "Aw, the hell with it!" The gunshot blasted through the tunnel, the closest people blinded by the flash and deafened by the concussion. Several seconds went by with everyone but Rork stunned. Still enraged, he kicked the door but it didn't move. More Gaelic curses erupted from him as he stood there glowering.

Oswaldo leaned over and looked at the lock. It was broken neatly in two by a jagged line. Timidly, he slid the bolt back. The door lurched open. Rork swore again.

Mocenni fell on his knees again, hands together, eyes heavenward, whispering. "From Satan's grasp to Saint Peter's feet. Thank you, Lord!"

Wake peered through the doorway, then entered the room. It was the one depicted in the map. Evidently the bishop was right, he surmised, the locked door had been added after the map was made. Just as the map showed, there were several tunnels leading out of the room. One had faint light in it and Wake guessed it to be the one leading to the cathedral above them. Mocenni was still trembling as he oriented the map according to the tunnels before him. When he spoke his words were overly loud from his deafness, his gestures looking like pantomime to the others as he pointed to a tunnel.

"This one. We go through here. That other one goes up into the cathedral. We should not go there. Move quickly. I think with the noise we may have attracted attention—yes, I know it had to be done, my son—but we should hurry."

Wake noticed the movement out of the corner of his eye before anyone else, but was too slow to react. The tunnel from the cathedral had someone emerging from it—a scowling man in a Chilean army uniform, obviously an officer, with a revolver in his right hand. It went off at the same as Rork's. The Chilean's pistol fell as he clutched his abdomen and staggered sideways into the wall, crumpling down to the floor.

The man behind him, a common soldier, tried to raise his rifle in the confines of the tunnel as he attempted to climb out. Rork shot him too, the headshot collapsing him where he was and effectively blocking the men behind him. The officer squirmed in the corner, his eyes burning with hatred even as his mouth tried in vain to speak. All that came out was blood. Children's screams pierced the fog in Wake's ears. Another soldier's shadow appeared in the tunnel, then backed up quickly as Wake fired a shot.

He yelled for the bishop to take the children and run, that he and Rork would stay behind and hold them off. Oswaldo gathered up his robes and plunged into the tunnel with the lantern with Mocenni pushing the seemingly endless line of frightened children in after him. Damian arrived at the end, took notice of the carnage in the murkiness, grunted approval, and whipped out his dagger.

*"Vamonos!"* Wake yelled into Damian's ear, pointing to the tunnel the children had entered. The monk shook his head no, pointing to the Chilean bodies. He picked up the pistol and rifle. Then he gestured for the Americans to head after the line of children, that he would stay. *"Es mi destino—para los niños . . ."*

Wake stood there, not knowing what to say, looking into those dark, determined eyes. He felt Rork's hand on his shoulder. "Peter, he knows what he is doin,' an' it's best we let him do it. Those children will be needin' the likes o' us when they get to the boat."

The last image Wake had of the soldier-turned-monk was the shadowed outline of him in the dark room, sitting back against the wall with the rifle at his shoulder, aimed at the cathedral tunnel.

# 29

# Wake's Namesake

Gradually Wake regained his hearing. The first thing he heard was the crying of the children. All composure and confidence gone, their whimpering filled the tunnel, echoing into a mind-numbing noise. When they'd gone what Wake estimated was a thousand feet, he felt the thudding vibration of three separate gunshots, followed by several rapid shots, reverberate up the tunnel from the room. The children silenced immediately and everyone stopped, listening. There were no more shots.

The line started moving again, this time as silently as they could, with older children carrying the young and hushing them. Last were the Americans. Wake turned and waited periodically, straining to listen for the sound of boots.

The word came back down the line that Oswaldo was in the sub-basement of the church of Santo Domingo. Then came the message to be quiet—he heard people above him.

Without explanation the line started moving again, this time the only sound was the heavy breathing and occasional whine of one of the littlest youngsters. Wake wanted to get up to the front, to see what was happening, but he stayed in his position. It would've been impossible to squeeze past the children anyway. He groaned in frustration.

The ones in front shushed the rear guard as the line slowed. Something was ahead. Wake couldn't see in the dark and strained to hear. Nothing. Then he saw a vague lightening of the tunnel. Minutes later they were in a sub-basement large enough to accommodate the entire group, illuminated by a torch sconce on a wall. Wooden stairs led up to a barricaded door and opposite them were two tunnels. On the far wall was the tunnel they had come from.

Mocenni and Oswaldo were bent over the map whispering as they rotated it this way and that, trying to determine which of the two tunnels to enter. Wake listened to them for a moment, puzzled. Neither wanted to go up the stairs to the church and Wake asked the bishop why.

"Because we listened at the door and heard many soldiers' boots and voices. That means the wagons I had hoped would meet us here will not be here. Perhaps the message was intercepted and read, I do not know. But this escape route is closed and we have no choice but to go into one of these tunnels. However, this ancient map does not show them. Do you have an idea, Peter?"

Wake looked at the map. There was no compass rose on it but he knew the geographic relationship of the Monastery of San Francisco to the Cathedral of Lima, so he forced himself to do a dead-reckoning plot, as he would in a fog along a coast. It was mainly deductive reasoning, a guess really, but it was all he could come up with at the moment.

"All right. From the monastery to the cathedral we generally ended up going southwest. From the cathedral to Santo Domingo we turned to the right sharply and went northwest. Of the two tunnels before us, the one on the left appears to go southwest and one on the right to the northwest. Hmm."

Wake turned the map. "Sir, what important building is close by, northwest of here?"

"There are no government or church buildings close to the northwest, Peter."

"And to the southwest?"

"The churches of San Augustin to the south and Las Nazarenas to the south and west. Maybe a kilometer to Nazarenas and more than that to Augustin. Both are relatively new compared to the church of Santo Domingo above us, so I am not sure if they are connected to the catacomb system."

Wake put himself in the enemy's position. "The Chileans obviously are going to the churches first, probably to loot but maybe also looking for us. So we can't go to those churches in the center of the city. How about to the *far* northwest of us, sir? What is out there?"

"Sanctuario de Santa Rosa de Lima!" said both clerics at once. Mocenni explained. "It is only about one hundred sixty years old and named after the first saint of the Americas. She was born in Lima. There could be a newer tunnel to that place that would not be on this map. It is at least two kilometers away, though."

"Looks like that's the direction of freedom, sir. We take the tunnel on the right and head there. Now."

His decision was punctuated by a thump against the door at the head of the stairs, followed by a distant muffled conversation. Mocenni quickly took the lantern and ordered Oswaldo to bring up the rear, then walked fast into the tunnel, the Americans right behind him. The children knew the procedure by this time and went into line as they were ushered forward by the monk.

This tunnel was different from the others, however, obviously newer, taller and wider with a smooth floor. Several places had bricked arches and niches in the walls and the air was noticeably better, which suggested to Wake that there were fewer if any doors cutting off circulation. They were able to make a better pace and were moving well when another thump on the church door behind them speeded the line up even faster until they were almost running. Wake began to feel more confident when he heard word passed forward from Oswaldo in the rear that everyone was out of the church's sub-basement.

They rounded a bend in the tunnel, Wake keeping track of

their direction better now, just as a crashing sound resonated behind them. The church door was breached. Soldiers would be entering the tunnel. He figured the other soldiers from the cathedral should be approaching Santo Domingo by then and would meet the ones from the church. They would warn the Chileans in the northwest part of the old city to the escapees' presence.

Now they were heading northerly and ascending. According to Wake's calculations, they still had at least a kilometer and a half to go. Soldiers could make better speed in the larger tunnel, so he realized it would be a matter of time. He didn't see how they could make it to the sanctuary of Santa Rosa de Lima ahead of them.

Mocenni unexpectedly stopped. There was a smaller passage to the right. He held the lantern up and squinted. It ran around a curve. He looked at Wake, who shrugged and said, "This side tunnel heads north. That's a better direction than any other."

Rork seized the lantern and took off up the passageway briskly, Wake and the bishop leading the line of children after him. The passage sloped up rapidly and Wake felt movement in the air. It was fresh! They were nearing the surface, but didn't know where. At that point Wake didn't care. He was desperate to get out of the catacombs.

Around two more sharp bends, they had to stop one more time. Wake felt his heart sink again. Rork cursed in Gaelic. Mocenni cursed in French. Wake sat on the floor and wanted to cry.

An iron grating was set across the tunnel and embedded into the rock. Beyond there was actual white daylight in the passageway, reflected from around another curve. The grating had a narrow gate with a padlocked handle. The padlock was a large affair, hanging on the other side. Rork reached through the bars and turned it toward him. Then he smiled.

"Ah, now this one's right up me alley. Jus' sittin' there awaitin' another skill from me misspent youth." He was the picture of innocence as he faced the others. "No, no. Not to worry! I'll be wee bit more subtle than the last."

Wake sighed. "All right, I'll ask. Why?"

"The last lock, me dear friend an' respected superior officer, had been corroded shut for centuries—like the attitude o' certain Englishmen I've known and hated. But this little darlin' is modern and will respond to me charms. An' now, me fellow fugitives, I need a hairpin, if someone would be so kind as to find one among the young ladies present."

Three hairpins were produced just as Oswaldo sent word many footsteps were behind them. Rork's face contorted in concentration as he worked the lock, all the while explaining his procedure like a teacher in class.

"Now you see the primary mechanism is the easiest. Any ol' ne'er-do-well can unlatch the first set o' cutouts. No, no, 'tis the secondary alignment that's the most difficult. An' this one's playin' hard ta get, but not to worry—"

Wake glanced behind them. He could hear the boots approaching. "Hurry it up, Sean."

"Said an' done!" Rork announced casually as the padlock clicked open and the gate swung. The bishop and children rushed through, running around the curve and up the incline where light shined wonderfully a hundred feet ahead. Light from the sun. Wake followed and felt real air. Energy surged through him. He saw it in all of them as they began to smile. They were emerging from the underworld! There were thick bushes across the entrance, trampled easily by the mob running out of the tunnel.

"My God in Heaven, thank you!" cried out Mocenni as he came out into a small garden lined with fruit trees. Everyone was sobbing with relief, bent over as they breathed in the clean air. The sky was filled with clouds that filtered the sunlight. Absentmindedly Wake checked his watch. Six o'clock. Then it struck him. It was morning. They had been running all night. The line of children was still emerging as he forced himself back to reality and quickly took stock of his surroundings.

The clouds weren't natural, they were oily black—smoke rising from fires everywhere. Gunfire formed an incessant background to shouts in the distance, some nearby. Unlike the odd tranquility of their temporary refuge, outside the garden the city of Lima was bedlam.

Thirty feet away was a wall that encircled them. A building was close by within the wall. It was three stories high with a tower even higher. Where were they? A church? he wondered, as Mocenni rose from his prayer of thanks and walked over. The bishop was haggard, looking nearly dead. He sat on a rock next to Wake.

"No soldiers here. I know this place. It is not a church, Peter, but the home of the Oquendo family. From the room at the top of that tower you can see the whole city, even the harbor at Callao. We are at the northern edge of the city, the river is two, maybe three, hundred meters away, across the railroad tracks."

Wake didn't have time to comment, for Rork and Oswaldo emerged from the tunnel at the end of the line. The monk doubled over to catch his breath. He gasped out in Spanish, nodding toward the bosun, "Rork closed the lock again and it worked, thanks be to God. If everyone is quiet they will not hear us and will go back to the main tunnel toward Santa Rosa de Lima."

Rork instantly went around telling everyone to be quiet. Motioning them to stay behind bushes, out of sight. The three men moved under a small tree. Wake whispered his own prayer of thanks, then scanned the area, scrutinizing the windows of the house to see if anyone was watching them.

"Bishop, I think we should hide the children until we know the situation here. Could you go to the house and see?"

"Certainly, my son. The Oquendos are friends of mine. We will be safe here for a while. Come with me, Oswaldo."

When they had left and the children were concealed by the foliage, Wake said to Rork, "Good work on the lock, Sean. That saved us."

"Aye, sir, 'twas a close-run thing there for a moment, but we're not out o' the woods yet. Methinks we'd better be gettin' along smartly now. Time's a wastin' an' we're surrounded by enemies."

"Take the river down to Callao?"

"Me very own thought exactly, sir. After all, water's our home."

The bishop and monk returned. The house was empty and locked. Wake told them his opinion. The plan with the wagons was ruined, but the fishing boat might still be there. The river could take them to Callao. All agreed and Rork suggested that he "open" the door to the house so that food and drink could be given to the children and a survey of the area be done from the top of the tower.

Five minutes later, Wake's idea of pushing on right away fell apart on the hard reality of an exhausted group of children. Oswaldo reported from the tunnel that the soldiers had not gotten through the locked gate and must have surmised that their quarry had kept on heading west to Santa Rosa de Lima. The direct threat to them had faded. The youngsters could barely stand and were in dire need of food, water, and rest. Mocenni counseled that perhaps spending the day hidden inside the house and later escaping in the dark might be best for all.

At night the vista from the tower of Casa de Oquendo was even more dynamic and far more frightening. The rancid smell of death and destruction hung in the air, so thick Wake imagined he could see it. The south and east horizons were a rim of fires. Flashes of Chilean artillery could be seen in the east, naval guns in the west. Eruptions of flames dotted the city, roiling up out of the buildings like volcanoes, the whole effect reminding Wake of Dante's vision of hell. He had seen small communities afire, but never a large city. It was terrifying and fascinating.

The incessant thunder of heavy guns was continually interrupted by the staccato of small arms fire in the streets, which was accompanied by high-pitched screams and drunken laughter. Order had completely broken down in the city. The Peruvian army had withdrawn to the hills in the east and the main Chilean combat units were in pursuit. That left the occupation of the city to the militia battalions brought up by sea and the pro-Chilean Chinese formations. Discipline evaporated. Everyone, on both sides, was on their own.

The children had seen it all before at Arica and their eyes broke Wake's heart. They knew they had to leave the house and expected to die that night. The odd sense of normality he had seen in them living underground amidst the bones of the dead had vanished. They were silent little scarecrows doing what they were told, beyond the point of crying or hesitation. They had lost hope and even Rork's best antics couldn't change that.

Wake and Rork had already slipped down to the river an hour earlier. They'd been prepared to have everyone swim downstream to Callao, but instead found to their astonishment three unloaded coal barges against the bank. Clambering aboard they discovered the large sweep oars neatly stowed.

They'd come back elated. No one was going to have to swim. The group could carry some food and water with it and make it downriver in about two hours by Wake's estimate. Then they'd cross from the mouth of the river to the docks, board the fishing boat, and try their escape to sea.

Wake and Rork were in the tower for the last time, carefully looking to the west and the sea, noting the locations of gun flashes from the Chilean ships in the far distance, checking the surrounding streets for signs of enemy patrols. It was nine o'clock and time to go by Wake's pocket watch. He nodded to Rork as the bosun descended and glanced over at Mocenni, who was sitting in a chair, fighting back tears as he gazed vacantly over the city he loved.

"I am the diplomatic servant of the longest reigning sovereignty in the history of the world, Peter. I have risen high and gone far. Leaders of nations listen closely when I convey the messages of the Holy Father in Rome." His frail hand waved over the scene. "I wear the robes of authority, but I was powerless to stop this. My heart is bleeding its life out at the sight of this, this cruel stupidity."

Wake turned to go down the steps but paused. "We made it this far because of you. Let's go. It's what God expects and it's all we can do at this point."

Mocenni's head hung low from stooped shoulders, the man was close to the edge of complete physical collapse.

"You know, my friend, for a Methodist you speak very much like a good Catholic. I see why my brothers in Christ like you. Indeed, my son, you are even named after our most beloved and strongest saint."

Wake didn't feel like giving or hearing a speech—he was exhausted too.

"Yeah, well, let's hope my namesake gives us some help tonight. We're gonna need it."

# 30

# Sacrifice

She would've walked, but there was a winter storm on and ice ruled the city. No tranquil blanket of snow, just a treacherous sheath of ice. Fortunately, on her last visit Dr. Purvis offered to send one of the hospital wagons to bring her. Linda had gratefully accepted. She had no money for a carriage and with the pain getting to the point where it doubled her over without warning, she was apprehensive of walking the four miles to the hospital.

Little Sean went to school that day, it was a Monday and he had an examination in mathematics, which he found dull and seldom did well in. Linda had him promise to do as well as he could and said she'd be home soon, after she healed from the "procedure." When he asked what it was for she said, "a female problem" that he wouldn't understand. He left it at that, knowing she'd been painfully sick and believing that whatever his mother was doing at the doctor's would end the problem. She never told him it was an operation.

Useppa knew everything. Linda felt she should, as a young lady that might have to face something like it herself someday. Useppa already knew two women from the neighborhood who had died in childbirth, and steeled herself to never let on that her mother's descriptions of the ailment had terrified her.

Together they rode the wagon, sitting on a box set up as a temporary seat on the cargo bed, as the black driver slowly drove through the streets. Bundled in coats and blankets against the cold, they listened as, with flamboyant hand gestures accented by clouds of vapor, the driver told them his life story. Sounding like a circuit preacher in full passion, he described his life as a slave from Virginia who had swum the Potomac at Harper's in the winter of '63, then made his way up to Pennsylvania and around to Washington.

There he'd enlisted in the Second Colored Infantry Regiment and ended up six months later "way down in de ocean. Place called Key West, some sorta part a' Florida, one a' them *seesech* states. Mos' terrible place I'd ever seen. Storms an' skeeters an' the yella death ev'ry summah."

Linda smiled. She'd been there then, a Southern island girl in love with a young Yankee naval officer named Peter Wake. Useppa knew most of the story and loved it. She nudged her mother and giggled as the man droned on. Suddenly, memories warmed Linda. It had all happened sixteen years earlier but it seemed like fifty, so much had happened since.

When the driver went on to describe the "yella death" and the funerals at some "African slave bury groun' by de ocean," Linda weighed in.

"I'm from Key West and know that cemetery well. My husband and I were married there since no church would marry a Yankee and a Key Wester. It was about the time you were stationed there."

The wagon driver gushed on for the rest of the long ride, but the mention of yellow fever deaths reminded Linda of her mother's horrible death from that disease. She'd held her mother's hand for days, nursing her as well as she could, but to no avail. Her father had blamed the Federal army occupation authorities for withholding medicines and it drove him even further into a secessionist frenzy—eventually compelling him to actions that landed him in prison. He later died a broken man. Their family was never the same.

Dr. Purvis leaned over closer to her. "Mrs. Wake, you will smell the ether, then I'll ask you to count down from fifty. After a few seconds you'll be asleep. Don't worry, you won't feel a thing through the whole procedure."

Linda thought her own voice sounded distant when she answered, "Thank you, Doctor. I trust you."

Then the other doctor's hand appeared from the opposite side of the table. It had several layers of gauze and descended to her face, resting gently on her nostrils. The smell was odd, overpowering. Linda heard Dr. Purvis reminding her to count.

The last thing she saw was two black men, gray-haired and serious, standing over her, staring at her. They appeared calm. Linda thought that a good sign. Then everything went dark.

"Brits seem to be in a quagmire down there in southern Africa, Bill. What's that name they're calling it?" Navy Secretary Thompson asked of William Evarts. They were in Thompson's office discussing world events.

"Boer War. Dutch Boer settlers're giving the British regular army hell down there. Like a certain revolution I remember reading about in North America. Say, Richard, I just got some information in from Lima. Is your man still missing in Peru?"

"Missing or dead. Don't know which. Admiral Stevens pulled offshore during the fighting in the city and hasn't heard from him. Admiral Porter's worried. You hearing anything from your office down there?"

"Yes. Today our legation in Lima just got a cable through to us the long way around, via the Chilean telegraph network, and I've wanted to let you know. They're reporting the situation as very confused. Included a bit about your man Peter Wake—that he was last seen at the legation office several weeks ago, just after he warned them to get out before the city fell. No sign of him since then.

"By the way, they wished they *had* gotten out. It's pretty bad. Rioting, looting, buildings burning, gangs on the streets, no food, short on water."

Thompson pressed. "They haven't seen him since then? We've been wondering what happened to him. Is he dead, caught in a battle somewhere, or maybe a prisoner? No one knows."

"Well, the message included some odd information that they weren't sure of, but thought they should send. There's a rumor that the Chilean army is searching the city for two men in uniforms similar to U.S. naval officers—that they've committed some kind of crime or attack and were hiding out in a church or churches. Did he have another American with him? The legation last saw him alone."

"Yes, he did," Thompson said. "A senior petty officer named Rork was with him. It's a bad deal down there, Billy. With no real information we haven't declared them dead or missing yet. Not sure what we should do. Fortunately the press doesn't know. Neither does Wake's family. But the president knows and is very upset about it."

Evarts leaned on Thompson's desk and folded his hands in thought. "Hmm. I knew the president was melancholy about something. So *that's* it. Understandable."

Thompson frowned, lost in thought. "Yes, embarrassing, isn't it?"

Evarts's face went crimson. "Embarrassing? He's not *embarrassed*, Richard—he's concerned. He liked Wake and sent him in harm's way down there. The man feels responsible."

*295*

Unfazed by Evarts's obvious disgust, Thompson stood to leave. There was a political meeting in ten minutes at the Willard. "Well, he'll only be responsible for another five weeks and then it'll be Garfield's problem, Bill."

"Richard, I'm afraid you don't understand. Rutherford Hayes was a soldier in combat during the war. He doesn't leave his men behind. And Peter Wake isn't some political sacrifice."

"Oh, get over the sentimentality, Bill," said Thompson as he walked out. "You and the president know full well that if he becomes an embarrassment, Wake will be sacrificed. That's the way of Washington."

Evarts buried his head in his hands—worried that Thompson was right, wondering just what they'd all become after they came to Washington years before.

# 31

# Guts

The run down the river was both frightening and easy. Frightening because of the scenery—the outskirts of the city in flames, the villages deserted, the stench and desperate sounds permeating the air, bodies floating downriver.

Easy because they weren't stopped. Wake was steering the lead barge, with Mocenni next to him. Oswaldo had the middle barge and Rork steered the last in line. With the children hidden down in the coal bins and only the helmsman showing on deck, they made their way around the bends and down through the low hills toward the sea. At midnight they reached the edge of Callao and Mocenni told Wake they should ground the barges on the southern side of the river, so they could walk to the main docks at the port.

It got far more complicated and dangerous as soon as they stepped ashore. Wake kept the children divided into the same groups under himself, Oswaldo, and Rork, while Mocenni acted as the scout ahead. Walking through the deserted streets, Wake tried to keep the children in the shadows, all of them hiding in alleys when groups of men were seen.

Artillery had ceased but rifle gunfire was constantly heard around them; there was fighting still in the area. Several times Mocenni came hurrying back to warn of mounted Chilean soldiers on patrols farther up the street. Everyone concealed themselves in dark side alleys as the Chileans rode by, Wake noticing the cavalrymen were wary, weapons ready. It was a combat area. He quickly prayed the children would do what they were told and would stay safe, though he feared the worst.

The inevitable finally happened. An older Chinese man peered out a window and saw the children. He called out to them but got no reply. Then came shouting from the man, more people came to their windows. More shouts in Chinese and Spanish. Wake thought he heard the words "reward money." He and the others began to run. The crowd of tiny refugees clattered down the cobblestone streets, the sound echoing off the buildings, as they ran the rest of the way to the docks, Wake expecting a volley of gunfire at any moment.

Near the docks, Mocenni met them out on the street and led them down some alleyways he had just examined. Wake followed him into an ancient stone building through a broken window. It was the only pane broken out in a row of windows. When Rork slyly grinned at him, the bishop shrugged. "You weren't the only one with a misspent youth, my son."

The building was a cotton warehouse. After threading their way through the window, everyone in the group collapsed onto the bales with groans. The fishing docks, and hopefully their boat, were two blocks away, Mocenni announced.

"Stay here with the children, Sean," Wake told Rork. "The bishop and I will go and see about the boat. Don't come out and for God's sake, keep them quiet."

"Aye, sir. Quiet as a trollop . . . ah, make that as a *mouse* . . . in a cardinal's church."

Wake and Mocenni made their way through the shadows down a side street. The bishop had never been to the boat, but knew where it should be. They rounded a building still smoldering from a direct hit and saw the dock. Two fishing vessels, both disheveled, were moored along the dock. From a distance neither looked in good shape.

The two men ran across the street to the boats, Mocenni tripping in the dark and letting out an oath against the devil while struggling to get up. He limped gradually over to where Wake already sat on a large bollard at the edge of the dock, gazing down at the boats.

"Oh, my. This is not at all what I expected," said Mocenni.

"It's *exactly* what I feared all along."

The fishing boats were riddled with holes, sitting on the bottom with their decks awash. Useless.

Mocenni sat down on the next bollard and put his head in his hands. Wake rubbed his shoulder, which had been throbbing all night and forced himself to think. It would be dawn in a few hours. They had made it against all odds to the docks. All they needed was something that could float with a hundred and ten people on it. He looked around. Nothing.

Asking the bishop to stay there, Wake trudged south along the docks toward the Peruvian naval station, now occupied by Chilean marines. Two hundred feet away, the silhouette of an armed steam launch, maybe fifty feet long with a four-pounder boat howitzer, showed against the flames. It was tied up to the wharf and steam was up in the boiler, periodically escaping with a hiss from the overflow valve. Wake darted over to a demolished storefront and watched the boat crew's manner, checking on their vigilance. The Chileans were as he expected—alert and well armed.

An idea formed in Wake's head. His mind debated the pros and cons. No, there was no way he could do it. It was preposterous. First of all—it was illegal. It was extremely dangerous. And even if it was successful and he lived, it would cost him his career. There was no way around *that*.

Then he weighed the alternative. The Chinese-Peruvian children would die when the gangs found them—murdered to cover up the previous atrocities. He knew their names now: Chen, the fourteen year-old boy with the perpetually sad face who struggled to be a man and older brother to the rest; Guang, the six-year-old boy who limped yet carried a baby girl through the tunnels; Li Wei, the ten-year-old girl who had the eyes of a old woman and never said a word. Their crime was to be the children of patriotic Peruvian Chinese and witnesses to their parents' murder.

Wake knew he couldn't abandon them. The only question now was how to overwhelm the launch's crew. His and Rork's revolvers wouldn't do it. He racked his mind. *How?*

Wake heard a footstep behind him and spun around in a crouch, revolver aimed gut high, hammer back, ready to kill.

Woodgerd didn't flinch. He looked too tired to move. "You, my little swabbie friend, were supposed to give me a decent warning of the collapse and some assistance for exiting this dung heap of a country." He paused. "Damn, you look like hell, Wake. What happened, *mon confrère?*"

Wake almost cried. Behind Woodgerd were thirty tough-looking Peruvian soldiers. He hugged the mercenary, who eyed him warily, and said, "You won't believe it when I tell you, but first things first—is the port being taken back by Peruvian forces?"

"Ha! What Peruvian forces? You're looking at the Peruvian army in Callao. We—mainly me, actually—are looking to steal a boat and get the hell out of here, post haste. Some very agitated Chilis are searching for us as we speak."

"Mike, am I glad to see *you.* I figured you'd take your men up into the hills with Cáceres and fight on as guerrillas. We've heard that thousands are gathering up there."

"Yeah, they are. Good for them. They fight for ideals, some sort of babble about love of country. On the other hand, I fight only for money and when the money stops—I stop. The money stopped."

Woodgerd was already eyeing the launch. So were the soldiers. Wake gauged his friend. He knew Woodgerd had a soft spot for animals. He'd seen the man kill a thug in Genoa who had abused a dog on the street. Maybe that soft spot applied to children, too.

"The steam launch is for my party, Mike. You and your men are welcome to come if there's room."

Woodgerd's eyes never left the launch. "How many in your party, Peter?"

"One hundred and ten. Hundred and seven are children. Peruvian-Chinese who witnessed their parents murder in Arica by the pro-Chilean Chinese there. The Catholic Church smuggled them to Lima. I've got them now. You can imagine what will happen to them when they are found here by the gangs."

Woodgerd blew out a breath and shook his head. "Oh, not again. Peter Wake, the Good Samaritan, strikes once more. Just how the hell did you get mixed up with that *mess*. No, never mind—we don't have time and I'd need a drink to hear it, anyway."

"*God just so happens to like Good Samaritans,* Colonel Woodgerd," announced Mocenni as he limped out of the shadows onto the scene. Even emaciated, crippled, and hoarse, he radiated authority. "I was worried about you, Peter. But I see you've found the colonel and reinforcements. How very fortunate."

Mocenni held out a hand. "Colonel, I am Bishop Mario Mocenni, Apostolic Delegate and Papal Envoy to Peru from the Holy See in Rome. We last met in November at a soirée at the presidential palace. You were regaling people with your experiences in Africa with the followers of Islam. I see you know my dear friend Peter Wake."

"Yeah, I remember you now. Didn't recognize you tonight, Bishop." Woodgerd didn't add why. By this point, Mocenni looked like a street beggar in his torn and bloodied robes.

"Quite all right, my son. These are trying times for us all. But you appear to be an instrument of God, does he not, Peter?" Mocenni turned back to Wake, who was once again astounded at the man's capacity to summon hidden reserves of energy. The bishop continued on as if they were at a cocktail party. "I presume, my friend, that you were thinking of using that nicely appointed vessel over there for our voyage, and that Colonel Woodgerd's providential appearance has solved the dilemma of how exactly to procure it from the Chilean navy. Am I correct?"

"Ah, yes, sir. That's the nice way to put it."

Mocenni graciously smiled. "Very good indeed, my son. Here is what I propose. I will accompany the good colonel and his soldiers over to the boat, and explain to the crew that it is most certainly the better part of valor to not contest ownership when outnumbered by desperate Peruvians. It is my fervent hope that no blood need be shed."

Wake grinned. The man was incredible. "Then we summon the children, get aboard and go!"

"Precisely. Simple plans really are the best plans."

Woodgerd leaned closer. "Excuse me, boys, but shouldn't I be consulted here? I think I'm part of this little show."

"Yes, of course, Colonel," agreed Mocenni. He turned back to Wake. "But I really think we should wait until Rork brings the children here from the warehouse to establish our ownership of that boat. More efficient use of our time, as it were."

Woodgerd physically fell back a step. "Rork's on this too? Tell me you've got more men to help, Peter. I'd even take sailors at this point."

"No, Mike, what you see is what I've got—except for one feisty monk. But now that you and your crew are here, I do have men to help. Bishop, please go back and bring the others up. Once you get back with the children we'll take the boat."

"Hey, wait a minute. Did anybody even *ask* me?" said Woodgerd.

"Why, whatever for, Colonel?" replied Mocenni, innocence dripping from his words. "There was absolutely no doubt in my mind you would help."

They marched across the street in platoon formation as if on parade. The dozen Chilean sailors on the launch didn't even realize it was the Peruvian army until the rifles were leveled at them. Woodgerd looked fiercely maniacal as Mocenni stood erect and stepped forward, addressing the boat crew in elegant Spanish.

"My dear gentlemen of the famous navy of the great Republic of Chile! Welcome to Peru, and thank you so very much for offering us your boat. I trust there will be no blood spilled over this minor matter, for you are greatly outnumbered by my angry Peruvian friends and any unpleasantness is really uncalled for. Now, if you would be so kind as to step off the boat and come over here."

The children, monk, and the Americans watched from the shadows in awe as the Chileans grudgingly walked across the street and were gagged and bound, then gently guided to sit on the ground. Oswaldo went to each and said thank you, eliciting grunting curses in response from the petty officer in charge.

Then, as easy as a Sunday yachting excursion, the entire mob of Peruvian soldiers, Chinese children, Catholic clergy, and American sailors boarded the launch. After making sure the children were safely seated and quiet, Mocenni called all to silence for a prayer of thanksgiving, which he gave in Spanish, Woodgerd scanning the harbor front and grumbling about wasting time.

As Wake was trying to get the clutch unstuck, the bishop climbed up to the dock and called out, "*Vaya con Dios, mis niños. Vaya con Dios.* And thank you so very much, my friends Peter, Sean, and Michael. May God bless each of you in your journey, and in your lives. You are angels."

"You're staying? Why?" asked Wake. "It's time to get out now."

"Oswaldo will stay with you and the children, Peter, but this city is where the Holy Father sent me." Mocenni grinned. "It's just like the navy, my friend. I go where they tell me to go."

In Wake's exhausted state his emotions got the best of him and he didn't trust himself to speak. Instead he nodded, then bent down and banged the clutch lever again. Finally it moved free and engaged. The propeller turned, Rork cast off the lines, and slowly the launch made its way across the harbor, laden to the point that it had only a foot of freeboard. The children waved goodbye to the bishop. Rork stood on the bow and watched the frail figure on the dock for a long time.

"Been called a lot of things, but never an angel," muttered Woodgerd. "Gotta admit though, the old boy does have class. And guts."

"Aye, that he do," said Rork as he came aft where Wake steered. "Guts in spades."

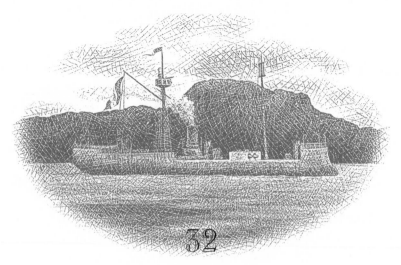

# 32

# In our Hearts . . .

D r. Purvis knew that his attitude would influence his patient, so he hoped to sound positive. "Mrs. Wake, it appears we didn't get it all. But after you've recovered from this operation we can go in again. Next time I'll take the lymph glands. Recent studies show that is the next step."

Linda was in excruciating pain—the morphine didn't touch it. Purvis had just prescribed opium, which a nurse was fetching. Linda propped herself up in the bed as Purvis wiped the sweat off her brow.

"How long to recover enough for another operation?" she asked.

"A month, at the very least. I'd like you to have more time, but—"

"—You're worried the cancer's growing too fast."

"Yes, ma'am," Purvis said gently. "We never know until we get inside and actually see the extent of the spread. The tumor was larger than I originally estimated, with tentacles spreading into your abdomen. We took all of that out, but you were losing blood fast so there was no time to remove the lymph glands. We had to close the surgical entry."

"And if you take the lymph glands that will be the end of the cancer?"

"We can never be sure, ma'am. Two British doctors, Handley and Beatson, have recently done pioneering work in this area, tracking how the disease spreads. Their success has been primarily achieved by removing the affected organs and isolating the cancer. That's what we are doing here at Howard. But Mrs. Wake, even though our modern techniques are increasing the chances of survival considerably, there are no guarantees."

Linda's voice was husky through gritted teeth. "So the choice to is do nothing and die, or try again and maybe live a little longer?"

Purvis nodded. "Yes, ma'am."

"Thank you for your candor, Doctor. Do the next operation."

The nurse entered with a cup and held it to Linda's lips. Purvis watched as her face relaxed and hand went limp from the maximum dosage.

Martha and Don Boltz had come across the river from Virginia and were sitting with Useppa in the anteroom when Purvis came out of the ward. Useppa stood, her eyes bloodshot, and was first to speak. "How is she? Was it successful?"

"She is in pain, but we've given her something for that. Yes, it was successful. We did remove the tumor. However, I am afraid it was larger than we expected and therefore it probably spread into areas we didn't have time to examine. She was losing too much blood and we had to end the procedure. We will do another operation in a month to examine those areas—if she can rest and recover enough to be able to handle it."

Useppa couldn't talk. She nodded her understanding as Don Boltz put his arm around her. Martha's voice was almost a whisper. "How long does she have?"

Purvis took a breath. "If we don't get it all, several months at the most."

Useppa sobbed. "I wish Daddy were here. He'd know what to do."

Martha was crying too. Her new husband Don tenderly

helped Useppa into a chair. He had grown to love the Wake family. A veteran of a Virginia regiment, he had seen too much horror in the war. It angered him that this should happen to Linda Wake, of all people.

"The only thing we can do is pray, Useppa."

"I want to know the moment you do, Admiral. Use this telephone contraption, that's why we have it in here," said President Hayes in the tone he'd learned commanding the 23rd Ohio Infantry at the battle of South Mountain.

"Aye, aye, sir."

Porter respected Hayes. And he fully understood that tone. He used it frequently himself. The president didn't know anything about ships or the sea, but he didn't pretend to either, and most importantly he didn't meddle in the navy affairs. Besides, Porter had developed a grudging like for Wake. The young officer reminded him of himself forty years earlier. He hoped Wake would show up alive. "Any specific orders regarding Wake, sir?"

"Yes, bring him home when he surfaces down there. I want to get a personal briefing from him about the situation as soon as he can be brought to me."

"We'll get him on the first available transport back, sir." The president's aide was hovering. Porter knew it was time to depart. "Is that all, sir?"

"Yes. No, wait!" Hayes shooed away the aide, then returned to Porter. "You mentioned something earlier about Wake's wife being ill at a hospital? I want Lucy to send her a note of support. The poor lady's got enough on her plate worrying about a missing husband. A note might be of moral value, would let her know we care."

"Yes, sir. We got word Mrs. Wake's at Howard University's hospital. Had an operation there."

"Oliver Howard's Negro school up on the north side? Why in tarnation is she there?"

"Lack of funds, I believe, sir. I heard about it through the Navy Yard commandant, who heard from the naval hospital doctors. Most think it's scandalous she decided to seek medical attention at Howard and had *black* doctors there do the operation."

That comment didn't sit well with the president. Hayes knew that several of the black teaching doctors at Howard University had been army surgeons during the war and learned their profession the hard way, under appalling conditions.

"Oh, what a load of horse crap that is! Let me tell you something, Admiral. If a good Christian man like Oliver Otis Howard believes in his school's doctors, then I do too. Tell your navy surgeons that for me. On second thought, I'll write that note of empathy to Mrs. Wake myself and have it delivered by presidential courier."

Porter knew the president was getting worked up now. The man was unstoppable once he perceived an attack on the Republican effort to assimilate the former slaves into society. Porter couldn't care less about blacks, but had sense enough not to indicate it at that point.

Hayes summoned his aide. "Get a courier. And get me the address of Major General Oliver Otis Howard. He's someplace out west keeping things calmed down with the Indians. No, I'm wrong on that—I think he's back east on leave. Come to think of it, he's due to take over at West Point soon so he's probably in New York."

The aide turned to leave but Hayes stopped him. "And get me what we have on Howard University. They were using federal funding from the Freedmen's Bureau at one point, unless those congressional Democrats ended that too—like they did on everything else we've tried to do for black citizenry. You know, Porter, they say we won the war, but sometimes I think we're losing the peace."

The admiral didn't have time to reply. Hayes' voice rose. "I'm sending a note of support to the doctor and to whoever's the head of Howard University too. You tell those hidebound navy medicos over there at the Washington Naval Hospital that I just might decide to inspect their institution one of these days and when I do, it'd better be absolutely perfect. I've still got another couple of months as their commander-in-chief and I'll make them know it!"

Porter seldom saw the president this way, and never regarding the navy. Usually these tirades were reserved for Democratic-Republican skirmishes, foreign intransigence, and army Indian-fighting incompetence.

"Mr. President, please. They didn't mean anything at all. You know that the Negro school is new and it takes awhile for a lot of people to get used to it. Especially a black doctor treating a white woman. I don't want you to get the wrong impression."

"Admiral, you're a good man and do a good job. And you also know that I have exactly the correct impression." Hayes pulled a pile of papers across the desk and took out reading glasses—the signal that the interview was over.

"Now, I've got other things to do, Admiral. Keep me apprised about Lieutenant Commander Wake and anything you hear about his wife and family's condition. Dismissed."

The admiral stood at attention. "Aye, aye, sir."

Porter hadn't had anyone talk to him like that for twenty years. As he marched out of the president's personal study he smiled. It seemed that Rutherford Birchard Hayes was going to be president all the way to his last day.

Useppa was in tears again, this time from joy. Don and Martha were touched beyond words. Even little Sean, finally allowed in to see his mother, was silent with awe—a naval officer in dress uniform had delivered the special message. Don had just read the note aloud.

*The Executive Mansion*
*of the President of the United States of America*
*Washington, District of Columbia*
*20$^{th}$ day of January, 1881*


Dear Mrs. Wake,

*Mrs. Hayes and I want to send our empathy for your illness and best wishes for a rapid recovery to full health. You are in our hearts and in our prayers to a most merciful God.*

*Your husband is a gallant and valued officer in our Navy and we also pray that he will be united with his loving family soon. That will be a joyous occasion, indeed.*

*When you are feeling better, we hope you will honor us with a special personal visit to the Executive Mansion. We remember well your last visit and eagerly anticipate the next.*

*Your very respectful friends and most obedient servants,*

*Rutherford B. Hayes, President of the United States and Mrs. Rutherford Hayes*


"Oh, Mama," said Useppa softly as she leaned over her mother. "It's extraordinary, just *extraordinary!*. The President and Mrs. Hayes remember you. What a wonderful note. And just look at the lovely flowers."

Linda was groggy from the opium, but managed a smile. "Yes, lovely. Nice of them."

"And they even remembered Daddy. He would love to be here and see this."

Linda feebly took Useppa's arm in her hand and pulled her

daughter closer. "He is, darling." She touched her chest. "He's right here, in my heart."

Linda raised her hand and waved around the room. "Peter's here, in all our hearts . . ."

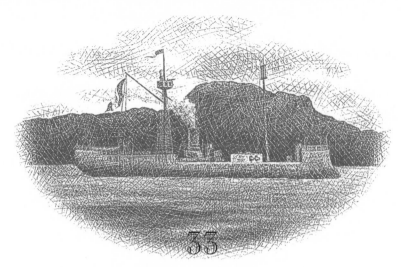

# 33

# Merci Beaucoup pour la Humanité

"We'll keep the speed low. I don't want any sparks showing from the stack," said Wake as they entered the darkness of the harbor away from the light of the burning city of Callao.

"Look at that," said Rork, pointing to the *Atahualpa*. The monitor was scuttled, sitting on the harbor bottom. Next to her was a barge with Chilean sailors trying to recover something from the water—the scuttled *Toro* submarine. Wake wondered where Gonzalez was, whether he'd ever received the cryptic message, hoping he was alive.

Minutes later they were in the outer harbor. The moon gave them enough illumination to see the shapes of ships offshore, black against the horizon. Once around the northern breakwater, Wake swung the tiller over and headed north.

The bosun climbed over sleeping bodies packed tight against each other and stood aft next to Wake. "Not headed south to go out around them, sir?"

"No, Rork. I don't think there's time left for fancy plans. We'll just have to chance it and try to get as far north along the coast as we can. Stay a mile or so off the coast. In about five hours or so until the sky will start to get light. We're doing about three or four knots, so that'll be fifteen miles maybe. At least there're no wind and waves to fight."

"Where're the Chilean lines north o' the city, do ya think, sir?"

"Not a clue, Rork."

"Aye, sir. The whole thing's been totally on faith so far, hasn't it? But we've done fair, an' as me sainted granny used to say, 'God may send ye down a stony path, Sean me boyo, but nary to worry, for He'll always provide ye wi' stout shoes along the way.' "

Just then the engine gasped and the crankshaft began to slow down. Wake checked the pressure gauge and found it dropping. They needed more fire. He looked next to the boiler. Two pieces of kindling. Frantically he peered around the boat. In the hurry of the escape they had forgotten to ascertain the fuel load.

"Break up the thwarts, anything, Rork. We'll feed the fire anything that burns."

"Aye, aye, sir." The bosun ripped two wooden seats out by brute strength. Oswaldo began looking for combustible items and held up an oar.

"No! Not them! We'll need them," yelled Wake.

The pressure was still dropping. A leak in the boiler tank? Wake was worried. He dared not touch it but got close and listened for the hissing of escaping steam, hoping his face wouldn't find it the hard way in the dark, by scalding. Rork shook his head at Wake so close to the tank.

"Paper, sir. Use paper to find the steam, not your face. Old engineer's trick."

Wake fished through his pockets. No paper. None of the men had any paper. Then Oswaldo held up his pocket Bible and asked if that would do? Yes, answered Wake.

The torn front page found the leak. It was by the girding strap just aft of the forward end of the boiler tank. The page was blown out of Wake's hand. He examined the seam of the strap.

The leak was at least six to eight inches long—too long to plug.

The engine barely turned over, even though the firebox below the boiler was full of wood that was starting to burn. The leaking steam was beginning to scream now. Wake looked at Rork and shook his head. The boat slowed.

"There's a mast an' a lanteen sailin' rig, sir. I'll have it up in a jiffy an' we'll sail the little darlin' out o' here."

Wake didn't say anything as he collapsed on the stern seat. He didn't have the strength to point out the obvious.

After much growling and swearing, the rig was set up five minutes later. Rork stood at the bow after shackling down the forestay and turned to look at his sail. It hung limp.

There was no wind.

The children and soldiers, along with the stoic Oswaldo, were sprawled in slumber, lulled by exhaustion and the motion of the sea as the boat drifted. In the bow, Woodgerd was snoring fitfully. To the east, the night had turned from black to dark gray with just a touch of mist. The distant jagged mountains of Peru were starting to silhouette, a warning that danger was growing with every hour.

Rork was on watch, arm wrapped around the mast, scanning the shoreline. He swung around the mast and surveyed the southern horizon at sea. There was a black shape in the gray loom. White water crinkled around it starkly. A bow wave. The shape was heading for them quickly. Rork made his way carefully over the collapsed bodies and whispered to a dozing Wake.

"Company comin', sir."

Wake jerked up and followed the bosun's finger. Letting his eyes adjust, he shook his head at what he saw. "Well, I guess we can't outrun them, so I'd better figure out a way to outtalk them, Sean."

"Yep, that's me thinkin' as well, sir. Now's the time for some blarney, if ever there was one. Uh oh . . ."

A group of winking flashes erupted from shadowy shapes on the horizon, well behind the approaching vessel. Faded thuds sounded seconds later. Wake couldn't tell if they were Chilean or the foreign neutral observer fleet, but the heavy guns of somebody's ships were firing. The sky was lightening fast and he could see the masts of the vessel coming toward them. More distant flashes from the horizon.

Woodgerd stumbled aft to join them. "Humph . . . Those damn Chilis are starting to see in the light and're firing again." He nodded toward the approaching vessel. "Any idea of who that is?"

"People that don't bloody fancy any o' us, Colonel Woodgerd," said Rork

Woodgerd's appearance suddenly gave Wake an idea. An idea he knew Woodgerd wouldn't like, not one bit, but that might buy them a little time to figure out something better.

"Get the Chilean flag down, Rork, that'll just complicate our situation." Then he turned to the colonel. "Mike, I've got an idea, but it's a little dicey."

"Most of yours are. What is it?"

Wake proceeded to tell him, watching the mercenary's eyes narrow in disbelief, then anger. Rork looked bemused.

"You're joking, right?" Woodgerd asked.

"This isn't the time for jokes, Mike. I know it sounds crazy—"

"It sounds suicidal, Wake—for me and my men."

"You're in a helluva tough spot anyway, Mike. Got a better idea?"

A string of foul oaths came in reply, after which Woodgerd said, "No, dammit, I don't."

"Aye, Colonel," Rork said cheerfully. "Now don't you worry a wee bit. Peter Wake's got a bit o' the Sainted Isle's gift o' gab in him, all right. Why, next to me, he's the smoothest talkin' man on the coast."

"I hope to hell he is, Rork."

In the distance Wake noticed the bombardment had stopped and briefly wondered why. Then his mind returned to the problem immediately at hand—the vessel was almost to them and there was no time to lose. Everyone aboard was woken up and quickly told the plan.

It was a Chilean gunboat. The lieutenant in command looked down at them and ordered his men to help them up to the gunboat's main deck. The children and Oswaldo were grouped aft, Woodgerd and his soldiers forward under gunpoint of the sailors. The Americans stayed amidship with the wary lieutenant, who spoke no English. Wake could see the man was not thrilled at his find of neutrals—especially American neutrals—and didn't know what to do. Wake explained the situation in his basic Spanish, hoping he was using the correct wording.

"*Teñiente,* I am Lieutenant Commander Peter Wake of the United States Navy, a neutral naval observer of the war. This is my servant, Senior Boatswain Sean Rork." He gestured to the bosun, who was wearing a fierce expression. "And we thank you for coming to our rescue, as well as that of the children. It obviously was God's will that you helped us, as did the great Chilean Navy men at the port last night."

"How is that, sir?"

Wake registered that the lieutenant was using the polite form of the Spanish language and that his features had softened somewhat. Evidently the lieutenant didn't know the boat was stolen. So far, so good.

"We were given this boat to go out to our American ship by your comrades ashore, then to return it. However, upon steaming out of the harbor we ran upon these rats leaving Peru—" He swept a hand toward Woodgerd and the soldiers, who didn't need pretension to look scared. "—in another boat, who had these innocent hostage children with them. I presume they were going to use them to bargain their way out of Peru, the scoundrels. Maybe to sell them as *slaves*. Who knows?"

Wake caught a glance of Woodgerd glaring at him, and went on.

"Fortunately the hand of God was with us and, amazingly, we surprised them and were able to liberate the children and their chaperon. The other boat was sinking so we put everyone in this one. But the engine died, as did the wind. We drifted at sea, but then God provided again! He provided *you* to our rescue. Thank you, again, on behalf of the United States Navy and these frightened children and this man of the Church."

The lieutenant was overwhelmed. It was an implausible story, but the man didn't want to take the chance of making a diplomatic *faux pas*. Not now, when victory was so close. He paused, then decided to do what Wake hoped he would. Nothing.

"This is a matter for my superiors, sir. We will proceed there. In the meantime the pirates will be put under arrest and the children cared for."

"Excellent, Lieutenant. The reputation of your navy is well deserved and my president shall hear of it. You are a hero and I am sure there is a medal for you in this. By the way, the leader of those men is, very regrettably, a former countryman of mine. He has violated several laws of our country, all of which are punishable by death."

Wake spat out the next words. He'd conjured them while waiting for the gunboat to come alongside the launch. This part had to be done just right. "I am going to *personally* put him to trial today and then have the pleasure of watching him die slowly aboard a United States Navy warship by stretching his neck. We have special knots that don't kill quickly. The scum will dangle and twist in the wind for a week, rotting in the sun as a warning to others."

Woodgerd's face went blank, his hand trembling uncontrollably as Rork chuckled and rubbed his hands with ominous relish. The Chilean sailors made a collective gasp as they muttered about the *yanqui's* gruesome vision. Even the Chilean navy, the most disciplined in Latin America, didn't have one of those barbaric hangman's knots that made a man die slowly.

Rork slowly nodded as Wake leered at the lieutenant. "I want that man in my eyesight at all times, under the firm guard of my petty officer here. I know that as a naval officer, you understand exactly what I mean."

"Commander, I regret to inform you that the United States warship has left station days ago. It is not off Lima now, sir. I think they went to Panama for dispatches and supplies and will probably be back in a day or two. Maybe three."

"Then the French flagship will do. Admiral Dupetit-Thouars is a dear friend and will be pleased to see me, take my prisoner, and hear of your professionalism."

The lieutenant decided that this *norteamericano,* even though he appeared in disheveled bloodied clothing and clearly hadn't had a shave in days, was not one to be trifled with. Plus, he obviously had influence in high places and there could be a medal, certainly an honorable mention, and perhaps a promotion. And what difference would it make—let him keep the prisoner.

"It is my honor to fulfill your request, sir. We shall now go to my admiral's fleet."

The sun had already burned off the mist when they arrived at the fleet off Lima two hours later. Wake's mind was whirling. He hadn't anticipated the absence of the American warship and he couldn't let the lieutenant take everyone to the Chilean admiral. Sooner or later, probably sooner, word would get out to the fleet that a *yanqui* had stolen a Chilean naval launch.

The British had three ships, the French two, loitering off

Lima by the Chilean blockading fleet. Wake observed that while enroute to the Chilean flagship the gunboat would pass by the warship flying an admiral's pennant and the huge tri-color of France.

He sensed many nervous eyes on him—especially Woodgerd and the soldiers. A desperate notion came to him. He didn't think it would work, but there was no choice. The lives of one hundred thirty-seven people were in his hands.

The lieutenant was pacing the deck, intent on his own view of events, and how he would present them to his admiral. Wake cleared his throat and spoke in his best quarterdeck command demeanor, translated as best he could into Spanish, "Ah-hhm, Lieutenant! There is the French flagship. I need to speak with Admiral Dupetit-Thouars at once, so that he knows of the gallantry of your actions and of my immediate requirements. It is a matter of the laws of war and I'll need a gig to take me across to him. Time is of the essence."

The lieutenant physically stopped in his tracks and stared at Wake, who hadn't stopped at all, but gave rapid orders in English to Rork to prepare the prisoners, gather their baggage, and spread the word for everyone to be ready to move quickly. Then Wake, acting as if the lieutenant had already acquiesced, went to the starboard rail and waved to the French officer of the deck. "*Bonjour, amis des Etats-Unis. Un message à l'amiral de Commandant Peter Wake! Vite, vite, s'il vous plaît!*"

The lieutenant walked up to Wake and stammered out in Spanish. "Sir, you want to go to the French ship *now?*"

"Of course. That is what I said. We are passing them. Stop now."

The lieutenant hesitated, then sighed, and gave orders for the gig to be put over the side as the gunboat lost speed. The *yanqui* was *loco*, of course, but perhaps there really was a promotion in it for him? Wake tried to stay nonchalant, amazed that it worked. Now all he had to do was convince the French to violate international law.

"Lieutenant Commander Peter Wake, a pleasure as always. Please forgive my regrettably bad English. What is the occasion? You appear to have had some difficulty," said Admiral Dupetit-Thouars as they lounged in the great cabin over snifters of Hennessy *Privilège* V.S.O.P. cognac. The admiral was referring to Wake's haggard appearance—he looked like one of the dregs off the docks. For a moment Wake let the cognac's warmth flood through him, feeling his muscles relax. Then the vision of Woodgerd, Rork, the soldiers, and the children came into his mind, bringing him back to reality. The gunboat was still close by, waiting for Wake to return.

"Got involved in a matter of honor, sir. Had to rescue some children, a monk, an American officer serving the Peruvians, some Peruvian soldiers, and myself and my petty officer assistant. It's been a very long couple of weeks and the last twenty-four hours have been a nightmare, as you can see by my less than impressive attire."

"It sounds like quite a story, Commander. I would like to hear it."

Wake told him the whole tale. Dupetit-Thouars cast looks of concern when hearing of the fugitives fleeing through the Catacombs of the Dead, and nodded approvingly at the points where Wake described making difficult decisions. Finally, Wake got to the end.

"And so, once we were captured, I bluffed my way here. And now I have the obvious request, Admiral, from one *officier* of the *Légion d'honneur* to another. I need you to insist that the children and monk be brought aboard here for their safety and Colonel Woodgerd and his men be brought aboard for future American prosecution of piracy."

"But technically Colonel Woodgerd and his men are not

pirates. They were at war. They are legitimate prisoners of war of the Chileans."

"The piracy story was a *ruse de guerre* on my part, sir, to get them away from the Chileans. Otherwise they would rot to death in a prison dungeon, or more likely suffer far worse than that at the hands of the enemy. They fought honorably for months, letting them die now at the hands of the Chileans is wrong."

Dupetit-Thouars stood and walked to the stern gallery window, drumming his fingers on the sill. "You ask a lot."

"I ask for a decision to do what is right, sir. To save lives in this region that has seen so many lives lost. I ask it of a naval officer who is well known as a man who knows what is right, and who does what is right."

"It is also a matter of honor, Commander. *My* honor. You are asking me to make a statement under . . . how do you say it in English? . . . *sous un prétexte faux* . . . under a false pretext."

Wake decided was time to be frank. "Yes, sir. I consider it a *ruse de guerre* to save lives."

Dupetit-Thouars continued to gaze out the window. "Do you know what I did this morning, Commander, with the Chileans?"

"No, sir."

Dupetit-Thouars turned on his heel and faced Wake. "The information from shore has been horrific. So this morning at dawn I informed the Chileans that I would not allow them to ransack and loot the city of Lima, and Callao, anymore. I informed them, accompanied by blank charges fired from my guns, that the Republic of France would oversee the safety of the foreign neutrals and the general civil population, and turn her guns upon anyone that was inclined to doubt or dispute that. The British warships have joined me. A joint landing force of a thousand men went ashore an hour ago. The Chileans have wisely backed away from confrontation."

Wake was astounded. It explained the brief gunfire he'd seen, the nervousness and compliance of the gunboat lieutenant. "The right decision, Admiral. You have saved thousands of lives by that decision already. I am asking for one hundred thirty more."

Dupetit-Thouars looked suddenly weary. "Yes . . . very well, you shall have it, Commander. I will write out orders immediately. My officer will present them to the Chilean gunboat commander and your people will be brought over here on one of our ship's cutters. Woodgerd and his Peruvian soldiers will be brought into our custody, officially to be turned over to the Americans for piracy, or something of that sort."

He smiled roguishly. "The Chileans will not protest. Not after this morning's events. We will transfer everyone to the American warship when she returns to her station here in a few days. Your admiral can arrange further transport onward from this place. I presume that is agreeable to you?"

Wake fought back tears. "Yes, sir. Thank you, sir. *Merci beaucoup pour la humanité.*"

"You are quite welcome, Commander," said the admiral. He called for his aide, gave the man his orders, then looked at Wake. "And one thing I would ask of *you*, if you please?"

"Of course, sir. What can I do?"

Dupetit-Thouars raised an eyebrow. "Perhaps a bath? We will give you a uniform. You really need to enhance your appearance." He paused and clucked disapprovingly. "After all, Commander Wake, you are not looking very much the part of an *officier* of the *Légion d'honneur* right now, are you? It is rather embarrassing— you know we *chevaliers* must keep up our image."

A bath and clean clothes. Heavenly luxuries. "Aye, aye, sir."

Dupetit-Thouars noted the tears on the American's cheek. He put a hand on Wake's shoulder. "*You* are the one who saved them, Commander. It seems that Bishop Mocenni picked the right man."

# 34

# Homeward

## February 1881

Three days later Admiral Dupetit-Thouars was relieved to have the unauthorized passengers off his ship, and Admiral Thomas Holdup Stevens was less than amused to find another hundred and thirty mouths to feed on board *Pensacola.* But that was the least of it for Stevens. Lieutenant Commander Wake had felt the need to report to Stevens all that he'd done since he'd been ashore. The admiral wished Wake would've kept his mouth shut.

Stevens knew that Wake's various violations while ashore and afloat could fill a court-martial book and most certainly would not look good if they ever got out to the hostile powers in this war. The very thought of that made Stevens' stomach knot up. His head throbbed as he added up the potential charges against a man nominally under *his* command.

Wake had violated the international rules of war for neutrals, specifically the Treaty of Paris of 1856, by actively taking sides in this conflict—good God, thought Stevens, the man had actually *killed* Chilean soldiers down in those catacombs, *stolen* a Chilean naval vessel, and *lied* to Chilean naval officers!

Wake had also violated United States foreign policy by offering refuge to Peruvian combatants and using them to further his violations of international law. Hell, it sounded like he had planned out their operation against the Chilean launch! And the man had violated Stevens' personal orders by going absent without permission for a month! In addition, some pompous ass named Kronburg at the legation ashore was making noises about how Wake hadn't helped the diplomats at all.

Not to mention that Wake had somehow connived the French admiral into being an accomplice in flaunting international law, complicating Stevens' relationship with the representatives of every nationality in sight. It was just one helluva damned mess and now the whole thing was in *his* lap.

Stevens groaned. His head felt like it would explode. If the press got ahold of Wake's exploits they'd have a field day and the wrath of Admiral Porter would head south toward him. He could see the questions now—why didn't he maintain control over this officer? Why didn't he insist on more frequent reporting in? Why didn't he send along one of his own staff to assist? Just how and when did he lose control of the naval observers in his area of responsibility?

And on top of everything he now had orders from Washington, received while reprovisioning at Panama, to send Wake home the moment he appeared. He looked up at Wake standing at attention three feet in front of his desk.

"Commander, I will reflect upon this situation and contemplate preferring the appropriate charges. There are so damn many that I'll need to try to keep track of them all and that may take awhile."

Wake kept staring at the after bulkhead. "Yes, sir."

"But first, fortunately for me, but perhaps unfortunately for you, the leadership in Washington—that would be the one and only Admiral Porter and the secretary of the navy—want you home as soon as possible, Commander. You will leave aboard the chartered steamer for Panama *today,* courtesy of the Catholic Church."

Stevens was still surprised by that particular turn of affairs. The same day he'd returned to the station and found Wake and his entourage, he'd been handed a formal letter from some high-ranking Catholic bishop ashore, asking him to find a steamer to transport the Peruvian soldiers to nearby neutral Ecuador; and Colonel Woodgerd, Brother Oswaldo Lento, and the one hundred seven Chinese-Peruvian children, with Lieutenant Commander Wake and Senior Boatswain's Mate Rork, all to Panama—that the Church would pay for it.

Happy to get the civilians off his ship, the Peruvian soldiers off American territory, and Wake out of his hair, Stevens had immediately sent a staff officer and an armed boat crew to coerce the cynical captain of a worn-down Mexican steamer heading north to take the passengers, based on the promissory note from the Church.

The other passengers were already disembarking the warship for the steamer. Only Wake and Rork were still aboard *Pensacola.* Wake cleared his throat.

"Aye, aye, sir. May I take Bosun Rork? He'll probably be a witness at my court-martial." Wake didn't elaborate further. He didn't have to.

"Yes, take that damn bosun with you."

"Aye, aye, sir."

A week later, in the glow of a glorious Pacific sunset, Bishop Vargas met the steamer at the dock, accompanied by a flock of nuns who gushed with joy over the children when they gingerly made their way down the gangway to the wharf. Oswaldo had a rapid conversation in Spanish, then herded the whole crowd toward the cathedral for a thanksgiving service. After that, the children were bound for the parsonage for clean clothing, a decent meal, and real beds. Wake was overjoyed to see the children chattering and laughing again in the care of the nuns. It had been months since they'd had any maternal influences.

Wake and Rork, in new uniforms, and Woodgerd, now attired in civilian clothes, came down to the wharf last and were greeted by Vargas. The bishop beamed as he took Wake's hand in both of his, pumping it in appreciation.

"Welcome back to Panama, my dear friend Peter Wake. Thank you so much for what you have done to save the children. They are finally safe and going to start their new lives here, under the protection of the Church. I hope in the future you will return and meet them as they grow and mature."

Vargas turned to Rork as the bosun walked up. "Oh! And this man must be the Irishman that I've heard so much about, Sean Rork. So pleased to meet you, sir. Thank you, sir."

"Very pleased to make your acquaintance, but I'm not a 'sir,' Your Excellency. I'm a bosun. Commander Wake here is a officer, an' that makes him a 'sir.' "

Wake introduced Woodgerd, but Vargas apparently already had heard of him too. "The famous Colonel Woodgerd? You have done a good deed, sir. You helped to save these children. God bless you, my son."

Woodgerd bobbed his head, muttered something about self-preservation and walked over to a street food vendor.

"How in the world did you know we were coming, and what's happened?" asked Wake.

"The cable is back up and working in Lima. My friend Bishop Mocenni sent me a telegraph message explaining what had happened. *Very* exciting, Peter."

That worried Wake. "An open message? That means the Chilean occupation authorities will know."

Vargas laughed. "It was in Jesuit code couched in classical Latin, Peter. We've been using it for a couple of hundred years now. The message's contents are safe."

"Well, sir, the navy wanted it kept quiet so I'd appreciate it if you would not tell anyone outside your chain of command."

Vargas displayed that knowing smile Wake remembered so well.

"We never do, Commander."

The bishop rubbed his hands together as Woodgerd reappeared with an enchilada stuffed in his mouth. "And now, my sons, it is time for some refreshment and relaxation, in honor of your good deeds. You have missed the train to Colón for today, so tonight the Diocese of Panama will have the honor and pleasure of being your host."

Vargas held up a hand and motioned forward. "Follow me, gentlemen. We are eating and drinking only the finest tonight—money is no obstacle. And I am the one buying."

Woodgerd gave Wake a look of awe. "Wake, I don't know how you do it, but someday I want you to teach me."

Wake laughed, then remembered his duty. "Bishop, thank you very much. We accept, but first I have to check in at the consulate."

"Peter, they closed an hour ago," explained Vargas. "It is time to enjoy an evening with friends, my son."

Rork gave Wake the "what-are-you-doing?" look while Woodgerd grumbled, "Wake, just say 'aye, aye'—or whatever it is you squids say. Come on, I need a drink—a *real* drink—and the chaplain says he's buying. Lead the way, Bishop."

The next morning Wake was feeling decidedly un-religious. A ray of light pierced the window, moving slowly across the room with the rising sun until it rested on his eyelids, rousing him from his rum-enhanced slumber. He opened his eyes and worked his jaw, slowly remembering where he was—a guest room in the bishop's rectory. Then he remembered the previous evening and grimaced.

Had he really drunk all that rum?

Wake's head felt fine until he tried to rise out of the bed and stand. Instantly, a pounding in his ears started and he fell sideways into a table against the wall, knocking a crucifix down off the wall and onto his head. A trickle of blood made its way down his nose as he sat on the floor. In the other bed, Woodgerd cackled with laughter, his voice hoarse from singing all night.

"God's punishment for a good man gone bad. One *helluva* a drunk last night, Peter Wake, and you were in it till the bitter end. Guess it's true what they say about sailors and drinking."

"Mike, please, we're in a church. Show some respect. No swearing. And don't talk so loud. Please . . ."

Rork staggered in from the room next door. "All hands doin' well here? Thought I heard a bit o' a crash. You officer lads ain't dancin' again, are ye?"

Woodgerd cackled again and pointed to Wake on the floor. "Our fearless friend fell down. God nailed him good on the head for his transgressions last night. Rork, you're Catholic, isn't one of the Ten Commandments against getting drunk?"

"No, sir. You're thinkin' o' the second o' the seven deadly sins. Gluttony. One o' me personal favorites." He helped Wake up. "I'm not feelin' so frisky me ownself this morn, gentlemen."

Woodgerd launched himself out of the bed, grunted, "Ooo*rrahhhh!*" loudly, and announced, "Up and at 'em! Takes a *man* to tackle the day after. Soldiers are tougher than you girly sailor boys." Then his eyes rolled back in his head as he swayed, collapsing back on the bed, out cold. Seconds later he was snoring.

Rork volunteered to check in at the consulate, saying the walk would do him good and that he'd meet the other two for the midday meal later. They could relax that morning, the train for the Caribbean side of the Isthmus didn't leave until two in the afternoon.

When Rork got to the consulate he was surprised Wake had no mail. He made the clerk look in the old mail filed away in a box in the cellar. It paid off, a dozen letters from Linda were found, dating back a month—they'd never made it to the *Pensacola*. The clerk apologized, mumbling that someone had apparently misfiled them in the dead letter box.

The bosun had an odd sensation, which he surmised was his Gaelic intuition, as he studied the envelopes. They appeared normal—he'd seen many of Linda's letters in the past eighteen years. Then why, Rork asked himself, did he have this bad feeling about them? Rork didn't pretend to be a devoutly religious man, but he suddenly had the feeling he should visit a church and do some thinking.

The closest was a tiny old sanctuary a block away from the consulate. It was empty except for some elderly nuns gathered in a corner. He stared at the envelopes in his hand and prayed for strength to make the right decision for his friend Peter, debating whether to open them. If it was bad news, would letting his friend know now, when he still had a long voyage home ahead of him, do any good? Or would it be better for him to not have that heartache until the last moment. But if the letters had good news, then they would cheer his friend up.

He beckoned a passing nun over to him. "*Buenas dias,* Sister, do you speak English?"

She shook her head but came back a few minutes later with another nun.

"I speak English. How can I help you, sir?"

"Aye, thank you, Sister. Would ye happen to have a pot o' tea on the boil?"

"Yes, we do. It is in the back room. Do you want some tea?"

"Aye, a cuppa would hit the spot nicely, Sister. But I'm mainly in need o' that steam . . ."

The Americans were lunching with Vargas and Blanchet before leaving, and the canal company was paying the bill. Gaston Blanchet's furrowed face appeared a decade older than when Wake had last seen him, in this same barroom of the Grand Hotel the previous year. Wake felt sorry for the man. The young French engineer still had his famous good looks, but was clearly far more subdued. Well, Panama will do that to you, thought Wake, remembering the yellow fever Panama had given *him*.

Blanchet flashed a smile. "Peter Wake, so very good to see you again. All the city is talking about the children you saved. Bishop Vargas here says you are quite the hero, my friend."

That kind of talk embarrassed Wake. "A lot of people worked to save them, Gaston. Thank you for inviting us to lunch. How are things going on the canal project?"

"Slow but sure. I must say that you were correct on the disease and the labor problems. But we will overcome them. And we are forging ahead on the financial aspects. The directors in Paris have signed on a new man in America to assist with the selling of investments in your country. Richard Thompson, the secretary of the navy who is soon leaving his office. Do you know him?"

"What? Did you say Thompson, the secretary of *our* navy?"

"Why yes. You seem to be surprised, Peter. Why is that?"

"Hmm, I am surprised. I thought he despised Latin American politics, and our president—his direct boss—wasn't exactly enthusiastic about the French building the canal. I'll bet he got a sweetheart deal to do the selling job. Got his money up front, didn't he?"

"Yes, I have heard that it is quite a lucrative financial agreement."

"I guess I'm not surprised, Gaston. Not surprised at all."

"But he is a man who has much influence with Americans, no?" asked Blanchet.

"Maybe a few in Indiana, but none anywhere else that I know. I thought he was going to retire to Indiana and grow corn or something."

"Oh, that is different than what I have been told. I think that Monsieur de Lesseps believes Secretary Thompson has many friends in Washington and New York. That he will be able to sell many bonds for the company."

What's President Hayes think of Thompson playing for the other team? wondered Wake. "Who knows, Gaston? Who really knows?"

After lunch Wake went to the Pacific Mail office and sent a brief cable to the Navy Department reporting his location, with no explanation of his past two months. That was best described in person.

TO: ADM D. PORTER
NAVY DEPT/WASH DC
09FEB81
FROM: LTCMDR P. WAKE/SPCL ASSGNMT/PAC SQDN
   XXX RCVD ORDERS TO RETURN XXX IN PANAMA
NOW XXX BOUND TO HDQTRS XXX ETA 2 WEEKS XXX
   LTCMDR WAKE

He sent a second cable to Linda with the same text, but ending with "Love, Peter." Afterward, Wake sighed and said, "All right, got a message to Linda and also did my friggin' duty to the bureaucratic bilge rats in Washington . . ."

He caught Rork looking at him oddly as they walked out. Rork had been eyeing him askance a lot lately and Wake was tired of it.

"So why're you looking all uppity, Rork? What's your *prob-lem?*"

Woodgerd had strolled on ahead. Rork let out a breath and slowed his pace. "I'm a-lookin' at me old an' dear friend, Peter

Wake, who's been changin' these last few years, an' not for the best. I've been meanin' to speak on it. Guess now's a good time."

Wake stopped. "Just what the hell are you talking about?"

"You're a cynical man, Peter. The last years, since Africa, you've gotten cynical about every wee thing. Oh, aye, ye still do the right thing, as you've always done—but now ye do it grudgin'ly. Your heart's gone dark, me friend. I don't know if it's duty in Washington among them politicos, or what we went through in Africa, or what we've been through down here, but I'm worryin' 'bout the man I've known for eighteen long years now. You used to steer clear o' that type. Now ye've become one. 'Tis even in yer words. Cursin' like a Ulsterman in Limerick all the time now—like that man ahead o' us. The good colonel is a tortured soul an' you're headed that way too."

Wake saw the concern in Rork's eyes and knew his old friend was right—he had been looking at everything darkly for some time. Was it Africa, where they'd both been beaten and sold as slaves, or was it working in Washington, where idealism died daily in the reality of politics?

"All right. Maybe you're right, Sean. I guess I have been swearing more lately. And being a bit cynical. I'll do some thinking on that." He put a hand on the bosun's shoulder. "Thanks for telling me."

Rork flashed a grin and shrugged. "Aye, what're friends for? Times get tougher the older we get, Peter—'tis our outlook that makes it better or worse. Your outlook was always inspirin' to the lads an' to me. I want you to get that back. You'll need it for gettin' through what life's got in store for us. It don't get easier. Sure as the green grass o' Cork it'll get tougher."

From a hundred feet ahead they heard Woodgerd's voice boom out.

"You two sorry friggin' squids've been lollygagging around back there long enough. Get your lazy damn carcasses the hell up here. We've got a train to catch and you're slowing me down!"

Wake nodded toward Woodgerd. "I was really starting to sound like that?"

"Aye, ye were. But not quite as *colorful* as the colonel."

Wake was tempted to backslide into an oath-filled rant when they got to the train station half an hour later. Their train wasn't late—it didn't exist. The train had gone off the track earlier that day near Gorgona, just short of the Barbacoas Bridge. The other two trains on the Pacific side had been sent with men and gear to recover it. No one knew how long it would be before the trains would be able to get through. Woodgerd swore creatively for five minutes without letup. Rork glanced at Wake and shook his head ruefully.

The only other way to get to Barbacoas Bridge so they could catch the train to the Caribbean side of Panama was by slow wagon train. None was scheduled, though there was a rumor one might be assembled *mañana*. The three men trudged back to the bar of the Grand Hotel, where they joined Blanchet and Bishop Vargas for dinner and drinks.

They stayed there another five days.

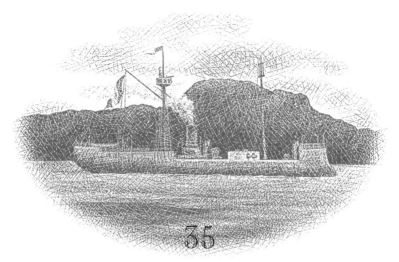

# 35

# The Last Delay

The six thousand-mile journey from Peru, with one peril or frustration after another, had mentally and physically exhausted him, but now Wake was so close to home he recognized the acrid foundry smoke from the iron-working shops of the Washington Navy Yard. Tired and melancholy as he was, though, when he stepped foot in his homeland Wake found out he couldn't go home to his family until he handled a final delay. The last obstacle was none other than Rutherford B. Hayes.

Beside him in the coach car sat Woodgerd, on the bench across was Rork and Lieutenant Charles Hostetler. An old shipmate and friend, Hostetler was newly stationed at the Navy Department. He'd been detailed to come to the Baltimore docks, present Wake with urgent orders, and escort him via first-class train cabin to an immediate private audience at the White House.

That boded ill and Wake was worried. His last telegraph cable message from Panama had predicted he'd be home in two weeks. It had taken three and a half weeks and was now late February. A hundred questions filled his mind as he sat there staring out the window, swaying with the motion of the train. All of them were unpleasant. None had answers his superiors would like.

Would the leadership be angry he was late, like before? That would be minor compared to their anger if they'd heard of what had happened, and what he'd done in Peru. Had Admiral Stevens recommended charges? Did he telegraph them ahead of Wake's arrival? Had it blown up into an international scandal? Did the press know already? It was certain that his career was in jeopardy, if not over. Would he be dismissed personally by the president? He'd never heard of that, but Hayes was no wallflower and had been known to lose his temper.

Wake pushed his sinking career out of his mind and concentrated on more important questions. Linda—how was she? He hadn't seen a letter from her in months. Why hadn't she written since November? Did she still have that pain or did the black doctors at Howard relieve her? And his children, his wonderful children—how were they? How much had they grown? What had he missed in their lives?

He asked Hostetler for news, but the man had none. He'd only been assigned to headquarters since early January. He and his wife Barbara lived outside the city in Maryland and hadn't seen Wake's family. It grew silent in the train cabin, each man occupied in his own thoughts as the train rumbled on.

The late afternoon vista outside the window was a beautiful white landscape in amber sunlight, completely the opposite of the environment in which Wake had just spent six months. Winter had descended mightily on Washington. Hostetler told him there had been two weeks of unending subzero temperatures, with ice paralyzing the city. He filled him in on the political atmosphere too. Hayes was going to be in office only a few more days—James Garfield would be inaugurated on March 4th. Big changes were in the air—changes having to do with the war in South America. No one knew for sure what, yet, but everyone was speculating.

They rattled their way along the Baltimore and Potomac Railroad's bridge onto Virginia Avenue. The snow inside the city was sprinkled with cinders and soot. Wake realized his three companions had gotten quieter with each mile closer to Washington. He wondered why. Woodgerd was going home to his wife in Alexandria and should be happy, Rork to his drinking cronies in the senior petty officers' quarters at the Navy Yard, Hostetler was going to have the excitement of visiting the president with Wake. None could be held responsible for Wake's decisions or actions. But all were looking glum. He'd seen them talking among themselves at the docks. They knew something—it was obvious to Wake. Something they didn't want to talk about. A court-martial, most likely.

Well, he'd been through that kind of mess before. Off the coast of Panama, eleven years earlier, a decision of Wake's ended in court-martial for mutiny six months later, ironically at the same Washington Navy Yard that was now sliding by outside the window. Wake had gotten through that because he'd decided to do the right thing for the right reasons.

His decision in Peru also was the right one and he had no regrets. He was getting angry just thinking about the possibility of a court-martial. If they wanted to hang him out to dry for it, then they damn well wouldn't do it without one hellacious fight. He caught Rork glancing at him with an odd look. More than concern, it was almost despair.

"Sean, come on over for dinner Friday night. We'll broach some of that old Royal Navy stuff I've saved. It's good rum."

Rork nodded. Wake decided to cheer him up.

"Come on, Sean, I've been in trouble before and gotten through it all right. I'll get through this too. You're too morose about this. What happened to that famous Gaelic wit?"

Wake saw all three were looking anywhere but him. Rork finally said, "Aye, sir. Me body's tired an' me mind's empty as a Saxon's heart. No riposte from an Irish bosun today, I'm afraid."

It was a ten-block walk to the White House from the Baltimore and Potomac depot at Pennsylvania Avenue and Sixth Street, usually only a fifteen-minute walk, twenty-five in bad weather like this, but a Navy Department landau waited to transport them as they walked out of the building. Wake realized it was the secretary of the navy's personal vehicle and thought that most unusual—especially for a mere lieutenant commander escorted by an even lower lieutenant. Hostetler mentioned that he heard Secretary Thompson had already left office and was out of town, his term ended in days anyway.

Wake didn't like surprises. He didn't like not understanding what was going on around him and to him. It made him wary, nervous. But perhaps he wasn't going to be court-martialed. If he was a political *persona non grata* they would have let him walk.

Woodgerd had to transfer to the local train to Alexandria. Before he departed, he shook Wake's hand. "You have my address. I'm just across the river. If you don't contact me, I'll be looking for *you,* squid."

Rork wasn't ordered to the White House, so he hailed a cab for the Navy Yard. As he got in, he stopped, turned to Wake and leaned over, squeezing his shoulder. "Never forget that a lot o' people are alive today because o' what you did, Peter."

Wake began to protest, but Rork held Wake's shoulder tight and spoke again, his eyes leveled at his old comrade. "Aye, we do what we can, then God takes over, me friend, an' sometimes works in mysterious ways. 'Tis that way in all things. Remember that. I'll see you the day after tomorrow, on Friday morn, an' we'll down some o' Nelson's Blood an' talk o' things."

Then he was in the cab and gone, Wake suddenly realizing Rork had said Friday morning instead of the evening. Plus, his friend's tone had been odd. Out of character, portentous. He was pondering that when the postern opened the door of the landau. Seconds later they were clattering along westbound for the White House, the same route he'd walked the last time back from South America. It was after the usual afternoon hour of congestion and traffic was light. They made good time and minutes later the landau was rounding the curved driveway of the White House.

The horses' hooves echoed in the mansion's portico as the massive double doors opened and a tall regal black man in black tie and tails walked out into the cold air. Wake recognized him from before, the head usher, one of the servants Linda had befriended the night President Hayes had debriefed her husband in the private office upstairs. The head usher looked inquiringly at the landau's crew and the postern called out the identity of the naval officers as the vehicle braked. As the two naval officers climbed down a gust of wind dusted their uniforms with powdery snow and Wake thought of the heat of the jungle.

The usher faced inside, bellowed out their names, and swept a long arm around in a flourish, beckoning them to enter the house of the president. The marine guards presented arms as the naval officers passed them, Wake returning the salute and marveling for the thousandth time at the directions his career had taken him.

An army major, doing duty as a White House staff aide, introduced himself and requested they wait in the Green Room, that it might be a few minutes. He motioned for them to sit down and relax. An attendant came in with juice and cookies. Wake sat at the large green satin chair across from the alabaster fireplace, where a low pile of kindling flamed. The mansion was empty of the usual social throng and oddly peaceful. Through a window he saw that the sun had set—it was just another Wednesday night in Washington. The bureaucrats had gone home for the evening. The same attendant came in and lit the gas table lamps and crystal glass gasolier above them, the white light bringing out the many shades of green in the room.

It was Hostetler's first time in the mansion and he stood, turning constantly and taking in the artwork, the furniture, the carpeting, and wall decorations. Wake remembered his first time and smiled at the memory. He and Linda had come for the annual Navy Ball in seventy-seven. There was no thrill in being there now, he just wanted to get it over with and go home to Linda. He closed his eyes and could smell her jasmine perfume, feel her soft hair and smooth skin, the warmth of her body, the curves.

Wake abruptly opened his eyes. A black man in the hallway

was watching him, then turned away. The man didn't look like a servant, he was dressed in a business suit. Next to him stood a large stern-faced army officer with the shoulder boards of a general. Thick eyebrows over a bushy beard accentuated his fierce mien. The two men were talking, the black man gently but the general's tone was like a growl, until the staff major appeared in the hallway and gestured for them to follow him. Wake saw that the general was missing his right arm and wondered who he was. There were several senior army officers who had lost their limbs during the war, but most had retired out not long afterward. This general was still serving.

From the opposite side of the room a voice suddenly boomed. "Commander Wake, I am so darn glad you're here."

With the army major in the background, President Hayes extended his hand to Wake, who had jumped to his feet and stammered, "Yes, sir. Glad to be here, too, sir. That is, I think I'm glad to be . . ." he stopped, not knowing what to say. Hayes smiled and nodded to the major, who disappeared out the door. Hostetler edged back into a corner by an ebony bust of Lincoln.

Hayes plopped down and pointed to the chair next to him. "Sit down and relax for a moment, Commander. You're not in trouble. Quite the opposite, in fact. The Peruvians think you're a hero, son. Made some tough decisions, I understand. I want to hear all about it, every bit of it, but first we need to get the Peruvian minister in here. He's been waiting for you to get in from Baltimore tonight. Needs to do something special."

"Me, sir? Ah, I thought Peru's minister to the United States would've been removed after the occupation."

"No, not yet. The Peruvian government hasn't formally capitulated yet and they're still fighting up in the hills. Piérola and his generals aren't doing much more than barely hanging on, but they've still got their man here representing Peru. Of course, the Chileans aren't thrilled that I still recognize him. They're installing their own puppet government down there and I'm not sure how it'll all play out."

The diplomat, Juan Alfonse Moroz, entered the room, accompanied by Admiral Porter, who nodded to Wake. Everyone rose, introductions were made, and afterward Hayes said, "Well, Juan, are you ready?"

"Yes, Mr. President. I am ready." Moroz unscrolled a long document and faced Wake, clearing his throat and speaking as if there were a hundred people listening, instead of four.

"Hear, all men present! Lieutenant Commander Peter Wake, esteemed officer of the Navy of the United States of America, by order of the president and commander-in-chief of the armed forces of the Republic of Peru, His Excellency Nicolás de Piérola, and in recognition of your successful heroic efforts against powerful foes while in mortal peril of your life, to save the lives of one hundred and seven beloved children of Peru; along with the lives of thirty of the republic's valiant soldiers, two respected clergymen of our most sacred faith, one of which is the renowned envoy and apostolic delegate of the Holy Father in Rome—you are hereby awarded the most valued medal of the republic and proclaimed to be a Commander of the Order of the Sun of the Republic of Peru. May all men know of this honor and show proper respect, now and forever."

Hayes beamed as Moroz removed a small box from inside his coat and took out a medal of shiny gold, shaped in an Inca vision of a glowing sun with rays emanating from it and suspended from a purple ribbon trimmed with the red and white colors of Peru. He pinned it on Wake's chest, stepped back and bowed. Then, tears running down his cheeks, he embraced Wake and said, "The people of Peru have endured the unendurable this last year and more, but your actions were a bright spot of humanity in a sea of despair. You are a brave man, sir. May I say on behalf of my people and myself, thank you for what you did."

"Ah, sir. Thank you, but I was only doing what anyone would—"

Hayes stepped forward and pumped Wake's hand. "Nonsense, son. You did far more than most would or could."

Admiral Porter spoke for the first time. "Commander Wake, you deserve the medal, so don't argue. That's an order."

"Yes, sir. Aye, aye, sir. Thank you, Señor Moroz, for this great honor."

Wake caught sight of Hostetler grimly watching from the corner and instantly knew there was something else going on. An ominous dread flooded Wake and his throat constricted as he forced himself to think it through. Obviously there would be no court-martial, but what else would happen? And why this nighttime charade of an award ceremony?

Hayes was already thanking Moroz as the army major guided the diplomat to the door. Wake started that way, about to ask if he could brief the president in the morning, but Hayes took Wake's elbow and said, "Come this way."

That was the last thing he wanted to do, but he answered. "Aye, aye, sir," walked behind Hayes out of the Green Room and up the back stairs to the president's private office on the second floor. Porter, Hostetler, and the major did not follow.

The black man and the general were sitting in chairs in the upstairs hallway. Neither got up as Hayes and Wake passed them and entered the office, but Wake felt their eyes on him as he shut the door and took the proffered seat.

"Commander, I know about the children and their escape with your help. Well done, son. The Chileans are upset, but I don't care—it was a question of life or death. Right now I need you to tell me about the military and political situation in Peru as you saw it personally or got reliable information about it. Be concise, but cover it all."

Knowing he'd probably be asked to do so, Wake had already outlined it all in his mind. Much of his information had come from Mocenni, who had given the Americans daily briefs of information during their month underground. The information had been gained from his network of clergymen throughout the city, impressing Wake with the man's ability to know what was happening at all levels of the society and government, and who was really making the decisions in Lima.

Wake began his briefing, starting with the disposition of forces, the attacks and ensuing retreat. Then he went into the political briefing, including the tensions within both warring sides, personalities, and attitudes toward the United States. Thirty minutes later he ended with what he had learned aboard the French flagship about the actions and outlooks of the neutrals.

Hayes listened intently and never asked a question until the end. "So we owe the French admiral for helping you. Very well. And what about Panama? Tell me about the French canal efforts and the views of the locals there."

Wake related his candid conversation with Blanchet about the company's challenges in building the canal; what he learned from Bishop Vargas about the Panamanian elite's outlook for the canal, the French, and the Americans; and his own observations as he traversed the Isthmus on the way home. He did not mention Thompson's business agreement with the French company.

"So, given all that you know, what do you think the foreign policy of the United States should be in those regions, Commander?"

"Sir, I believe we should have a very close observation of the French canal endeavor in Panama to ensure the government in Paris doesn't take it over out of Gallic pride if and when it fails privately. That would violate our nation's stated goals.

"We should be pro-Peru and anti-aggressor on the Pacific coast of South America. The other countries there are watching to see what we do. So is Europe."

Hayes paused pensively. "I see. Hmm . . . I'll give President-Elect Garfield your recommendations at our meeting tomorrow. He may want to hear them from you in person, later on in a few weeks. Be prepared to give them."

"Aye, aye, sir," Wake said with relief as he imagined his bed at home. The last delay was over and Linda was only minutes away.

Hayes called for his aide, who peeked inside the door. The

president bobbed his head quickly and the aide disappeared. Seconds later the general, the black man, Porter, and Hostetler walked into the office. Except for Hostetler, who stood back in the corner, they sat in chairs without introductions. None spoke. Seeing the look on their faces, Wake felt a terrible dread crushing his chest. He suddenly guessed the reason for everyone's glum attitude earlier on the train. Frantically hoping he was wrong, he looked at them all again, searching for a sign.

Hayes reached out and put a hand on Wake's arm. The president's face suddenly looked ancient and slack, the eyes sad. He let out a long doleful sigh as he indicated the others.

"This is Major General Howard and Doctor Purvis. Now I have to talk to you about something else, Peter."

# 36

# Why?

"It's your wife, Linda." Hayes paused for a breath. Wake felt the walls closing in. He couldn't speak, couldn't think, as the president continued. "She's been sick, very sick, lately."

"Where is she? What's wrong? I need to see her!" Wake turned angrily to Hostetler. "Get me to her now, Chuck."

Hostetler's eyes filled as President Hayes said, "You can't, Peter. She's gone. She died of her illness, even after the doctors did everything they could do. God took her home two weeks ago."

Wake's hand clutched his aching chest. "No! It was just a pain, a little heartburn she said! They were going to take care of it. She's not *dead*, she can't be. *No!*"

Hayes shook his head slowly. "No, Peter, she's gone home to the Lord. She's not feeling any pain now. Linda's not in any pain now."

Hostetler reached over and put a hand on Wake's shoulder. "I'm sorry, Peter."

"What happened? I don't understand. It was just a little pain . . ."

The president glanced at the black man and general. "I think you've heard of General Howard's service in the war, his work with the freedmen, and the university he founded here in Washington. It's a good university with a good medical school. Their doctors are more versed in ailments of women than the navy doctors, so Linda went there for treatment. The university surgeons cared for Linda, particularly Dr. Purvis. They can explain."

A well-known lay preacher, General Howard's words came out in a sermonlike tone, "Commander, my heart goes out to you for your loss, but as a Christian I rejoice that your beloved Linda is in a better place now, a place without pain or fear. She was a believer all her life and therefore she shall have ever-lasting life. You will meet again, in heaven, son. It's hard to understand now, but you know in your heart it's true. You and Linda will meet again in heaven."

Wake didn't want a sermon, he wanted someone to tell him this was a mistake. It *must* be a mistake. "But she was just in a little pain. She told me so . . ."

Dr Purvis walked over and knelt beside Wake's chair. "I am Charles Purvis, Mrs. Wake's physician, Commander. Yes, she did have a little pain at first, but it got worse and worse as time went on. She finally came to us and we determined the source of the pain was probably a cancerous tumor of the ovarian region. The only option was an operation to remove the tumor. That was successful in mid-January and the tumor was removed.

"But we found that the cancer had already spread beyond that tumor. A second operation was performed as soon as Mrs. Wake had recovered from the first. That was three weeks ago. We couldn't get all of it out. She lived for a week after that, was able to see and talk with her family and friends, to get prepared and say goodbye. Everyone at the hospital loved her, sir. Mrs. Wake died on February fourteenth."

Hostetler had tears on his cheeks. "There was a memorial service for her a week ago, Peter. It was beautiful, with hymns and remembrances from her church and friends. It was just as she requested. The president and Mrs. Hayes, Admiral Porter, and many of your friends in the navy, all attended."

Wake still didn't understand. They were saying that Linda was *dead*. But she couldn't be dead, she was too young. He must be in a dream and would wake up out of this nightmare. All this would be gone.

Then he studied their distraught faces. Oh God, it was true. Somehow, it was true. Linda was gone. His beautiful wife was gone.

"We are all so sorry, Peter," murmured President Hayes.

"Commander, it is a tragedy and all the navy here in Washington is grieving for you, son. We're here to help in any way that we can."

Hostetler said, "Useppa and Little Sean are all right. They handled this as well as could be expected. They're living with Mr. and Mrs. Boltz down by Fairfax." He looked at Hayes, who nodded to go ahead.

"Peter, I have three letters from Linda that you never got. They were mislaid in Panama and missed the *Pensacola*. Rork got them for you but waited until now. There was no reason to put you through this until you arrived here."

Hostetler put them in Wake's hand.

"It's true? Linda's . . ."

"Yes, Peter, it's true."

"My children?"

"They are being well cared for by your friends the Boltzes. Martha and Don love them like their own and they're doing fine."

"Linda . . ." He couldn't say the word. "She's . . ."

"Her soul is in heaven, Peter. Her remains are at the church, awaiting your return. She left instructions." Hostetler was barely able to say the next. "She also left a final letter to you. Here it is."

President Hayes stood. "It's too late to go to Fairfax now and there is no reason for you to go home to an empty house, Peter."

In a more assertive tone, he spoke to Admiral Porter,

"Commander Wake and Lieutenant Hostetler are staying here, tonight. That's not a suggestion, it's an executive order. The major has their room ready."

Purvis reached into a bag and handed Hostetler a vial of pills. "Three to start. Two more in six hours if he's awake. I'll be back here in the morning to check in on him."

Hostetler gently lifted Wake by the shoulder out of the chair. "Come on, Peter. Time to lie down for a while. President's orders. We can talk later."

Wake's terrified eyes searched around the room. "Rork. Sean knew about this?"

"Yes, in a way. Sean's suspected since Panama. He had a bad premonition and checked the letters that he got down there. The last one from Linda warned she might not live. There was nothing you could do, so he didn't give it to you. Sean and Colonel Woodgerd found out when I met you all at the ship. Sean'll be here in the morning to take you home."

"This is *real?*"

"Yes. God help us, it's real."

Hostetler helped his old shipmate down the hallway and into the Prince of Wales's bedroom, across from President and Mrs. Hayes' suite. The purple and faded gold motif seemed funereal to Hostetler. He guided Wake to the bed, took off his friend's uniform coat, pulled off the shoes, and handed him the pills with a glass of water. "Drink this down, Peter."

Wake mechanically did as told and lay back. Only then, lying in the famous bed both Lincoln and his little son Willie had occupied in death, did Wake lose control of his emotions. The words became clear. It was real.

Hostetler watched from the army camp cot set up beside the big bed as Wake's body convulsed in sobs. There was nothing more to do, other than let human nature take its course. At two in the morning Hostetler saw by the dim lamp that his friend was awake, lying there on his back and staring at the canopy over the bed. He gave the next two pills.

The president came in as the sun rose. The room was cold even though a fire was burning. Hostetler was draped in a chair facing the bed, haggard and groggy. Wake's eyes were red-rimmed and dulled, and still staring at the canopy. His uniform shirt was crumpled. Over a coat rack near the door the Peruvian medal on his coat caught a ray of the morning sun.

Hayes went to the bedside. Wake tried to get up but the president gestured to stay down. "Commander, your old friend Bosun Rork will be here in an hour with your children. He'll take you all home. You are now on full-pay leave for six weeks. I want you to use that time to take care of your family. At the end of that time, the new president will be needing you, so your tour of duty in Washington has been extended for at least a year. Understood, son?"

"Yes . . . sir."

"Very well. Always know that I personally appreciate your efforts on behalf of the United States for the last year and a half down there in South America. Never forget you saved lives of innocent children there. And also know that you and Linda will always be in the hearts of Mrs. Hayes and me. We're grieving too."

Hayes paused, then turned to go. He stopped when he heard Wake saying something.

"*Why Linda?*"

The man who had seen thousands die horribly in war felt the tears coming as haunting images from the past filled his mind. He'd asked that same question so many times and never found an answer.

"I wish I knew, son. I wish to God I knew."

# 37

# Consequences

## May 1881

Wake, now living in several rooms at Boltz's Inn on Chain Bridge Road near Fairfax on the Virginia side of the Potomac with his children, had been back at work for two months. He boarded a train in Fairfax each morning and in the city each evening for the swaying noisy ride—a situation he didn't like, but one that was best and certainly safer for Useppa and Sean. He wanted them to live in the countryside, breath clean air, and be around decent, positive-minded people. Now that they were getting older, he also wanted them away of the seedier influences of Washington. Most of all, he wanted to be out of the apartment. He couldn't sleep there. It was part of his past.

Still on the ship survey board, he was working on a demoralizing assessment of the USS *Vandalia* when he got the summons from Admiral Porter one morning. The reason was simple—Wake was to be at the executive mansion at three that afternoon to brief the new president and cabinet members on the Panama Canal and the Peruvian war. At exactly three he marched into

President Garfield's office, the same room on the second floor of the White House that Hayes had used, and stood at attention in front of the same rollup desk.

"Lieutenant Commander Wake reporting as ordered, sir."

Garfield said nothing, but tilted back in the swivel chair, unsmoked cigar clamped in his teeth, his hooded eyes studying Wake. Garfield was a combat veteran who led troops from his native Ohio in the first two years of the war, and a classically educated intellectual who could use one hand to write in Latin while using the other to write Greek. Wake had heard that in 1876 the man even found a new proof for the Pythagorean theorem. But above all, Garfield was known as a consummate lawyer and politician, the dark horse who beat all comers in the election of 1880. Wake had never met him and was there because Hayes had recommended Garfield listen to his opinions of South America and Panama.

In the chair opposite was the new secretary of the navy, William Hunt, an anti-secession Southerner who had actually served during the war, ostensibly with reluctance, as a Confederate officer in Louisiana until Farragut captured New Orleans. Afterward, Hunt became a well-known Republican in the South. Wake found it incredible that a former enemy was now in the presidential cabinet—times had obviously changed. Hunt had no naval experience. Neither did Garfield.

In a chair in the corner sat Garfield's new secretary of state and former political opponent, James Blaine, a fair-haired white-bearded fifty-year-old former newspaperman, educator, and state and national politician from Maine who was so adept at electoral campaigning for Republicans that his supporters called him the "Plumed Knight." Wake knew that Blaine was a brilliant and principled man who had championed the fourteenth amendment that guaranteed black rights in the South, but wondered what he would promote as policy regarding the war between Peru and Chile. There were all kinds of rumors on the subject. A pronouncement was expected soon.

"You may sit, Commander Wake," said the president. "President Hayes suggested I listen to you, that you had sound ideas regarding the Latin people's problems down south of us. Please be brief."

Wake reiterated his previous briefings for Hayes, adding at the end that the present was a perfect opportunity to try to break the deadlock in the War of the Pacific. The Peruvians were still fighting on in the mountains and the Chileans had consolidated their hold over the coast. Commerce was stifled, European influence was growing, American interests in the region were getting angrier at Washington's inaction, and Latin American liberals were waiting for the new president to do something.

Wake concluded and asked for any questions. He was dismayed when none of them had any. Garfield thanked and dismissed him. Wake was exiting the room when he was further astounded by a last-minute comment by Hunt.

"Oh, Commander, please wait a moment for a simple question. Is our navy strong enough to influence anyone down there?"

Was it a trick question? Or was the man that ignorant? He considered Hunt's face for an instant—there was no outward sign of guile.

"No, sir."

Hunt appeared genuinely surprised. "Please explain."

"Sir, for the last fifteen years the navy hasn't been funded adequately to keep up to comparable strength with any of the larger nations of South America. Most especially Chile. The Europeans are vastly superior and openly snicker about us. We've got the right officers and men, sir, but our ships are antiquated and no match for any potential enemy. They deter no one."

"My God. I didn't know that," blurted out Hunt, who looked at the president.

Garfield shook his head and growled, "Heard that a couple times over the years. Maybe we can do something." He held up a hand. "No promises, though, money is up to Congress."

"The foreign policy of this republic must be accompanied by

a credible strength," announced Blaine. "That is a basic tenet of international relations. And, for the record, I agree with the commander's assessment of the situation in Peru. We need to back up the victim in this, Peru; be coldly neutral toward the aggressor, Chile; and show the other South Americans we mean business. Sitting on the fence hasn't worked. I'd like to try a new diplomatic approach to spur an end to this ridiculous situation, maybe even go there myself."

Wake tried not to show his reaction—Blaine was bluntly saying what Wake had been suggesting for the last year. Was this going to turn around? Would someone actually face up to the Chileans?

"You sound pretty convinced, James. You really think you can break that impasse down there? The Chileans are in a strong position," asked Garfield.

Blaine leaned forward, his voice angry as his eyes bored into Garfield. "Yes, Mr. President, I think we can and damn well should. This is our hemisphere and we need to take care of this mess. It's gone on for long enough and the British are the ones reaping all the benefits. Our whalers and cargo shippers have been frozen out of the area, our mercantile interests are dwindling, and our political influence is next. The Brits have moved in lock, stock, and barrel, and mark my words, as time goes by it'll only be harder to dislodge them. I worry about their political influence more than anything, though."

Garfield noticed Wake still standing in the doorway.

"You may go, Commander. Thank you for your briefing."

Wake said, "Aye, aye, sir," and escaped, his mind turning over the implications of the discussion, wondering what would happen when it became public.

Two weeks later the public found out. A press report described the new United States' effort in Latin America: The secretary of state's son, Walker Blaine, and William Trescott, would lead a peace mission that would force the Chileans to the table.

The Blaine-Trescott Peace Mission made headlines for weeks. Wake waited for another assignment to South America, but it never came. The mission met with the same parties, slogged through the same pontifications, and was stopped by the same Chilean intransigence. Secretary of State Blaine's peace idealism died slowly, but his nationalistic view of the European interlopers in the Western Hemisphere was strengthened. In the end, it came to naught for the American endeavor, but Wake's life was changed forever by that one briefing and the unforeseen consequences of it.

The first consequence was Walker Blaine's report back to his father. It contained two important things. First, that Wake's description of the personalities and politics of the situation was correct. And second, that Wake was respected by the Peruvians and despised by the Chileans. Secretary Blaine duly let President Garfield know.

The second consequence was a presidential conversation. Garfield mentioned in passing to his vice-president, Chester Arthur of New York, Wake's accurate briefing and the deep trust Hayes had held in the naval officer. These conversations cemented Wake's reputation in the area of naval/political assessment. Unbeknownst to Wake initially, his credibility was now assured at the highest levels of the American government.

The third consequence was that Secretary Hunt was sufficiently startled by Wake's candid description of the navy to begin to delve into the department for which he had assumed responsibility. Hunt asked for opinions and suggestions from younger officers, passing them along to the president, pondering how he could implement them, spreading the word that the navy needed to be modernized. Even taciturn old Admiral Porter, a veteran of decades in the Washington political arena, smiled inwardly with hope. Maybe the navy would get help now.

The final consequence, and the most important, was that Wake was moved out of his assignment at the survey board and installed in an office on the lower level, in the northeast corner of the building. His official title was Special Assistant to the Senior Admiral of the Navy—his real job was to collate and peruse scraps of information coming in from squadrons around the world regarding naval, military, and political developments that could affect the Unites States, alerting the leadership to potential problems and opportunities. The idea was to change American strategy from one of being reactive to world events to one that was predictive and proactive.

He was given an assistant, Lieutenant Theodorus Bailey Myers Mason. Mason was an inquisitive, clean-cut young officer with extensive foreign naval observations to his credit. He was also the nephew of the famous Rear Admiral Bailey, whom Wake had served under during the war, and the son of a prominent New York family.

Wake liked the work, in which he submerged himself and his private grief. The mounds of incoming data exercised his mind, consuming his days and many of his evenings. His correspondence with the overseas squadrons grew immense, and he devoured diverse bits of information, in time becoming the man to go to with questions, to ask for opinions, to test theories.

Each week he briefed Admiral Porter. He briefed the navy secretary and the president four times on the situations in Korea, South America, and the Mediterranean. Now they asked questions. More significantly, he had the answers.

Sitting in bed in his room late one night in late May, Wake did a lot of soul-searching about his career. He knew that without the naval academy ring on his finger his chances for major command and promotion were limited in a navy that had few ships. It was a fact of naval life he had known for a long time.

But he also knew that he enjoyed his work and that he could, and frequently did, make a positive difference for the navy. His career would never be glorious, but he was confident it would be secure and productive. And the very best thing about his current assignment was that it allowed him to live a normal life with his children, to watch them grow into young adults, and to help them as much as he could.

The introspection that night illuminated his personal feelings too. He knew he had to outwardly let go of Linda, to stop referring to her constantly, to allow his children to look ahead. He read Linda's final letter to him again, the one containing her last wishes. He read it over and over for hours by the bedside lamplight, lashing out in anger, sobbing in his grief, until he was weak from emotional exhaustion. Wake noticed the three other letters piled on the bedside table that he had received a week earlier. They had forced him to confront himself, to stop ignoring reality.

One was from Bishop Ferro in Genoa, who sent Wake sympathy for his loss and wrote that he would be in the priest's prayers. Ferro wrote that he had heard the sad news from the bishop in Washington and passed it on to Father Muñosa in Sevilla, Bishop Vargas in Panama, and Bishop Mocenni in Lima. Wake saw that it was postmarked in late February—Ferro had learned of Linda's death very quickly. The Jesuit's global connections still amazed Wake.

The second letter was from Bishop Mocenni. He sent his profound sentiments of empathy, wishing he could be there to comfort his friend. He also said the Chilean occupiers were not acknowledging that Wake and Rork had stolen a naval launch—they were too embarrassed that it could happen at all. Lima was still sad, but getting more orderly. Christiancy was still leading the U.S. legation, but Kronburg had departed. Rumor had it he was heading for a post in Paris.

The third letter was the most surprising, and unsettling. It was from Wake's dear friend in North Africa, Mu'al-lim Sohkoor, Royal Scholar of the Court of Hassan, Sultan of Morocco, Lion of the Atlas. Somehow he'd gotten word about Linda.

*2nd day of April, in the Christian year 1881*
*Year 1298 of The Hijra of Muhammad*
*At Rabat, in the Kingdom of Morocco*

*My Dear Friend Peter,*
*I have learned with infinite sadness of the cruel passing of your lovely wife Linda, of whom you were so enamored and to whom so devoted. I know that, as People of the Book, you both believe in an afterlife. As a man who has studied such things for all my life, I want you to know that God in His wisdom has provided many heavens, and that surely your Linda is resting in the Christian heaven now, by the side of Jesus, Blessed be His Name.*

*I must also tell you this, my friend—that grief can make one stronger or can achieve the opposite effect. Use it to strengthen your family and your faith. But do not allow it to become your banner. There is a time to put it aside.*

*Be alert for a special sign sent by God. Through it He will express His wonder at your character, give you a balm for your wound, and salve your pain. It will come soon from the east for all to see, but it is painted for you. See the sign and know that He cares for you personally, Peter. Understand it now as you have understood them in the past. Use the sign as a call to go forward in life. It is time.*

*Love never dies. It urges us onward. Live life, my friend.*
*Ssalamu' lekum—Peace be upon you . . .*
*Sohkoor*

Wake shuddered. Sokhoor was one of the most brilliant men he had ever met. The man knew things about life and the world, about God and the universe—strange, incredible things that no one else knew. Wake had seen him predict the future and explain the past. Together, they had looked into the abyss of death and emerged. It was Sokhoor who had tended Wake's wounds in Africa, who had saved his life. It was Sohkoor who had predicted that Wake's marriage would not fail and that it would grow stronger, at a time when Wake himself thought it was over. Now, somehow, Sohkoor understood his pain, and was reaching out to him again.

It was time to take that step forward.

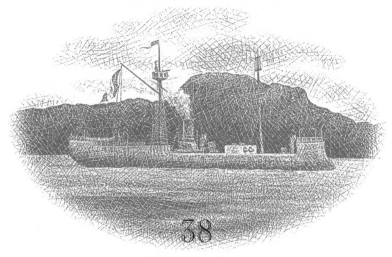

# 38

# Useppa

## June 1881

The urn was a pale green that brought back memories of the water on the Gulf coast of Florida. It was trimmed in a fili-gree of rich forest-green that reminded him of her eyes. Linda had written out her last wishes in the perfect cursive of the letters he'd slept with every night when at sea. Wherever he had been sta-tioned in the world for almost two decades, she'd been with him in her letters. Even now he slept with them close by.

It was a final wish that was pure Linda Donahue Wake. She wanted her ashes to go home, and for her husband to show their children that special place. Not to Key West, where she had been raised and had so many bad memories from the war, but to the islands a hundred and twenty miles due north, and specifically to the one island that had meant so much to them both when she and Peter were young and scared and newly in love. It had been a refuge from the hate of a civil war, a lovers' tropical hideaway, the place where their marriage blossomed and their daughter was conceived and born.

Wake was finally ready. He had secured leave and was going to take Linda's last remains home, a journey of a thousand miles southward and eighteen years into the past. But it was more than just that. Wake was going to show his children their heritage.

Rork had obtained leave also and was going too—he had his own wonderful memories of that oasis of tranquility during that cruel war. Wake knew he'd need his friend along to make it through what had to be done. All four of them set out for Florida's Useppa Island. The urn had its own place on the seat, a location insisted upon and guarded by little Sean. Useppa sat next to her father on the opposite seat. Rork was next to his godson. All four had crammed into the day salon coach of a Norfolk and Carolina Railroad train, watching the low country of South Carolina rumble by.

When they got to Jacksonville, Florida, the family switched to a Florida Railroad train and rode on the new line through the gentle sand hills of the central peninsula to Tampa on the Gulf coast. At Tampa they embarked on a steamer and arrived late the next afternoon at a ramshackle dock at Punta Gorda on the Peace River. Memories filled Wake's mind as he looked at the village of shacks. He'd fought a desperate little battle on that river during the war—the scar on his right temple was one of the results.

The crudely built tavern near the dock had two rooms for rent, which Wake obtained for the night. After a dinner of fish stew and red mangrove tea, they all retired to the dock, where a smudge pot belched smoke to keep the bugs away. The children had never seen such a thing and thought it intriguing, especially young Sean, who was given the job of finding green wood for it.

Wake and Rork sat there drinking stale beer, remembering the war when suddenly the sound of laughter and music came from the tavern. It was Florida swamp music. Rork looked at Wake, grinning. "Do me ancient ears deceive me, or is that—?"

Wake completed the thought with glee. "—*The Yard Dogs!* Well, I'll be, Sean. Last I heard they were in jail in Key West."

The rest of the evening was spent in raucous fun with the

disheveled band of troubadours known as The Yard Dogs—an old swamp term for an alligator—playing their homemade gitjo, squeezebox, and Jamaican thumpbox, singing ballads and regaling Wake's children with tales of the exploits of their father and Rork during the Civil War in Florida. The musicians were former Union soldiers who never went back north after the war, assimilating into Florida's rough coastal life and becoming popular at fish camps from Key West to Tampa.

And they were great storytellers. Brian included Wake's role in the Great Bar Riot of 1864 in Key West, Kip told the children of their parents' wedding at Key West's African cemetery, and Charlie added the story of Wake's liberation of a slave ship at the end of the war. Wake cringed, glad that his old friends hadn't included *too* much in front of his children—some things Useppa and Sean didn't need to learn. Wake found himself wishing Linda was snuggled up next to him, watching their children's eyes sparkle as they laughed at Charlie's antics as he danced atop a table. It had been a long time since Wake had laughed that hard, and that night he went to sleep truly relaxed and content.

The following morning they were aboard a thirty-foot sloop-rigged fishing smack, the *Nancy Ann*. Rork had haggled for the charter with the boat's owner, a Mr. Addison, a flint-eyed Florida cracker and veteran of the Confederate dismounted cavalry company Wake had faced at the Battle of Myakka River in 1863. Rork had bought him a drink the night before and explained the reason for the charter. The old man, who remembered Wake from the war as a man of honor, charged half what he usually got for carrying passengers out to the islands.

It was a pretty Florida summer afternoon, something out of a *Harper's Monthly* illustrated story. A steady warm breeze out of the east propelled puffy clouds across the sky as the *Nancy Ann*

rounded up into the wind at the old navy anchorage east of the big hill. Rork dropped the jib as the gaffed mainsail shook in the wind and the sloop eased slowly to a stop, her stern a hundred feet off the beach. Wake called out, "Let go, now," and young Sean loosed the anchor into the luminescent green water, immensely proud that he'd done it perfectly. Useppa cast loose the mainsail halyard and peak lift from the pinrail, letting the gaff and sail slide down the mast.

While Rork lowered the dinghy Wake surveyed the island. Useppa was different, completely different, from the way it looked during war. He remembered a pro-Union refugee village of crude palm-thatched and scrap board huts—a place where over a hundred Floridians who had stayed loyal to the United States were brought by the navy after they'd fled to the coast.

The village had been spread along the beach and hills, with cooking pits and rickety docks and communal tables. The refugees had lived on fish and fruit, barely making it and always worried about lack of rain water or a Confederate attack from the mainland. It had been a desperate time, with people who had lost everything but their national loyalty and personal dignity. But it had also been a time of intense camaraderie and joy at the little victories of life.

Linda moved there from Key West shortly after their marriage in 1864. Useppa had been born there the next spring, as the war was ending. Wake had last been there in June of 1865, when he took his young family away from the island to Pensacola, where Sean was born two years later.

But now there was no village, no sign of human life except for the lean-to of a Cuban fisherman at the northern point. Even that looked abandoned. The village had been left to rot when the war ended and the refugees returned to their homes at Tampa and Gainesville and Cedar Key. The huts had blown away in storms since then, with creeper vines and strangler figs gradually covering the ruins.

Useppa had reverted to its primordial self, just another jungle-clad island in a bay of jungle-clad islands. Wake's children glanced from the island to their father. It didn't appear anything like the stories they'd heard.

"*This* is where you and Mama lived as newlyweds?" asked Useppa, unable to keep the surprise from her voice.

"Yes, dear. And up on that hill is where you were born."

The children had never seen anything like it—the ending of a day in the tropics. The sun had transformed into a ball of seething molten copper, its liquid edges pouring out onto a leaden Gulf of Mexico, spreading luminescently along the dark line of the horizon. Above was a pastel canvas of yellow and rose-colored clouds brushed against a powder-blue sky, with a tinge of faded green barely discernible way high up. Wake heard a little Carolina wren cry out his sunset call from a nearby sable palm. An osprey floated along the wind, scanning the water for food as his plaintive screech echoed around the island.

The island was getting dark now as shadows covered the eastern beach and the sloop beyond—only the top of the high hill where they all stood was still bathed in sunlight. Wake had taken them around the island, pointing out the places he'd known. The rainwater cistern, the ruins of the old Indian war fort, the rotted remnants of Linda's hut, the residue of the communal cooking pits and eating tables on the ridge. He saw them as they were before, both smiling and tearing up at the memories so real that he once again felt Linda's softness in his arms, smelled the grouper roasting, tasted the sweet palm wine, and heard the laughter and banjos and guitars, saw women and men around the firelight, sharing a desperately light-hearted moment in the nightmare of a civil war, far from their real homes. Wake remembered it all.

Rork remembered too. How the single girls watched him

come ashore back then, silent except for their eyes that said it all—the war had taken away their lives and hopes and innocence. How their eyes turned him wary, forced him to think of consequences, made him behave differently than he usually did when ashore. Useppa was an island of wounded people during the war—wounded in their spirit.

Except for Linda Wake. She had loved this place. Her best years of life had started here. Rork's face eased into a smile as he remembered Linda and Peter hand in hand where he now stood, coming from their hut to a dinner celebrating some Union victory up north, sharing a rare drink of real Cuban rum, having something Rork had never known—a shared love forever.

Wake's children didn't see any of that as they looked around, only piles of rubbish and rotted lumber and thickly matted jungle. But they knew that their father and honorary uncle could see it all again, and listened closely as the tales were told. They'd never seen their father this way, misty-eyed and sentimental.

The four of them were sitting on the crushed shell ground at the top of the hill, around the fire that Rork and young Sean tended, just finishing up the grouper and stone crab the old bosun had gotten two hours before—the old fishing holes from sixteen years earlier still worked. Next to young Sean was the urn, under his protection. There were no bugs, unusual for that time of year. The easterly wind stayed steady and cleared the island of mosquitoes and no-see-ums. It was a beautiful evening.

Several times, while telling stories of him and Linda, or of Rork or the navy battles along the coast, or of Useppa when she was a baby, Wake would look up into the sky and say, "Isn't that right, Linda?" or "Remember that, darling?" He wasn't maudlin, just reminiscent, asking her as if she were right there, standing above them.

Rork pulled out an old jug he had been carrying and glanced at the sun. It had lost its strength now. Not much left. It was time to do what they had come a thousand miles to do. He looked at his old friend, who nodded slowly and stood. Wake faced west and gazed out beyond Palmetto and Lacosta Islands, toward the distant horizon. Rork took a pull from the jug and passed it up to Wake, who let the rum slide down his throat and fill him with warmth. Then everyone stood, young Sean instinctively knowing to pick up the urn. Wake's hands trembled as he lifted it up from his son's hands.

"Children, your mother isn't in this urn. You are Christians and you know that." He spread his arms wide across the sky. "Linda is all around us. She's free now, her soul is in heaven. She's smiling down on us now. And she always will. She'll always be there to listen whenever you want to talk."

The boy and his sister bobbed their heads in understanding, sniffling while they followed their father's gaze west, snuggling up close to him as the evening breeze strengthened.

"In this urn is what remains of your mother's earthly body. She wanted these ashes to be scattered here, where she knew not just war, but love and friendship. Where you were born, Useppa."

Wake took the urn and unscrewed the top, scattering the ashes in great arcs, borne by the breeze across the island. He cast three arcs and then the ashes were gone, and he handed the urn back to little Sean. The sun's last flicker of light flashed on the horizon, an instant of green, as Rork sounded his beat-up old conch shell, the one he'd carried all around the world for years after receiving it as a present from a grateful Useppa refugee. It was a slow mournful wail. Repeated three times, it echoed around the bay, the traditional farewell to the sun by the islanders.

From a mile away at Patricio Island came a reply. Then from nearby Palmetto Key. All the way from distant Pine Island came another. Wake and Rork shook hands, then everyone embraced, each feeling Linda's presence and an indefinable sense of contentment with what they had done.

"It'll be all right, won't it, Daddy?" murmured Useppa.

"Yes, honey. It'll be just fine. You and Sean have nothing to worry about. It's time to keep on *living* life. And you both have a lot of living to do."

Young Sean was still holding onto his father. "I don't want to leave the island yet. Can you tell us more stories, Daddy? About Mama and this island? Uncle Sean, can you tell some too?"

Wake sat down close to the fire, his two children next to him. He was tired, but wanted to stay a little longer. "More stories? Well, son, there's a thousand stories about these islands in the war. Uncle Sean and I were right smack dab in the middle of most of it, so I suppose we could remember a few more. What say the bosun of our crew?"

Rork grinned. "Oh, I'm from a long line o' storytellers, Seanie, an' me tongue's nicely facilitated by this rum for talkin'— jes' try to stop me. But first I'll need a wee bit o' help in gatherin' some kindlin' for the fire. These stories'll need a good *roarin'* fire. You come an' help me, lad."

When they had moved off into the forest, Useppa leaned over hugged her father, then looked at him. She had Linda's eyes. "I wasn't asking earlier about Sean and me, Daddy. I was asking about you. I'm worried about you."

He almost lost his composure. She seemed so mature. His voice choked and came out husky. "Thank you, honey. But I'll be all right. As long as I know you and Sean are safe and happy, then I'll be all right."

Her tone grew solemn. "Well, Sean and I have been talking about you, Daddy. We both agree that you need to stay in the navy—you're a naval officer, not some boring land dweller. You need to go to sea sometimes. Mama understood that and so do we. We want you to know that."

It was something Linda would say. He couldn't hold back the tears anymore. He was so very proud of his daughter. "Thank you, Useppa."

The stories went on and on. Each person around the fire told them. Stories about their friend, mother, and wife, Linda. Stories of the war, stories of their own lives. Hilarious tales, hesitant admissions, poignant remembrances. Wake learned things about his children and Rork he never knew, and was moved to tell them some of his past that had been kept hidden away. They ate fruit from the remaining trees and drank juice and talked all night.

Wake pointed at the stars in the east, showing them an odd vertical lineup of orange-tinged Mars and Saturn, with bright Venus above. A crescent moon and the cluster of the Pleiades and Jupiter floated off to the left of the line as if they wanted to join. He remembered that night almost two years earlier—was it really that long ago?—in the southern Pacific Ocean off the Bolivian coast when he'd seen another line of stars pointing ominously to the enemy on the horizon coming for them. This line of stars pointed down to the horizon too.

Then he recalled Sokhoor's letter, which he'd told Rork about on the trip down. Could it be? The night was lightening in the east, but it was too early for dawn. Rork saw Wake looking at something low on the horizon, then shushed the children and pointed it out to them. Tiredness evaporated as they all watched the eastern sky. It was a faint line at first, gray against the black nothingness of space, rising up from the spot on the horizon where the star line led, past the Pleiades. Starting as a thin line it widened gradually into a wide shimmering path of cosmic light, like a great fountain of golden water erupting from the Earth, somewhere far to the east.

Little Sean sat up, pie-eyed with wonder. "*Wow . . .*"

"Is that a comet, Daddy?" asked Useppa.

"Yes, darling. It's a comet." He glanced at Rork, who raised an eyebrow and shrugged. Wake swallowed hard. This was eerie. How did Sokhoor *know?*

Useppa was fascinated. "It's so beautiful. I've read about them. Some are famous. Did anybody know it was coming, Daddy? Do the men at the naval observatory know about these?"

Wake took a breath. It was beautiful, the largest comet he had ever seen. He was a friend of the men at the Washington naval observatory. They frequently would tell him of interesting celestial events that were anticipated in coming months. They never mentioned this. This comet was completely new.

"No, honey. The naval observatory didn't know it was coming. Only one man knew this comet was coming and told me in a letter. He lives on the other side of the world, in northern Africa, right about the direction of that comet, and he knows things that other people don't. He wrote me that a sign was coming from God just for us. This is it."

"From God! What's it mean, Daddy?"

Wake reached his arms around both his children and held them close. He couldn't answer her just yet as he was overcome by emotion. The comet began fading now as the sky lightened from the coming sunrise. It diminished back into the light gray of the sky. A new day was coming. He felt Rork's hand on his shoulder.

"It's a sign to live our lives for the future, children. To remember the past, remember your mother and love her, but to always look forward. Never waste your life and the time you have on Earth. A new day is coming."

Useppa quietly nodded agreement with her father. Young Sean looked so grown up as he tried to not cry. "It's gone now, Daddy."

Wake stood and helped the others up. "Let's go home now. We've got lives to lead."

# 39

# ONI

## October 1881

When Wake returned to duty in Washington on the last day of June he was resigned to his fate, a paper pusher reading about other naval officers' work, vicariously imagining their challenges, their decisions, the minor victories of peacetime warriors.

Three days later everything changed. On July second, Wake was at the train station, leaving work early that day to make sure he could attend Useppa's recital of the Declaration of Independence at her school in Fairfax. He noticed a commotion and saw President Garfield with Secretary of State Blaine and an entourage making their way across the platform. He also saw a wild-looking young man heading for the president from behind. Two shots cracked the air.

Garfield fell to the floor, clutching his back. Blaine rushed to his president's side. The shooter screamed something about "Stalwarts!" as he was subdued by Wake and beaten by the angry crowd.

Vice President Arthur took over the reins of government as

Garfield lingered from his severe wounds at a summer cottage in New Jersey, doing well one day then failing the next. It went on until mid-September, the country following every story, until it was obvious Garfield would not survive. Infection had set in. He died on September nineteenth, with Wake in the naval contingent of the funeral procession down Pennsylvania Avenue the next week. Chester Arthur, the career bureaucrat once fired for suspicion of bribery, the backroom politician who had partnered with a dark horse at the Republican convention and never thought they'd win—was sworn in as the twenty-first president of the United States. He was the country's third president in six months.

He kept the cabinet on for a while and continued Garfield's policies. But Arthur did something more, something that affected Wake directly. Arthur had been collector of customs in the port of New York. He understood the need for a strong navy and by September had started promulgating his belief that the United States needed to protect her commerce by modernizing her navy. Without waiting for Congress, he started by calling upon Porter to make sure the officer corps would be ready with new ideas, innovative technologies, and global strategies. Members of the seven-year-old United States Naval Institute, of which Wake was a member, urged that post-academy advanced naval science courses be offered for officers. Others suggested a dedicated formal intelligence organization, like many of the European navies had. Thus, one of the first places changed was Wake's office.

Wake's assistant Mason was a New Yorker and friend of President Arthur's family and had attracted the attention of the man in the White House across the lawn from the Navy Department. Both Mason and Wake briefed the president during the fall, until their foreign intelligence became one of the primary sources of information for presidential decision-making.

Porter called Wake in at the end of October.

"What I'm about to tell you is completely confidential,

Commander. Understood?"

"Yes, sir."

"There are changes in the wind for our navy. Good changes. We are starting a new office, of which you'll be a *quiet* part. It'll be located up here near me. The assignment will be a refinement of what you're already doing, receiving intelligence from distant squadrons and presenting it, with proper analysis, to the executive leaders of the country. But there will be important changes."

Porter paused, weighing his words.

"The new endeavor will be designated the Office of Naval Intelligence—ONI. It will be formalized in the 1882 budget year with Lieutenant Mason as the apparent head. He, assisted by three clerks, will work here, gathering the reports from overseas and preparing his own analysis. You'll have a desk in that office, but you won't be sitting at it very often. You'll be out there." Porter waved his hand toward the window.

"Out there, sir? I don't understand that."

"You're getting out of the building and heading for distant shores, Commander. And please don't pretend that *that* prospect doesn't cheer you up. You'll be going back to sea on missions for ONI to places in the world that interest or affect us. Mason is good at the data, but not as good as you are in the field and at sea."

Wake's mind was overwhelmed by the news. He remembered Mason's connection with the president's family. Mason, back in the office, would get the credit. "Ah, now I'm starting to see, sir."

"No, not entirely. You will have various *ostensible* public assignments, Commander, but the new Office of Naval Intelligence won't be one of them. You will have to complete your openly known tasks and also accomplish the covert intelligence functions I assign you. It won't be easy. Many times you will be alone. That's another reason it's you out there—I trust your judgment."

"Yes, sir."

"And you probably won't get much public acknowledgment

for your work, however I want you to understand this part very well—I will know and so will the president. It will be a different kind of honor, Commander. The quiet kind . . ."

Porter lightened his tone. "Of course, you'll also have a lot of time between missions, working in Washington and staying at home, close to your children."

"Yes, sir."

"One last thing. This is a *volunteer* situation, Peter. Do I hear you volunteering? Take a moment and think it through."

Wake knew he could refuse. Stay in Washington and work at a desk. Ride that train every night and every morning. See his children every day. In effect, become a permanent clerk. Everyone at headquarters knew what he'd been through and no one would blame him. Someday, with a little luck, he might make full commander just before retirement.

Images flashed through his mind—young Useppa on the island urging him to stay a sailor and go to sea; Sokhoor's comet heralding a new day; President Arthur appreciating a briefing on French activities in Panama; and then Linda, sweet Linda, years ago standing on the beach at the island and gently smiling that it was all right.

"Aye, aye, sir. Count me in."

Porter eyed him carefully, then nodded knowingly. "Very good. Tomorrow morning you and I will meet with President Arthur. Seems there's a thorny problem brewing over in the Dutch East Indies. . . ."

# Chapter Notes

The Honor Series is historical fiction. Here, arranged by chapter, is some information about the actual history Peter Wake encounters. Also added are some notes about events of previous and future novels in the series that tie into this one.

## Chapter One—Make Them Understand

Rear Admiral Miguel Grau is revered to this day in the navies of Latin America for his courage and skill that summer of 1879. For the rest of his life, Wake will consider his brief relationship with Grau one of his greatest professional honors.

Wake wasn't the only one stunned by what he saw in the night sky—this very unusual celestial event startled astronomical observers around South America.

## Chapter Two—Washington, DC

Incredibly, Admiral Porter stayed in service until he died at age 77 in 1891. He was in the U.S. Navy for 62 years. Known for his Civil War victories on the Mississippi, after the war he shepherded his beloved navy through the lean 1870s and 1880s. In the 1880s Porter became a prolific writer, penning half a dozen books on various topics. Peter Wake hasn't really liked Porter for much of his career, but he'll soon find himself working closely under him and grudgingly admiring him.

The *Washington Post* was unabashedly pro-Democrat in those

days. Other papers were pro-Republican. The notion of a neutral, professionally written newspaper is a relatively recent phenomenon of the twentieth century. Calista Halsey was one of the first females in the news reporter business. For more information about the early years of the *Post* visit their interesting website: www.washpost.com/gen_info/history/timeline/index.

**Chapter Three—*Una Leyenda Heroica***
The Battle of Angamos was the first in the world between ocean-going ironclads. Wake was professionally fortunate to observe it and personally lucky to escape aboard *Union*. Grau's decision saved his life that morning. When in Talcahuano, Chile, you can still visit *Huascar* (built in 1865) at anchor off the naval station. She is in pristine condition—a testament to the professionalism of the Chilean Navy, the finest in Latin America.

**Chapter Seven—*Le Grand Français***
Recipients of the French Légion d'honneur still form an influential network in the world. It is a network that will be beneficial for Wake. For details on why and how he was awarded the medal, read *An Affair of Honor* (2006).

De Lesseps had never been to Panama before this and must have been alarmed by what he saw, even before Wake spoke candidly. But it was too late for him to stop the momentum he had started. De Lesseps continued down the path he had chosen, to his eventual profound regret. He should have listened to Peter Wake.

**Chapter Eight—The Palace**
The State, Navy, and War Building still stands in full splendor next to the White House. It is now known as the Eisenhower Executive Office Building and serves as office space for presidential staff. In the 1980s the building was renovated and many of the famous rooms were returned to their original appearance. Wake will meet many modern technological wonders in this building over the years to come.

## Chapter Nine—Room 274

Room 274 still exists. Secretaries of the Navy used this magnificent room several decades into the twentieth century. Peter Wake will get to know it, and the men who preside there, very well in his career. Now it's used as the ceremonial office of the Vice President of the United States.

## Chapter Ten—Homeport

The Bureau of Ordnance's Naval Gun Factory dominated the Washington Navy Yard in the post–Civil War years, when fewer ships were built. The famous John Dahlgren, friend of Lincoln, did some of his best work there before and during the Civil War. The imposing Latrobe Gate is still there.

The United States Naval Institute still exists and is the primary independent forum for the nation's sea services. Peter Wake was one of the first members and will continue so for his entire life. Visit them at www.usni.org.

## Chapter Eleven—An Officer and a Gentleman

Foundry Methodist Church, begun in 1815, still exists and is going strong. It will be Peter Wake's home church for the rest of his life. Many presidents and their families have attended it over the years. President Roosevelt and Winston Churchill attended a special service there on 25 December 1941. The Clintons attended frequently. Originally on 14th street, it is now on 16th Street.

Wake loved to tell the story of the Anglo-American desk—symbolic of the unity of the two nations. The desk has served in the Oval Office of every president (except Johnson, Nixon, and Ford) since. Many Americans remember the famous photo of President John F. Kennedy's young son emerging from behind the hinged front panel.

The White House interior didn't change that much in the years after the Civil War. Lincoln would've recognized it two decades later. Wake will be a frequent visitor over the coming years.

**Chapter Twelve—Perceptions**
Already becoming well-known in the naval world, Jacky Fisher is destined to become one of Great Britain's greatest admirals. When they first met, Wake was quite wary, but soon learned to respect the feisty Brit, who later became known for using dancing as a form of exercise among his subordinates, and for his promotion of a ship design that would alter world history—the dreadnought. He and Wake will remain friends into the twentieth century, with interesting consequences.

And so, in this chapter a question of history is answered—how did the United States administration decide to get deeply involved diplomatically in a Latin American war at the bottom side of the world? Peter Wake influenced history by influencing the decision-making of the president. It is his first time, but not his last.

**Chapter Thirteen—Politics**
The Royal Navy fought pirates in the Straits of Malaaca for centuries, the U.S. Navy since 1839. That area still has the highest piracy rate in the world and the U.S., Royal, and Royal Australian navies are still combating it to this day. It was Lt. Allen of the Royal Marines who got Wake in trouble, and almost killed, in the Spanish Alcázar in 1874—read *An Affair of Honor* to find out more about it.

**Chapter Sixteen—Desperation**
Unlike its international predecessors, Peru's *Toro* was the first true deep-diving combat submarine in any navy. Wake, always interested in naval technology, is fascinated with the possibilities of submarines. But his newly discovered claustrophobia means he'll have to leave future underwater adventures to others.

**Chapter Seventeen—The Striped-Pants Crowd**
The mercenary Michael Woodgerd, formerly of the U.S Army, is one of those men who can turn up anywhere there is trouble—

usually as a participant. To find out how Wake first met him, read *An Affair of Honor.* Since both are in the profession of war they will no doubt meet again at far-flung places in the world. As morally nebulous as Woodgerd is, Wake respects him as a first-class warrior—besides, the man loves dogs and children.

### Chapter Nineteen—No Time to be Sick
Howard University is still there, one of the most respected institutions of higher learning in the nation. However, with the mores of the time being what they were, it was scandalous of Linda Wake to choose Howard for her medical care in 1880. But what else could she do? Many others were in similar situations and didn't have her courage.

### Chapter Twenty—Unwritten Worries
When in Lima, Peru, I urge my readers to visit this monastery and the library—a charming place with a very interesting four-hundred-year history.

### Chapter Twenty-two—Good News and Bad News
All of these Latin American diplomats later rose to the highest level of government in their own countries. Wake's network of acquaintances who will turn into future leaders is growing.

### Chapter Twenty-five—All in the Same Boat
Certain sections of the Catacombs of Lima can still seen, especially by way of the Monastery of San Francisco. There are many legends, some very frightening, about the Catacombs. No one knows how many bodies were buried there, but it numbers at least in the tens of thousands. I shared Wake's claustrophobia when exploring this eerie, ominous, and mystical place.

### Chapter Twenty-nine—Wake's Namesake
The Oquendo Mansion is still standing. When in Lima, visit it on Superunda Street.

## Chapter Thirty—Sacrifice
To get the flavor of Key West during the Civil War and under-
stand Peter and Linda's dilemma, read the award-winning *At the
Edge of Honor* (2002) and *Point of Honor* (2003).

## Chapter Thirty-two—In our Hearts . . .
Medical care for women, particularly regarding cancer, was
abysmal in this period, with treatments that now seems barbaric.
There were very few specialists and most physicians were ignorant
of women's health issues, a problem that Linda Wake, like so
many women then, had to face. Handley and Beatson were two
pioneering doctors trying to understand the problem and come
up with potential solutions, but it still took another century to
get the medicine and the treatments that would save lives.

## Chapter Thirty-three—*Merci Beaucoup pour la Humanité*
Dupetit-Thouars was not known as a gentle or sentimental man,
but on that day in 1881 he saved thousands of people's lives by
his decisive move to stand up against the sacking of Lima. It is
indeed fortunate that Wake caught him at that moment, when
the French admiral had the naval and political strength at hand
to accommodate this strange request.

## Chapter Thirty-four—Homeward
Sadly, Gaston Blanchet, talented engineer, project leader for de
Lesseps and newlywed husband, died in Panama of the malarial
fever Wake had warned him about.

Readers of the Honor Series will have noticed by now that
Peter Wake, an Episcopalian turned Methodist, has an intriguing
relationship with senior Jesuits on several continents. That network will expand in the future, both helping Wake and putting
him in harm's way.

## Chapter Thirty-five—The Last Delay
Hostetler first served with Wake during the tumultuous end of

the Civil War described in *Honorable Mention* (2004) and was on the defense team during Wake's court-martial for mutiny in 1869, as told in *A Dishonorable Few* (2005).

The Order of the Sun of the Republic of Peru is still awarded today for outstanding achievement. This is Wake's third foreign medal. His awards will be a constant source of envy and jealousy among his fellow United States naval officers, few of whom ever received one prior to the First World War.

## Chapter Thirty-six—Why?

The Prince of Wales slept in that room on a visit to Washington in 1860. Mary Lincoln extensively redecorated it after moving in the following year. During the Civil War the room gained its maudlin reputation: young Willie Lincoln died in the room in 1862 and his father Abraham was laid out there after he died from his wounds in April 1865. No longer a bedroom, it is now the First Family's private kitchen, installed by the Trumans.

## Chapter Thirty-seven—Consequences

Mu'al-lim Sohkoor was indeed a remarkable character in Peter Wake's life, a man who could read and speak Greek, Hebrew, Latin, and several other languages; knew the mysteries of the celestial universe; the hidden secrets of science; and the lessons of history. More about this Islamic friend of Wake's can be found in *An Affair of Honor.*

## Chapter Thirty-eight—Useppa

Useppa Island is one of the highest on the southwestern coast of Florida, with manmade hills constructed as temple mounds during the pre-Colombian Calusa Empire. In the middle of the Civil War, the pro-Union refugee settlement on Useppa raised a militia unit that fought from 1863 to 1865 along the west coast of Florida. *At the Edge of Honor* (2002) tells this story. After the war the island lay dormant until the turn of the century, when Barron Collier made it a famous tarpon fishing resort. It still exists today and is the most beautiful of the islands in Pine Island Sound.

The Great Comet of 1881 was a tremendous surprise to astronomers and was one of the brightest comets in history. How Sokhoor knew it would come is one of the mysteries that always intrigued Wake.

**Chapter Thirty-nine—ONI**
The legendary Office of Naval Intelligence was officially started in 1882 with Lt. Mason in charge of collecting the information gathered from various sources. Many American naval officers around the world contributed intelligence to ONI and a few went on special assignments to gather it. Peter Wake is one of the latter. His career will never be the same again.

# Acknowledgments

As my longtime readers know, I do quite a bit of research while working on my writing projects. This includes sifting through published material and also "eyeball recon," where I actually do the voyages, see the places, and experience the cultures that are described in my novels. This novel took two years to research and involved three voyages along the Pacific coast of Latin America, with repeated visits to ports in Chile, Peru, Ecuador, Colombia, and Panama.

A lot of folks helped me along the way. Here are some who went beyond the call of duty.

In Ecuador, Captain Marco Toledo, formerly of the Chilean Navy, gave me insight on navigation conditions of the coast and on the Chilean Navy, one of the finest in the world.

In May of 2004, Lieutenant Juan Sebastian of the Chilean Navy at Talcahuano, showed me around *Huascar,* the legendary vessel from 1865 that is still a commissioned warship in the Chilean Navy. And in 2006, Denise Fuentés, of Santiago de Chile, cut through the bureaucracy and got me to my ship on time. *¡Muchas Gracias!*

In Peru, Juana Castro and Pepe Soto showed me the monastery of San Francisco and the *catacombas* under Lima in 2004. I returned in 2006 and was lucky enough to have Milagros Vargas and Miguel Rivas provide valuable assistance in Lima. On that second journey, shipmates Chris Glaser, Helen Szuluk, and Barbara Roadcap helped make my "eyeball recon ashore" far more enjoyable than it usually is.

Eljohn Cervantes, third mate of the M/V *Hamburgo,* shared

with me coastal conditions and navigation during the course of our 10,000-mile voyage along the Pacific coast of Latin America.

In Panama, Sandra Campinas shared very good background information on the railroad. Over the last ten years, several Zonians have shared with me a tremendous amount of information about Panama and the Canal, also giving me the opportunity to have some incredible hands-on experiences. Ron, Craig, and Fran Myers, Mike Stabler, and Bonnie Davis were absolutely wonderful.

In Washington, historian Jan Herman helped immensely with my understanding of late nineteenth century Washington DC, especially celestial matters at the original Naval Observatory. The Naval Historical Center (as always) was a big help. Dennis Gurtz of the Washington Map Society at the Library of Congress gets my thanks as well for finding a good map of Washington. Fascinating information about the old State, War, and Navy Building (now the Eisenhower Executive Office Building) was provided by Lonnie Hover, Director of Preservation in the Executive Office of the President at the White House. Thank you, Lonnie, for the great help.

No one is better at historical astronomy than my dear friend, the lovely Nancy Glickman of Pine Island, who has helped me with several novels by tracking down significant events that occurred long ago in the night sky at far-flung locations around the world. She did it again for this book and has my sincere thanks. Ted Connally of Fort Myers gets my thanks for coming up with the title. Look for him as a character in the next novel.

My academic research yielded a huge amount of material. Here is some that proved to be of salient importance. Bruce W. Farcau deserves a special mention for his definitive history of the War of the Pacific in English—*The Ten Cents War*, published by Praeger in 2000. David McCullough's *Path Between the Seas* is still *the word* on the Panama Canal. David F. Long's *Gold Braid and Foreign Relations* helped immensely, as did Dr. Jorge Gumucio Granier's excellent work on the War of the Pacific, *The United*

*States and the Bolivian Seacoast.* Thanks to the folks at Cornell University Library—your *Making of America* section provided some great nineteenth-century media information.

I also want to say a big thank you to Head Librarian Randy Briggs and his assistant, Lillian Bradley, at the Pine Island Library, and to Eileen Downing, head of the Interlibrary Loan Section for the Lee County Library System, who provided crucial assistance in my research by finding and obtaining special reference books for me.

*Bob Macomber*

Here are some other books from Pineapple Press on related topics. For a complete catalog, write to Pineapple Press, P.O. Box 3889, Sarasota, Florida 34230-3889, or call (800) 746-3275. Or visit our website at www.pineapplepress.com.

*An Affair of Honor* by Robert N. Macomber. In this fifth novel in the Honor series, it's December 1873 and Lt. Peter Wake is the executive officer of the USS *Omaha* on patrol in the West Indies. Lonely for his family, he is looking forward to his return to Pensacola—but fate has other plans. He runs afoul of the Royal Navy in Antigua, then he's suddenly sent off on staff assignment to Europe, where he finds himself running for his life after getting embroiled in a Spanish civil war and gets caught up in diplomatic intrigue. The real test comes when he and Sean Rork are sent on a no-win mission in northern Africa. Not the least of his troubles is Madame Catherine Faber de Champlain, wife of a French diplomat; her many charms involve Wake in an affair of honor. (hb)

*A Dishonorable Few* by Robert N. Macomber. Fourth in the Honor series of naval fiction, this historical thriller takes the reader from the Caribbean to the halls of power in Washington, D.C. It is 1869 and the United States is painfully recovering from the Civil War. Lt. Peter Wake heads to turbulent Central America to deal with a former American naval officer turned renegade mercenary. As the action unfolds in Colombia and Panama, Wake realizes that his most dangerous adversary may be a man on his own ship, forcing Wake to make a decision that will lead to his court-martial in Washington when the mission has finally ended. (hb)

*Honorable Mention* by Robert N. Macomber. This third book in the Honor series covers the tumultuous end of the Civil War in Florida and the Caribbean. Lt. Peter Wake is now in command of the steamer USS *Hunt,* and quickly plunges into action, chasing a strange vessel during a tropical storm off Cuba, confronting death to liberate an escaping slave ship, and coming face to face with the enemy's most powerful ocean warship in Havana's harbor. Finally, when he tracks down a colony of former Confederates in Puerto Rico, Wake becomes involved in a deadly twist of irony. (hb)

*Point of Honor* by Robert N. Macomber. Winner of the Florida Historical Society's 2003 Patrick Smith Award for Best Florida Fiction. In this second book in the Honor series, it is 1864 and Lt. Peter Wake, United States Navy, assisted by his indomitable Irish bosun, Sean Rork, commands the naval schooner *St. James.* He searches for army deserters in the Dry Tortugas, finds an old nemesis during a standoff with the French Navy on the coast of Mexico, starts a drunken tavern riot in Key West, and confronts incompetent Federal army officers during an invasion of upper Florida. (hb, pb)

*At the Edge of Honor* by Robert N. Macomber. This nationally acclaimed naval Civil War novel, the first in the Honor series, takes the reader into the steamy world of Key West and the Caribbean in 1863 and introduces Peter Wake, the reluctant New England volunteer officer who finds himself battling the enemy on the coasts of Florida, sinister intrigue in Spanish Havana and the British Bahamas, and social taboos in Key West when he falls in love with the daughter of a Confederate zealot. (hb, pb)

*Black Creek: The Taking of Florida* by Paul Varnes. This novel is set in the midst of the historical upheaval caused by the Seminole Wars. White settlers Isaac and his son, Isaac Jr., serve as scouts in the Second Seminole War—one of the bloodiest, costliest, and least successful wars in American history. Isaac Jr. is torn between his loyalty to his family and white neighbors, on the one hand, and his unique understanding and appreciation of the Indian way of life, on the other. The characters in *Black Creek* are based on the author's family members a generation before those he used for his first novel, *Confederate Money*, set in Florida during the Civil War. (hb)

*Confederate Money* by Paul Varnes. Two young men from Florida set out on an adventure during the Civil War to exchange $25,000 in Confederate dollars for silver that will hold its value if the Union wins. Training to be physicians, they get mixed up in some of the war's bloodiest battles, including the largest battle fought in Florida, at Olustee. Along the way, they meet historical characters like Generals Grant and Lee, tangle with criminals, become heroes, and fall in love. (hb)

*A Land Remembered* by Patrick D. Smith. This well-loved, best-selling novel tells the story of three generations of MacIveys, a Florida family battling the hardships of the frontier, and how they rise from a dirt-poor Cracker life to the wealth and standing of real estate tycoons. (hb, pb)